HOUSE OF KAREDES

Two Crowns

**A royal family, torn apart by pride and
a lust for power, reunited by passion**

The coronation diamond is missing!
Whether by seduction, blackmail or
marriage, the jewel must be found.
Secrets and sins from the past are revealed
and desire, love and passion war
with royal duty.

KATE HEWITT
CHANTELLE SHAW
MELANIE MILBURNE

THE ROYAL HOUSE OF KAREDES

The Royal

HOUSE OF KAREDES

Two Crowns

Kate
HEWITT

Chantelle
SHAW

Melanie
MILBURNE

MILLS & BOON

Published in Great Britain 2014
by Mills & Boon, an imprint of Harlequin (UK) Limited,
Eton House, 18-24 Paradise Road, Richmond, Surrey, TW9 1SR

THE ROYAL HOUSE OF KAREDES: TWO CROWNS
© 2014 Harlequin Books S.A.

The Sheikh's Forbidden Virgin © 2009 Harlequin Books S.A.
The Greek Billionaire's Innocent Princess
© 2009 Harlequin Books S.A.
The Future King's Love-Child © 2009 Harlequin Books S.A.

Special thanks and acknowledgement are given to Kate Hewitt, Chantelle Shaw and Melanie Milburne for their contribution to The Royal House of Karedes series.

ISBN: 978 0 263 24577 6

026-0214

Harlequin (UK) Limited's policy is to use papers that are natural, renewable and recyclable products and made from wood grown in sustainable forests.The logging and manufacturing processes conform to the legalenvironmental regulations of the country of origin.

Printed and bound in Spain
by Blackprint CPI, Barcelona

The Sheikh's
Forbidden Virgin

KATE HEWITT

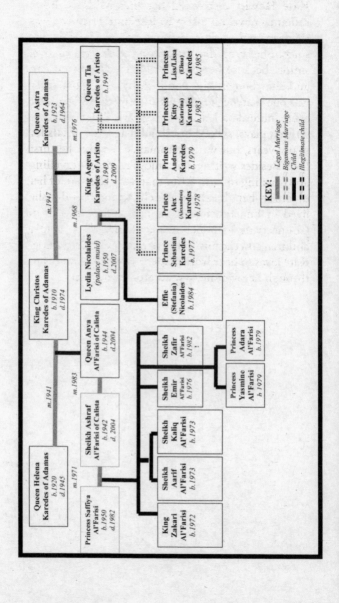

Kate Hewitt discovered her first Mills & Boon romance novel on a trip to England when she was thirteen and she's continued to read them ever since. She wrote her first story at the age of five, simply because her older brother had written one and she thought she could do it, too. That story was one sentence long. Fortunately, they've become a bit more detailed as she's grown older. She has written plays, short stories and magazine serials for many years, but writing romance remains her first love. Besides writing, she enjoys reading, travelling and learning to knit. After marrying the man of her dreams—her older brother's childhood friend—she lived in England for six years and now resides in Connecticut with her husband, her three young children and the possibility of one day getting a dog. Kate loves to hear from readers; you can contact her through her website, www.kate-hewitt.com.

CHAPTER ONE

THE dream came to him again. It was an assault of the senses and of memory, a tangle of images, grasping hands, the choking sea. Aarif Al'Farisi slept with his eyes clenched shut, his hands fisted on his bed sheets, a sheen of sweat glistening on his skin.

'Help me...help me...Aarif!'

The desperate cry of his name echoed endlessly, helplessly through the corridors of time and memory.

Aarif woke suddenly; his eyes opened and adjusted to the darkness of his bedroom. A pale sliver of moon cast a jagged swathe of light on the floor. He took a deep, shuddering breath and sat up, swinging his legs over the side of the bed.

It took a moment to calm his racing heart. Each careful, measured breath steadied him and made the shadows retreat. For now. He ran a hand through his sleep-tousled hair, still damp with sweat, and rose from the bed.

From the balcony of the Calistan royal palace he could see an endless stretch of moonlit sand, arid desert, all the way to the Kordela river with its diamonds, Calista's lifeblood, mixed treacherously in its silt. He kept his gaze on the undulating waves of sand and the promise of the river with its guarded treasure, and let his breathing return to normal as a dry desert wind cooled the sweat on his skin.

He hated his dreams. He hated that even now, twenty years

later, they left him shaken, afraid, helpless. Weak. Instinctively Aarif shook his head, as if to deny the dream. The reality. For the truth, stark as it was, was that he'd failed his brother and his family all those years ago, and he was destined to relive those agonising moments in his mind whenever the dreams visited him.

He hadn't had a dream like this for months, and the respite had lulled him into a false sense of security. Safety. Yet he would never have either, he knew. How could you be safe from yourself, secure from the endless repercussions of your own failures?

Letting out a sigh of frustrated exasperation, Aarif turned from the balcony and the inky night spangled with stars. He moved to the laptop he'd left on the desk by his bed, for he knew sleep was far off now. He would redeem the night through work.

He opened the computer and the machine hummed to life as he pulled on a pair of loose-fitting cotton trousers, his chest and feet still bare. In the mirror above the bureau he caught a glimpse of his reflection, saw the remembered fear still etched in harsh lines on his face, flared in his eyes, and he grimaced in self-disgust.

Afraid, after all these years. Still. He shook his head again, and turned to the computer. He checked his e-mail first; there were several clients he had appointments with in the next week who needed careful handling. Calista's diamonds were precious, but the island did not possess the vast reserves of Africa or Australia, and clients needed to be counted—and treated—carefully.

Yet there were no e-mails from clients in his message in-box, he saw, just one from his brother, King Zakari of Calista. Aarif's brows snapped together as he read his brother's instructions.

I must follow a lead on the diamond. Go to Zaraq and fetch Kalila. Ever your brother, Zakari.

The diamond…the Stefani diamond, the jewel of the Adamas Crown, split in two when the islands' rule had been divided. Aarif had never seen the diamond in its unified whole of course; the Calistan crown held only half of the gem. The other half, meant to be in the Aristan crown, was missing, and proving to be utterly elusive. By tradition, uniting the diamond was believed to be the key to uniting the kingdoms of Aristo and Calista for ever. Aarif had seen how determined Zakari was to retrieve that precious stone, and with it gain a kingdom.

So determined, in fact, that he now delegated this new responsibility to Aarif. Zakari's e-mail message contained a simple directive, yet one fraught with decisions, details, and potential disaster. For Princess Kalila Zadar was Zakari's betrothed and their wedding was in a fortnight.

The retrieval of a royal bride was a complex and cautious affair, one that rested on ceremony, courtesy, and tradition. Aarif knew he would have to play his hand—and his brother's hand—very carefully so as not to offend Kalila, her father King Bahir, or the people of Zaraq. The alliance with Zaraq was important and influential, and could not be treated lightly.

Aarif pressed his lips together in a hard line before touching his fingers to the computer keys. His reply was simple: *I will do as you instruct. Your servant, Aarif.*

There was never any possibility of questioning Zakari, or refusing his brother's demand. Aarif did not even consider it for a moment. His sense of obedience and responsibility were absolute; his family and kingdom came first. Always.

Aarif glanced up from the screen. Dawn was beginning to streak across the sky, pale fingers of light that illuminated the mist-shrouded dunes below. In that eerie grey half-light Aarif caught another glimpse of his face in the mirror, and for a moment he was startled by his own reflection, still surprised even now by the puckered finger of scar tissue that ran from his brow to his jaw, for ever a reminder of how he'd once failed in his duty to his family and kingdom.

He would never do so again.

* * *

Kalila woke from a restless sleep as the sun slanted through the window of her bedroom in the Zaraquan palace, the gauzy curtains stirring lazily in the hot breeze.

Nerves jumped and writhed in her belly, and one hand stole to her middle and rested there, as if she could calm the thoughts and fears that raced through her.

Today she would meet her husband.

She swung her feet over the side of the bed and padded barefoot to the window. The sky was already hard and bright, an endless stretch of blue without a single cloud. Beneath the sky the desert rolled away to the sea, little more than a pale blue-green shimmering on the horizon, marked by the slim stretch of verdant fields by the water's edge. The rest of Zaraq, a small kingdom, was desert. Dry, barren, and unproductive save for a few copper and nickel mines that now provided nearly all of the country's revenue.

Kalila swallowed. And that, she reminded herself, was the reason she was marrying at all. Zaraq needed Calista. Her father needed the security of Calista's diamond mines, and Calista needed Zaraq's stability of over a hundred years of uninterrupted independent rule. It was simple, depressingly so. She was a pawn, a bargaining chip, and she'd always known it.

Kalila rested her forehead against the mellow, golden stone of the window frame, still cool with the memory of night, although the sun slanting onto her skin was hot.

What would Zakari look like after all these years? What would he think of her? She knew he wouldn't love her. He hadn't seen her since she was a child, skinny and awkward, with too much hair and a gap-toothed smile. She barely remembered him; her mind played with shadowed memories of someone tall, powerful, commanding. Charismatic. He'd smiled at her, patted her head, and that was all.

Until now…when the stranger would become the bridegroom.

Today she would see him at last, and would he be pleased with his intended spouse? Would she?

A light, perfunctory knock sounded on the door and then her childhood nurse, Juhanah, bustled into the room.

'Good! You are awake. I've brought you breakfast, and then we must ready your beautiful self. His reverence could be here by noon, or so I've been told. We have much to do.'

Kalila suppressed a sigh as she turned from the window. Her father had told her yesterday just what kind of reception Sheikh Zakari must have.

'He must see a traditional girl, well brought up and fit to be a royal bride. You need not speak or even look at him, it would be too bold,' King Bahir warned, softening his words with a smile, although his eyes were still stern. 'You understand, Kalila? Tomorrow's meeting with Sheikh Zakari is important, and it is crucial that you present the right image. Juhanah will help you with the preparations.'

Not even speak? Every Western sensibility Kalila had ever possessed rose and rankled. 'Why can't Sheikh Zakari see me as I am?' she protested, trying to keep a petulant note from entering her voice. She was twenty-four years old, a university educated woman, about to be married, yet in her father's presence she still felt like an unruly child. She moderated her tone, striving for an answering smile. 'Surely, Father, it is just as important that he knows who his bride really is. If we present the wrong impression—'

'I know what the wrong impression is,' Bahir cut her off, his tone ominously final. 'And also what the right one is. There is time for him to *know* you, as you so wish, later,' he added, and Kalila flinched at the blatant dismissal of her desire. Bahir lifted one hand as though he were bestowing a blessing, although it felt more like a warning, a scolding. 'Tomorrow is not about you, Kalila. It is not even about your marriage. It is about tradition and ceremony, an alliance of countries, families. It has always been this way.'

Kalila's eyes flashed. 'Even for my mother?'

Bahir's lips compressed. 'Yes, even for her. Your mother was modern, Kalila, but she was not stubborn.' He sighed. 'I gave you your years at Cambridge, your university degree. You have pursued your interests and had your turn. Now it is your family's turn, your country's turn, and after all this waiting, you must do your duty. It begins tomorrow.' Despite the glimmer of compassion in his eyes, he spoke flatly, finally, and Kalila straightened, throwing her shoulders back with proud defiance.

'I know it well, Father.' Yet she couldn't help but take note of his words. Pursue her interests, he'd said, but not her dreams. And what good were interests if they had to be laid down for the sake of duty? And what *were* her dreams?

Her mind wrapped itself seductively around the question, the possibility. Her dreams were shadowy, shapeless things, visions of joy, happiness, meaning and purpose. Love. The word slipped unbidden in her mind, a seed planted in the fertile soil of her imagination, already taking root.

Love…but there was no love involved in this union between two strangers. There was not even affection, and Kalila had no idea if there ever would be. Could Zakari love her? Would he? And, Kalila wondered now as Juhanah bustled around her bedroom, would she love him?

Could she?

'Now eat.' Juhanah prodded her towards the tray set with a bowl of *labneh*, thick, creamy yoghurt, and a cup of strong, sweet coffee. 'You need your strength. We have much to do today.'

Kalila sat down at the table and took a bite. 'Just what *are* we doing today, Juhanah?'

Juhanah's chest swelled and she puffed out her already round cheeks. 'Your father wants you to be prepared as a girl was in the old days, when tradition mattered.' She frowned, and Kalila knew her nurse was thinking of her Western ways, inherited from her English mother and firmly rooted after four years of independent living in Cambridge.

When Kalila had discarded a pair of jeans on the floor of her bedroom Juhanah had pinched the offending garment between two plump fingers and held it away from her as if it were contaminated. Kalila grinned ruefully in memory.

'His Eminence will want to see you as a proper bride,' Juhanah said now, parroting her father's words from yesterday.

Kalila smiled, mischief glinting in her eyes. 'When shall I call him Zakari, do you think?'

'When he is in your bed,' Juhanah replied with an uncharacteristic frankness. 'Do not be too bold beforehand, my love. Men don't like a forward girl.'

'Oh, Juhanah!' Kalila shook her head. 'You've never left Zaraq, you don't know what it's like out there. Zakari has been to university, he's a man of the world—' So she had read in the newspapers and tabloid magazines. So she *hoped*.

'Pfft.' Juhanah blew out her cheeks once more. 'And so, do I need to know such things? What matters is here and now, my princess. King Zakari will want to see a royal princess today, not a modern girl with her fancy degree.' This was said with rolled eyes; Kalila knew Juhanah thought very little of her years in England. And in truth, she reflected, sitting at the table with the breakfast tray before her, those years counted for very little now.

What counted was her pedigree, her breeding, her body. Zakari wanted an alliance, not an ally. He wasn't looking for a lover, a partner. A soulmate.

Kalila's mouth twisted in bitter acknowledgement. She knew all this; she'd reminded herself of it fiercely every day that she'd been waiting for her wedding, her husband. Yet now the waiting was over, she found her heart was anxious for more.

'Aren't you hungry, *ya daanaya*?' Juhanah pressed, prodding the bowl of *labneh* as if she could induce Kalila to take a bit.

Kalila shook her head and pushed the bowl away. Her nerves, jumping and leaping, writhing and roiling, had returned, and she knew she would not manage another bite. 'I'll just have coffee,' she said, smiling to appease her nurse, and took a sip of the thick, sweet liquid. It scalded her tongue and burned down to her belly, with the same fierce resolve that fired her heart.

The bridal preparations took all morning. Kalila had expected it, and of course she wanted to look her best. Yet amidst all the ministrations, the lotions and creams and paints and powders, she couldn't help but feel like a chicken being trussed and seasoned for the cooking pot.

There was only Juhanah and a kitchen maid to act as her *negaffa*, the women who prepared the bride; the Zaraquan palace had a small staff since her mother had died.

First, she had a milk bath in the women's bathing quarters, an ancient tradition that Kalila wasn't sure she liked. Supposedly the milk of goats was good for the skin, yet it also had a peculiar smell.

'I wouldn't mind a bit of bath foam from the chemists',' she muttered, not loud enough for Juhanah or the kitchen maid to hear. They wouldn't understand, anyway.

As Juhanah towelled her dry and rubbed sweet-smelling lotion into her skin Kalila felt a sudden pang of sorrow and grief for her mother, who had died when Kalila had been only seventeen. Her mother Amelia had been English, cool and lovely, and it would have been her loving duty to prepare Kalila for this meeting with her bridegroom.

She, Kalila acknowledged with a rueful sorrow, would have understood about bath foam. They could have teased, laughed, enjoyed themselves even with the pall of duty hanging over her, the knowledge of what was to come.

Still, she reminded herself, she could be modern later. She could be *herself* later, when she and Zakari were alone. The thought of such an occurrence turned her mouth dry and set her nerves leaping once more.

Yet they would not be alone today. Today was for the formal meeting of a royal king and his bride, a piece of theatre elaborately staged and played, and she was merely a prop… one of many.

'No frowns,' Juhanah chided her gently. 'Only smiles today, my princess!'

Kalila forced a smile but she felt a pall of gloom settle over her like a shroud. The future loomed dark and unknowable ahead of her, a twisting road with an uncertain destination.

She hadn't seen or spoken to Zakari since she was little more than a child. There had been letters, birthday presents, polite and impersonal inquiries. Tradition demanded there be no more, and yet today she would meet him. In two weeks she would marry him.

It was absurd, archaic, and yet it was her life. The rest of it, anyway. Kalila swallowed the acidic taste of fear.

'Look.' Juhanah steered her towards the mirror, and even after the hours of preparation Kalila wasn't expecting the change. She looked…like a stranger.

The red and gold kaftan swallowed her slight figure, and her hair had been twisted back into an elaborate plait. Heavy gold jewellery settled at her wrists and throat, and her face…

Kalila didn't recognise the full red lips, or the wide, dark eyes outlined in kohl. She looked exotic, unfamiliar. Ridiculous, she thought with a sudden surge of bitterness. Like a male fantasy come to life.

'Beautiful, yes?' Juhanah said happily, and the kitchen maid nodded in agreement. Kalila could only stare. 'And now, the final touch…' Juhanah slipped the veil over her head, the garment of feminine pride, the hijab. It covered her hair and a diaphanous veil spangled with gold and silver coins covered her face, leaving nothing but those wide, blank, kohl-lined eyes. 'There,' Juhanah sighed in satisfaction.

Gazing at her exotic reflection, it seemed impossible that only eight months ago she'd been in Cambridge, debating philosophy and eating pizza with friends on the floor of her student flat. Wearing jeans, completely unchaperoned, living a life of freedom and opportunity, intellectual pursuit and joy.

Joy. She felt utterly joyless now, standing, staring there, utterly alien. Who was she? Was she the girl in Cambridge, laughing and flirting and talking politics, or was she this girl in the mirror, with her dark eyes and hidden face?

Eight months ago her father had come to England, taken her out for a meal and listened to her girlish chatter. She'd thought—deceived herself—that he was merely visiting her. That he *missed* her. Of course there had been a greater plan, a deeper need. There always had been.

Kalila still remembered the moment she'd seen her father's face turn sombre, one hand coming to rest lightly on hers so the spill of silly talk died on her lips, and her mouth went dry. 'What…?' she'd whispered, yet she'd known. Of course she'd known. She'd always known, since she had been twelve, when she'd had her engagement party.

She and Zakari had exchanged rings, although she barely remembered the ceremony. It was a blur of images and sensations, the cloying scent of jasmine, the heavy weight of the ring, a Calistan diamond, that Zakari had slipped on her finger. It had been far too big, and she'd put it in her jewellery box, where it had remained ever since.

Perhaps, Kalila thought distantly, she should wear it again.

'I know the wedding has been put off many times,' Bahir said, his voice surprisingly gentle. It made Kalila's eyes sting, and she stared down at her plate. 'Family obligations on both sides have made it so. But finally King Zakari is ready to wed. He has set a date…May the twenty-fifth.'

Kalila swallowed. It was the end of September, the leaves just starting to turn gold, flooding the Cambridge backs with colour, and the start of her term. 'But…' she began, and Bahir shook his head.

'Kalila, we always knew this was your destiny. Your duty.

I have already spoken to the registrar. Your course has been cancelled.'

She jerked her head up, her eyes meeting his, seeing the implacable insistence there. 'You had no right—'

'I had every right,' Bahir replied, and now she heard the hard implacability, felt it. 'I am your father and your king. You have received your degree—the post-graduate course was merely a way to pass the time.'

Kalila swallowed. Her throat ached so much the instinctive movement hurt. 'It was more than that to me,' she whispered.

'Yes, perhaps,' Bahir allowed, his shoulders moving in a tiny shrug, 'but you always knew what the future held. Your mother and I never kept it from you.'

No, they hadn't. They'd spoken to her before that wretched party, explained what it meant to be a princess, the joy that lay in fulfilling one's duty. Propaganda, and Kalila had believed it with all her childish heart. She'd been dazzled by the crown prince of Calista, although now she didn't remember much of Zakari, no more than a tall, charismatic presence, a patient—or had it been patronising?—smile. She'd only been twelve, after all.

'You will come home with me,' Bahir finished, beckoning to the waiter to clear their plates. 'You have a day to say goodbye to your friends and pack what you need.'

'A day?' Kalila repeated in disbelief. Her life was being dismantled in an instant, as if it had been meaningless, trivial—

And to her father, it had.

'I want you home,' Bahir said. 'Where you belong.'

'But if I'm not getting married until May—'

'Your presence is needed in your country, Kalila.' Bahir's voice turned stern; she'd worn his patience too thin with her desperate, fruitless resistance. 'Your people need to see you. You have been away nearly four years. It is time to come home.'

That evening, packing up her paltry possessions, Kalila had considered the impossible. The unthinkable. She could defy her father, run away from her so-called destiny. Stay in Cambridge, live her own life, find her own husband or lover…

Yet even as these thoughts, desperate and treacherous, flitted through her mind, she discarded them. Where could she run? With what money? And what would she do?

Besides, she acknowledged starkly, too much of her life—her blood—was bound up in this country, this world. Zaraq's future was bound with Calista's; to risk her country's well-being for her own selfish, feminine desires was contemptible. She could never betray her father, her country in such a manner. It would be a betrayal of herself.

So she'd returned home with her father on his private plane, had settled back into life in the empty palace with its skeleton staff. She drifted from day to day, room to room, at first trying to keep up with her studies in history and then discarding them in depression.

She'd attended to her civic responsibilities, visiting sick children, new businesses, shaking hands and cutting ribbons, smiling and nodding. She enjoyed the interactions with the people of Zaraq, but at times it felt like only so much busy work, a lifetime of busy work, for that was her duty.

Her destiny.

Now, gazing into the mirror, she wished—even wondered if—her destiny lay elsewhere. Surely she'd been made for, meant to do, more than this. Be more than this.

'Princess?' Juhanah said softly. 'Beautiful, *n'am?*'

Kalila had a desperate, intense urge to rip the veil from her face. She'd never been veiled before—her mother had refused, wearing only Western clothes, her nod to old-fashioned propriety no more than a scrap of head covering on formal occasions. Her father hadn't minded. He'd married his English rose as part of an attempt to Westernise his country. Yet now, Kalila thought with renewed bitterness, she looked like something out of the *Arabian Nights*. Like a harem girl. The coins tinkled when she moved.

'Lovely,' Juhanah murmured. Kalila's fingers bunched on the gauzy material of her kaftan and a fingernail snagged on a bit of gold thread.

Juhanah tutted and batted her hand away. Just then a knock sounded on the door of the bedroom, and Juhanah went to answer it while Kalila continued to stare.

What would Zakari think of her like this? Was this what he wanted? Was this what her future looked like?

She swallowed, forcing the fears and doubts back. It was too late now, far too late. She understood her duty.

She just hadn't known how it would *feel*.

Juhanah padded back into the bedroom and flitted around Kalila, tugging a bit of material here, smoothing it there. 'You are radiant,' she said and beneath the veil Kalila's lips twisted sardonically. Was Juhanah blind, or just blinded by her own happiness? Her nurse was thrilled Kalila was fulfilling her duty and destiny as a crown princess. A queen. 'And it is time,' she continued, her eyes lighting, her plump cheeks flushed with excitement. 'The sheikh has just arrived. He's coming directly from the plane.' And as if she didn't understand already, her heart already beginning to hammer a frantic, desperate beat, Juhanah added in satisfaction, 'Finally, he is here.'

Aarif was hot, dusty, and tired. The short ride in an open Jeep from the royal airstrip to the palace itself was enough to nearly cover him in dust. He'd been met by a palace official who would take him to the palace's throne room, where he would extend Zakari's formal greetings to his bride and her father.

Aarif swallowed and the dust caught grittily in his throat and stung his eyes. Already he'd seen the official sweep a cautious gaze over his face, linger on that damnable line from forehead to jaw. His scar. His reminder, and everyone else's, of his flaws, his failures.

The palace emerged in the distance, long and low, of mellow golden stone, with towers on either end. In every other direction the desert stretched to an empty horizon, although Aarif thought he glimpsed a huddle of clay and stone buildings to the west—Makaris, the nation's capital.

The Jeep pulled up to the front entrance, a pair of intricately carved wooden doors under a stone canopy.

'I will take you to wash and prepare yourself, Your Highness,' the official said, bowing. 'King Bahir awaits you in the throne room.'

Aarif nodded, and followed the man into the palace, down a cool, stone corridor and to a waiting chamber with benches and a table. There was a pitcher of lemon water, and Aarif poured a glass and drank thirstily before he changed into his *bisht*, the long, formal robe worn for ceremonies such as this. In the adjoining bathroom he washed the dust from his face, his eyes sliding away from his reflection in the mirror before returning resolutely to stare at his face, as he always did.

A light, inquiring knock sounded on the door, and, turning from that grim reminder, Aarif left the bathroom and went to fulfil his brother's bidding, and express his greetings to his bride.

The official led him to the double doors of the throne room; inside an expectant hush fell like a curtain being dropped into place, or perhaps pulled up.

'Your Eminence,' the official said in French, the national language of Zaraq, his voice low and unctuous, 'may I present His Royal Highness, King Zakari.'

Aarif choked; the sound was lost amidst a ripple of murmurings from the palace staff that had assembled for this honoured occasion. It would only take King Bahir one glance to realise it was not the king who graced his throne room today, but rather the king's brother, a lowly prince.

Aarif felt a flash of rage—directed at himself. A mistake had been made in the correspondence, he supposed. He'd delegated the task to an aide when he should have written himself and explained that he would be coming rather than his brother.

Now he would have to explain the mishap in front of company, all of Bahir's staff, and he feared the insult could be great.

'Your Eminence,' he said, also speaking French, and moved into the long, narrow room with its frescoed ceilings and bare walls. He bowed, not out of obeisance but rather respect, and heard Bahir shift in his chair. 'I fear my brother, His Royal Highness Zakari, was unable to attend to this glad errand, due to pressing royal business. I am honoured to escort his bride, the Princess Kalila, to Calista in his stead.'

Bahir was silent, and, stifling a prickle of both alarm and irritation, Aarif rose. He was conscious of Bahir watching him, his skin smooth but his eyes shrewd, his mouth tightening with disappointment or displeasure, perhaps both.

Yet even before Bahir made a reply, even before the formalities had been dispensed with, Aarif found his gaze sliding, of its own accord, to the silent figure to Bahir's right.

It was his daughter, of course. Kalila. Aarif had a memory of a pretty, precocious child. He'd spoken a few words to her at the engagement party more than ten years ago now. Yet now the woman standing before him was lovely, although, he acknowledged wryly, he could see little of her.

Her head was bowed, her figure swathed in a kaftan, and yet as if she felt the magnetic tug of his gaze she lifted her head, and her eyes met his.

It was all he could see of her, those eyes; they were almond-shaped, wide and dark, luxuriously fringed, a deep, clear golden brown. Every emotion could be seen in them, including the one that flickered there now as her gaze was drawn inexorably to his face, to his scar.

It was disgust Aarif thought he saw flare in their golden depths and as their gazes held and clashed he felt a sharp, answering stab of disappointment and self-loathing in his own gut.

CHAPTER TWO

HE HADN'T come. Kalila gazed blankly at the stranger in front of her, heard the words, the explanations, the expected flattery, the apologies and regrets, but none of it made sense.

She couldn't get her head—her heart—around the fact that her husband-to-be hadn't bothered to show up. Would he even be at the wedding? Hadn't he realised she'd been waiting, wondering, hoping…?

Or had he even bothered to think about her at all?

She swallowed the bubble of hysterial laughter that threatened to rise up and spill out. Her father was speaking, his voice low and melodious, inviting this man—who was he? Kalila's brain scrambled for the remembered words, fragments—Prince Aarif. Zakari's younger brother, sent on this *glad errand*. Her lips twisted cynically, but of course no one could see her smile behind this damned veil.

Her fingers clenched at her side. She longed to rip off the veil, destroy the entire charade, because that was all it was. A charade, a façade. False.

A piece of theatre, and she no longer wanted the role.

She wanted to run, to run and never stop until she was somewhere safe and different, somewhere she could be herself—whoever that was—and people would be glad.

Where, she wondered hopelessly, was that place? She didn't think she had found it yet.

Her father had risen, and Kalila knew this was her cue to gracefully withdraw. This pretty little part had been scripted, rehearsed. She bowed, lowering her head with its heavy plait and awkward veil, and backed slowly out of the room, trying not to trip over the embroidered hem of her kaftan. She couldn't wait to get out of this get-up, to be *free*.

She tore the veil from her face as soon as she was out of the room, grabbing a fistful of the kaftan to clear her feet as she strode to her bedroom. Juhanah followed, tutting anxiously.

'The fabric—it is delicate!' she protested, reaching for the veil Kalila had fisted in one hand.

'I don't care,' she snapped, and Juhanah clucked again, prising the veil from Kalila's fingers and smoothing it carefully.

'You are disappointed, of course. But the king is a busy man, with many demands. It is just as well you become accustomed to this early, *ya daanaya.*'

'Even before we've met?' Kalila heard the sarcastic edge to her voice and was glad. She needed to vent her feelings, her frustration, for Juhanah was right, she was disappointed. Disappointed and hurt.

And she had no reason to be, because she had never thought Zakari loved her. How could he? So what had she been hoping for? She didn't know, couldn't answer, yet she felt deep in her belly, her soul, that something had been irretrievably lost today. She just didn't know what it was.

Back in the sanctuary of her bedroom she took a deep, steadying breath. She knew there was no point in acting like a petulant child; she was a woman, with a woman's life ahead of her. A woman's duty, a woman's burden.

Her mind slid back to the night eight months ago, alone in her Cambridge flat, when she could have walked away. She could have cut herself off from her father, her family, her country and culture. A small part of her would have welcomed it.

Yet she hadn't, and she knew in her heart she never would

have. Despite the endless, aching uncertainty and regret, she had a duty to her family. To herself.

And yet. And yet she hadn't expected this. This hurt, this disappointment, so fresh and raw and painful.

She had been nourishing dreams without even realising it. Those shadowy dreams took form now as she acknowledged her own folly. She'd wanted Zakari to come here, to be eager for this day, and then to be speechless at the sight of her. She'd wanted him to be enchanted, enamoured, in love.

And all without even knowing her! She really was a fool. A child, to believe in such childish dreams, such fairy tales. To have let herself hope even when she thought she was being realistic, responsible. She'd fooled *herself*.

Kalila sighed wearily as she stared at her painted face in the mirror. A fan whirred lazily above her but the heat of midday was oppressive, made even more so by her heavy garments.

'Please help me, Juhanah,' she said. She pulled at the kaftan. 'I want to get this off.'

'Of course, of course,' Juhanah soothed, hurrying to her side. 'You will want to rest, to be fresh for this evening.'

Kalila frowned. 'Why? What's happening this evening?'

'Did you not hear? Your father invited Prince Aarif to dine with you both tonight. Informal, he said.' Juhanah's smile glinted knowingly. 'No kaftan, no hijab.'

Kalila breathed a sigh of relief as she pushed the heavy mass of hair away from her neck. 'Good.'

Juhanah slipped the kaftan from Kalila's shoulders. 'You know this was your mother's?'

'It was?' She turned in disbelief. 'I never saw her wear anything like it.'

'No, she didn't, not very often.' Juhanah ran one finger along the gold thread. 'But she wore this to her own engagement party—your father chose it as a wedding gift. She looked very beautiful.'

Kalila tried to imagine her mother, tall, slender, blonde,

wearing the outfit she had. Weighed down by its heaviness and expectations. She wondered how her mother had felt wearing it. Had she been as stifled and suppressed as Kalila had? Or had she seen it only as a costume, and a beautiful one at that?

Her mother had chosen to marry Bahir, she knew. It had been, against all odds, a love match.

So why, Kalila wondered as Juhanah quietly left the room and she stretched out restlessly on her bed, couldn't she have the same?

Surprisingly, she slept, although she'd felt too anxious and upset to even close her eyes at first. Somehow she fell into an uneasy sleep, where even her dreams were tinted with a vague unhappiness.

When she awoke, the sun was low in the sky, and the breeze blowing in from the window was blessedly cool.

Kalila pushed her hair away from her eyes and moved to the window. The sun was a fiery ball of orange, sending vivid streaks of light across a sky just darkening to dusk. It was a stark yet beautiful sight, and one she never tired of. She'd missed sunsets like these in England. She'd missed the purity of light and air, the violent brightness of the colours.

A glance at the clock told her she needed to ready herself quickly. The woman Prince Aarif saw tonight would be nothing like the vision of traditional womanhood he'd seen this afternoon, Kalila would make sure of that. The time for pageantry and play-acting was over. And besides, she reminded herself as she stepped into a scalding shower, there was no one to impress. Zakari wasn't even here.

She scrubbed away the kohl and the red lipstick, the scents of jasmine and sandalwood. She scrubbed until her face was clean and bare and her skin smelled only of soap.

She dressed in a simple cocktail dress, modest by Western standards, although glaringly different from her earlier outfit. It was a simple silk sheath in pale lavender, skimming her body and ending mid-calf. She slipped on a pair of matching pumps and pulled her hair up into a quick and careless chignon. The only nod to make-up was a bit of lip gloss.

Taking a deep breath, wondering just why nerves had started their restless fluttering once more, Kalila headed downstairs.

Prince Aarif was already in the palace's smaller, less formal dining room, drink in hand, when she arrived. Kalila paused on the threshold, taking in the table set intimately for three, and then the prince standing by the window, his back half to her. Her father was nowhere in sight.

She hadn't given their unexpected guest more than a passing thought since she'd seen him that afternoon; it had been Zakari's absence that had occupied her thoughts rather than Aarif's presence.

Yet now she found her gaze resting on him, sweeping over him in open curiosity. He wore a Western suit in charcoal grey and it fitted his long, lithe form with gracious ease. He looked so different in these clothes than in his *bisht*, Kalila realised, so much more approachable and human. She wondered if she did as well.

Then, as if he sensed her presence, he turned to face her fully, and Kalila drew in a breath at the sight of his face, his eyes curiously blank although his lips were curved in a smile of greeting, the scar curving along his cheek. He looked formal, forbidding, almost angry even though he smiled.

Kalila forced herself to smile back. 'Good evening, Prince Aarif.'

Aarif nodded once. 'Princess.'

She stepped into the room, strangely conscious of the fact that they were alone, although even that was a fantasy. Servants were within earshot and her father would undoubtedly arrive in a few minutes. 'Did you have a good afternoon?' she asked, and heard the bright falsity in her own voice.

Aarif's mouth flickered in something not quite a smile. 'An

enlightening one,' he replied, and took a sip of his drink. He gestured to her own empty hand. 'Would you like a drink?'

As if on cue, a servant came forward and Kalila asked for a glass of fruit juice. She wanted to keep her head clear.

'I'm afraid I don't remember you,' Kalila said, smiling ruefully. 'You must be Zakari's younger brother, but I know he has many, and sisters too…'

'Yes, there are seven of us.' Aarif's hard gaze settled on her as he added, 'I remember you. You were quite young at that engagement party, weren't you? You wore a white dress, with a bow in your hair.'

'I was twelve,' Kalila replied, her voice coming out in almost a whisper before she cleared her throat. She was touched—and unsettled—that he remembered her dress, her hair.

'You looked as if you were going to a birthday party.' Aarif glanced away. 'Perhaps it felt like that at the time.'

Kalila nodded, surprised and unsettled again that he could understand just how she'd felt. 'Yes, it did. And I was getting the best present of all.' The trace of bitterness in her voice must have alerted him, for he glanced at her with faint censure now, the moment of unexpected closeness shattered by her own confession.

'Marriage is an honour and a blessing.'

He sounded so much like her father, Kalila thought. Like every man who lectured about a woman's duty. 'Are you married, Prince Aarif?' she asked, a note of challenge in her voice.

Aarif shook his head. 'No,' he said flatly, and any further discussion was put to an end by the arrival of her father.

'Ah, Prince Aarif. And Kalila, you look well rested. I am glad.' He came forward, rubbing his hands together, every inch the beneficent ruler. 'I was telling Prince Aarif earlier that we do not rest on formality here, especially among family and friends.'

Then what, Kalila wanted to ask, was the point of that spectacle today? Of course she knew: tradition, ceremony. Pride. She saw her father's gaze move speculatively between her and Aarif and instinctively she took a step away from the prince. A new, hidden meaning to her father's words making her uncomfortably aware of the potential impropriety of their brief conversation. 'Yes, of course,' she said with a perfunctory smile. 'We are very glad to welcome you to Zaraq, Prince Aarif.'

'And I am very glad to be here,' he returned, his voice low, pleasant and smooth, yet somehow devoid of any true expression. Kalila glanced at his face and saw his eyes looked blank. He was wearing a mask, she thought, a veil, as much of one as she had worn this afternoon. She wondered what he was trying to hide.

Bahir drew Kalila's chair, before sitting down, and Aarif followed.

'Earlier Aarif was explaining to me why King Zakari could not be here today,' Bahir said as he poured them all wine. Kalila took a sip; it was light and refreshing and bubbled pleasantly through her.

'Oh, yes?' she said, raising her eyebrows.

'He is, of course, a busy man,' Bahir continued. 'With many royal duties. He is not, in fact, on Calista at the moment…' He let his voice trail off in delicate inquiry, and Kalila watched with a flicker of interest as Aarif's mouth tightened.

'He is not?' she asked. 'Where is he, Prince Aarif?'

'Please, call me Aarif.' There was a thread of tension in his voice that Kalila heard with growing curiosity.

'Then you must call me Kalila,' she returned as a matter of courtesy, yet this pleasantry caused Aarif's sharp gaze to rest briefly on her face and something unfurled deep in her belly and spiralled strangely upwards.

He wasn't, she reflected, taking another sip of wine, a classically handsome man. The scar put paid to that, but even without it his face was too harsh, too hard. There was no kindness in it, no humour or sympathy. The only emotion she saw in his dark eyes, in the flat line of his mouth, was determination.

She wondered just what Aarif was determined to do.

The first course, stewed chicken seasoned with coriander and paprika, was served, and they all began to eat.

'I have heard,' Bahir said after a moment, his voice mild and easy, 'rumours of diamonds.'

Aarif paused for only a fraction of a second before he smiled and shrugged. 'There are always rumours.'

'This rumour,' Bahir continued, his voice turning hard for only a second, 'is that half of the Stefani diamond is missing.' He paused, and Kalila watched as Aarif continued chewing with what looked like deliberate unconcern. 'I wonder if that is what concerns your brother, Aarif?'

Aarif swallowed and took a sip of wine. Tension crackled in the air and Kalila's gaze flickered from one man to the other, both smiling and genial, yet too much shrewd knowledge in their eyes.

What was going on?

'My brother is indeed concerned about the Stefani diamond,' Aarif said after a moment. 'It has long been his desire to unite the diamond, and of course the kingdoms of Calista and Aristo.' His gaze rested once more on Kalila, and again she felt that strange unfurling, as if inside her something had taken root and now sought sunlight, life and air. 'This, of course, is of benefit to you, Princess. You shall be Queen not only of Calista, but of Aristo also.'

Kalila tried to smile, although in truth she hadn't considered herself queen of anything at all. She'd only been thinking of herself as someone's wife, not queen of a country, or even two.

Queen. She tried to feel the obligatory thrill, but disappointment and fear were too pressing. She didn't aspire to titles; she aspired to love.

'I wish your brother every success,' she finally said, keeping her voice light, and a servant came to clear their plates.

'My brother will be successful,' Aarif said, smiling, although there was an odd flatness to his voice, his eyes. 'When one is determined, one is also successful.'

There was a tiny pause, and the servant came to clear the dishes. 'Indeed, an excellent maxim to live by,' Bahir said lightly, and poured more wine.

Kalila toyed with the next course, a salad made with couscous, cucumbers, and tomatoes. Her appetite had vanished and she felt unsettled again, uneasy even though she was in comfortable clothes. Even though she was herself.

She didn't know what caused this sense of unease, a needy sort of dissatisfaction. Was it Zakari's absence or Aarif's presence? Her gaze flitted to the prince's hard profile, lingered briefly on the strong curve of his jaw, the livid line of his scar, and she felt again that strange spiralling within, upwards, something happy and hungry. He interested her, she realised with a spark of surprise. Fascinated her.

Would Zakari have done the same? The shadowy figure from her childhood held little appeal compared to the enigmatic presence of this man…this man, who was not and was never going to be her husband.

Aarif turned, his eyes clashing with hers, and Kalila jerked her gaze away, feeling exposed, as if he'd somehow witnessed her disturbing thought process.

'Kalila?' Bahir raised his eyebrow, drawing her back into the conversation.

'Please excuse me,' Kalila said quickly, forcing herself not to flush. 'My mind was elsewhere. Father?'

'Prince Aarif was just inquiring about bringing you to Calista. He wanted to leave tomorrow, and I was explaining to him about our customs.' Bahir smiled apologetically at Aarif. 'You see, Prince Aarif, there is a tradition here in Zaraq. The people love the royal family—it has always been so.' He paused and took a sip of wine. 'It is, perhaps, why we have enjoyed over a hundred years of peaceful rule.' It was, Kalila knew, a delicate reminder of the power and prestige Zaraq brought to this marriage alliance. 'The people of Makaris, our capital, like to hold a little festival when a member of the royal family is going to be married.' Bahir held up one smooth, well-manicured hand, anticipating Aarif's response, although he hadn't moved or spoken. He simply waited. 'I know this festival would normally occur after the wedding, but Kalila will be in Calista then, and it is important to the people that they see the happy couple…or at least the radiant bride.' There was no censure in Bahir's voice, but Aarif must have felt it for his mouth tightened once more.

'If my brother had been aware of such traditions, I am sure he would have made every effort to be here,' he said after a moment, and Bahir inclined his head in gracious acknowledgement.

'Of course, of course. As it is, he is not, and you are. And for the sake of our beloved people, as well as the peace of our happy country, the festival must go forward as planned. It is a small affair, a simple matter. Food, music, dancing. I thought, considering—' he paused delicately '—you could stop in Makaris on your way to the airport, and enjoy the festivities for an hour, two, no more. The people like a glimpse of the royal family, that is all.'

'On the way to the airport?' Aarif repeated, his voice scrupulously polite. 'It was my understanding we would depart from the palace's airstrip.'

Bahir waved a hand. 'Yes, yes, I can see how you would think that. But as I said, the people of Zaraq care very much for the royal family, and in truth Princess Kalila, being my only heir, is much loved. They will want to wish her well, say farewell, you know how it is.' He smiled, but no one could mistake the shrewd glint in his eyes.

Aarif dabbed his mouth with a napkin before smiling easily, although Kalila saw that his eyes were just as hard and shrewd as her father's. 'Yes, of course. We must satisfy the people, King Bahir. Let it be as you wish.'

Bahir smiled in satisfaction, and Kalila felt a sudden wave of numbing fatigue crash over her at the thought of several hours of mingling, chatting, waving, smiling. Indulging everyone's need for a fairy tale.

Yet it had to be done; it would be done. It was, she knew, all part of her duty as princess. As queen.

'I am sorry to rush you from your home, Princess,' Aarif said, turning to her. 'But as you know, the wedding is in two weeks, and there will be preparations to complete there.' He paused before adding almost as an afterthought, 'And of course King Zakari will be eager to see you, his bride.'

'Of course.' Kalila stared down at her untouched plate. At that moment she had trouble believing Zakari was eager for anything but another diamond in his crown.

The rest of the evening passed with more ease, and Bahir made sure the wine and conversation flowed smoothly.

'I have heard that many of the Al'Farisi princes have been educated at Oxford,' he said as dessert, roasted plums seasoned with cardamom and nutmeg, was served. 'I went to Sandhurst myself, which is how I happened to meet my late wife, Queen Amelia, God rest her soul. Her brother was one of my best friends.' Bahir smiled in inquiry. 'Did you attend Oxford, Aarif?'

'I did, and then returned to Calista to oversee our diamond industry.'

'You are a man of business.'

'Indeed.'

And he looked like one, Kalila thought. All about hard facts and figures, details and prices. Even his eyes had the hardness of diamonds.

'Kalila went to Cambridge,' Bahir continued. 'As I'm sure you, or at least your brother, knows. She studied history, and enjoyed her years there, didn't you, my dear?'

'Yes, very much.' Kalila smiled stiffly, disliking the way her father trotted out her accomplishments as if she were a show pony. A brood mare.

'An education is important for any ruler, don't you think?'

Bahir continued, and Aarif swivelled slightly to rest that harsh and unyielding gaze on Kalila.

She stilled under it, felt again that strange warmth bloom in her cheeks and her belly at his scrutiny. Strange, when his expression was so ungenerous, his eyes so dark and obdurate. She should quell under that unyielding gaze, yet she didn't. She flourished. She wanted more, yet more of what? What more could a man like Aarif give?

'Yes,' he said flatly, and then looked away.

Finally the meal was over, and Bahir invited Aarif to take a cigar and port in his private study. It was a male tradition, one that took different guises all around the world, and all it took was for her father to raise his eyebrows at her for Kalila to know she'd been excused. It usually annoyed her, this arrogant dismissal of women from what was seen as the truly important matters, but tonight she was glad.

She wanted to be alone. She needed to think.

She waited until Bahir and Aarif were ensconced in the study before she slipped outside to the palace's private gardens, an oasis of verdant calm. She loved these gardens, the cool shade provided by a hundred different varieties of shrub and flower, the twisting paths that would suddenly lead to a fountain or sculpture or garden bench, something pleasant and lovely.

She breathed in deeply the surprising scents of lavender and rose, imported from England by Bahir for the pleasure of his homesick wife.

The air was damp and fresh from the sprinkler system Bahir had installed, although Kalila could still feel the dry, creeping chill of the night-time desert air. She wished she'd thought to bring a wrap; her arms crept around her body instead.

She didn't want to marry Zakari. She acknowledged this starkly, peeled away the layers of self-deceit and foolish hope to reveal the plain and unpleasant truth underneath. She didn't want to travel to a foreign country, even one as close as

Calista, to be a queen. She didn't want to live the life that had been carefully chosen for her too many years ago.

She didn't want to do her duty.

Funny, that she would realise this now. Now, when it was too late, far too late, when the wedding was imminent, the invitations already sent out even. Or were they? Funny, too, that she had no idea of the details of her own wedding, her own marriage, not even about the groom.

Kalila sighed. The path she'd been walking on opened onto a sheltered curve bound by hedgerows, set with a small fountain, its waters gleaming blackly in the darkness, the newly risen moon reflected on its still surface. She sank onto a bench by the fountain, curling her legs up to her chest and resting her chin on her knees, a position from childhood, a position of comfort.

From the ground she scooped up a handful of smooth pebbles and let them trickle through her fingers, each one making a tiny scuffling sound on the dirt below. She hadn't realised the truth of her situation until now, she knew, because she hadn't separated it from herself before.

Since she was a child of twelve—half of her life—she'd known she was going to marry King Zakari. She'd had a picture of him—from a newspaper—in her underwear drawer, although she made sure no one saw it. When she was alone, she'd taken it out and smoothed the paper, stared at the blurred image—it wasn't even a very good shot—and wondered about the man in the picture. The man who would be her husband, the father of her children, her life partner.

In those early years she'd embroidered delicate daydreams about him, his beauty and bravery, intelligence and humour. She'd built him up to be a king even before a crown rested on his head. Of course, that youthful naiveté hadn't lasted too long; by the time she went to Cambridge, she'd realised Zakari could not possibly be the man of her daydreams. No man could.

And even when she'd thought she was being realistic,

nobly doing her duty, accepting the greater aims of her country, she'd still clung to those old daydreams. They'd hidden in the corner of her heart, dusty and determined, and only when Aarif had shown himself in the throne room had she realised their existence at all.

She still believed. She still *wanted*. She wanted that man…impossible, wonderful, somehow real.

Because that man loved her…whoever he was.

For a strange, surprised moment, Aarif's implacable features flashed through her mind, and she shook her head as if to deny what a secret part of her brain was telling her. The only reason she thought of Aarif at all, she told herself, was because Zakari wasn't here.

Yet she couldn't quite rid herself of the lingering sense of his presence, that faint flicker of his smile. *You wore a white dress, with a bow in your hair.*

Such a simple statement, and yet there had been a strange intimacy in that memory, in its revelation.

'Excuse me.'

The voice, sharp and sudden, caused Kalila to stiffen in surprise. Aarif stood by the fountain, no more than a shadowy form in the darkness. They stared at each other, the only sound the rustling of leaves and, in the distance, the gentle churring of a nightjar.

'I didn't realise,' Aarif said after a moment, his voice stiff and formal, 'that anyone was here.'

Kalila swallowed. 'I thought you'd still be with my father.'

'We finished, and he wished to go to bed.'

More time must have passed than she'd realised, lost in her own unhappy reflections.

'I'll go,' Aarif said, and began to turn.

'Please. Don't.' The words came out in a rush, surprising her. Kalila didn't know what she wanted from this man, so hard and strange and ungiving. Yet she knew she didn't want him to go; she didn't want to be alone any more. She wanted, she realised, to be with him. To know more about him, even if there was no point. No purpose.

Aarif hesitated, still half-turned, and then as Kalila held her breath he slowly swivelled back to her. In the darkness she couldn't see his expression. 'Is there something I can help you with, Princess?'

Kalila patted the empty seat next to her. 'Please sit.'

Another long moment passed, and in the darkness Kalila thought she could see Aarif gazing thoughtfully at that empty space before he moved slowly—reluctantly—and sat down next to her, yet still far enough apart so his body did not touch hers at all.

The constraint of his behaviour, Kalila realised, was revealing in itself. Was he aware of the tension Kalila felt, that heady sense of something unfurling within her, something she'd never felt before?

Did he feel it too?

He couldn't, Kalila decided, or if he did, he was not showing it. He sat rigidly, his hands resting on his thighs, unmoving, and it amazed her how still and controlled he was, giving nothing away by either sound or movement.

'This is a beautiful garden,' Aarif said after a moment, and Kalila was glad he'd spoken.

'I have always loved it,' she agreed quietly. 'My father designed it for my mother—a taste of her homeland.'

'Like the Gardens of Babylon, built by Nebuchadnezzar for Amytis.'

'Yes.' Kalila smiled, pleased he'd recognised the connection. 'My father used to call my mother Amytis, as an endearment.' She heard the wistful note in her voice and bit her lip.

'I'm sorry for her death,' Aarif said, his voice still formal and somehow remote. 'The loss of a parent is a hard thing to bear.'

'Yes.'

'When did she die?'

'When I was seventeen. Cancer.' Kalila swallowed. It had

been so unexpected, so swift. There had only been a few, precious, painful weeks between diagnosis and death, and then the raging emptiness afterwards. Going to Cambridge had been a relief, a new beginning, and yet Kalila knew the ache of her mother's loss would never fully heal. It was something you carried with you, always.

'I'm sorry,' Aarif said quietly, and Kalila knew he meant it. Above them the nightjar began its steady churring once more.

'I know you lost your father and stepmother a few years ago,' she said hesitantly. 'I…I heard of it. I'm sorry.' She'd written to Zakari, she remembered, expressing her condolences, and she'd received a formal letter back. Now she wondered if he'd even written it.

'Thank you. It was…difficult.' Aarif said nothing more, and Kalila did not feel she could brave the intimacy of asking. He shifted slightly, and she wondered if he was uncomfortable. There was a strange, quiet intimacy provided by the cloak of darkness, the sounds of the night gentle and hypnotic around them. She wished she could see his face, but the moon had gone beyond a cloud and she could see no more than the shadowy outline of his shoulder, his jaw, his cheek.

'Tell me about Calista,' she finally said. 'You know, I've never been there.'

Aarif was silent for so long Kalila wondered if he'd heard her. 'It's beautiful,' he finally said. 'Much like here.' He paused, and Kalila waited. 'Of course, not everyone sees the beauty of the desert. It is a harsh loveliness. Was it difficult for your mother to live here?'

'Sometimes,' Kalila acknowledged. 'Although she took trips back to England—I spent my first holidays in Bournemouth.'

The moon glided out from behind a cloud, and in the pale light Kalila saw his teeth gleam, and she realised he was smiling. Faintly. The gesture surprised her; he hadn't smiled properly since she'd met him. She wished she could see more of it. She wondered if the smile lit his eyes, softened the hard planes of his face, and realised she wanted to know. 'And she had the garden, of course,' she finished after a moment, her voice sounding stilted. 'She loved it here.'

'And you?' Aarif asked. 'Will you miss your homeland?'

Kalila swallowed. 'Yes…I think so.' He said nothing, but she felt his silent censure like a physical thing, tautening the small space between them. And, of course, why shouldn't he be surprised? Disappointed even? Here she was, admitting that she didn't know if she'd miss her own country! She opened her mouth, wanting to explain the jumble of confused emotions and disappointed dreams to him, but nothing came out. What could she say, and what would this man want to hear?

Yet somehow, strangely, she felt as if he might understand. Or was that simply the wishful thinking of a woman with too many disappointed dreams?

'I'll miss Zaraq, of course,' she said, after a moment, wanting, needing to explain. 'And my father. And friends…' She trailed off, unable to put words to the nameless longing for something else, something deeper and more instrinsically a part of herself, something that had no name. Something, she realised despondently, she wasn't even sure she'd ever had.

'It is a strange time,' Aarif said after a moment. His voice was still neutral, yet in the shadowy darkness Kalila saw him lift his hand and drop it again—almost as if he'd been going to touch her. Her heart beat harder at the thought. 'Once you are in Calista, you will feel more settled. The people will welcome you.' He paused before adding, his voice still flat, 'I'm sure they will love you.'

The people. Not Zakari. And what of him? What of Aarif? The question was ludicrous, so ridiculous and inappropriate that under the cover of darkness Kalila's cheeks warmed. 'Thank you,' she whispered. 'I suppose I sound like I am full of self-pity, but I hope—I know—' she swallowed painfully '—that it will be better with time.'

'Time heals most things,' Aarif agreed, yet Kalila felt he was saying something else, something far from a platitude. Most things…but not all.

Aarif stirred on the bench and Kalila knew he wanted to leave. The night had grown quiet, their conversation too close. Yet the thought of his departure alarmed her, and she held out one hand, the moonlight bathing her skin in lambent silver. 'Tell me about your brother.'

The words fell in the silence like the pebbles from her hand, disturbing the tranquil stillness. Kalila wished she hadn't spoken. Why had she asked about Zakari? She didn't want to know about him. She didn't even want to *think* about him.

But you need to know. He is going to be your husband.

'What kind of man is he?' she asked, her voice trailing to a whisper. It shamed her that she had to ask. She felt as if she'd exposed something to Aarif without even realising it, as much as if she'd shown him that faded photograph in her lingerie drawer.

'He is a good man,' Aarif said after a long moment when he'd remained still and silent, his head half turned away from her. 'A better man than I am. And a good king.' Kalila started at his admission. *A better man than I am. Why? What kind of man are you?* She wanted to ask, but she was silent, and Aarif finished, 'He will do his duty.'

His duty. Highest praise, no doubt, from a man like Aarif, but to Kalila it had the ring of condemnation. She wanted so much more than duty. Summoning her spirit, she tried for a laugh. 'Can't you tell me more than that?' she asked, keeping her voice light.

Aarif turned to look at her, his eyes and face carefully expressionless. 'I fear I cannot tell you the kinds of things a bride would like to know about her groom. And in truth, you will know soon enough.'

'I thought he would have come. To see me.' Kalila bit her lip, wishing the words back. Then she shrugged, a sudden spark of defiance firing through her. 'He should have.'

Aarif stiffened, or at least Kalila felt as if he had. Perhaps he hadn't moved at all. Yet she knew she'd gone too far; she'd almost insulted King Zakari. Her husband. She closed her eyes, opening them once more when Aarif spoke.

'It was my fault that you were expecting King Zakari,' he told her flatly. 'I should have explained the arrangements before my arrival.'

Kalila glanced at him, curiosity flaring within her. Aarif held himself rigidly now, and although he was still unmoving she felt his tension emanating from him in forceful waves. He was not the kind of man to make such a mistake, she reflected, so what had happened? Why was he taking the blame?

'It is no matter,' she said after a moment. She could hardly explain how much it had mattered, or why. 'King Zakari will be waiting for me in Calista. The wedding has already been delayed several times—what is a few more days?'

'It seems,' Aarif replied, his voice carefully neutral, 'that it matters to you.'

Kalila looked away. That afternoon, it had mattered. She had been disappointed, hurt, like the child at a birthday party Aarif had thought her, waiting for a present only to find it empty inside. Yet now she felt worse; she was numb, indifferent. She'd finally realised there had never been a present, or even a façade of a present. There had only been an empty box.

And there was nothing she could do about it.

'Princess Kalila, I should go.' Aarif rose from the bench. 'It is not seemly for us to be like this.'

'Why not? We shall be as brother and sister in a matter of weeks,' Kalila replied, raising her eyebrows in challenge.

Aarif paused. 'True, but you know as well as I do that in countries such as ours men and women who are unattached do not spend time alone together, unchaperoned.'

'Are you unattached?' The question slipped out without much thought, yet Kalila realised she wanted to know. He wasn't married, but was there a woman? A girlfriend, a mistress, a lover?

She shouldn't ask; she didn't need to know. Yet she wanted to. Something about that still, considering gaze, the carefully neutral tone, made her want to know the man that must be hidden underneath.

'Yes.' Aarif made to turn. 'And now I must bid you goodnight. I trust you can find your way safely back to the palace?'

'Yes—' Half-turned as he was, the moonlight bathing his cheek in silver, illuminating that livid line from brow to jaw, Kalila found another question slipping out. 'How did you get that scar?'

Aarif jerked in surprise, and then he turned slowly to face her. From the surprised—almost trapped—look on his face Kalila realised it was not a question she should have asked. It was not one Aarif wanted to answer. Still, she waited, her breath caught in her throat, her mind a flurry of questions.

'A foolish accident,' Aarif finally said, stiffly, as if he were not used to explaining. Perhaps he wasn't.

'It must have been.' She regarded him solemnly, longing to lighten the moment, to make him smile again—somehow. 'You look as if someone came at you with a scimitar,' she added, letting a teasing note enter her voice. 'Did you win?' She held her breath, waiting for his reaction.

After an endless moment Aarif's mouth curved in a tiny, reluctant smile. That hint of humour caused Kalila's heart to lurch, her insides to roil in a confused jumble, for suddenly he did not seem like the man he'd been before. Suddenly he seemed like someone else entirely. Someone she wanted to know, the man underneath she'd wondered about coming to the fore.

'Would you believe me,' he asked, 'if I told you I took on three camel rustlers by myself?'

His gaze was steady on hers, his mouth still curved. Kalila smiled and nodded. 'Yes, I would.'

And suddenly the moment of levity took on a deeper, disquieting meaning; suddenly something was stretching between them, winding around them, drawing them closer though neither of them moved.

Aarif's eyes held hers and she didn't look away. She reached one hand out in farewell, and to her surprise Aarif clasped it, his fingers, dry and cool, wrapping around hers, sending a jolt of startling awareness along her arm and through her whole body.

Her fingers tightened on his, and as the moment stretched on—too long—neither one of them let go. Neither of them, Kalila felt, wanted to. She should have pulled her hand away. Aarif should have loosened his grip.

Yet neither of them did, and the moment stretched on suspended and endless, as they remained, linked by their clasped fingers, holding each other's gaze with a silent, suppressed longing. Kalila felt a clamour of different emotions rise within her: the need to be understood, cherished. Loved. The idea, strange and impossible, that this man could be the one who would.

Then, as if rousing himself from a dream, Aarif shook his head, the light in his eyes replaced by an even more disquieting bleakness, his mouth returning to its familiar, compressed line. He dropped her hand so suddenly Kalila's arm swung down helplessly in the darkness, landing in her lap with a thud. She curled her fingers, now burning with the memory of his touch, against her thigh as Aarif turned away.

'Goodnight, Princess,' he said, and disappeared silently into the darkness of the garden.

CHAPTER THREE

BY THE time Kalila awoke the next morning the city was alive with excitement and activity. She could sense it from the window of her dressing room, which faced east towards Makaris. She smelled it on the wind carried from the city, the scents of frying meat and spices, felt it in the air as if it were a tangible thing.

Kalila felt an answering excitement in herself, although her mind skittered away from its source. She was not looking forward to her marriage, yet she found herself eagerly anticipating the journey to Calista. With Aarif.

Stop. She shouldn't think like this, want like this. Yet the desires she felt were formless, nameless, and Kalila knew it was better for them to stay that way. Safer. In a fortnight, she would marry Zakari. There was no escaping that fate. Yet if she could afford herself a few brief, harmless moments of pleasure before then—

Stop.

'Kalila! It is time you dressed!' Juhanah bustled in, clapping her hands as she beamed in excitement. She would be accompanying her to Calista, and would stay for as long as it took for Kalila to settle.

And how long would that be? Kalila wondered, feeling the familiar despair settle over her once more. Days, months, years? Ever?

'Kalila, my princess.' Juhanah knelt by her side as Kalila sat on the window seat, one shoulder propped against the stone frame. 'It is time. Prince Aarif wishes your bags to be loaded, everything is prepared.'

'Already?' She turned away from the window. Her clothes and personal items had already been packed; many of them she'd left in boxes, shipped from England. She did not have too much to bring, clothes, a few books and photographs, nothing more. They felt like scraps being brought to a feast, a humble and pathetic offering.

'Juhanah, I don't want to go.' The words tumbled from her and her lips trembled. She pressed them together tightly, willed herself not to cry. Tears, now, would do no good. Still, she had to speak. She needed to give voices to the nameless terrors clamouring within her. 'I don't want to marry him,' she whispered.

Juhanah was silent for a moment. Kalila couldn't look at her; she felt too ashamed. 'Oh, *ya daanaya*,' Juhanah finally said, and rose to put her arms around Kalila. Kalila rested her head against Juhanah's pillowy bosom, let herself be comforted like a child. 'Of course you are afraid now. If King Zakari had come, perhaps it would be different. It is a hard thing, to travel to a strange country and wed a strange man.'

'But I don't think it *would* be different,' Kalila whispered. 'I realised that last night. I don't want to do it, Juhanah. I don't care what he's like. He doesn't love me.'

'In time—'

'In time comes affection, understanding, kindness,' Kalila cut her off. '*Maybe*. I've been telling myself that for years. But why should I settle for such things? My father was able to have a love match. Aarif's father and stepmother—Anya and Ashraf—had a love match. Why not me?'

Juhanah released her, her mouth pursed thoughtfully. '*Aarif's* father?' she repeated, and Kalila flushed.

'Zakari's father as well. Why must I settle?'

'You are doing a great thing for your country,' Juhanah told her, and there was a warning note in her nurse's voice that reminded Kalila of when she'd been caught stealing honey cakes from the kitchen. 'You must act like the princess you are, Kalila, and do your duty.'

'Yes. I know.' She'd accepted that many years ago, had told herself it many times. Yet all those resolutions crumbled to dust in face of the harsh, present reality. 'I know,' she repeated, and if Juhanah heard the damning waver of doubt in Kalila's voice, she did not comment on it.

'Now, come. You must dress.'

'I'm not wearing another costume,' Kalila warned. 'I won't truss myself up like a harem girl so the people of Makaris can be satisfied.'

'Of course not,' Juhanah soothed. 'Besides, it wouldn't be sensible for travel.'

Kalila gave a little laugh, and Juhanah smiled encouragingly. She was wound so tightly, so desperately, she realised, and that little laugh reminded her of who she was. Who she used to be. She was a girl who laughed, who loved life, who embraced each opportunity with pleasure, abandon.

She was not this skittish, frightened, desperate creature. She would not let herself be.

In the end she chose a pair of loose cotton trousers and a matching tunic in palest green, embroidered with silver thread. She plaited her hair once more, and wore silver hoops on her ears, a silver locket that had been her mother's around her neck.

Juhanah went to supervise the packing, and Kalila was left alone in her childhood bedroom. In a few moments she would say goodbye to the palace, the staff, and then her father. Bahir would fly to Calista for the wedding, but it wouldn't be the same. When she walked out of the palace, she would be leaving this life for ever.

The thought saddened her. She'd grown up here, explored the echoing, shadowy corridors, curled up in a sunny window seat, sneaked into her father's library or the palace kitchen. The first time she'd been away from home for any length of time had been when she'd gone to Cambridge.

And what a different life she'd had there! A shared flat with a few other girls, nights out at the pub or takeaway pizza and a bottle of wine, everything casual and messy and fun.

She felt as if she were two people, the princess and the person. The queen-in-waiting and the modern girl who just wanted to be loved.

Yet you couldn't be two people and still be happy. Still be yourself. So how would she survive in the coming months and years, when she took on the mantle that was so foreign to her, queen, wife? How could she be happy?

Again Aarif's image flittered through her mind, tempting, treacherous. She'd been happy in his presence. She shook her head as if to deny herself that forbidden truth, and left her bedroom. From the window in the upstairs corridor she saw a motorcade assembled in the palace courtyard. There was a van for her cases, a car for Aarif, another for her father, a car for her and Juhanah, and another for the palace staff accompanying them to the airport.

It was a parade, and she was the centrepiece. Kalila closed her eyes. Her fingers curled around the sun-warmed stone of the window sill, and she held onto it like an anchor.

'I can't do it,' she whispered aloud, though there was no one to hear. Her own heart heard, and answered. *I won't.*

The sun beat down on Aarif as he stood in the palace courtyard, waiting for Kalila to arrive. A light wind blowing from the desert eased his discomfort, and he was grateful for the refreshment. He'd been up since dawn, seeing to arrangements; he wanted nothing left to chance or circumstance, no more mistakes to be made.

The first one had been bad enough.

Aarif's mouth twisted in a grimace as he recalled his private interview with King Bahir last night, after dinner. The king was too shrewd and politic to be overt about his displeasure, but he'd made his disappointment over Zakari's absence known.

Aarif had done his best to be apologetic without weakening his own position, or that of his brother. He half-wondered if Bahir was making a bigger to-do about Zakari's absence than perhaps was warranted; it could be, in future, a necessary bargaining chip.

And what of Kalila? His mind drifted back to the evening in the garden, the scent of roses mixed with a heady scent that he felt—feared—was the princess herself. He'd watched her out of the corner of his eye as he'd sat on the bench, less than a foot away from her. He'd seen how the moonlight had gleamed on her heavy, dark hair; he'd found his eyes drawn to the bare, graceful curve of her neck.

He'd felt her fingers in his, and he had not wanted to stop touching her. It had been a balm, that gentle touch, as if she'd understood him. As if she'd wanted to.

Yet even more than her appearance or touch had been her words, her smile. *You look as if someone came at you with a scimitar.* No one talked about his scar, no one asked him to remember. No one made him smile.

Except, somehow, inexplicably, she had. She'd slipped under his defences without even knowing she'd done so, and it made him both uneasy and strangely glad.

Stop. His mind clamped down on these wandering thoughts with the precision and power of a steel trap. He had no business thinking of Kalila's neck or hair, wondering what she smelled like, remembering the feel of her fingers. He had no business thinking of her at all.

She was to be his brother's wife. He was here as a proxy, a servant, and he would do his job, fulfil his task.

He wouldn't fail.

There was a flurry of movement at the palace doors, and Aarif saw Kalila come out into the courtyard. Her father was behind her, dressed simply as Aarif was, in a white cotton shirt and tan chinos.

It was too hot, Aarif acknowledged, for formal dress. And his sense of the festival in Makaris was that it was a fun, light-hearted affair, a celebration rather than a ceremony.

Kalila approached him, looking fresh and cool, her eyes bright and clear, her smile firmly in place. As she came closer he saw shadows under her eyes, and her smile started to look a little fixed. She was bound to be a bit nervous, he supposed, a bit uncertain.

'Good morning, Princess.'

'Prince Aarif.' She gave a small, graceful nod. 'Thank you for helping with these arrangements. You do me a great service.'

Aarif sketched a short bow back. 'It is my honour and pleasure.'

The formalities dealt with, she lowered her voice. 'Thank you for your conversation in the garden last night. It helped me immeasurably.'

Aarif felt himself grow cold, his formal smile turning rigid. He felt as if her simple thanks had cast a sordid, revealing light on that innocent conversation—for it hadn't been innocent, had it? His thoughts hadn't, his touch hadn't.

He nodded brusquely, saw the flicker of disappointed hurt in her eyes before she nodded back, accepting. He turned to gaze at the line of shiny black cars. 'The day grows old and the sun high. We should not delay, for the people of Makaris are eager, I am sure.'

Kalila folded her arms protectively across her middle before becoming aware of the defensive position and dropping them. 'Tell me, will King Zakari be in Calista when I arrive?' Aarif hesitated, and she met his gaze knowingly. 'Will he be waiting at the airport with a bouquet of roses, do you think?' He heard the thread of mockery in her voice and felt equal stabs of annoyance and alarm. Did the girl actually expect a love match? Was she that naive, or simply hopeful?

Didn't she deserve one?

He made his voice non-committal. 'I am sure King Zakari will be pleased to renew your acquaintance.'

'If you ring him to tell him,' Kalila said, and now he heard laughter in her voice, brittle and sharp, 'tell him I don't actually like roses. Irises are my favourite.'

Aarif did not answer, and she moved away, her body held with stiff dignity. He suppressed another prickle of irritation. The last thing he needed was a royal princess's hurt feelings to deal with. Surely she'd known this was an alliance of countries, not some great romance! Yet apparently she'd been hoping for something of the sort, or so it had seemed last night, when he'd heard the aching disappointment in her voice...

Aarif turned his mind resolutely away from the memory of last night, the quiet, forbidden intimacy of the garden. He turned to one of the palace staff who waited patiently for orders.

'Have the cases been loaded?' he demanded, hearing his tone and knowing it was unnecessarily surly and abrupt.

The aide lowered his eyes. 'Yes, Prince Aarif.'

'Good.' Aarif glanced at the sky, the endless blue smudged by a faint streak of grimy grey on the horizon. 'It looks like a wind is kicking up. We should leave without delay.'

It was another half-hour before they actually began to drive the five kilometers to Makaris, as servants and staff hurried to and fro, remembering this, forgetting that, while Aarif waited and watched, curbing his irritation with effort.

He wanted this whole spectacle to be finished. He wanted to be back in Calista, in his offices, away from the distractions, the temptations—

Again his mind clamped down, and he shook his head. No, he wouldn't think of it. Of her.

As the motorcade moved into Makaris people lined the road, and the cars slowed to a crawl. Ahead of him Aarif saw Kalila's car window open, and a slender, golden arm emerge to accept ragged bouquets of flowers, scraps of paper printed with blessings and prayers, and other well wishes. The crowd smiled, cheered, and called their blessings, children and dogs trailing the cars as they went under the main arch of the city into the Old Town, with its crumbling buildings of red clay, before emerging into a large square lined with food stalls and filled to near overflowing with a joyous throng.

The cars drew to a halt, and King Bahir emerged from the front car, smiling and waving while aides stayed close to his side. Aarif looked around the ragged crowd with a deepening unease.

It was crowded, dirty, impossible to keep track of Kalila. Anyone could accost her, anything could happen. Aarif knew how quickly it could all go desperately, dreadfully wrong. And he, Aarif, would be responsible. Again.

He threw open the door of his car, snapping to an aide behind him. 'Stay close to the princess. Don't let her out of your sight.'

The man nodded, scurrying off, and Aarif stood in the centre of the square, shielding his eyes from the glare of the sun as people pressed close, desperate for a glimpse of the royals, a blessing from the princess.

A space had been cleared for dancing, and Aarif watched as some local women put on a little show, a band of men in colorful robes and turbans playing instruments, the bandir drum, the maqrunah, the garagab. Together the instruments made a reedy, dissonant, not unpleasing sound, yet with the crowds and the heavy, spicy smell of fried food from the stalls, Aarif found himself annoyed, tensing, on alert.

There was too much risk. Too much danger. It kicked his heart-rate up a notch, made his palms slick with sweat. He despised himself for it; he despised his fear.

He despised the uncertainty, the unknown.

Anything could happen here.

He glanced around, his eyes sifting through the crowds, and saw Kalila standing at the front of the cleared space, watching the little dance as if it completely captured her attention. Her hair fell down her back in a dark, gleaming plait, and the breeze moulded her loose clothing to her body, so Aarif could see the gentle swell of her breast and hip. He swallowed, dragging his gaze away.

Next to him a ragged little boy tugged on his leg, and Aarif glanced down at his smiling face and reached for a coin, glad for the distraction.

The presentation ended, and once again Aarif found his gaze pulled relentlessly back to the princess. She clapped and smiled, speaking to each woman in turn, her arm around them as if they were equals. Friends.

Aarif felt a reluctant tug of admiration for her poise. He knew she was under strain, nervous and tense, and yet she acted with an innate grace. She acted like the princess she was, the queen she would be. His brother's wife.

He turned away, scouring the crowds on the other side for any sign of danger, darkness—

'The king wishes you to join him and the princess,' an aide murmured in his ear, bowing low, and Aarif was left with little choice than to make his way through the crowds to King Bahir's—and Kalila's—side.

She glanced at him sideways as he approached, smiling slightly, and Aarif gave a tiny bow back. Her smile deepened, but her eyes, those deep golden pools of reflected emotion and light, were sad, and Aarif felt something inside him tug, something start to unravel. He wanted to make her smile. He pushed the feeling away, and when Kalila looked back at the dancers so did Aarif.

The dance was followed by another, and then a performance by children. Aarif watched, feeling himself grow weary even as Kalila continued to smile and applaud, speaking individually to each man, woman, and child. Finally the performances ended, and Aarif realised a meal of sorts was to be served. Perhaps after they'd eaten they would be free to continue to the airport, and finally home. Safety.

Makeshift tables and benches, no more than rough planks, had been set up by the food stalls, and Kalila and her father sat down with a few other important dignitaries from the palace. A few well-placed individuals from the city crowd had been chosen as well, Aarif saw with a cynical smile, a pretty child, a smiling old woman, a fat merchant.

The food was served, dish after dish of beef kebabs and chicken with raisins and rice, stewed prunes and eggplant salad. Aarif ate a bit of everything so as not to offend, although his nerves were wound too tightly to enjoy what was a surprisingly delicious meal.

The plates were cleared and the music and dancing began once again in the square, with no sign of the festivities abating. Aarif suppressed a sigh of impatience, nerves tautening like wire. He was hot and sticky, tense and irritable, and they'd already been there too long. It was time to take charge.

He wove his way over to Bahir, who was smiling at some of the more energetic dancing that was now going on, men in a circle with their arms crossed, stamping their feet. Instinctively Aarif looked around for Kalila, but her slight figure was nowhere to be seen.

He scanned the crowded market place, the crush of bodies, searching for her distinctive figure, that gleaming plait of hair, knowing instinctively if she was there, certain he could find her.

She wasn't there. He knew it, felt it like a shock to his system, rippling unpleasantly through him. Somehow, somewhere, she had gone. A sharp pain stabbed him in the gut, memory and anger and fear. Aarif's mouth tightened, his eyes narrowed against the dazzling glare of the sun.

He saw Bahir glance at him in question, but Aarif did not want to see the older man now. He wanted to see Kalila. He wanted to know she was safe. He needed to.

He pushed away from Bahir, through the crowds, scanning the strange, smiling faces for a glimpse of the untarnished loveliness he'd seen in the garden last night.

Where was she?

He caught sight of the aide he'd assigned as her babysitter, and grabbed the man's elbow. 'Where is the princess?' he demanded roughly.

The aide flinched under Aarif's rough grasp. 'She went into the church for some cool air. I thought there was no harm—'

Aarif swore under his breath and let the man go. His gaze searched the square before he found what he was looking for—an ancient church in the Byzantine style, made of a startling white stone with a blue cross on top of its dome. He moved towards it with grim purpose.

The door was partly ajar, and Aarif slipped inside quietly. The church was refreshingly cool and dark, and empty save for a few benches and some icons adorning the walls. Kalila sat on one of the benches, her back to Aarif. Something about her position—the rigid set of her shoulders and yet the despairing bowing of her head—made Aarif pause.

He took a breath, waited for the rush of fury to recede, acknowledging to himself it had been unwarranted. Too much. And yet for a moment he'd thought—he remembered—

He cleared his throat, and Kalila turned her head so her face was in profile, her dark lashes sweeping her cheek. 'Have you come to take me away?' she asked, her voice soft, as if it were being absorbed by the stone.

Aarif took a step towards her. 'I wondered where you were.'

'I wished for some air.' She paused, and Aarif waited. 'I've always liked this place. My parents were married here, you know. It was founded when the Byzantines went down to Africa—well over a thousand years ago now.' She gave a little sigh as she looked around the bare walls. 'It survived the invasion of the Berbers, the Ottomans, the Turks. A noble task, don't you think, to keep one's identity amidst so much change?'

Aarif took a step closer to her. 'Indeed, as your country has done,' he said, choosing to guide the conversation to more impersonal waters. 'I know the history of Zaraq well, Princess, as it is a neighbour of my own homeland, Calista. When nearly every other kingdom was invaded and taken over the centuries, yours alone survived.'

'Yes, because we didn't have anything anyone wanted.' She gave a little laugh that sounded cynical and somehow wrong. 'Ringed by mountains, little more than desert, and inhabited by a fierce people willing to fight to the death for their pathetic patch of land. It's no wonder we survived, at least until the French came and realised there was nickel and copper to be had under our barren earth.'

'Your independence is no small thing,' Aarif said. He saw Kalila's hands bunch into fists in her lap.

'No, it isn't,' she agreed in a voice that surprised him; it was steely and sure. 'I'm glad you realise that.'

Aarif hesitated. He felt the ripple of tension and something deeper, something dark and determined from Kalila, and he wondered at its source.

In an hour, he reminded himself, they would be on a plane. In three hours, they could be at the Calistan palace, and Kalila would be kept in the women's quarters, safe with her old nurse, away from him. The thought should have comforted him; he'd meant it to. Instead he felt the betraying, wrenching pain of loss.

'We have enjoyed the festivities, Princess,' he said, 'but you were right, we must go. The hour grows late and a storm looks to approach, a sirocco, and living in the desert you know how dangerous they can be.'

'A storm?' Interest lifted Kalila's voice momentarily. 'Will the plane be delayed, do you think?'

'Not if we leave promptly.'

She hesitated, and Aarif resisted the urge to take her into his arms. He wanted to scold her, tell her to stop feeling sorry for herself, and yet he also wanted to comfort her, to breathe in the scent of her hair—

Irritated by his own impulse, he sharpened his tone. 'I

regret to disturb your tranquillity, Princess, but there is a duty to fulfil.' There always was, no matter how crippling the weight, how difficult the task.

'I'm coming,' she said at last, and there was a new resolute determination to her tone that relieved Aarif. She rose gracefully, glanced at him, her eyes fastening on his, and once again Aarif was transfixed by that clear gaze, yet this time he couldn't read the expression in it.

'I'm sorry, Prince Aarif,' she said in a quiet, steady voice, 'for any trouble I've caused you.' She laid a hand on his arm, her fingers slender and cool, yet burning Aarif's skin. Branding it, and he resisted the desire to cover her hand with his own, to feel her fingers twine with his once more. A simple, seductive touch.

He raised his eyebrows in surprise before managing a cool smile. 'There has been no trouble, Princess.' Carefully, deliberately, he moved his arm away from her touch.

Her hand dropped to her side, and she smiled back as if she didn't believe him, going so far as to give her head a little shake, before she moved out of the cool church into the dusty heat of the crowded square.

The festivities were blessedly winding down by the time they found their way back to the royal party. Aarif was glad to see Kalila's—and his—absence had not been noted, although Bahir gave them both a quick, sharp glance before indulging the crowd in a formal farewell of his daughter. He kissed both her cheeks and bestowed his blessing; while they went on to the national airport, he would return to the palace.

Kalila accepted his farewell with dignity, her head bowed, and then turned to enter her car. Everyone followed suit, the doors closed, and with a sigh of relief Aarif saw they were at last on their way. Surely nothing could go wrong now.

The cars moved slowly through the crowded streets of the Old Town, still chased by a merry crowd of well wishers, then back onto the main boulevard, a straight, flat road lined with dusty palm trees that led to the airport.

The airport was only ten kilometres away, but Aarif noted the darkening smudge on the horizon with some dismay. How long would it take to load all of the cases, make any arrangements? He knew well enough how these things could drag on.

As if to prove his point, the cars slowly drew to a halt. Aarif rolled down his window and peered ahead, but through the dust kicked up by the line of cars he could see nothing.

A minute passed and nothing moved. With another muttered oath, Aarif threw open his door and strode down the barren road to the princess's car.

He rapped twice on the window and after a moment Kalila's nurse, a plump woman with bright eyes and rounded cheeks, rolled down the window.

'Prince Aarif!'

'Is the princess well?' Aarif asked. 'Do you know why we are stopped?'

'She felt ill,' the nurse gabbled. 'And asked to be given a moment…of privacy…'

A sudden shadow of foreboding fell over Aarif, far more ominous than the storm gathering on the horizon. He thought of his conversation with Kalila only moments ago in the church, her talk of independence, her apology for troubling him, and the shadow of foreboding intensified into a throbbing darkness.

'Where is she?' he asked, and heard the harsh grating of his own voice. The nurse looked both alarmed and offended, and drew back. Aarif gritted his teeth and tried for patience. 'This is not a safe place, madam. I do not trust her security in such an inhospitable location.' He glanced up; the smudge on the horizon was growing darker, wider. Makaris was at least five kilometres behind them, and rocky desert stretched in every direction, the flat landscape marked only by large, tumbled boulders, as if thrown by a giant, unseen hand.

The nurse hesitated, and Aarif felt his frustration growing. He wanted to shake the silly woman, to demand answers—

'She's over there.' The woman pointed a shaking finger to a cluster of rocks about twenty metres away. A perfect hiding place.

Aarif strode towards them, his body taut with purpose and fury. He didn't know why he felt so angry, so afraid. Perhaps Kalila did indeed need a moment of privacy. Perhaps she was ill. Perhaps this was all in his mind, paranoid, pathetic. Remembering.

Yet he couldn't ignore his instinct; it was too strong, too insistent, a relentless drumming in his head, his heart.

Something had gone wrong. Something always went wrong.

Still, as he approached the rocks he hesitated. If Kalila was indeed in an indelicate position, it would not do to disturb her. Yet if she was in danger, or worse…

What was worse? What could be worse than danger?

Yet even as Aarif turned the corner of the rocky outcropping, he knew. He knew just what nameless fear had clutched at him since Kalila had apologised in the church, or perhaps even before then, when he'd heard her unhappy sigh in the garden.

For on the other side of the rocks, there was nothing, no princess. But on the horizon, riding towards the storm, was a lone figure on a horse.

Kalila, Aarif realised grimly, was running away.

CHAPTER FOUR

KALILA knew where she was going. It was that thought that sustained her as the wind whipped the headscarf around her face and the gritty sand stung her eyes. She pictured the scene behind her, how quickly it would erupt into chaos, and felt a deep shaft of guilt pierce her.

How long would it take Aarif to realise she had gone? And what would he do? Even with her brief acquaintance of the man, Kalila knew instinctively what the desert prince would do. He would go after her.

The thought sent a shiver of apprehension straight through her, and she clenched her hands on the reins. Arranging her disappearance had not been easy; the plan had crystallised only that morning when she'd looked down at the courtyard, seen the dismantling of her life, and realised she couldn't do it. She couldn't ride like a sacrifice to Calista, to marry a man she didn't love, didn't even know. Not yet, anyway.

Yet even as she rode towards a grim horizon, an uncertain future, she knew this freedom couldn't last for ever. She couldn't live in the desert like a nomad; Aarif would find her, and if he didn't someone else would.

Yet still she ran. That was what fear did to you, she supposed. It made you miserable, sick, dizzy. Desperate. Willing to do anything, try anything, no matter how risky or foolish, how thoughtless or selfish.

So she kept riding, heading for the one place she knew she'd be safe…at least for a little while.

Two kilometres behind her Aarif grimly wound a turban around his head to protect himself from the dust. Already the wind was kicking grit into his eyes, stinging his cheeks. What was she thinking, he wondered furiously, to ride out in weather like this? He'd warned her of the storm, and surely, as a child of a desert, she knew the dangers.

So was she stupid, he wondered with savage humour, or just desperate?

It didn't matter. She had to be found. He'd already sent an aide back to fetch a horse and provisions from the city.

The aide had been appalled. 'But King Bahir must be notified! He will send out a search party—'

Aarif gestured to the darkening sky. 'There is no time for a search party. The princess must be found, and as soon as possible. I will go…alone.' He watched the aide's eyes widen at this suggestion of impropriety. 'Circumstances are dire,' he informed the man flatly. 'If the princess is not found, it will be all of your necks on the line.' And his. He thought of Zakari, of Bahir, of the countries and families depending on him bringing Kalila back to Calista, and another fresh wave of fury surged through him.

'Prince Aarif!' A man jogged up to his elbow. 'There is a horse, and some water and bread and meat. We could not get anything else in such a hurry—'

'Good.' Aarif shrugged into the long, cotton *thobe* he wore to protect his clothes from the onslaught of the sun and sand. He'd exchanged his shoes for sturdy boots, and now he swung up onto the back of the horse, a capable if elderly mount.

'Drive to the airport,' he instructed the aide, 'and shelter there until the storm wears out. Do not contact the king.' His mouth curved in a grim smile. 'We don't want him needlessly worried.'

The man swallowed and nodded.

Turning his back on the stalled motorcade, Aarif headed into the swirling sand.

The wind was brisk, stinging what little of his face was still unprotected, but Aarif knew it could—would—get much worse. In another hour or two, the visibility would be zero, the winds well over a hundred miles an hour and deadly.

Deadly to Kalila, deadly to him. It was the princess he cared about; his own life he'd long ago determined was worthless. Yet if he failed to bring the princess back to Calista, if she died in his care…

Aarif squinted into the distance, refusing to let that thought, that fear creep into his brain and swallow his reason. He needed all his wits about him now.

The old horse balked at the unfamiliar terrain. She was a city animal, used to plodding ancient thoroughfares before heading home to her stable and bag of oats every night. The unforgiving wind and rocky ground were terrifying to her, and she let it be known with every straining step.

Aarif had always been kind to animals; it was man's sacred duty to provide for the beasts in his care, yet now his gloved hands clenched impatiently on the reins, and he fought the urge to scream at the animal, as if she could understand, as if that would help. As if anything would.

Where was Kalila? He forced himself to think rationally. She'd had a horse hidden behind the rocks, so someone had clearly helped her. She'd had a plan, a premeditated plan. The thought caused fresh rage to slice cleanly through him, but he pushed it away with grim resolution. He needed to think.

If she had a horse, she undoubtedly had some provisions. Not many, perhaps not more than he had, a bit of food, some water, a blanket. She was not an unintelligent woman, quite the contrary, so she must have a destination in mind, he reasoned. A safe place to shelter out the storm she knew about, the storm he'd *told* her about.

But where?

He drew the horse to a halt, scanning the horizon once more. Through the swirling sand he could just barely see the outlines of rocks, dunes, the ever-shifting shape of the desert. Nothing seemed like a probable resting place, yet he knew he would investigate every lone rock, every sheltered dune. It was his duty.

His duty. He wouldn't fail his duty; he'd been telling himself that for years, yet now, starkly, Aarif wondered when he *hadn't* failed. He shrugged impatiently, hating the weakness of his own melancholy, yet even now the memories sucked him under, taunted him viciously.

If you hadn't gone...if you hadn't said Zafir could come along...if you hadn't slipped...

If. If. If. Damnable, dangerous ifs, would-have-beens that never existed, never happened, yet they taunted him still, always.

*If...*your brother would still be alive.

Aarif swore aloud, the words torn from his throat, lost on the wind. The horse neighed pitifully, pushed already beyond her limited endurance.

And then he saw it. A dark grey speck on the horizon, darker than the swirling sand, the clouds. Rock. Many rocks, clustered together, providing safety and shelter, more so than anywhere else he could see. He knew, knew deep in his gut, that Kalila was making her way towards those rocks. Perhaps she was already there; she must have known the way.

He imagined her setting up her little camp, thinking herself safe, smiling to herself that she'd fooled them all, fooled *him*, played with their lives, with his own responsibilities and code of *honour*—

Cursing again, Aarif raised the reins and headed for the horizon.

She hadn't ridden so fast or furiously in months, years perhaps, and every muscle in Kalila's body ached. Her mind and heart ached too, throbbed with a desperate misery that made her wonder why she'd ever taken this stupid, selfish risk. She pushed the thought away; she couldn't afford doubt now. She couldn't afford pity.

Aarif had been right. A storm was blowing, a sirocco, the wet winds of the Mediterranean clashing with the desert's dry heat in an unholy cacophony of sound and fury. She had, Kalila guessed, maybe half an hour to set up shelter and get herself and her horse secure.

She murmured soothing endearments to her mare, As Sabr, and led her to where the huge boulder created a natural overhang, the small space under the shadow of stone enough for a tent, a horse.

Her father had taken her camping here when she was child; it was a no more than twelve kilometres from the palace, less even from Makaris, yet with the blowing sands it might have been a hundred.

Kalila set about her tasks, mindless, necessary. The tent was basic, with room only for two people.

Two people. Kalila's mind snagged and then froze on the thought, the realisation. If Aarif came after her…if he found her…

But, no. He had no idea where she was going, had never been in this desert before, didn't know the terrain, if he was out here at all. Surely in this storm he would turn back, he would wait. Any sensible man would do so, and yet…

Aarif did not seem a sensible man. He seemed, Kalila realised, remembering that hard look in his eyes, her heart beating sickly, a determined man.

What would she do if he found her? What would he do?

She pushed the thought, as she had a host of others, firmly away. No time to wonder, to fear. Now was the time for action only.

With the wind blowing more ferociously every second, it took Kalila longer to assemble the tent. She was furious with her own ineptitude, her soft hands and drumming heart. She'd assembled a tent like this—this tent even—a dozen, twenty times, yet now everything conspired against her; her hands cramped and slipped, her muscles ached, even her bones did. Her eyes stung and her mouth was desperately dry. Her heart throbbed.

Finally the tent was assembled and she took the saddlebags from As Sabr—food, blankets, water—and shoved them inside. She covered the horse with a blanket, drawing her closer against the rock for safety.

Then she turned to make her way into the tent, and her heart stopped. Her mouth dropped open. For there, only ten metres away, was a man. He was turbaned, robed, veiled except for his eyes, as she had been yesterday. He looked like a mythical creature, a hero—or perhaps a villain—from a fairy tale, an Arabian one.

It was, Kalila knew, Aarif.

He had found her.

Her mind froze, and so did her body. Kalila stood there, the winds buffeting her, the sand stinging her eyes, flying into her open mouth. She closed it, tasted grit, and wondered what would happen now. Her mind was beginning to thaw, and with it came a fearful flood of realisations, implications. Aarif looked furious. Yet with the realisation of his own anger was her own, treacherous sense of relief.

He had come.

Had she actually wanted him to find her? She was ashamed by the secret manipulations of her own heart, and she pushed the thought away as Aarif slid off his horse, leading the pathetic animal towards the shelter of the rock. His body was swathed in cloth, and she could only see his eyes, those dark, gleaming, angry eyes.

Kalila swallowed; more grit. Aarif came closer, the horse stumbling and neighing piteously behind him. Kalila still didn't move. Where could she go? She'd already run away and he'd found her. He'd found her so very easily.

He dealt with the animal first. From the corner of her eye

Kalila saw him soothe the horse, give her water and a feed bag. He patted her down with a blanket, his movements steady, assured, yet Kalila could see the taut fury in every line of his body; she could feel it in the air, humming and vibrating between them with the same electricity that fired the storm.

The horse dealt with, he turned, and his gaze levelled her, decimated her. She swallowed again, choking on sand, and forced herself to keep his gaze, even to challenge it. Yet after a long moment she couldn't, and her gaze skittered nervously away.

The wind whistled around them with a high-pitched scream; in half an hour, less perhaps, the storm would be at its worst, yet still neither of them moved.

'Look at me,' Aarif said. His voice was low, throbbing, yet even with the shrieking wind Kalila heard it; she felt its demand deep in her bones, and she looked up.

Their eyes met, fought, and Kalila felt the onslaught of his accusation, his judgment. Aarif stared at her for a full minute, the dark fury of his gaze so much more than a glare, so much worse than anything she'd ever imagined.

She'd been so stupid.

And he knew. She knew.

Aarif muttered something—an expletive—and then in two quick strides he was in front of her, one hand stealing around her arm, the movement one of anger yet control.

'What were you thinking, Princess?' he demanded. His voice was muffled by the cloth over his face and he yanked it down. Kalila saw sand dusting his cheeks, his lips, his stubble. She swallowed again, desperate for water, for air. 'What were you thinking?' he demanded again, his voice raw, 'to come out here in a storm like this? To run away like a naughty child?' He threw one contemptuous arm towards the tent. 'Are you playing house, Princess? Is life nothing but a game to you?' His voice lowered to a deadly, damning pitch. 'Did you even think of the risk to you, to me, to our countries?'

Kalila lifted her head and tried to jerk her arm away, but Aarif held fast, his grip strong and sure. 'Let go of me,' she said. She would keep her pride, her defiance now; it was all she had.

He dropped her arm, thrust it away from him as if she disgusted him. Perhaps she did.

'You have no idea,' he said, and there was loathing and contempt in his voice, so great and deep and unrelenting that Kalila felt herself recoil in shame. 'No idea,' he repeated, shaking his head. 'And I thought you had.'

'You have no idea,' Kalila shot back. 'No idea what has gone on in my head, my heart—'

'I don't care,' he snarled and she jerked back proudly.

'No, of course not. So why ask what I was thinking? You've condemned me already.'

His gaze raked her and Kalila kept her shoulders back, her spine straight. She wouldn't cower now.

'Maybe I have,' Aarif said.

Another piercing shriek of wind, and then a louder, more horrifying crack. Aarif glanced up but before Kalila's mind could even process what she heard he'd thrust her back against the rock, her back pressed against the uneven stone, his body hard against hers.

The rock above them had broken off, a stress fracture in the stone that had finally given way in the wind, and fallen below with a sickening thud. Kalila swallowed. That could have—would have—fallen on her if Aarif had not pushed her out of the way.

She looked back at Aarif, and with a jolt of alarmed awareness she realised how close he was, his face inches from hers. His eyes bored into hers, his gaze so dark and compelling, yet with a strange, desperate urgency that caused an answering need to uncoil in her own belly.

His eyes searched her mind, her soul, and what did he find? What did he see? What did she want him to see?

She was suddenly conscious of his heart beating against

hers, an unsteady rhythm, a staccato symphony of life. And with a knowledge of his heartbeat came another, more intimate awareness of his body pressed against hers. Even through the layers of dusty cloth she could feel the taut length of his torso, his thighs, his—

She gasped aloud, and with a curse Aarif jerked away as if she'd scorched him. Kalila stood there, her back still hard against the rock, stunned by her new knowledge.

Aarif had desired her.

'It is not safe out here,' he said brusquely, his eyes not meeting hers. 'You must go into the tent.'

Kalila nodded, her mind still spinning with this new, surprising knowledge. Even facing the bleak prospects of her future, she had no desire to be left for dead in the desert, pinned by a fallen boulder.

She opened the tent flap and struggled in, only to realise after a prolonged moment that Aarif was not coming in with her.

He'd strode towards the horses, and, squinting, she could see him crouched on his haunches in the Eastern style between their lathered bodies, his back against the rock, his expression undeniably grim.

Exasperation, relief, and disappointment all warred within her. Of course a man like Aarif wouldn't want to share the cramped intimacy of the tent. Of course he would stoically insist on weathering a sandstorm outside, with the horses for company. It almost—almost—made her want to laugh.

But then she remembered the feel of his body against hers, the betrayal of his own instinct, as well as her answering need, and she pressed her hands to her hot cheeks.

Desire. It was a strange, novel thought. She hadn't felt desire for anyone; not what she thought of as desire, that inexorable tug of longing for another person. She'd never been close enough to another person to feel that yearning sweetness. Even in her years of freedom in Cambridge, she'd known she must be set apart. A princess had to be pure.

Yet in that moment, feeling the evidence of his own desire and need, she'd felt an answering longing for Aarif and it had been as sweet, as sensuous a pleasure as a drug. It had uncoiled in her belly and spiralled upwards like warm wine through her veins, until all she'd been aware of was him.

Him.

It was the same feeling she'd felt at dinner, in the garden... since she'd met him. She just hadn't recognised it, because she'd never felt it before. Yet now it was so apparent, so obvious, what that feeling was. That hunger, that need. She knew enough about nature and humanity to recognise what Aarif had felt for her moments ago, and she understood the physical reaction of his body—and hers. She might be innocent, but she was not a child.

She did not feel like one.

She took a deep breath; it hurt her lungs. She needed water. Kalila scrabbled through the saddlebags for her canteen, taking only a few careful sips to ease the raw parching of her throat.

Another breath and reason began to return. It had been a heated moment, she acknowledged, a moment of passionate anger. That was all it could be, what it had to be. It wasn't real; she didn't think Aarif even liked her. At least, he certainly didn't after what she'd done today.

She wasn't even sure she liked herself.

Kalila peered out of the tent flap. Even though Aarif was only a few metres away she could barely see him. Sighing in exasperation, she struggled out of the tent and stumbled in the near-darkness towards Aarif.

'You shouldn't be out here.'

'I've experienced worse, Princess,' Aarif told her flatly. He sat crouched on his haunches, his arms crossed. 'Go back in the tent where you belong.'

'You know the desert as well as I do,' Kalila returned. 'It is foolish to wait out here, not to mention dangerous. Why do you think I brought a tent?'

'I can only assume,' Aarif returned, his voice still tight with suppressed fury, 'that you had been planning your little escapade for some time.'

Kalila sighed, then sat down. 'Not as long as you think. If you're going to stay out here, then I am too, and it's likely the tent will blow away.'

She folded her arms, squinting to see him, the wind whipping her hair in tangles around her face. Aarif was silent, and Kalila waited, determined to win this battle of wills.

It was incredibly uncomfortable, though; the ground was hard, the wind merciless, the sand stinging every bit of exposed skin, and Aarif's glare was the harshest element of all. Still, she waited.

'You are the most stubborn woman I have ever met,' he said at last, and, though it wasn't a compliment, not remotely, Kalila smiled.

'I'm pleased you're beginning to realise that.'

A long moment passed as the wind shrieked around them. Muttering something—Kalila couldn't quite hear—Aarif rose fluidly from the ground and fetched his own saddlebags. 'Come, then,' he said, his voice taut. 'I will not risk your own foolish life simply because you choose to be so stubborn.'

Kalila rose, and his arm went around her shoulders, a heavy, strangely comforting weight, as he guided her back to the tent. They crawled through the flap in an inelegant tangle of limbs, half-falling into the small space.

And it was small, Kalila realised with a thrill of alarm. It would be difficult to avoid touching each other.

Aarif turned back to the tent flap. 'We must find a way to secure this, or you will have half the Sahara in here by morning.'

'I have some duct tape,' Kalila said, and dug through her saddlebags to find it.

He slotted her a thoughtful glance as she handed him the tape, although his eyes were still hard and unforgiving. 'You came prepared.'

She shrugged. 'I've camped in the desert many times. I simply knew what to bring.'

Aarif began to tape the flap shut, and it occurred to Kalila that they were locked inside. Trapped. Of course, she could remove the tape easily enough, but it still gave her the odd feeling of being in a prison cell, and Aarif was her jailor.

He turned to her, his eyes sweeping her with critical bluntness. 'You are a mess.'

'So are you,' she snapped, but she was instantly aware of her tangled hair, the sand embedded into her scalp.

'I imagine I am,' Aarif returned dryly. 'I was not prepared to go haring off into the desert in the middle of a sandstorm.' He shook his head, and when he spoke his voice was resigned. 'I don't know whether to think you a fool or a madwoman.'

'Desperate,' Kalila told him flatly, and then looked away. The silence stretched between them, and she raked her fingers through the tangles in her hair, needing to be busy. She felt Aarif's eyes on her as she began to unsnarl the tangles one by one.

'Is marriage so abhorrent to you?' he asked eventually.

'Marriage to a stranger, yes,' Kalila replied, still not looking at him.

Aarif shook his head; she saw the weary movement out of the corner of her eye. 'Yet you knew you would marry my brother since you were twelve. Why choose your escape now, and such a foolhardy one?'

'Because I didn't realise how it would feel,' Kalila said, her voice low. She pulled her fingers through her hair again, attacking the tangles with a viciousness that she felt in her soul, her heart. 'When it came to the actual moment, when I thought Zakari would be there—'

Aarif exhaled, a sound of derisive impatience. 'Is this all simply because he did not come to fetch you? Your feelings are hurt too easily, Princess.'

Kalila swung her head around to meet his gaze directly.

'Perhaps, but yesterday—it clarified everything for me. I'd been going along waiting, hoping, believing I would do my duty, and then—all of a sudden—' She shook her head slowly. 'I thought, well, maybe I won't.'

'The thought of a child,' Aarif replied. 'What did you think? That you would flee into the desert for the rest of your life, live with the Bedouin? Did you think no one would ever find you?'

'No,' Kalila admitted slowly. 'I knew someone would. And even if they didn't, I would have to go back.'

'Then what—?'

'I just wanted to be free,' she said simply, heard the stark honesty, the blatant need in her voice. 'For a moment, a day. I knew it wouldn't last.'

Aarif eyed her unsympathetically. Freedom, to him she supposed, was unimportant. Unnecessary. 'And do you know how much you put at risk for an afternoon's *freedom*?' he asked. 'If your father discovers it—if Zakari does—'

'There's been no harm done,' Kalila objected. 'We're safe.'

'For now,' Aarif replied darkly. 'All is uncertain.'

'You have a grim view of things,' she replied, lifting her chin, clinging to her defiance though he picked at it with every unfeeling word he spoke. 'When you found me in the church, you were the same. Do you always think the worst is going to happen, Aarif?'

He reached for the canteen from his own bag. 'It often does,' he told her and unscrewed the top. Kalila watched him drink; for some reason she found she could not tear her gaze away from the long brown column of his throat, the way his muscles moved as he drank. He finally lifted the canteen from his mouth and she saw the droplets of water on his lips, his chin, and still she could not look away. She gazed, helpless, fascinated.

Slowly her eyes moved upwards to meet his own locked gaze, saw the intensity of feeling there—what was it? Anger? Derision?

Desire.

The moment stretched between them, silent, expectant, and Kalila again remembered his body against hers, its hard contours pressed against her, demanding, knowing. She swallowed, knowing she must look away, she must act, if not demure, then at least dignified.

'We should eat,' she said, and the words sounded stilted, forced. 'You must be hungry.'

Aarif said nothing, and Kalila did not risk looking at him again, seeing that unfathomable darkness in his eyes. Her hands trembled as she reached for bread and cheese, breaking off a bit of each and handing it to Aarif.

He took it with murmured thanks, and they ate quietly, neither speaking, neither looking at the other.

Was she imagining the tension coiling in the room, a far more frightening force than the wind that howled and moaned outside, rattling the sides of the tent as if it would sweep the shelter, and them inside, all away?

No, she was not, at least not in herself. She had never been so aware of another human being, the sounds of him chewing, of the cloth stretching across his body, even his breathing. She'd never had such an insane, instinctive desire to touch someone, to know what his hair, his skin felt like. Would his stubble be rough under her fingers? Would his hair be soft?

Horrified yet fascinated by the train of her thoughts, Kalila forced down a dry lump of bread and finally spoke, breaking the taut silence. 'Haven't you ever felt like that?'

'Like what?' Aarif's tone wasn't unfriendly, but it was close to it.

She swallowed again. 'Wanting to be free, if just for a moment. Haven't you ever wanted to…escape?'

He was silent for so long Kalila wondered if he was going to answer. When he finally spoke, his voice was heavy with a dark finality that Kalila knew she couldn't question. Wouldn't.

'Perhaps, when I was a child,' he said. 'But I outgrew such childish desires, and so must you.'

Kalila said nothing. Yes, she knew running away had been a childish, desperate desire, a moment's insanity, perhaps, and yet it had felt so good to be out on the desert, alone, in charge of her destiny, if only for an hour…even with the churning fear and regret, it had been good.

For a moment, she had been free.

She wondered if Aarif could ever understand that.

'Besides,' he continued, still unsympathetic, 'you had your years in Cambridge to be free, if this *freedom* is so important to you. Do you think my brother will veil you and lock you in the women's quarters? He is a modern man, Princess.'

'Yesterday you called me Kalila,' she blurted, and his lips compressed into a hard line.

'Yesterday was not today,' he said flatly, and Kalila wondered what he meant. She almost asked him, but then she remembered again the feel of his body against hers, his eyes pleading urgently—angrily—with hers, and she thought perhaps it was better not to know. Safer, anyway.

'What will happen?' she asked instead, heard the unsteadiness in her voice. 'Where is everyone?'

'God willing, they are sheltered at the airport. The storm will not die down until morning, I should think. We will return then.' His voice was grim, determined, and Kalila knew what he was thinking.

'And how will you explain our absence?'

'How will you?' he challenged. 'What will you say to your nurse, Kalila? She believed you were unwell. What will you say to all the civil servants of your country who have sworn to give their lives to protect you? Will you talk about *freedom* to them?' His voice rang out, contemptuous, condemning, and Kalila closed her eyes.

'Don't. I know…' She drew a shaky breath. 'I know I acted foolishly. Selfishly. I *know*!' She swept the crumbs off her lap, suddenly restless, needing activity, needing the freedom she had so desperately craved. Tears stung her eyes as she realised the full depth of her situation, her mess. And she'd caused it. Everything, she thought miserably, was her fault.

'How did you arrange it?' Aarif asked after a moment. 'Who brought the horse? The provisions?'

Her eyes flew to his even as her mind replayed the frantic, whispered conversation with a stableboy that morning. 'I don't want to tell you.'

He shrugged, no more than the arrogant lifting of one powerful shoulder. 'I could find out easily enough.'

She thought of the shy, young boy, how she'd determinedly twisted him around her little finger, and felt another hot rush of guilt. 'I don't want—that person—punished.'

'You are the one who should be punished,' Aarif returned harshly. 'Not some frightened servant girl—or was it a besotted stableboy? Either one too weak to disobey your bidding!'

More condemnation. They piled on her head, a crippling burden she had to bear alone.

'It hardly matters,' she whispered. 'You've as good as guessed anyway.' She raised her eyes to his, seeking mercy from the one person who was least likely to give it. 'But tell me this, Aarif. Was it really so terribly selfish, so unforgivable, to allow myself one day—one afternoon—of freedom, when the rest of my life is spoken for?'

Her question was like a penny being dropped into a fountain, sending ripples through the stillness. Ripples of awareness, of feeling.

Aarif said nothing, but Kalila thought she saw a softening in his glance, however small, and it compelled her to continue. 'I don't want an arranged marriage. I'm willing to go through with it, and I'll do my duty by Zakari. I'll do my best. But I want to be loved, Aarif, and I think that's a natural desire. Human beings were created for love. To love and be loved. And even if Zakari grows to love me—and that, I know, is only an if—it's not the same. We weren't able to choose. Your father and stepmother chose love, and so did my parents. Why can't I?'

Her question rang out in a helpless, desperate demand, one that Aarif did not answer. 'Your destiny lay elsewhere,' he replied after a moment, his voice expressionless. He looked away.

'My destiny,' Kalila repeated, unable to keep the scorn from her voice. Not even wanting to. 'A destiny shaped by my father and yours, not by me. I want to choose my own destiny, or at least believe it could be different.'

'We do not always have that choice, Kalila.' His voice was low, almost gentle, although he still did not look at her.

'And what about you?' Kalila forced herself to ask. 'Don't you want love? To love someone and be loved back?' She knew it was an impertinent question, an imprudent one. It hinted at shadowy thoughts, memories, desires, nudged them to the light. It was, she realised, her heart fluttering in anticipation of his response, a dangerous question.

Yet she wanted to know. She *needed* to know.

'It doesn't matter what I want,' Aarif finally said, and it was clear he was ending the conversation. 'It never has. What matters is how best I can serve my family and country.'

'You don't take your own desires into consideration at all?' Kalila pressed, and when his eyes met hers they were flat and hard.

'No.'

Kalila felt as if she'd touched on something darker, some hidden memory or regret that suddenly filled the small space of the tent with its poisonous presence.

Aarif busied himself taking off his boots and spreading his blanket as far away from her as he could.

'We should sleep. We will ride out as soon as the storm breaks.'

Nodding slowly, Kalila reached for her own blanket. Aarif lay on his side, his back to her, his body still and tense.

She spread her own blanket out, removing her boots, stretching out gingerly. If she so much as moved her arm it would brush against Aarif's back, and as much as she was tempted to feel the bunched muscle underneath his shirt—a desire that surprised her with its sudden, unexpected urgency—she pressed backwards instead.

The wind still whistled and shrieked shrilly, and the flapping of the tent's sides was a ceaseless sound. On the wind she heard the horses neighing and moving in animalistic anxiety.

Tomorrow she would be back in civilisation, in Calista. She would meet Zakari. And what would she say? How would she explain what she had done? And why?

Kalila closed her eyes, unwilling to consider the impossible answers to those questions. Tomorrow, she determined miserably, would have to take care of itself.

Kalila had no idea how either of them could sleep in this situation, yet even so fatigue fell over her in a fog. Still, her body was too tense, too aware, too miserable to relax into sleep. She lay awake, listening to the wind and Aarif's steady breathing.

Had he actually managed to fall asleep? It wouldn't surprise her. He was a man of infinite, iron control. Sleep, like everything else, would follow his bidding.

Finally, after what felt like several hours, she fell into an uneasy doze, woken suddenly in the middle of the night.

All was dark and silent; the storm had abated and the stillness of the aftermath carried its own eerie tension. Yet there was a sound, a faint moaning, and Kalila wondered if it was the wind or one of the animals, still uneasy in the unfamiliar surroundings.

But no, she realised, the sound was coming from inside the tent. From right next to her, little more than a tortured breath, a whispered plea of anguish. She shifted, the blanket rustling underneath her, and squinted through the moonlit darkness.

Aarif lay on his back, the blanket twisted around him, a

faint sheen of sweat glistening on his skin. His lips were parted in a grimace, his eyelids twitching as he battled his nightmare.

For surely it was a nightmare that held him in its grip, Kalila realised, for the sound, that piteous moan, was coming from Aarif.

CHAPTER FIVE

IT WAS the same, it was always the same. Agonisingly, torturously the same, where he could never change what had happened, what *would* happen, replaying again and again in his mind as he watched, helpless, hopeless…

He knew it was a dream, and still he could not wake himself from it. The nightmare grabbed him by the throat, swallowed him whole in its cavernous jaws, so all he could hear was his brother's choked cry of desperation.

'Aarif…'

And he did nothing. He felt the searing heat across his face once more, his hands reaching out to grasp—to save—his brother, but Zafir was too far, and farther still, his face pale and terrified as Aarif fell into the water and it rushed into his mouth and nose, closed over his head…

'Aarif…' The voice was softer, sweeter now, a whisper from another world, the real world, yet still the dream did not let him go. He shook from the force of it, great tremors that racked his body with emotional agony.

'Aarif…' It was Zafir again, his voice trailing away, the cry of a boy, a child, and yet holding the relentless ring of condemnation. 'Save me…'

The voice rang in his eyes, faint and desperate, and there was nothing Aarif could do. There was nothing he could ever do.

* * *

Aarif shifted restlessly on his blanket, his face contorted with both pain and anguish.

'Aarif…' Kalila whispered, but he didn't hear her. Couldn't. He was locked in a far more terrible world than the one they currently inhabited. Tentatively Kalila reached over to touch his shoulder, wanting to stir him into wakefulness, but Aarif jerked away from her light touch.

'No…*no*!' His desperate scream ripped through the still-ness of the tent, the night, and caused Kalila's hand to freeze inches from his shoulder. That agonised shriek was a sound she would never forget. It was the sound of a man in mental agony, mortal pain.

Aarif let out another shuddering breath, his hands bunching on the blanket, and Kalila saw the faint, silvery tracks of tears on his cheeks.

Her heart twisted painfully at the sight of so much suffering. What kind of dream could hold him in such terrible captivity?

'Aarif…' she tried again, her voice stronger now. 'It's all right. It's just a dream.' Yet even as she spoke she realised it was not just a dream. A mere figment of imagination could not hold Aarif so strongly in its thrall. This was something far more terrible, far more real.

Kalila couldn't bear to see him suffering so; it cut at her heart and she felt near tears herself. She leaned over him, smoothing the damp hair away from his forehead. *'Aarif,'* she said again, her voice breaking, and then he opened his eyes.

Their faces were close, so close that when his eyes opened it felt as if he touched her with his gaze. Kalila was conscious of her hand still stroking his hair as if he were a child to be comforted.

Aarif stared at her, the vestiges of his private torment still visible on his ravaged face, and then he let out a choked cry and tried to roll away.

He couldn't; she wouldn't let him. She didn't know why she wouldn't, only that she acted on instinct. No one deserved to bear that kind of pain alone. 'Don't,' she whispered. Her fingers threaded through his hair, drawing his gaze back to hers. 'What torments you so?' she whispered. Aarif said nothing. She could feel his racing heart, heard him swallow back another cry. Gently, a movement born still of instinct, she trailed her fingers down his cheek, tracing the path of his scar as if her touch could heal that grim reminder of what—?

Kalila didn't even know, but she felt it, knew the pain Aarif was experiencing must be a personal memory, a private grief. His hand clamped over hers, his fingers trapping and yet clinging to hers, and he shook his head, trying to speak, but unable to.

Kalila stilled, her fingers on his face, and Aarif closed his eyes. A shudder went through his body, a tremor of remembered emotion, and naturally—too naturally—Kalila put her arms around him and drew him to herself.

His head was on her shoulder, his silky hair brushing her lips, his body, hard and muscular, against hers. His arms came around her, and Kalila realised she had never been so close to a man, every part of their bodies in intimate contact. It felt natural, right, this closeness, their bodies wrapped around each other in an embrace born of comfort and need. It humbled her that a man like Aarif would accept her caress, that he might even need it.

Neither of them spoke.

His still-racing heart pounded against her own chest, and after many long moments where the only sound was Aarif's ragged breathing she felt it slow. She stroked his hair, felt his fingers tighten reflexively on her shoulder. Still neither of them moved beyond those tiny gestures, neither of them spoke.

Kalila knew that to speak, to even think would break the moment between them, with its precious fragility, its tenuous tenderness. In a day and night of unreality, this felt real. It felt, she thought distantly, before her mind turned hazy and still once more, right.

Another long moment passed and Aarif's breathing

steadied. Now was the time, Kalila knew, for them to roll away, to close their eyes, to forget this brief and wonderful intimacy, this moment of desire stolen from a lifetime of duty.

Yet she didn't, and she knew with a sudden, thrilling certainty that Aarif wouldn't. She knew as he lifted his head, his eyes gazing darkly, hungrily into hers, what he would do.

He kissed her.

It was not the hard, urgent kiss she'd been half expecting, something born of the reckless desperation of this stolen moment. Instead it was sweet, tentative, his mouth moving gently over hers until it bloomed into something stronger and sweeter still as he deepened the contact, his tongue exploring her lips, her mouth, his hands reaching to cup her face, to draw her even closer, as if he was seeking something from her— and she gave it.

Kalila gave herself up to that kiss, let it reverberate through her heart and mind, body and soul. It was, she thought hazily, a wonderful first kiss. For she'd never been kissed before, not like this, not like anything.

She'd kept herself apart, pure, as she'd always meant to do, as she'd had to do as a princess betrothed since she was twelve. Yet now her mind drifted away from that realisation, for with it came the ugly knowledge that this was far more wrong and selfish an act than running away in the first place.

This was betrayal of the deepest kind, yet her mind—and heart—skittered away from that word for this felt too wonderful. Too right.

The kiss deepened, lengthened and grew into hands and touch, their bodies a living map to be explored and understood.

Aarif fumbled at first with her clothes, but somehow the buttons and snaps gave way and her skin was bare to his fingers, his hands gliding over her flesh before his lips followed, and Kalila gasped at the intimacy, the exposure that made her feel vulnerable and yet treasured.

Loved.

They moved as one, in silence, the only sound a drawing of breath, a sigh of pleasure, the whispering slide of skin against skin. It felt like a dream, a wonderful and healing dream, as Aarif's hands moved over her, touching her in places that had known no man's caress.

She opened herself up to him, parting her legs, arching her back, wanting his touch, needing this new caress, this forbidden intimacy.

And then she touched him, tentatively at first, her hands exploring, seeking, discovering the hard, muscled plane of his chest and stomach, the surprisingly smooth curve of his hip, the ridges on his back—more scars.

Now was not the time to ask where they came from, what terrible memory Aarif kept locked in his heart. Now, Kalila thought, her lips touching the places her hands had gone, brushing over that satiny skin, was the time for healing.

She wouldn't think about what this meant. She pushed the thought, the implications, firmly away, and let herself drift in a haze of feeling and emotion, let Aarif's hands and mouth seek her as she gave herself up to him and the maelstrom of pleasure and wonder he caused to whirl within her.

She'd never imagined the feelings to be strong—sharp— she gasped as he touched her, gasped in surprise and wonder, and felt Aarif smile against her skin. She loved that she'd made him smile, that there was a joy to be found here.

And yet a moment came—as Kalila knew it would have to—when they could have stopped. Should have. Clothing bunched and pushed aside, their bodies bare and touching, Aarif moved on top of her, poised to join his body to hers in an act so intimate, so sacred and precious and unfamiliar, and yet so right. His eyes sought and met hers, a silent agreement. They gazed at each other, neither speaking, both complicit, and then their bodies joined as one.

Kalila gasped at the feeling, her hands bunching on his back, the twinge of discomfort lost in the exquisite sensation of this union, the fullness of him inside her, the sense of completion that reverberated through her body and heart.

Aarif buried his head in her shoulder, his hair brushing her lips, his body straining for both of their releases, and she clasped him to her, gasping in wonder and shock. She never wanted the moment to end, never wanted to feel alone again—

The realisation was as wonderful as the sensation of his body moving in hers, and as her body finally gave itself up to the spiralling pleasure and the joy she found that at last, now, she felt free. That she knew who she was.

What she'd been meant for.

The aftermath, she thought as Aarif rolled away from her, was as eerie and silent as that of the storm. Aarif lay on his back, one arm flung over his face. The silence that had wound its seductive spell around them moments before now stretched taut as a wire, and just as sharp.

Kalila was suddenly conscious of the sand in her scalp, the stickiness on her thighs. Moments before she'd felt only joy, and now it was replaced by something far worse. Something sordid. She felt used and cheap and dirty, and she didn't want to.

Yet, a whisper within her mocked, *isn't that just what you are? You just betrayed your fiancé with his brother.*

She closed her eyes, felt the flood of remorse that she'd kept at bay while pleasure had reigned in her body and heart, still turned her bones to runny wax. She felt the regret wash over her in engulfing waves, and could only imagine how Aarif felt.

Aarif…a man bound by duty and honour. A man with whom responsibility weighed heavily, endlessly. What could he be thinking now?

She sneaked a glance at him and saw he hadn't moved. Only moments ago she'd touched his skin, kissed him, *loved* him.

Love.

Could she love Aarif? *Did* she?

She barely knew him; he was unforgiving, unemotional, *unpleasant*, and yet when she'd held him in her arms…

When he'd touched her as if he knew her, not just her body, but her heart. Her mind.

When he'd smiled.

Kalila swallowed. She couldn't possibly love Aarif, yet what had happened between them was real, it was *something*—

'Aarif.' Her voice came out in a croak. She had no idea what to say, where to begin—

'Don't.' The one word was harsh, guttural, savage. Aarif rolled up in one fluid movement, his face averted from hers, and with a vicious jerk he peeled the tape away from the door. Kalila watched him, her heart starting to pound with a relentless anxiety, and a deep misery settled coldly in her bones.

Another jerk and the tape was off; he flung it to the floor before pushing through the flap and out into the desert's darkness.

Kalila could hear the crunch of his bare feet on the sand, the low nicker of one of the horses and Aarif's soothing murmur back. Tears—stupid tears—stung her eyes. He was kinder to the horses than he was to her.

And yet, that insistent whisper protested, *the horses didn't do anything. They are innocent. You are not.*

Innocence. So prized, so precious. So important for a woman like her, a woman poised to marry a king, and she was innocent no longer. Instinctively Kalila glanced down, saw a faint rusty smear of blood on her thigh. In another age that bit of blood would have been proof of her innocence, her purity, her whole reason for being a wife. It would have been displayed with bawdy jokes and satisfied smiles. In another age, she realised, swallowing down a hysterical laugh, she would have been killed for what she had just done.

Her innocence was gone.

And yet even so, despite the regret and shame and even fear coursing through her, she couldn't forget the feeling of

Aarif in her arms, in her body. She couldn't forget, and she didn't want to.

What kind of woman did that make her?

She took a shuddering breath, tried to calm her racing thoughts, her racing heart. She needed to think, to plan. She needed to speak with Aarif.

With a bit of water from the canteen she cleaned herself up as best she could and dressed, combing the tangles from her hair with her fingers.

Then, taking another deep breath for courage, she slipped through the flap and out into the cool night.

The air was cold and sharp, the sky glittering with stars. The sand dunes were cast in silver by the moonlight, and the air after the storm was perfectly still.

Signs of devastation could be glimpsed, shadows of broken rocks, twisted roots. Briefly Kalila offered up a prayer for the rest of her party, sheltering at the airport. She prayed no one would lose a life because of her own folly.

Her own selfishness.

She moved gingerly across the sand to Aarif; his back was to her, one arm braced against the rock overhang. His head was bowed, every taut line of his body radiating anguish. Anger.

She stood a few metres behind him, her arms creeping around herself in the cold, and waited.

What could she say? What could he say?

What, she wondered distantly, could happen now?

A long moment of silence passed; the horses shifted fretfully and a slight breeze stirred the hair lying limply against her face. Then Aarif spoke.

'What we'll do,' he said in a cold, flat voice, as if they were in the middle of a conversation, 'is tell everyone I found you this morning. You sheltered here alone, and I found a protected place of my own. Then at least your reputation will not be called into question. I don't think there is anyone in the party who wishes to cast doubt on you or this marriage union.'

Kalila heard his words echoing relentlessly through her, but they didn't make sense. He was sticking a plaster on a wound that required major surgery.

'That's all very well,' she finally said when she'd found her voice, 'but it hardly addresses the real situation.'

'I hardly think you want your father's staff knowing what happened,' Aarif replied, his voice still cold and so horribly unemotional. 'I am trying to salvage this mess, Princess.'

'How? By lying?'

'By protecting you!' Aarif turned around, and Kalila took an instinctive step backwards at the anguished fury twisting his features. 'God knows I made this mess, and I will be the one to clean it up.' He spoke with such a steely determination that Kalila quelled.

'How?' she whispered.

'I will have to tell Zakari.'

She closed her eyes, not wanting to imagine that conversation, or what it meant for her. For her marriage. 'Aarif, if you do that, you will ruin my marriage before it even begins.'

'I will tell Zakari that it is my fault—'

'And you think he will believe that? That you *raped* me?' She shook her head, disbelief and disappointment warring within her. She didn't want this, this sordid discussion of what had just happened between them. She couldn't bear to talk cold logistics when her heart cried out for him now—still—

'I was responsible,' Aarif insisted in a low voice. 'I should have stopped, turned away—' He shook his head. 'I accused you of being selfish, Kalila, but it is I who have been the most selfish of all.' He muttered something under his breath and stalked away, his body so taut his muscles almost seemed to be vibrating with a seething self-loathing.

Kalila took a few tentative steps towards him. She wanted to touch him, to reach him, yet every instinct told her she couldn't. He had shut himself off completely, walled himself with his own sense of responsibility and guilt.

Still, she tried.

'Aarif, I could have protested. I could have stopped. We are both to blame.' His back was to her, and he said nothing. Dragging a breath into her lungs, she forced herself to continue, to lay her heart open to him as her body had been. 'The truth is, I didn't want to. I wanted to be with you, Aarif, from the moment you touched me. The moment I touched you, for if we are going to apportion blame, then I was the one who first—'

'Don't,' he cut her off, 'romanticise what was nothing more than a bout of lust.'

Kalila blinked. She felt as if she had been slapped. Worse, she felt as if he'd taken the handful of memories they'd just created and crumpled them into a ball and spat on them. 'No,' she whispered, 'it wasn't.' Aarif was silent, and she spoke again, her voice wavering and then finally breaking, 'Aarif, don't make this into something sordid—'

'It is sordid!' he snapped. 'Everything about it is sordid, Kalila, can't you see that? My brother trusted me, *trusted* me, with your care. He asked me to come fetch you because he believed he could depend on me, and I did the worst thing— the only thing—that would betray him utterly.' He swivelled to face her, his face pitilessly blank. 'There is nothing good about what happened, Kalila. Not one thing. You might have felt a brief pleasure in my arms, but it was cheap and worthless, and if you had any sense of honour or duty, you would know it.'

Kalila opened her mouth but she couldn't think of a single thing she could say. Tears rolled slowly, coldly, down her cheeks. Aarif watched her with such an obvious lack of sympathy that she felt as vulnerable and exposed as she had underneath him, her body open to his caress.

'I know what you're thinking,' he said, his voice as sharp and cutting as a razor. 'You're thinking you've fallen in love with me.' He spoke the word—love—with such contempt that Kalila could only blink. 'You told me you wanted love.

Not an arranged marriage, you said. And so now you think this is it. Love.' He shook his head, holding up one hand to stop her from speaking, although Kalila's mind was too shocked and numb to frame even a syllable. 'Oh, I don't think you realised what you were doing. You were caught up in the moment as much as I was, but now you're desperate to make it into something, to believe we *have* something.' He spoke with a sneer that reverberated through her. 'Well, we don't, Princess. All we have is a mistake, and it is my duty to rectify it. As for your marriage—Zakari is a kind man. He can forgive.' He paused, his lip curling. 'He'll have to.' He turned to walk away, to leave her alone with his harsh words, his cold condemnation.

Kalila's head was bowed under the weight of his judgment, and she spoke through stiff lips. 'You are saying this because it's the only way you can accept what happened.'

Aarif stilled, stiffened. 'Still clinging to fairy tales?' he mocked, but she heard—hoped she heard—a current of deeper hurt and even need beneath his sneering tone.

'This doesn't feel like much of a fairy tale to me,' Kalila replied, lifting her head, her chin tilted at a proud, defiant angle. 'I'm not going to cheapen what happened between us, Aarif, simply because it was wrong. And, yes, I know it was wrong. I accept that, but I also accept that for a few moments you clung to me, you needed me, and I needed you. And we found something together that I can't believe everyone finds.' Tears sparkled on her lashes, she felt another one drip onto her cheek, but she kept his gaze. 'Believe what you want, if it makes you feel better,' she said. 'Believe your own version of the fairy tale, Aarif, but I know the truth.'

Aarif's mouth tightened in a hard line, his eyes dark and angry. Kalila looked up and saw the stars were fading into an eerie grey dawn, the first pale pink finger of daybreak lighting the flat horizon. 'It's morning,' she said. 'Time to go.'

They packed up in stiff silence. Kalila wrapped herself in

numbness; the pain and the realisation, the repercussions and the bittersweet memories, could all come later. They would come, she knew; she wouldn't be able to stop them.

For now, she busied herself with mundane tasks of rolling blankets and folding the tent, feeding the animals and making herself as presentable as she could given their limited resources.

She had no mirror, but she didn't need one to know her hair was in a wild tangle, her eyes dry and gritty, her face wind-reddened, her hands rough and chapped.

Would Zakari be waiting at the Calistan airport? Would he see her like this?

Would he *know*?

For the first time she hoped he was still seeking after his precious diamonds. The longer he stayed away, the longer the reprieve she had. The longer until the reckoning.

And yet it would come. She knew it would come, and the thought had the power to dry the breath in her lungs and cause her heart to pound with relentless anxiety until she surrounded herself in numbness once more.

It took them three hours to ride to the airport. Kalila was weary and saddle sore, conscious of the new tenderness between her thighs, the utter, aching weariness in every muscle, sinew and bone.

She followed behind Aarif as the sun rose higher in the sky, its rays merciless and punishing. Aarif did not falter once as they made their way through the shifted sand, a landscape utterly changed from yesterday, and yet he rode with an unerring sense of direction, of rightness.

Of course, Kalila thought with a weary wryness, of course he would know just how to get to the airport, an airport he'd never even been to. A man like Aarif never strayed off the path, never made a wrong turn—

Except once. Last night he had.

What had caused him to stumble? To reach out for someone, for her? Kalila's heart ached as she thought of it, remembered how it felt to hold Aarif, to be held by him. To be needed, touched, loved.

You're thinking you've fallen in love with me.

Her mouth compressing into a grim line, Kalila lowered her head and focused on the rough trail, her mare plodding wearily after Aarif's mount.

When the airport, a low, humble building of tin and concrete, came into view, Kalila almost felt relieved. She was tired of the waiting, the tension. She wanted to get it over with, the explanations, the lies. Then she wanted a hot bath.

Juhanah came running out first, her face grey with anxiety. 'Oh, *ya daanaya!* My child! We feared you were dead, both of you!' Even as Juhanah wrapped her in an embrace the old nurse's eyes slid speculatively to Aarif and Kalila saw it.

So it begins, she thought, closing her eyes and letting herself be comforted. The whispers, the rumours. Her reputation couldn't be protected, not from imaginations, minds.

And it didn't even deserve to be.

'I found Princess Kalila a few hours ago,' Aarif said. He'd slid off the horse and handed the reins to an aide, giving terse instructions for both horses to be returned. 'She'd taken shelter in the storm, as I had, and when the winds died down I came upon where she had been waiting out the storm.' He spoke coolly, impersonally, his gaze flicking not even once to her. And stupidly, irrationally, Kalila felt hurt.

She almost started to believe the terrible things he'd said to her that morning.

'Thank God,' Juhanah said, clutching Kalila to her bosom once more. 'Thank God you found her, Prince Aarif.' She took Kalila by the shoulders, giving her a little shake as if she were still an unruly child to be disciplined. 'What were you thinking, Kalila? To run off like that? If your father had discovered—'

'King Bahir does not need to know about a young woman's moment of foolishness,' Aarif cut in smoothly. His voice was pleasant although there was a warning hardness to his eyes.

'The princess explained to me that she had a moment of folly, of fear. It is a fearsome thing, for a young woman to meet a husband she has never seen. For a moment—a moment only—the princess thought to run away. She did not go far, and in truth she was planning to turn around when the storms caught her. She knew she wouldn't make it back to the caravan, so she sheltered by a rock. I found her in the morning, and we returned at once.' Aarif smiled, this recitation of lies so easily given that even Kalila was almost convinced, despite the obvious evidence to the contrary. Yet if anyone thought of it, no one dared to ask why her mare, As Sabr, was there with saddlebags and provisions.

It would be better for everyone, Kalila acknowledged, to pretend this hadn't happened. Unfortunately, she wasn't sure she could do that. Her glance slid to Aarif, but he wasn't looking at her. His face was hard, blank, resolute, and Kalila wondered if she would ever see the other side of him again.

Conscious of an uncomfortable silence and the many pairs of staring eyes, she forced herself to give a weak nod before bowing her head. 'It is true, Juhanah. I had a moment of weakness, and I regret it deeply. It was wrong of me.' Her head still bowed, her gaze slid once more to Aarif—wanting something from him, even now—but he was staring fixedly ahead, a cool and remote look on his face even though he smiled.

'Poor darling,' Juhanah murmured. 'At least no one has been harmed.'

'Everyone sheltered safely here?' Aarif surmised, and when this was confirmed he gave a brisk nod and moved towards the airport, already taking out his mobile and punching in some numbers. 'Then it is time to return to Calista.'

Juhanah made a squeak of protest. 'But Prince Aarif! The princess is tired and dirty. She cannot meet her intended this way. We must return to the palace so she can wash, prepare—'

Aarif turned around. 'I fear that would not be wise, madam. The princess's place is in Calista now. As for the king seeing her in disarray, never fear.' He held up his mobile. 'I have just received a message that he has been delayed, so there will be time for the princess to prepare herself—' he glanced at Kalila, who jerked under his cool gaze '—as she sees fit.'

With a little nod, Aarif turned and walked into the airport.

'Poor darling,' Juhanah fussed again. 'To not even bathe or change your clothes—'

'There is a washroom in the airport,' Kalila said with a shrug. She didn't want Juhanah's motherly fussing, didn't deserve it. 'I'll wash my face and comb my hair and be myself in no time.'

Yet the words held a hollow ring, for Kalila knew she would not be herself again. She'd found herself—her freedom—in Aarif's embrace, and she was unlikely to do so ever again.

CHAPTER SIX

THE plane left the barren desert of Zaraq to glide over a smooth expanse of jewel-toned sea, the sky cloudless, blue, and perfect, the water calmed after the storm that had ravaged both land and sea in its ferocious grip.

Kalila leaned her head against the window and feigned sleep. She was weary—exhausted—yet the sanctuary of sleep eluded her. Still, she wished to avoid questions, and next to her Juhanah seemed poised to ask them.

Only Juhanah, herself, and Aarif were on the plane, as the other staff had returned to the palace with their own version of events. Kalila wondered what her father would think of her mad escape, yet even the thought of his anger failed to rouse her from her numb lethargy. She was beyond his reach now. The person to fear now was Zakari, and yet she couldn't quite summon the energy. He was not in Calista yet; she was safe. For a while.

Once she glanced back at Aarif, seated in a deep leather seat behind her, papers spread out on his lap. A pair of spectacles perched on his aquiline nose, and for some reason that little sign of human frailty touched her, made her remember the man who had reached out to her, who had buried his head in her shoulder. The man who had needed her.

Juhanah glanced at her, sharply, and Kalila realised she'd let her gaze linger too long. She turned back to the window and was about to close her eyes again when a stretch of land—desert once more—came into view.

Calista.

Her home.

Kalila craned her neck to take it in, the stretch of sand so similar to Zaraq, the winding blue-green of a river, twisting through rocky hills, where she knew Calista's famous diamonds were mined. Then, the Old Town, similar to Makaris yet somehow imposing in its unfamiliarity. She glimpsed a huddle of buildings, flat roofed, with a wide market square in the middle.

And finally, the palace. Made of a similar mellow, golden stone as the Zaraquan palace, its simple and elegant design speaking of centuries of rule, of royalty.

The plane glided past the palace and approached the airport, and Kalila sat back in her seat once more.

Aarif did not speak to her as they disembarked from the plane. A black sedan from the palace met them and again Aarif avoided her, sitting in the front with the driver while she and Juhanah shared the back.

Kalila was barely aware of the passing scenery, more desert, scattered palm trees, and then, closer to the city, the island's polo club, and the newer part of town with a sign for Jaladhar, the island's resort.

Exhaustion, emotional and physical, was crashing over her in wave after merciless wave and all she wanted was to sleep. To forget…if only for a few minutes or hours.

The car pulled up to the palace on the edge of the Old Town, and a servant dressed in official livery came out to greet them. The man's bland expression faltered for a moment as he took in Kalila's appearance, for, though she'd repaired some of the damage, she was hardly the royal presence he'd expected.

She smiled and he swept a bow, launching into a formal speech of obsequious flattery that Kalila barely registered.

'The Princess Kalila is much fatigued,' Aarif said, not

looking at her, and the servant straightened. 'Please show her and her nurse to their rooms and afford them every comfort.'

And then, without a backward glance, he swept into the palace. Kalila watched his back disappear behind the ornate wooden doors and wondered when she would see him again. She had a feeling that Aarif would make every effort to avoid her.

She followed the servant into the palace, and a waiting maid led them up a sweeping staircase to the second floor, a narrow corridor of ancient stone with open windows, their Moorish arches framing a view of azure sky and endless sand.

Although the palace was situated in the island's main city, Serapolis, on the edge of the Old Town, the women's quarters faced the private gardens, a verdant oasis much like the one back in Zaraq, although, Kalila reflected from the window of her bedroom, not as familiar.

Everything was strange. Even she felt strange, a stranger to herself. She'd acted in ways she'd never imagined herself acting in the last twenty-four hours, and she had no idea what the repercussions would be, only that they would be severe and long lasting.

She sighed, a sound that came from the depths of her soul, and Juhanah looked at her in concern. 'You must be tired. Let me run you a bath.'

Kalila nodded, grateful for her nurse's tender concern. 'Thank you, Juhanah.'

While Juhanah padded into the en suite bathroom, Kalila glanced around the bedroom that had been assigned her. It was a simple room, yet no less sumptuous for it. A wide bed with a white linen duvet, a cedar chest at its foot. A matching bureau and framed mirror, and two arched windows that framed the view of the gardens outside.

A few minutes later Kalila entered the bathroom, outfitted with every luxury from the sunken marble tub to the thick, fluffy towels, and sank into the hot, foaming water with a little sigh of relief. From behind the closed door she could hear Juhanah moving around, and realised her bags had arrived.

It felt good to wash the dirt and sand away, yet no amount of washing would make her feel clean again. Whole. Even now a pall of misery settled over her, into her bones, so that she wondered numbly if she would ever be apart from it—be herself—again.

Yet who was she? Caught between two worlds, two lives, two dreams. Duty. Desire. It had only been in Aarif's arms, under his caress, that she'd felt whole. One. With him.

Juhanah knocked on the door. 'All right, *ya daanaya*?'

'Yes, I'm fine,' she called. Her nurse's maternal worrying was sweet, yet it also made Kalila feel guilty. She didn't deserve Juhanah's concern. What would her nurse say if she told her...?

Kalila closed her eyes. She wouldn't tell her, wouldn't tell anyone. And yet Aarif would tell someone. He'd said as much. He would tell his brother.

What had she been expecting to happen? she wondered. Had she thought Aarif would tell her he loved her, that everything had changed? Had she actually believed, even for a moment, that an hour or two of passion changed everything? Anything?

Yet it had seemed so much more than that. When she'd held him in her arms, felt his heart beating against hers, felt that they were *one*...

That was what she wanted, she realised. That was why her heart and mind resisted marriage to Calista's king. She wanted love, and for a few moments it had felt as if she'd found it with Aarif.

You're thinking you've fallen in love with me. His words that morning mocked her. How could she believe it was love when she barely knew him? And what she knew, she wasn't entirely sure she liked.

He was hard, unrelenting, grim-faced, determined. Yet she'd seen flickers of humour, tenderness, need.

No, she didn't love him, Kalila knew. Yet she wondered if she *could*.

She also wondered about the dream that had tormented him so, what horrible memory still held him in its grip. Understanding that memory, Kalila felt, would be a key to understanding Aarif.

Yet how could she understand him when he would spend the next few weeks avoiding her at all costs? And, she reminded herself bleakly, when she was still engaged to his brother?

The water had grown cold and Kalila soaped herself quickly, her hands suddenly stilling on her flat belly. Yet another repercussion of those few moments with Aarif occurred to her with icy shock.

Pregnancy. A baby.

Aarif's child.

Yet even as her lips curved in a helpless smile at that thought, her mind recognised the disastrous consequences of such a possibility. A royal bastard, conceived before she'd even been married.

Of course, Kalila knew, Zakari could think the baby was his, conceived on their still-to-be wedding night, but if Aarif told him—

She closed her eyes again. This was such a mess. A mess, a mistake, and she had no idea how to fix it or where to begin. She thrust the thoughts away, all of them, to untangle later. It was too much to deal with now, and Kalila had a feeling it would *always* be too much.

The bath had made her sleepy, and when Kalila emerged from the bathroom swathed in a robe and saw the wide, comfortable bed with the duvet turned down, it seemed only natural to slip between the crisp, clean sheets and let herself be lulled to sleep by the lazy whirring of the ceiling fan. The last sound she heard was the gentle click of the door as Juhanah let herself out.

When she awoke to the sound of a knock on the door, the sun

was low in the sky, the room cast in shadow, the air sultry and still. Kalila pushed the hair out of her eyes and called, 'Juhanah?'

'Yes, Princess,' Juhanah replied, and entered. Kalila watched her nurse bustle around the room, a fixed smile on her face, yet something had clearly ruffled her.

Kalila sat up in bed. 'What time is it?'

'Past five o'clock,' Juhanah replied.

'When are we to dine?'

Juhanah pursed her lips briefly before replying, 'Prince Aarif has suggested we eat privately tonight, here in your rooms. He said the journey will have fatigued you too much to bear a formal meal.'

Kalila's lips twitched at Juhanah's barely disguised expression of outrage at this perceived slight. 'How very thoughtful of him,' she said dryly, knowing full well why Aarif would issue such a suggestion.

'Indeed,' Juhanah agreed huffily, 'although hardly a fitting reception for a royal princess!'

Kalila shrugged. 'I don't—'

'Of course you don't mind,' Juhanah cut her off, clearly too outraged to let her complaints go unspoken. 'You are young and easily pleased. But I do not know what to think of a palace that is shut up like a box with no one inside, no one to greet you but a lowly servant—'

'Actually, he looked quite important—'

'Pfft!' Juhanah made a dismissive gesture with her hand. 'It is not right.'

'You must remember there has been a great deal of upheaval in the royal family,' Kalila replied, the words as much a reminder to herself as to Juhanah. 'With King Aegeus of Aristo dying, and the rumours of the missing diamond—'

'And is that where they all are? On a wild goose chase for some jewel?' Hands on hips, Juhanah looked thoroughly disgruntled, and Kalila found herself smiling, her heart suddenly, surprisingly light.

She rose to embrace her nurse, who returned the hug with some surprise. Kalila had never been an overly affectionate child, yet now she felt a rush of gratitude, a need for touch. 'I'm glad you're here, Juhanah,' she said. 'I don't think I could bear this all alone.'

Juhanah patted her head, stroking the tangled curls. 'And you shouldn't have to. I shall stay in Calista as long as you want me, *ya daanaya*.'

'Thank you,' Kalila whispered, and felt a sudden wave of homesickness, followed by the sting of unexpected tears. She choked them both back down and moved away. 'Even if we're dining right here, I should dress,' she said, and opened the bureau where Juhanah had already put away her clothes.

A short while later a servant wheeled in a domed trolley with a three-course meal set on porcelain plates. Even if most of the royal family was not in residence, the cook clearly was and after twenty-four hours of riding rations Kalila was grateful for the rich offerings: sweet peppers stuffed with lamb, a tangine of chickpeas and tomatoes, and semolina cakes made with dates and cinnamon.

After the meal had been cleared away, Kalila told Juhanah she was sleepy again and the nurse retired to her own room.

Yet sleep, for now, eluded her. Outside her window the moon hung like a silver sickle in the sky, and the gardens beckoned, fragrant and cool. Kalila thought of stealing out there, wandering along the winding stone paths, but she decided against it. The garden could be explored in the light of day.

Yet she refused to be shut up in her room like a prisoner. Aarif might prefer it, but at this point Kalila was not inclined to make things easier for him.

She checked her appearance in the wide mirror and then softly so as not to disturb—or alert—Juhanah in the next room, she opened the door and tiptoed down the hall.

The palace was quiet, deserted. Kalila remembered Juhanah's words about it being 'shut up like a box' and thought now that was an apt description. Where was everyone? Aarif had brothers and sisters; were they all searching for treasure? Had she really been left alone for nearly two weeks to await her errant groom?

Kalila sighed, then shrugged. She didn't mind being alone. In fact, considering everything that had happened, she actually preferred it.

Yet right now, in the darkness and the quiet, she felt just a little bit lonely.

She tiptoed gingerly down the main staircase into the front foyer. Even down here everything was quiet and dark. She peeked in a few ornate reception rooms; they all looked formal, unwelcoming. For receiving dignitaries, not for living.

She wandered down another corridor, towards the back of the palace, where the private quarters were more likely to be. It wasn't until she saw the spill of lamplight from a half-open door that she admitted to herself she hadn't just been exploring; she'd been looking for Aarif.

And as she peeked round the door she saw she had found him.

He sat in a comfortable, silk-patterned chair, his spectacles perched on his nose, his head bent over a book.

She took a step into the room, but Aarif was too engrossed in whatever he was reading to notice. What weighty tome was he perusing now? Kalila wondered with a wry smile. The current market prices for diamonds? Some boring business text? It wasn't until she was only a few feet from him that he saw her, and by then she'd read the title of his book, a bubble of laughter rising in her throat and spilling out before she had a chance to suppress it.

'*Agatha Christie?*'

Aarif closed the book, a look of guilty irritation flashing across his face. 'Occasionally I enjoy a respite from the cares of work,' he said stiffly. 'And fiction provides it.'

'Undoubtedly,' Kalila agreed, smiling. The fact that he read light mysteries made him seem more human, more real.

Warm. 'I like Agatha Christie too. Tell me, do you prefer Poirot or Miss Marple?'

A smile flickered and died, but even that tiny gesture gave Kalila some hope. Hope of what—? She wouldn't answer that question, but she knew she was glad for whatever link had been forged between them.

'Poirot, of course,' Aarif said. Again the smile, like sunlight breaking through the shadows. He paused. 'And you?'

'Poirot. I always thought Miss Marple a bit stuffy.'

He chuckled, little more than a breath of sound, and then the smiles died on both of their faces as the silence between them stretched into tension, memories. Aarif glanced away.

'Is there something I can help you with, Princess?'

'Are you going to take that tone with me all the time?' Kalila demanded, and Aarif turned back to her with a cool smile, his eyebrows raised.

'I don't know what you mean.'

'That indifferent tone, like you don't know or care about me,' Kalila snapped, goaded into more honesty than she wished to reveal.

Aarif hesitated. 'I think, perhaps,' he said quietly, 'it is better for both of us. Safer.'

Now it was her turn to challenge him with a cool smile of her own. 'I think the time for safety has come and gone.'

Aarif's expression hardened. 'Perhaps, but just because I made one mistake does not mean I wish to repeat it. I think it is wiser for us to maintain our separate existences in the palace, Kalila. At least until my brother returns.'

Kalila pursed her lips. 'And what shall I do for the next two weeks?'

For a moment—a second—Aarif looked discomfited. 'Do…?' he began, and Kalila cut him off with a sharp laugh.

'Other than languish in my bedroom, eating bonbons,' she filled in for him. 'There's no one here, Aarif. I'm alone, and I'm sure there are things I should do before my wedding. You told my father there were preparations, it was why I had to leave so suddenly! Yet now I'm supposed to wander this palace like Bluebeard's bride?'

Aarif's mouth twitched in an involuntary smile even though the rest of his expression remained obdurate. 'It is not my job to entertain you.'

'Isn't it?' she challenged. 'What would your brother say if he knew you were ignoring me? Didn't he instruct you to take care of me?'

'He instructed me,' Aarif bit out, 'to protect you, and I failed. I prefer not to do so again.'

Kalila took a step back at the savagery of his words, his tone. She'd been enjoying their verbal sparring for a moment, had found a freedom in words. She was restless, edgy, unfulfilled, yet release would not come this way.

'Where are you brothers and sisters?' she asked after a moment, and Aarif shrugged.

'Busy.'

'Will they return for the wedding?'

'Undoubtedly.' He did not sound concerned.

Kalila sank into a chair across from him, gazing blankly around the room, a library she realised distantly, taking in the shelves of leather-spined books, the comfortable chairs. It was a room to curl up, to lose yourself, in, amidst many of the stories housed here.

Her gaze found its way back to Aarif, his face still hard, unyielding, and she felt a stab of wounded disbelief that she'd held this man in her arms, had kissed him, touched him. It seemed so incredible now, as if the entire episode were a dream.

Perhaps it was, or as good as.

'I didn't expect it to be like this,' she confessed quietly.

'Nor did I,' Aarif returned, and she thought she heard a current of sorrow in his voice, underneath his carefully neutral tone.

She sighed. 'Aarif, I know—considering what has happened between us—things are difficult, but couldn't you at least extend your hand to me these next weeks? I would like to see this island, the city.' She swallowed, feeling vulnerable and needy and not liking it. 'I want to know the country where I am to be queen, and I can't explore it on my own.'

Aarif was silent, but she saw the reluctance in his eyes, in the tightening of his mouth. She knew the battle warring within him: the desire to serve his brother best, and the duty to stay away from her. And perhaps, with that, a desire to spend time with her? To get to know her, the real her, whoever that was?

She wasn't sure herself; she only knew she'd felt more real and sure and right when she'd been in Aarif's arms.

'Yes, I could do that,' he finally agreed, the reluctance pronounced now, the words drawn slowly out of him. 'I could take you round Serapolis tomorrow if you like.'

Kalila smiled, suddenly feeling light. It was silly to feel so hopeful, as if he'd given her far more than an unwilling tour of the town, yet she did. She had time with Aarif…only hours, and who knew what could happen?

What did she *want* to happen?

The question unsettled her, made her uneasy.

You're thinking you've fallen in love with me. Aarif's warning, an ever present, insistent echo in her heart. She hadn't, she knew she hadn't.

But she could.

Kalila swallowed. 'Thank you,' she whispered, and Aarif jerked his head in the semblance of a nod.

There was no reason to stay in the warm, lamp-lit intimacy of that room, the sound of cicadas a loud chorus through the open windows. Yet she wanted to. She wanted to curl up in a chair and tell Aarif things she'd not told anyone else.

Sometimes I feel like I don't know who I am. I'm caught between two worlds, two lives, and I wonder if I chose the wrong one.

She bit her lip to keep from spilling such secrets, for she knew Aarif did not want to hear them. Worse, he would think less of her if he knew she thought such things. Wouldn't he? Or would he perhaps understand? She'd seen that flicker of compassion before, had felt it like a current between them.

She wanted that feeling again; she didn't want to go. She didn't want to leave him.

'Perhaps I'll get a book,' she said, and stood up, roaming the shelves. 'Any more Agatha Christies here?' she asked, trailing a finger along the well-worn spines.

Aarif sighed. 'I'm afraid not.'

No, she saw, the shelves were filled with dusty old classics, and, like Aarif, she wanted something light. She wanted escape.

'Ah, well,' she said with a little smile and a shrug, and selected a volume at random.

She plopped down into a chair across from him and with a sunny smile opened the book.

It was in German. She stared blankly at the words, fixing a look of interest to her face, although why she was pretending she had no idea.

Aarif sighed, a smile lurking in his eyes even though his mouth was still no more than a hard line. 'Can you read German, Kalila?'

She glanced up, the answering smile in her heart finding its way to her lips. 'No, can you?'

'No, but my father could. Most of these books were his.' His lips twitched. 'How long were you going to stare at that book, pretending you could read it?'

'I'm not sure.' Kalila closed the book with both reluctance and relief. 'I don't want to be alone,' she said quietly, and saw Aarif stiffen.

'It is not appropriate for—'

'Oh, Aarif, hasn't the time for such things passed?' Kalila cut him off. 'What harm can come of us sitting here, in a library?' Yet even as she said the words she heard the answer in her own heart. The room was cast into pools of light and

shadow by the little lamp and the thick, velvety darkness
outside. It was an intimate environment. A dangerous one, and
as Kalila watched Aarif's eyes flare with awareness she knew
he realised it too.

She felt it herself, coiling around her heart, making her
body tingle. It would be so easy, she thought, to rise from her
chair and go to Aarif, to take the spectacles from his nose and
the book from his hands, and—

'Go to bed, Kalila,' Aarif said quietly. 'It is late.'

It wasn't that late, only nine o'clock or so, but Kalila knew
what he was really saying. *Stay away from me.*

And yet she couldn't. She didn't want to, even though it
was dangerous. Even though it was wrong.

Aarif continued gazing at her, his expression steady and
becoming cold, the warm, sensual atmosphere dissolving into
arctic awkwardness. After a moment Kalila rose from the
chair, trying to keep her dignity although it was hard. Aarif
said nothing, just watched as she took a step backwards.

'Goodnight,' she finally whispered, and turned around and
fled.

It took her a while to find her way back to the bedroom,
and Kalila was glad. For a few minutes she lost herself in the
darkened corridors, her footsteps a whispery slapping sound
against the worn stone. She didn't want to return to her
bedroom, her prison.

This is my life now. All of this, my life.

She closed her eyes. How could she have not realised how
this would feel? A loveless marriage, born of duty? Hadn't she
realised in Cambridge, back when she had had a choice or at
least the semblance of one, how this would feel?

How miserable she would be?

And yet, it didn't matter, because in the end, even when
she'd found something different, deeper with Aarif—
maybe—she would still do her duty, would have to, and so
would he. That was what hurt most of all.

She slipped into her bedroom, a cool evening breeze blowing in the scent of jasmine from the gardens.

Kalila went to the window seat and curled up there, her flushed cheek pressed against the cool stone. She gazed down at the shadowy tangle of bushes and shrubs below, and it reminded her so much of her garden at home—a garden she'd loved, a garden she didn't know when she'd see again—that she let out an involuntary choked cry of despair.

I don't want to be here.

A tear trickled down her cheek, and a knock sounded on the door.

Kalila slid from the window seat, dashing that one treacherous tear from her face, and went to open the door. Aarif stood there, his face drawn, as ever, into harsh lines, his eyes dark and almost angry, his mouth pursed tightly.

'Is something wrong...?' Kalila asked and Aarif thrust something at her.

'Here.'

Kalila's hands closed around the object as a matter of instinct and she glanced down at it. It was a book, a mystery by Agatha Christie, one she hadn't read. Her lips curved into an incredulous, hopeful smile and she glanced up at Aarif.

'Thank you.'

'I thought you might want something to read, and I had some in my room.' Then, as if he'd said too much, he shut his mouth, his lips pressed tightly together once more.

Yet Kalila could not keep from smiling, couldn't keep the knowledge from blooming inside her. Somewhere, somehow, deep inside, Aarif cared. About her. Maybe just a little bit, a tiny bit, but—

It was there.

'Thank you,' she said again, her voice dropping to a whisper, and Aarif looked as if he might say something. He raised his hand, and Kalila tensed for his touch, wanting it, needing it— but he dropped it again and gave her a small, sorrowful smile.

'Goodnight, Kalila,' he said, and turned and walked slowly down the darkened hallway.

He needed to stay away from her. Aarif knew that, knew it with every instinct he possessed, and yet he denied what his mind relentlessly told him, denied and failed.

Failed his brother, failed himself, failed Kalila. Was there any test he would not fail? he wondered cynically, his mouth twisting in bitter acknowledgement of his own weakness. Was there anything—anyone—he could be trusted with?

The last time he'd been entrusted with another's care, his brother had died.

Take care of him.

He hadn't.

This time, he'd stolen a princess's innocence, her purity. He had, Aarif acknowledged with stark clarity, ruined her life. For even if Zakari could forgive his bride, the chances of Kalila gaining what she so wanted with him—love, happiness— were slim. How could those be built on a basis of betrayal?

It was with a rare irony that Aarif acknowledged how this tragedy had sprung from the first. If he hadn't had his old nightmare, Kalila wouldn't have comforted him. He wouldn't have found a moment's peace, a moment's sanctuary in her arms, and sought more.

More.

He'd denied himself for so long, kept himself apart from life and love, and yet for a moment he'd given in, he'd allowed himself to feast at a table where he was not even a guest.

And he wanted more.

Even now, he wanted to feel her in his arms, breathe in the sweet scent of her hair, watch the impish smile play about her mouth before he kissed her—

He strode into his bedroom, his fingers threading through his hair, fists clenched, feeling pain—

How could he make this right? How could he make anything right?

Or was he condemned to the hell of living with his mistakes and their endless repercussions, without any chance for healing or salvation?

Outside the cicadas continued their relentless chorus and the moon rose in the inky sky. He was condemned, Aarif decided grimly, and he deserved to be.

CHAPTER SEVEN

THE next day dawned bright and clear, with a refreshingly cool breeze blowing in from the sea. A perfect day for sightseeing, Kalila decided happily as she dressed in loose trousers and a tunic top in a pale mint green.

'What shall we do today?' Juhanah asked, bustling in just as Kalila began plaiting her hair.

Kalila's heart sank. In all her vague imaginings of the day ahead, she had not considered Juhanah, but of course her nurse would expect to accompany her into town, and of course Aarif would demand such a chaperone. Suddenly the day took on a whole new complexion, as Kalila envisioned the many ways Aarif could keep from engaging with her at all.

And wasn't that really the right thing to do? Kalila's conscience suffered yet another pang. If she had any sense of honour or duty, any sense at all, she would keep her distance from Aarif, just as he was determined to keep it from her. Surely learning more about him—growing closer, if such a thing were possible—would only lead to complications. Disappointment. Danger.

And yet. And yet…she still wanted to know him, wanted to discover what drove him, as well as what made him smile or laugh. Wanted to feel that closeness, that connection again. Right now it felt like the only pale ray of hope and happiness in an otherwise dull and disappointing existence.

'Prince Aarif is taking us into Serapolis,' Kalila said, finally answering her nurse. She kept her gaze on her own reflection in the mirror, although she was conscious of Juhanah stilling behind her. 'He realised he has certain duties as host, especially considering there is no one else here at the moment.'

Juhanah gave a small grunt of satisfaction. 'Did you speak to him?'

Kalila hesitated, and in the mirror she saw Juhanah's eyes narrow. 'He gave me a book last night,' she finally said lightly. 'An Agatha Christie, actually. You know how I like mysteries.'

Juhanah still looked suspicious, but she set about folding clothes and rustling the bed sheets, although Kalila was sure there was a palace maid who could see to such things. 'Did he tell you when King Zakari will be returning?'

'No, we didn't speak of it,' Kalila replied, then bit her lip at that unintentional admission. Juhanah's eyes narrowed speculatively once more.

'Didn't you?' she said, but left it at that.

Aarif met them in the palace courtyard. He looked fresh and cool, dressed in a cream-coloured shirt, open at the throat, and dark, belted trousers.

'We can take a car into the Old Town,' Aarif said, 'which will be comfortable and more private. Or, if you prefer, we can walk. Serapolis is a small city, and we do not have many formal customs here.'

'Let's walk,' Kalila said immediately, and the corner of Aarif's hard mouth twitched upward in a tiny smile.

'I thought you'd say that,' he murmured, and just from his look Kalila felt a dart of electricity shoot straight through her belly, tingling upwards and outwards to every finger, toe, fibre and sinew. She smiled back, but Aarif had already turned away and began to address Juhanah.

That was how the first hour passed as they walked down the narrow, winding street from the palace into the heart of the Old Town. Aarif pointed out various landmarks on the way, but as this was more for the benefit of Juhanah than her, Kalila found her mind drifting.

This was her town, her country. Her life. Her mind skittered away from that thought, although it was difficult to ignore the admiring gazes and bows of passers-by who recognised Aarif, some also guessing who Kalila must be. Within a short while she had collected a handful of ragged posies, and the edge of her tunic was grimy from the hands of children who had come begging for a blessing, some speaking in Arabic, some in Greek, some even in English.

Something softened and warmed inside her at the genuine goodwill of the Calistan people, and she smiled and touched the children's heads, grateful for their spontaneous affection. If she couldn't have the love of her husband, perhaps she would satisfy herself with the love of her people. Many a queen had done the same.

But I want more. The protest rose within her, unbidden, desperate. More.

Out of the corner of her eye she saw Aarif watching her, and there was a strange, arrested look in his eyes, something she didn't understand. She didn't know whether to be alarmed or appreciative of that look, yet it warmed her to know he was looking at her, thinking of her. Conscious of her eyes upon him, he jerked his own gaze away, focusing on the view of the market square ahead of them.

The market was lined with stalls and filled with the raucous shrieks of the peddlers determined or perhaps desperate to sell their wares. Kalila walked along the stalls, revelling in the variety of sights, smells and sounds. It had only been two days ago that she'd been in Makaris, enjoying a sight just like this one, and yet it felt an age, a lifetime ago. Two lifetimes—for surely she was not the same woman she had been then.

She knew she wasn't.

Juhanah was already exclaiming over a bolt of red damask threaded with gold, and Kalila paused before a display of lavender silk, threaded with a rainbow of shades of blue and purple. It looked and felt like water, clean and cool.

'You like that?' Aarif asked, coming up behind her, and Kalila smiled.

'It's very pretty.'

Aarif barked a few instructions in Arabic to the peddler, who, giving him a rather toothless smile, said something back. They were speaking too fast for Kalila to catch what they were saying, and her Arabic wasn't very good anyway, but she knew they were haggling, and she enjoyed seeing the glint of amused determination in Aarif's eyes, the way the simple exchange lightened his countenance.

Finally they reached an agreed price, and Kalila couldn't help but murmur, 'Did you get a good deal?'

Aarif turned to her with a smile and a shrug. 'He would have been offended if I hadn't haggled.'

'Of course.' She paused, watching as the peddler bundled the silk up and Aarif gave instructions to deliver it to the palace. 'You didn't have to buy it for me,' she said quietly.

He shrugged, yet this time the movement lacked the easy familiarity of a moment before. Instead it was tense, straining towards indifference, and his gaze did not meet hers. 'It will look lovely on you. Besides, it is custom in Calista to offer a wedding gift for the bride.'

'Shouldn't that be Zakari's providence?' Kalila asked, then wished she hadn't when Aarif's expression closed up.

'Perhaps, but he is not here to do it,' he replied, and there was a surprising note of acerbity to his voice. For a second Kalila wondered if Aarif was actually criticising his brother.

'Thank you,' she said, and dared to lay a hand on his arm. Aarif stilled, glancing down at her hand, and Kalila was conscious of the warmth of his skin on her fingers, the awareness that surged through her from the simple touch. Would he always affect her this way? she wondered. It was a wonderful and yet frightening thought.

'You're welcome,' Aarif replied, and he raised his gaze so his eyes were steady on hers, like a rebuke. Blushing a little, Kalila removed her hand.

They moved on, past the cloth and fabric stalls with their bolts of silks and satins, as well as the cheaper and more serviceable cotton and corduroy, and onto the spice stalls, with their exotic scents and deep colours of ochre and umber, canisters full of cinnamon, cardamom, paprika and the precious saffron.

There were more stalls, some selling postcards, some cheap American knock-offs and dodgy-looking electronics.

Kalila enjoyed the shouting and shrieking, the bargaining and haggling, the pulsing sense of energy and excitement that a crowded market created. She felt alive, part of something bigger than herself, and it was a blessed escape from the prison of her bedroom and, worse, of her own mind.

Aarif suggested they have lunch at a highbrow-looking restaurant with private rooms and deep, plush chairs, but Kalila refused, wanting to stay out in the noise and tumult of the market. She had a sudden fear that she would lose him in the oppressive formality of such a place; out here, in the market, he was more accessible, more free, and so was she.

They ate greasy, succulent kebabs at a food stall, licking their fingers and washing it down with bottles of warm Orangina, and yet Kalila found it to be one of the best meals she'd ever eaten, with the sun warm on her head, Aarif's eyes warm on her face.

He didn't smile, didn't even unbend, and yet she felt something had changed, shifted imperceptibly between them, and she was glad. It reminded her of how his skin had felt against hers, his lips on hers, and with an inward shiver she knew she wanted to feel that again.

To feel the intimacy of touch, and yet a deeper intimacy too, one of spirit. It amazed her even now that she'd felt that with Aarif…Aarif, who was so hard and dark and harsh. And yet she had; she knew she had, and it felt like something precious, something sacred.

After lunch they wandered around the other side of the market square, where the common hucksters performed their stunts to a half-indifferent, half-enchanted crowd: snake charmers, with the dozy cobras coiled in their baskets, weaving their heads sleepily upwards, the flame-throwers and fire-eaters, and a grinning 'dentist', armed as he was with a basket of pulled, yellowed teeth and a pair of rusty pliers.

'He's just there to scare what tourists come our way,' Aarif murmured in her ear. 'We have a national health service, and I can assure you he is not employed by it.'

Kalila smothered a laugh. 'You mean you haven't used his services yourself?'

Aarif's smile gleamed, white and whole. 'Most assuredly not.'

His hand came around her elbow, guiding her to the edge of the market square. 'Your nurse is flagging,' he remarked quietly. 'I think it might be time to sit down. She looks as if her feet are killing her.'

Guiltily Kalila threw a look behind her, where Juhanah lagged back a few paces. Her nurse did look tired, and her pinched expression suggested that she would indeed prefer a rest.

'Why don't we take tea?' Aarif suggested. 'You might have preferred eating standing up in the street, but I don't think your nurse did.'

'I'm sorry, Juhanah,' Kalila said, coming to take the older woman's arm. 'I've been so enjoying the sights, I haven't thought enough of you.'

'And enjoying more than the sights, it would seem,' Juhanah huffed under her breath, and Kalila shot her a sharp look. Were her feelings for Aarif so obvious? She barely knew what they were herself.

Aarif guided them to a flat-roofed café on the north end of the square. Once inside they were greeted with a flurry of excited chatter interspersed with bows, and then they were taken up a narrow staircase to the roof, open to the sun and sky.

They sat down at a shaded table and a dark-coated waiter soon arrived with glasses of mint tea and a plate of salted pistachios.

They sipped and nibbled in silence for a moment, the sounds of the market below carried on the breeze.

'Thank you,' Kalila said at last, 'for showing me Serapolis.'

'There's much more to see,' Aarif replied with a tiny smile and a shrug. 'Although nothing is quite as exciting as the central square on market day.'

'I'm glad to have seen it.'

Aarif raised his eyebrows. 'You must have seen similar sights back in Zaraq. Makaris's market looked quite like ours.'

'Yes,' Kalila agreed slowly, 'it is, and yet there is something different here.' She looked around at the market below them, and then at the sea, a glinting jewel-green on three horizons. 'There's more of an international flavour here,' she said at last, 'an energy. In Zaraq, we are cut off from most of the world by mountains. It is what has kept us from being invaded, but it has also kept us isolated.'

'Yet your country is very Western and progressive.'

'On the surface,' Kalila agreed after a moment, 'if not in reality.' She pressed her lips together and looked away, but she was still conscious of Aarif's frown.

'What are you speaking of?' he asked after a moment. He rolled the tall glass of mint tea, beaded with moisture, between his palms as he looked at her thoughtfully. 'Are you referring to your marriage?' he continued quietly, although Kalila thought she heard an edge to his voice. 'Arranged as it has been?'

She shrugged. 'Not very Western, that.'

'But necessary.'

'Yes.'

'You could have refused your father,' Aarif said after a moment. 'When you were in Cambridge.' He leaned forward, his expression suddenly intent. 'You could have said no.'

Kalila glanced up from her drink, her eyes widening as she realised what he'd said. What he'd guessed. For that was exactly the temptation that had assailed her in Cambridge, that forbidden, wonderful thought of what could be…but never would.

'Yes,' she said slowly, 'I could have, I suppose. But I knew I never would.'

'Why not?' Aarif demanded, and Kalila shrugged.

'Because. I couldn't betray my family, my heritage,' she stated simply. 'It would be the same as betraying myself.'

Aarif looked away again, yet Kalila had the strange sensation that her answer had somehow satisfied him. She glanced at Juhanah and saw that the older woman had succumbed to the pleasures of a drowsy afternoon in the sun, and was now dozing, her chin nodding against her chest. She turned back to Aarif, a smile glimmering in her eyes, playing around her mouth.

'We wore her out.'

Aarif smiled faintly. 'So it would seem.'

She couldn't resist taking advantage of the privacy afforded by Juhanah's momentary nap. Kalila leaned forward. 'What about you, Aarif? What brought you back to Calista? Were you ever tempted to stay in Oxford, make a life there?'

His fingers flexed around his glass. 'No.'

'Not at all?' Kalila persisted, trying to tease, yet sensing a deeper darkness to Aarif's words, seeing it in his frown.

'No, my duty has always been here. There was never any question of anything else.' He spoke flatly, his eyes on the horizon, or perhaps lost in a memory.

'You always wanted to manage Calista's diamonds?'

He shrugged. 'Always, no. But for many years…' he paused, and Kalila felt as if he was weighing his words, his thoughts. 'Yes,' he finally said, and left it at that.

'What about one of your other brothers?' Kalila asked. 'Are they interested in the diamond industry?' She snagged on a sudden memory. 'Don't you have a twin?'

'Yes, and he has his own affairs to occupy him,' Aarif replied. He drained his glass and set it on the table. 'Now the day is late and it is not good for any of us to sit out too long in the sun. Why don't you wake your nurse and we can go.' He rose from the table to settle the bill, leaving Kalila feeling dismissed. She'd asked too many questions, she knew. She'd tried to get too close.

And yet she'd been closer than this—and closer still—the night in the desert. She couldn't forget that wonderful moment of surprising intimacy, yet, watching the indifferent expanse of Aarif's broad back as he moved through the tables, she felt with a pang of weary sorrow that he could.

Kalila roused Juhanah, who insisted she'd not been asleep at all, but merely resting her eyes, and they made their way back to the palace in rather sombre silence.

A liveried servant swept the front door open and as soon as they were in the foyer Aarif bowed and, with a polite, formal thanks for their company, he took his leave.

Kalila watched him go with a sense of disappointed loss. She had a feeling Aarif would make sure she didn't see him again any time soon. He'd done his duty and taken her out, shown her the city. Now he would find excuses to stay away, and Kalila couldn't think of any to see him again. She envisioned a week of meals in her room, followed by a sudden and inexplicable wedding, and felt the loss intensify inside her.

Back in her bedroom the late afternoon sunlight sent long, lazy shadows across the floor, and the ceiling fan whirred slowly above them, creating barely a stir of air.

There, on her bed, was a paper-wrapped package, and before she'd even touched it Kalila knew what it was.

Her silk. The silk Aarif had chosen for her, had said would look lovely on her—

Kalila choked back a sudden sob, pressing her fist to her mouth. She couldn't cry now, not when it was too late, when nothing could be done—

'Oh, Kalila.' Juhanah stood in the doorway, her fists on her hips. 'What foolish thing have you done, my child?'

Kalila blinked back tears. 'N-n—nothing—'

'You have fallen in love, haven't you?' Juhanah closed the door, shaking her head as she moved closer to Kalila and laid a heavy, consoling hand on her shoulder. 'You miss the king, and so you have taken the prince instead.' Kalila heard both sympathy and censure in Juhanah's voice. 'Haven't you?'

Kalila closed her eyes. She was too tired and heart-sore to deny it, so she said nothing. Juhanah clucked her tongue and sighed.

'It is unfortunate, of course, but it will pass. It is only because the king was not here to see you, and in your disappointment you looked to someone else.'

Kalila kept her eyes closed, her face averted. She wasn't in love with Aarif, she told herself fiercely. He had moments of kindness, of softness, but that was all—

'I'm not in love with him.' There. That had come out strong, sure. She opened her eyes and blinked back the last sting of tears. 'He has been kind, Juhanah, and I'm homesick and lonely. But it is no more than that.'

'No, indeed.' Juhanah's voice was sharp with suspicion and her fingers tightened on Kalila's shoulder. 'Nothing happened when you ran off?' she asked. 'You were gone a full night—'

'Juhanah!' Kalila made herself sound shocked. She shrugged off her nurse's hand and moved to put the silk away. 'What are you talking about? Prince Aarif found me in the morning. He told you that himself.'

'Yes…' Juhanah let her breath out slowly, and then gave a little nod, seemingly satisfied.

Kalila didn't realise how hard and fast her heart was beating until her nurse left the room. She moved to the window, her hands pressed to her flushed cheeks, and tried to still her racing heart.

If Juhanah discovered what had happened, she trusted her nurse not to say anything, yet she didn't think she could bear her disappointment. And yet what did it matter if Juhanah found out? If anyone found out?

The only person who couldn't find out was Zakari, and Aarif was determined to tell him. And what would happen then? Any chance of happiness—she'd given up on love—would be destroyed. Zakari would hate her, and even if he forgave her their relationship would always be tainted with betrayal, *her* betrayal—

She would live under a shadow, a stain that could never be cleaned away. The thought was crippling, devastating.

She couldn't let that happen. Not for her sake, for Zakari's sake, for the sake of the country. Not for Aarif's sake.

Taking a deep breath, Kalila felt her determination harden into resolve. Tonight she would find Aarif again, and make him understand.

After another quiet meal in her bedroom with Juhanah, Kalila dismissed her nurse, insisting that once again she was tired and wished only to sleep. Juhanah, however, was less likely to believe this tale, and left with only the greatest reluctance and eyes narrowed in suspicion.

Kalila waited a full hour before she slipped from her room; by that time the dark, quiet corridors were lit only by moonlight and she could hear Juhanah's snores through the door of her bedroom.

It took her a while to find her way through the winding corridors of the palace, and when she did finally stumble upon the library it was dark and empty. Disappointment echoed through her as she surveyed the silent room. She'd been counting on Aarif being there.

Waiting for her? a sly inner voice mocked, and Kalila pushed it away resolutely.

She turned away, at a loss. The night stretched emptily, endlessly in front of her.

'Princess?' A disembodied voice floated through the darkness, and Kalila stiffened. The lights flickered on, bringing a mundane yet welcome reality to the situation, and a servant bowed before asking, 'May I help you, Princess?'

'I…' She licked her lips, her cheeks flushing. She felt as if she'd been caught sneaking around after bedtime, and yet in little more than a week she would be mistress of this place. The realisation made her straighten and look at the man with dignity. 'I was looking for the gardens,' she said. 'I would like some fresh air.'

The servant's face was professionally blank as he inclined his head. 'It is dark out, Princess.'

'I think I can manage,' Kalila returned a bit tartly, and, nodding again, the servant led her down another tangle of corridors to a heavy wooden door that clearly led outside.

'I'll wait for you here,' he said, and Kalila replied a bit sharply.

'Thank you, but that's not necessary. I'm quite sure I can find my way back.' In fact she wasn't, but she didn't want a guardian.

Once out in the cool darkness of the garden she wandered down a twisting path lined with palm trees, the cloying scent of jasmine heavy on the air. What to do now? Where to go? She felt as lonely and lost as a little girl, and wished she didn't. Suppressing a sigh that would just tumble her straight into self-pity, Kalila wandered for a few moments until the surprising sound of splashing pulled her curiously in the direction of the noise.

She came round another corner, half expecting to see a pool or fountain, and instead came face to face with Aarif.

He wore only a towel around his hips, his chest bare and brown and beaded with droplets of water. Kalila stared. She'd never seen his chest, only felt it against her own skin, and now she was transfixed by the sight of the lean, hard muscle.

Aarif muttered an oath under his breath when he saw her, and whirled around, jerking the shirt he'd held in his hand over his head. Yet still in that brief moment Kalila saw his back, watched as the moonlight bathed the scars there that she'd felt with her fingertips. They were old scars, long, jagged lines, and instinctively she knew what they were.

Aarif had been whipped.

She opened her mouth to say something, ask—what?—but Aarif had already turned around, and was buttoning up his shirt with stiff fingers. 'What are you doing out here, Princess?' he asked tightly.

'What were you doing?' Kalila challenged. 'Is there a pool out here?'

Aarif raised one eyebrow in surprising, sardonic amusement. 'There must be, unless I jumped in a fountain.'

Kalila smiled at the mental image. 'Can you show me it?'

'Do you want to go swimming at this hour?'

She shrugged, not willing to admit she just wanted to be with him. 'Why not? You did.'

'You're not wearing a swimming costume.'

She smiled, the gesture innately coy. 'Do I need one?'

Aarif's expression froze, and Kalila wished she hadn't been so provocative. Then he swivelled on his heel and she followed him down the shadowy path.

They came out into an open courtyard, and in the darkness the pool was no more than a glint of moonlight on the water, the sound of the water lapping against the sides. Kalila regarded it for a moment, feeling slightly silly. She was not about to go swimming.

'Do you like to go swimming?' she asked, and her voice sounded false and bright.

'I have made myself like it,' Aarif replied, which was a strange enough answer to make Kalila curious and want to know more.

'Made yourself? You didn't before?'

'I nearly drowned as a young man. It left an impression.'

Kalila could just imagine how resolutely Aarif would conquer his fears, forcing himself to swim even when it was the last thing he wanted.

'It looks like a lovely pool,' she said lamely, and in the moonlight she could see Aarif's hard expression. All the things she'd been wanting to say—confront him with—died too, withered under that expression.

'Have you heard from Zakari?' she finally asked in a small voice.

Aarif's tiny hesitation told her all she needed to know. 'No,' he admitted, 'but he is likely to be in contact soon.'

'How thoughtful of him,' Kalila snapped.

Aarif shrugged. 'Considering the circumstances, I would've thought you'd be grateful for a reprieve.'

A reprieve. It sounded so grim, so grisly. 'Perhaps,' Kalila allowed, 'but I don't like feeling completely unimportant, either. I feel like I've been discarded—' she took a breath, daring, needing '*twice*—'

Aarif stilled. 'There was nothing between us, Kalila,' he said quietly. 'Do not make it so simply because you are unhappy and alone.'

The truth of his words stung, and yet she also knew it was more than that, deeper than that. 'Do you feel anything for me, Aarif?' she asked, grateful for the darkness that hid her burning cheeks. She hated having to be so open, so vulnerable, knowing it would only lead to a rejection painful in its bluntness. Still, she had to ask. She needed to know. 'Did you feel anything for me that night?' she whispered.

Aarif was silent, and in the moonlight Kalila could barely see his face, yet she knew even in the blazing daylight no emotion would be revealed there. He had closed himself off from her already. He was good at that. 'Even if I were in love with you,' Aarif said slowly, heavily, 'it would not matter. Your duty is to my brother, and so is mine.'

'It would matter,' Kalila whispered, her throat aching, 'to me.'

For a moment—a second—she thought he looked torn, perhaps in as much anguish as she was herself. Kalila took advantage of what might be her only opening to reach for him, her hand bunching on the front of his shirt, damp from his skin.

'Aarif, please—' She didn't know what she was asking for, only that she needed him. Needed this, and to her amazement and joy he gave it to her, his hands curling tightly around her shoulders and drawing her to him.

Kalila's head fell back, her lips parting, her eyes closed, waiting—and she felt Aarif hesitate. She knew, even now, that he was struggling, at war with himself, and that the wisest decision, the *right* decision, would be to pull away and leave them both with their dignity and duty.

Yet she didn't. Couldn't, because she wanted this—him— too much. And when he lowered his head and his lips finally brushed hers, she couldn't keep back the sigh of both pleasure and relief.

How she'd missed this—this closeness, this connection, and of course the pleasure, running through her like honey in her veins, heating her blood, firing her heart. His mouth moved on top of hers, his tongue seeking hers, and then, all too soon, it was over, and he released her with such sudden, savage force that Kalila stumbled backwards.

Still dazed by his kiss, she blinked in the darkness and saw rage flash across his features, spark in his eyes. 'What do you want from me, Kalila?' he demanded, his voice raw. 'You want me to swoon over you, make a fool of myself over you? Do you want my *soul*? Will that help anything? Will it help you when you are married to my brother?' His words were harsh, grating, judging. Desperate. Kalila took a step back.

'No—'

'Here is the truth. I hate myself for what happened between us. I hate myself for betraying my brother, my family, myself, and whatever I could feel for you, if I let myself, is nothing, *nothing* compared to that.' His voice and body both shook, and Kalila could only stare, horrified and humbled by the torrent of emotion pouring through him and into his words.

'Aarif—'

'*That* is how it is between us,' he said flatly, cold and unemotional once more. 'And how it will always be.' He began to stride away, and, desperate not to lose him now, now, when she still felt the taste of him in her mouth, Kalila called after him.

'And what if there is a child?'

Aarif turned around slowly. 'Is that likely, do you think?' he asked in a voice devoid of anything, a voice so cold and distant that it made Kalila cringe.

'I...I don't know,' she admitted, and then, goaded by his cool silence, she added quietly, 'probably not.'

'Then we will, as they say, cross that bridge when we come to it.'

'And you are still determined to tell Zakari?'

'It is hardly something I can keep from him. I am not a liar.'

'I know. I'm not...' Kalila licked her lips. 'Could I tell him instead?'

Aarif stiffened. 'It is my duty—'

'Forget your damned duty!' she cried, her throat hurting from the force of the words, the feeling. 'Nothing is more important to you than that, I *know*, but can you think about what is best for Zakari, for me, for our marriage?' Her voice broke on the word—marriage. 'Instead of using this overblown sense of duty as a salve for your conscience?' she added, knowing she'd said it just to wound, and seeing with savage satisfaction Aarif blink in surprised hurt.

'If you would prefer to tell him,' he said stiffly, 'you may do so.'

Kalila let out the breath she hadn't realised she'd been holding. 'Thank you.'

Aarif nodded, and they were both silent, a silence that ached with sorrow and loss. Kalila wondered why Aarif did not walk away; he simply stood there, staring, as she was, and she wondered what was going through his head, what, apart from his duty, he really wanted.

Did he want her, want more than a stolen kiss in the darkness? Had that night in the desert been a thing apart, born of the storm and the frightful clutch of a nightmare? Had it been no more than a dream?

It had been more. For her, it had been more. Kalila took a breath. 'If you were able to tell me the truth,' she said, 'then I will tell you the truth also. That night in the desert—when I held you in my arms—that was not simply because I was lonely and afraid. It was more than that to me, Aarif. It was real. I didn't love you, because I didn't know you enough, but when you touched me I felt like I *could* love you, and I've never felt that before.' Aarif was silent, and from behind a haze of tears Kalila saw a muscle jerk in his jaw.

She took a step towards him, and then another, until she was close enough to touch him, which she did. She ran one fingertip along the livid line of his scar, traced it as she had that night before cupping his cheek. 'I don't know what haunts you, Aarif,' she whispered. 'What drives you to this sense of duty and despair. Is it guilt? Shame?' She shook her head slowly. 'I wish I could take it from you. I wish I could bear it for you.' His face was still and unyielding under her fingers yet she saw with a little shock that his eyes were closed, as if in pain or anguish, and she felt the connection between them like a current, conducted by her hand on his cheek. 'I wish you would let me,' she added quietly. 'But instead I fear I've only added to it, and of all the reasons to regret what happened between us, that is the greatest of all.'

Underneath her hand she felt Aarif shake his head, and then for the briefest of moments his fingers touched hers, pressed her hand against his cheek before he released her, stepping back.

Kalila swallowed past the lump of misery crowding her throat. 'Goodnight,' she whispered, and then turned and stumbled down the path back to safety. Solitude.

Loneliness.

CHAPTER EIGHT

KALILA awoke from a dreamless yet discontented sleep as Juhanah bustled in with her breakfast tray. After thanking her nurse, she stared dispiritedly at the coffee and *labneh*, her appetite utterly vanished.

Pushing her breakfast away, Kalila clambered out of bed and went to the window. The sun was rising above the sea, sending long golden rays across the gardens. Kalila took a deep breath of the still-cool, dry air and turned to Juhanah.

'I'm not going to stay in the palace today. I'll go crazy if I wait in here all week. I want to go out.'

'We went out yesterday,' Juhanah objected mildly. 'There are the gardens and the pool, Kalila. You could pass the day quite pleasantly.'

An image of Aarif, wet and bare from his swim, rippled across Kalila's mind and she pushed it away. For riding on the heels of that image was another, that of his voice, flat and terrible, as he spoke to her.

Whatever I could feel for you, if I let myself, is nothing, nothing *compared to that.*

Kalila swallowed and shook her head. 'No, I need to do something. Go somewhere—' Her gaze fell on a cluster of buildings in the distance, part of the palace compound, and she smiled. Stables. 'I'm going to ride,' she said resolutely. 'I want to ride.'

'Is that wise, Princess,' Juhanah murmured, 'considering—?'

'I'm not running away,' Kalila cut her off. 'It's too late for that. Anyway, Juhanah, this is an island.' She managed to smile wryly. 'There's nowhere really I can go.'

'We could ask Prince Aarif, I suppose…'

'No.' She didn't want another confrontation with Aarif, not when his judgment was still ringing in her ears. 'We don't need to bother the prince with such a matter,' she said, not quite looking at her nurse. 'He is not my jailor.'

'He is concerned for your welfare—'

'I've been on a horse since I was five. I think I can take care of myself.' Kalila knew she sounded petulant, but she couldn't bear the thought of going to Aarif to seek his permission, seeing him hesitate, perhaps even refuse her request. 'I'm sure there is someone at the palace besides Aarif who can arrange a mount for me,' she said. She'd made arrangements for her own mare, As Sabr, to be transported to Calista, but she knew she would not arrive for some days or weeks.

'I'll see what can be done,' Juhanah said quietly and left the room.

It took over an hour to finally track down a servant who had access to the stables, and then to find and saddle a suitable mount. Kalila was afraid Aarif would round a corner, coldly furious that she would even think of riding out considering what she'd done the last time she'd been on a horse. But he did not appear, and with the sun shining in a dazzling, hard blue sky, she left the palace compound for the flat, open stretch of the desert, undulating endlessly to the horizon.

It felt good to be out beneath the sun and sky, the wind stinging her cheeks, the air fresh in her lungs as she drew breath after deep, cleansing breath. It felt good to be free.

Aarif stared mindlessly at the contract he held in his hand before he shoved it away with an impatient sigh. He had not been able to work this morning; he felt hardly able to think.

He was restless and anxious and a little bit angry, and he knew the reason why.

Kalila. He couldn't get her out of his mind. He'd enjoyed their day in Serapolis too much, had felt something lightening and loosening inside him, something that had been held so tightly he'd forgotten how it felt to be free. To smile, to enjoy life.

His mind drifted to last night, that stolen kiss—it had been so tempting, so sweet, and if he'd let himself he would have made it into more. He'd wanted to drag her down to the wet tiles by the pool and have her right there, bury himself inside her warmth and *forget*…forget for a few moments everything that had made him who he was.

Yet even more wrenching than the memory of the kiss was that of the open, vulnerable honesty in her eyes, the tremulous smile on her face, the tear glistening on her cheek in the moonlight. The way her fingers, cool and smooth, had felt on his face, caressing his scar.

His scar. As a matter of habit and instinct, Aarif's own hand went up to his cheek to trace that grim reminder of his failure. He had never told Kalila about that day, there was no way she could know, and yet somehow she did.

I wish I could bear it for you. It was a testimony to her kindness, her generosity of spirit, that she would wish such a thing. If only she could! Aarif smiled grimly. No one could bear his burden, because it was his guilt, his shame, just as she'd said. And no matter how many times he tried to throw it off, it always came back to settle heavily on his soul.

Aarif…help me…

It was a cry that had been seared into his mind, his heart. A cry he would—could—never forget, and that desperate plea haunted him every day of his life.

Aarif…save me…

And he hadn't.

Aarif pushed away from his desk and stalked out of his

office, still restless. He passed a palace servant and barked, 'Do you know where the Princess Kalila is?' He didn't even know why he was asking; he wasn't going to see her, he wasn't—

The servant stiffened and turned. 'She has gone riding, Your Highness.'

'Riding?' Aarif repeated, the word one of disbelief and then dawning fury. 'She has gone riding and no one thought to tell me?'

Fear flickered faintly across the man's features. 'I thought—it was acceptable—'

Aarif jerked his head in a nod, realising how controlling he must sound. Of course it was acceptable. Kalila could do what she liked. She was a princess, soon to be a queen. No one here knew about her attempted escape, and Aarif doubted she would try such a thing again. Where could she go?

And yet his gut churned with anxiety at the thought of her out there alone. Stupid, when she was a capable horsewoman, a grown woman who could—must—make her own decisions. Her own choices. Still, he could not keep back the fear. Always, the fear.

He turned back to the servant who waited uneasily. 'Make arrangements to saddle my horse,' he said brusquely, and strode down the corridor.

The sun was hot on her bare head, the wind sending her hair streaming behind her in a dark curtain. Kalila urged her mount on, faster, needing the speed, the blur of motion and activity like a drug.

For a moment, she wanted to forget the cares that threatened to topple over, drag her under; for a moment she wanted to be like a child and race the wind.

A fallen palm tree, bleached to bone-whiteness, lay in her path, and, digging her heels into the horse's flanks, she urged the mare onwards. It was a simple, easy jump, and the horse cleared it without trouble. Then a little sand cat scuttled out from under the fallen palm, and the horse reared in surprise.

Kalila could have kept her seat—she almost thought she had—but she'd already cleared the log and had let herself relax. In that unguarded moment she felt herself sliding off, saw the ground rushing to meet her, yet everything seemed to be happening so slowly—then she felt the sharp, sudden pain of her head hitting a rock.

She lay there, dazed and breathless for a moment, thinking she was all right, blinking up at the blue sky. Then, like a dark curtain being drawn slowly across her mind, unconsciousness overtook her.

Later, in the hazy dream-state between sleep and wakefulness, she was aware of someone bending over her, gentle fingers smoothing her hair away from her forehead, a voice, low and sure, murmuring soothingly. She felt herself being lifted into capable arms, and then she slid mercifully back into darkness again.

Some point later, she was in a car, lying down on the back seat, and she felt the cool leather against her cheek. Then darkness again, yet before it drew her in once more she was conscious of one thought—one comfort—Aarif.

He was there. He had found her, and he had taken care of her.

'You're good at that, aren't you?' she half-mumbled, and heard him distantly ask her what she said. 'You take care of people,' she said, the words sounding slurred to her own ears. 'You take care of me.' Her eyes flickered open, and she saw Aarif's face bent over her, his jaw working, a strange sheen in his eyes, but then she was lost again to the comforting darkness of sleep.

When she awoke, sunlight was streaming in a small, bare room from a window high on the wall and she lay in a bed, an unfamiliar bed with crisply starched sheets. A hospital bed.

Kalila tried to move her head, and winced at the pain that sliced through her skull. She tried again, and her gaze rested on the man sitting in a chair by her bed, his head braced against one hand, his thick, luxuriant lashes fanning his cheeks. Aarif, his features softened into sleep, the stubble glinting on his jaw. Kalila wanted to reach out and touch him, but she couldn't summon the energy so she satisfied herself instead with letting her gaze rove hungrily, unfettered, over his profile, the crisp dark hair, the harshly arched eyebrows, the aquiline nose.

Then his eyes fluttered open and captured her gaze with his own, so she was trapped, exposed in her shameless scrutiny of him. A sleepy smile curved Aarif's mouth, and the gaze that stretched between them seemed to wrap Kalila in something warm and safe, like a cocoon.

Then awareness came with wakefulness, and Aarif sat up, running a hand through his hair. 'You're awake.'

Kalila smiled faintly. 'So it would seem. What happened?' Her voice sounded rusty, and she realised her mouth was as dry as dust.

'Would you like some water?'

She nodded gratefully and Aarif poured a glass of water from the pitcher by her table, then held the straw to her lips, the simple gesture somehow tender and intimate. She drank thirstily for a moment before she leaned back against the pillow once more.

'How did you find me?'

'I rode out after you,' Aarif replied, replacing the glass on the table, his face averted.

'Did you think I was running away?' Kalila asked, and though she'd meant the question to be a teasing one she heard the note of hurt that crept into her voice. Aarif heard it too, and he turned to her with a faint, wry smile.

'No. But you are under my care, and I wanted to make sure no harm came to you.'

Kalila nodded. She could hardly chafe at that, when in fact he might have very well saved her life. Who knows what might have happened if she'd been out in the desert heat, alone, unconscious?

'Thank you,' she said. 'For once, I am glad of your sense of duty.'

Aarif's smile deepened briefly before it died. 'For once, so am I,' he agreed.

Kalila lifted one hand to feel the bandage on her head, a thick pad of gauze that seemed to cover half her skull. 'Am I badly hurt?' she asked, and Aarif shook his head.

'A concussion, and they wish to keep you here overnight for observation. But it is no more than that, and there should be, if any, a very little scar.'

She didn't care how big a scar there was, and yet she wondered if Aarif thought she did. His face had reverted to its more usual, expressionless mask, and the sight saddened her.

For a moment, he'd seemed close. For a moment, it had seemed as if he felt for her what she felt—

But what did she feel? What could she feel for this man who was to be her husband's brother? Fatigue and an overwhelming sense of hopelessness crashed over her in a wave, and Kalila turned her head away.

'Thank you,' she said again, stiffly. 'You can go now. I am sure there is much you have to do, and I don't need a nursemaid.'

She waited, half expecting Aarif to leave with a murmured farewell. Wanting him to leave, because it hurt to have him here, hurt to be near him when she couldn't be with him as she wished, as she needed—

'I don't want to go,' Aarif said in a low voice, and Kalila turned her head back to face him, wincing at the pain the sudden movement caused.

Aarif's expression was one of both anguish and honesty, and it tore at her soul. He was admitting something both wonderful and terrible, and he knew it.

Smiling a little, the expression somehow sad, he reached

forward and brushed a tendril of hair away from her face, his fingers trailing gently along her cheek. 'I don't want to go,' he said again, his voice no more than a whisper.

Silently she reached her hand out to clasp his, still on her cheek, pressing his fingers against her face as he had done to her only the night before.

He returned the clasp, his fingers tightening on hers, and they remained like that, silent and touching, for a long time, as the shadows lengthened in the room and the day turned to dusk.

She left the next day. Aarif had spent the night next to her in his chair, although they had not spoken beyond the trivialities. Yet something had shifted, Kalila knew. Something had loosened, and she wondered if it was a good or a bad thing.

It felt good, she knew that. It felt wonderful. Aarif did not speak or even act in a way so different from how he had before, yet it *felt* different. He had acknowledged to himself what he felt for her—or so Kalila hoped—and it broke down the barricade he had erected as a defence between them.

Yet still, she reminded herself bleakly, it changed nothing. Still, in a week she would marry Zakari. She pushed the thought away, desperate to cling to the hope that somehow something could change, that even at the eleventh hour rescue would come.

Her knight in shining armour, she thought wryly, and knew the only knight—the only man—she wanted was Aarif.

He drove her back to the palace that morning and she spent the days mostly resting, regaining her strength for the celebrations and events that lay ahead.

There had still been no word from Zakari, and in a moment of bitterness Kalila remarked to Juhanah that he was like a phantom prince, never to arrive.

'A king,' Juhanah corrected her with surprising grimness, 'and when he arrives, *ya daanaya*, you will know it.'

Three days after her accident Kalila ventured out to the

pool. It was set amidst the luxuriant gardens, surrounded by tumbled rocks and a cascading waterfall so Kalila felt as if she'd stumbled on a bit of Eden, rather than a man-made enterprise. She stretched out on a chaise, fully intending to read the Agatha Christie Aarif had lent her, but it lay forgotten in her hand as she warmed her self and soul under the dry desert sun, lulled to a doze by the tinkling of the waterfall and the swaying of the palms above her.

'You look much better.'

Kalila's eyes flew open. She didn't know how long she'd been lying there, half-asleep, but now she was most certainly wide awake, and aware of Aarif standing above her. He was dressed in crisp trousers and a polo shirt, and he looked clean and fresh. Even though her swimming costume was modest by Western standards, Kalila felt exposed under his bland gaze.

'I feel better,' she allowed.

Aarif was silent for a moment, his expression guarded, and then when he spoke his voice was abrupt. 'I wondered if you'd like to leave the palace compound for a bit. I could show you where the diamonds are mined, as well as a few other of Calista's sights.'

Kalila's heart leapt at the thought. Away from the palace— with Aarif. It was tempting; it was dangerous. 'Yes, that would be nice,' she replied, her voice amazingly level and calm.

'Good.' Aarif nodded. 'We can go after lunch if you like.' Kalila nodded her agreement, and without another word he turned and left.

Her nerves were too highly strung even to consider lounging by the pool with a paperback, so Kalila returned to her room to shower and dress.

A few hours later she had eaten in her bedroom, as usual, and was waiting in the foyer of the palace, dressed in a sleeveless cotton blouse in pale lavender and loose trousers.

She heard footsteps and turned to see Aarif, keys in hand,

coming down the stairs. He didn't smile when he saw her, just nodded. 'Good. You're ready.'

He led her outside, and Kalila saw that an open-top Jeep had been driven round. Aarif opened the passenger door for her, and a few minutes later they were speeding away from the palace, away from the narrow, crowded streets of Serapolis, to the open stretch of desert.

They drove in silence, companionable enough, Kalila decided. She was content to simply enjoy the warm, dry breeze on her face, and the sight of the desert stretching away in graceful waves to a jewel-green sea.

'We'll drive to the river first,' Aarif said after a few moments. 'That's where the diamond workshops are.'

Kalila nodded, pushing a strand of hair away from her eyes and wishing she'd brought a hat, or at least a hair clip.

Aarif saw the movement and gave her a sideways smile. 'I'm used to seeing you a bit of a mess,' he said, his voice low. 'I suppose I like it.'

It wasn't really a compliment, yet it still sent delight fizzing through her veins, filling up her head and heart with impossible hopes.

They didn't speak again until the river, a winding stretch of muddy green, came into view, along with a few low, long sheds where Kalila assumed the diamonds were polished and honed.

Aarif parked the Jeep, and as they got out she saw where the diamonds were mined, a side of the rocky bank that was covered with a system of scaffolding and drainpipes.

'The diamonds are difficult to access,' Aarif told her, his hand under her elbow as he guided her along the uneven ground. 'And at present they are mined only by skilled artisans. There is too much corruption in the world of diamond mining as it is.' There was a hard note to his voice.

Kalila nodded, and Aarif led her past the river to the sheds. Aarif explained the process to her, how the diamonds had to be separated from the silt and gravel, then carefully polished and cut. He unlocked a case to show her a diamond in the rough—it looked no more than a piece of dirty glass, yet once honed it would, Aarif assured her, be quite spectacular.

'I prefer them like this, sometimes,' he said with a small, wry smile. 'Nothing gaudy or showy. All the potential—the best—still to come. The hope.'

Kalila nodded, her throat suddenly tight, for she under-stood what he meant. There was so much more excitement and hope in possibility, rather than in the finished product, known, certain, dull. She handed him back the diamond. 'Yes, I see what you mean.'

'I'm boring you,' Aarif said as he locked the case up again, and Kalila shook her head. 'I forget sometimes that most people are not interested in this as I am.'

'No, you're not,' Kalila said. 'I like learning about the diamonds—about you.' Aarif kept his face averted, and Kalila took a breath and continued. 'What made you first interested in diamonds?'

Aarif shrugged. 'Someone needed to do it.'

'But you clearly have a passion for it,' Kalila persisted. It had been obvious from his voice, the bright gleam in his eyes.

His hands stilled for a moment on the case, then he tucked the key back in his pocket and shrugged. 'It is important to me,' he said, his voice strangely cautious.

'What did you study at Oxford?' Kalila asked, genuinely curious.

He frowned, then replied, 'Geology.'

It made sense if he were to go into the diamond trade, Kalila supposed, yet with the conversation she felt as if she'd touched something hidden, forbidden. Something Aarif didn't want to talk about.

'What about you?' he asked. 'What did you study at Cambridge? History, your father said, I think?'

Kalila nodded. 'Yes, and then I started my MPhil in medieval social history.' She smiled wryly. 'Not very useful, but I enjoyed it, learning about people and the way they used to live.'

'You started?' Aarif repeated with a frown, and Kalila shrugged.

'I would have finished around now, but—'

'The wedding was delayed so many times,' he murmured. 'I suppose your father wanted you home.'

'Yes.'

His gaze was distant, his hands still in his pockets. 'And so you went.'

'You're not the only one with a sense of duty,' Kalila said, trying to be rueful but sounding a bit sharp. Aarif sent her one swift, searching glance.

'No,' he agreed quietly, 'I'm not.' He moved towards the door. 'There is a restaurant on the beach with a superlative view of the ocean. We can rest there.'

They drove in silence down the long, winding coast road, the sun starting its descent towards the sea, turning its surface to shimmering gold.

The restaurant was perched on a cliff top, with just a few rickety chairs and tables on a terrace, and the lone waiter, agog at serving royalty, nearly tripped over himself to provide them with glasses of orange sharbat and a plate of sticky sesame-coated buns, plump with raisins and sweetened with honey.

They ate and drank, chatting with comfortable ease that soon drifted into companionable silence. After a while, that silence became strained with unspoken tensions, memories, and thoughts. Strange, Kalila thought, how without a word spoken or a look given silence could become charged, dangerous, a palpable energy swirling around them.

Aarif's eyes were on the distant, shimmering sea, his gaze hooded and thoughtful. At that moment he hardly seemed aware of her existence.

Kalila lay a hand on his sleeve, yet he seemed unaware of her touch. 'Aarif, what are you thinking?'

He turned to her slowly, his expression still distant, as if he had yet to wake from the snarl of a dream, or perhaps a memory. 'I was thinking about the sea,' he said after a moment. 'It is so peaceful now, a thing of beauty. And yet it can be so treacherous.'

Despite the warmth of the sun on her shoulders, the gentle maritime breeze teasing her hair away from her face, Kalila wanted to shiver. She did not know what held Aarif in its terrible thrall, yet she sensed it had come to grips with him again.

'The hour is late,' Aarif said abruptly, draining his glass. 'We should return to the palace before people wonder where we are.'

Kalila followed him from the café, the waiter bowing and murmuring thanks behind them. Back in the Jeep, they drove back along the coast road in silence, and as the daylight faded into dusk so, Kalila thought, did that easy, companionable silence she hadn't even realised she'd been cherishing.

She suppressed a sigh, and then turned in surprise when just a mile or two from the palace Aarif pulled off the road onto a lonely stretch of beach.

'What…?'

'I want to show you something,' he said, his voice strangely brusque, and Kalila followed him across the rocky, uneven ground. The sun had faded, leaving only livid purple streaks across the sky and long shadows on the sand.

Aarif walked to within a few feet of the sea, which lapped against the sand with a soft, shushing sound. He gazed out at the sea, his hands thrust deep in his pockets, while Kalila waited behind him, conscious of the now-cool breeze that ruffled her hair and set goosebumps rising along her bare arms.

'I haven't come to this little beach in a while,' Aarif said after a long moment. He turned around, and in the shadowy darkness Kalila saw that he was smiling, although it didn't feel like a smile, and she didn't relax.

Aarif came and sat down on the sand, his elbows resting on his knees. Kalila sat next to him. The sand was cold and hard, and she waited, the only sound the continual lapping of the waves against the shore.

'Sometimes,' Aarif said quietly, 'I feel that my whole life has been bound up in a single moment. Here.' He raised one hand to gesture to the darkening beach before letting it fall once again. 'Everything has been held hostage to what happened here.' He shook his head, and Kalila waited, apprehension seeping through her with the chilling sand. 'When I was fifteen,' Aarif finally continued, 'my brother Kaliq and I decided we wanted a little adventure. We were bored, I suppose, and restless.' He paused, and Kalila wondered if he meant to go on. She could barely see him now, even though he was next to her. Darkness was falling fast. 'We built a raft,' Aarif continued finally. 'Out of driftwood and some rope. It wasn't a particularly handsome craft, but it did the job.' He shook his head, lost once more in memories, and Kalila was left groping in a darkness that had nothing to do with the setting sun. Why was Aarif telling her this now? Was this—an innocent, boyish adventure—the dark memory that snared his dreams and even his desires? She couldn't understand, and she wanted to.

'I don't know what might have happened,' Aarif said slowly, 'if Zafir hadn't found us out. He was my little brother, six years old, and he insisted that he come along with us.' Kalila heard the *was*, and felt another, deeper chill of apprehension. 'I said he could. You see, I was in charge. I always had been. Kaliq and I might be twins, but I was born first and those eight minutes have made all the difference. I've never forgotten that it was my responsibility to look after the younger ones, and especially little Zafir, the apple of my father's eye. There wasn't a soul alive who couldn't love him.' Aarif's voice took on a ragged edge and he turned his head away from Kalila, tension radiating from every taut line of his body.

She raised her hand, wanting to touch him, to take away some of his pain she felt like a physical thing, but he flinched, and she dropped her hand again.

'That raft took us out to sea,' he continued, his voice toneless now. 'We had no idea what we were doing, and before we could even credit it we were over a mile from shore. Then we saw a ship in the distance, and we thought it was our salvation. We flagged it down—took off our shirts and waved them. The ship came closer, and even then we didn't realise…'

'Realise what?' Kalila whispered.

'Diamond smugglers,' Aarif said. 'Modern-day pirates. Perhaps they would have left us alone but Zafir—little Zafir— told them we were the sons of the King of Calista and they would be rewarded for rescuing us.' He smiled bitterly. 'Well, they exchanged reward for ransom, and took us aboard.'

'Oh, Aarif—'

'They took us to a deserted island, one of the many scattered around here, and tied us up like animals. I'd never seen Zafir looking so…so *bewildered*. He'd only encountered goodness in his life, love and warmth, and now this…! At six years old. Those men were fiends. Demons.'

Kalila shook her head, unable to even imagine the terror and helplessness they all must have felt.

'After a few days,' Aarif resumed, 'Zafir loosened his ropes. He managed to untie us both—he was so brave! When our captors were busy—drunk, most like—we tried to escape.' Even in the dusky half-light Kalila could see the bleakness in his eyes, and she felt it in her own soul.

'And?' she whispered, for she knew the story did not end there.

'And we almost made it,' Aarif said. 'We made it back to the raft—they'd left it on the shore, most likely to use for firewood. Then…' he took a breath and let it out slowly. 'They saw us leaving, and they knew if we escaped, they were all dead men. My father would see to it. They had nothing to lose, and so they began shooting. One bullet hit me—little more than a graze, but I fell into the water.' His hand went to touch the scar on his face, although Kalila doubted he was aware of the action. 'I couldn't see for the blood, but I could hear. I heard Kaliq fall in the water too, and Zafir…Zafir…' He broke off with an almost-shudder. A full minute passed and a cold breeze blew off the water. When Aarif spoke again, it was in that terrible, toneless voice that made Kalila want to both weep and shiver. 'The smugglers dragged both Kaliq and me back to shore. But Zafir was lost on the raft. The last thing I saw was him on the horizon, nothing more than a speck. And I *heard* him…' His voice choked before he continued. 'I always hear him, asking me to help him. Save him. Me. He looked to me…and I failed him. I did nothing.' He shook his head, lost in the terrible tangle of his own thoughts.

'What happened then?' Kalila asked eventually, for, although all she wanted to do was put her arms around Aarif and smooth the furrows from his forehead, kiss and comfort his pain and sorrow away, she knew the tale had not ended.

'The smugglers took us prisoner. They were furious—and desperate. They took that out on us, but nothing, *nothing* seemed to matter any more.' Kalila remembered the scars on his back, and knew just what Aarif meant. 'My father paid the ransom, and we were returned. The smugglers were brought to justice, though they sought to escape it. But—' he drew in a breath '—we never saw Zafir again. Not even a trace.'

Kalila swallowed, her eyes stinging. 'I'm so sorry, Aarif.'

'I don't speak of it,' he told her. He turned his head so he was facing her, his eyes dark and determined. Kalila felt a quiver of apprehension ripple through her. 'None of us wish to remember. My father—and even my stepmother—were never the same again after we lost Zafir. It was as if all of our lives had lost an easy joy, and we were never to know it again.'

'It must have been—'

'I'm telling you now,' Aarif cut her off, 'because I want you to understand. When I told my father I would look after Zafir that day, I took it as an oath. A sacred duty, and I failed in the most horrific, spectacular way that I could.'

'But it wasn't your—'

Aarif held up a hand, and the sharp movement silenced her as if he'd put that hand over her mouth. 'I failed, and I shall never forget that I failed. It is a burden I carry to this day, and I shall carry it until I die. But I have alleviated its weight and pain by striving to never fail so again. I devoted my life to my family and this island, and the business of diamonds so that men such as the ones who kidnapped us might not profit and sail freely as they did that day. I honour Zakari as my brother and my king, and now that my father is dead my duty is—always—to him.' He paused, and Kalila knew this was what she did not want to hear. 'No matter what sacrifices I must make, or what pain it causes me.'

Her throat was tight, too tight, so it hurt to swallow. 'Are you talking about me?' she asked finally, her voice no more than a strangled whisper.

'Yes.' Aarif spoke heavily. 'Kalila, I will not lie. When you held me in your arms, I wanted you. I needed you.' His mouth twisted, and Kalila blinked back a haze of tears. 'I've never felt…so…*right* as I did then.' He shook his head. 'Perhaps in time I could have loved you. I have not known many women…I have not allowed myself to. But you…you were different.'

Kalila felt the cold trickle of tears on her cheeks. She held out one hand in supplication, but it was ignored. 'Aarif—'

'No. I tell you this now to spare you pain. I realise in these last few days you have thought yourself in love with me, although I can hardly believe you would love a man such as me—' He stopped, swallowed, and then shook his head when Kalila made to speak. 'And I have reacted with small kindnesses because I still wanted to be near you, to—' he swallowed again, his voice low '—even just to see you smile, to see the light in your eyes. But such things were unfair to you, because they gave you hope. There is no hope, Kalila, for us. There *is* no us. There never can be.'

Kalila's mouth was dry, her heart pounding even as it seemed to break. She forced herself to speak, her voice low and aching. 'Because I am engaged to your brother?'

Aarif nodded. 'Yes, of course.'

'And if I wasn't…?' Kalila asked.

Aarif's brows pulled together in a dark frown. 'There is no point even considering such a thing.'

Kalila knew she shouldn't say it—say anything—but she felt desperate and reckless and so very sad. 'What if I broke the engagement? What if I refused to marry him?'

Aarif's breath came out in a surprised rush, yet he did not speak. The night had fallen completely now, and the sky was inky and scattered with stars. 'If you did such a thing,' Aarif said slowly, 'then you would not be the woman I love.'

The woman I love. Was he saying he did love her? How could such a wonderful thing cause her such emotional agony? Kalila closed her eyes briefly, and she felt Aarif's fingers caress her face. She leaned into his hand, craving his touch, needing the comfort.

'Come now, *ayni.*' The Arabic endearment slipped off his tongue and made Kalila feel somehow all the more bereft. 'The hour grows dark and we must return to the palace.'

And with that return, Kalila knew she would lose Aarif for ever. Yet how could she lose something she'd never really had in the first place?

Except now, with the lingering memory of his fingers caressing her face, his words *the woman I love* echoing through her heart, she felt as if she'd lost something very precious indeed.

Wordlessly she allowed him to help her up from the hard sand, and they walked in silence to the Jeep.

The lights of Serapolis glittered on the horizon, and in only a few minutes they had driven to the front of the palace. A servant leapt to open their doors, and Aarif handed him the keys. Silhouetted by the light spilling from the open palace doors, he turned to Kalila with a sorrowful smile.

'Goodnight, Princess.'

Kalila's throat was too clogged with tears to respond, and in desperate silence she watched him walk away.

CHAPTER NINE

THE days slid by in a miserable, endless blur. Kalila was conscious of things changing as the wedding day drew nearer. People arrived, guests, more servants, Aarif's brothers and sisters, although not Zakari. He, at least, still saw fit to stay away, and Kalila could only be glad.

Her heart was too full—too broken—to even consider her future, or the wedding that loomed closer every hour. And yet she could not stop the marriage from taking place, the future slowly and surely becoming the present.

The long, empty days in the palace were gone, replaced with a sudden, frenetic activity as everyone in Calista began to prepare and anticipate one of the biggest events of the decade. Her marriage.

There was a flurry of dinners, parties, lunches and teas. The parade of faces were no more than a nameless blur, although Kalila tried to commit them to memory, to greet and chat with Aarif's siblings, although it felt like a parody, no more than play-acting.

Aarif stayed distant, never approaching or addressing her. It was, Kalila thought numbly, as if the past were nothing more than a dream…a wonderful yet terrible dream, for she knew it would torment her every hour of her life.

Two days before the wedding her father, King Bahir, arrived at the palace by helicopter. Along with half a dozen

palace servants and Aarif and Kalila met him at the helipad
in the palace courtyard. She sneaked a glance at Aarif, but he
was turned away from her, standing to attention as the helicopter made its descent.

Her father emerged from the helicopter, and the sight of
his familiar face with its kind, dark eyes and ruddy cheeks,
the sparse white hair blowing in the wind, made sudden tears
sting her eyes and she started forward.

'Papa!' The endearment from childhood sprang naturally
to her lips. 'I'm so glad to see you.'

Bahir embraced her before holding her away from him,
his eyes narrowing as he took in her appearance. 'And I am
glad to see you, daughter.' But Kalila saw the displeasure
flash in his eyes, his lips tightening, and she wondered what
had made him angry. Had he heard of her desert escapade...
or worse?

Aarif cleared his throat before sketching a bow. 'King
Bahir, we are honoured.'

'Indeed.' Bahir's gaze was still narrow. 'I may assume by
your presence that King Zakari is still away on business?'

'Unfortunately, yes.' Aarif's voice was toneless, and his expression did not flicker for a moment.

'I see.' Bahir nodded, his eyes ever shrewd. 'Then I will
take tea in my room, if it can be arranged, Prince Aarif. It was
an unsettling flight and I detest flying in helicopters.'

Aarif nodded briskly. 'It shall be done.'

'And the princess,' Bahir continued, 'shall take tea with me.
I'm sure we have much to say to one another.'

Upstairs in her father's suite of rooms, Kalila stood nervously by the door while a servant wheeled in a tea trolley.
Her father sat at a table by the window, the late afternoon sun
creating a golden halo around his head, one leg crossed ele-
gantly over the other.

He waited for the servant to depart before he gestured for
Kalila to pour them both tea. She moved forward, her hands

shaking just a little bit as she poured the tea out. Bahir watched her silently, and Kalila kept her gaze averted from his all too knowing one.

'You are well?' she finally asked, handing him his glass. Bahir accepted it and took a sip, his eyebrows arched over the rim.

'Yes, I am,' he said after a moment. 'But I would rather hear if you are well.'

Kalila's startled gaze flew to his. 'Y-y-y-yes,' she said, wishing she hadn't stuttered like a guilty child. 'I am.'

Bahir set his glass down carefully. 'Because, Kalila,' he continued gently, 'you don't look well.'

Kalila's gaze moved inadvertently to the mirror hanging above the bureau and she was surprised by her reflection. She hadn't looked at herself properly in days; she'd been moving through the hours like a ghost or sleepwalker, simply tracking time. Now she saw how wide and staring her eyes were, her face pinched and pale. She looked back at her father and saw him looking at her with far too much perception. Perception, she realised, and compassion.

Whatever her father might have heard about her escape to the desert—and Aarif's finding her—he was not angry. He was worried.

'Naturally I am a little tense,' Kalila finally managed. She sat down across from her father and forced herself to take a sip of tea. 'The wedding is only in two days and—'

'You still have yet to meet your bridegroom,' Bahir finished, and there was a hard, grim note to his voice that surprised her. Of all people, she would have expected her father to understand where Zakari's duties lay. Bahir wouldn't expect a king to waste time paying court to his fiancée, not when there was royal business to attend to, diamonds to find, kingdoms to unite.

Bahir was silent, his gaze shadowed and distant. Kalila knew her father well, and she understood now that he would speak in his own time. She was content to sit in silence and watch the sun's last golden rays sink to the endless stretch of sand, painting the desert in a rainbow of vibrant yellows and oranges.

'When your mother and I arranged your marriage, Kalila,' Bahir finally said, his gaze still focused on a distant memory, 'we did so with your best interests at heart.'

'Of course, Father—'

He held up one hand, and Kalila fell silent. 'We chose Prince—King—Zakari not only because he was from a good family and heir to an important principality, but because he was young and handsome and from what we could see, a man of honour.' He turned to face her, and there was a sorrow— and regret—in his eyes that took Kalila aback. 'Kalila, we wanted the best for you, for your happiness. Of course there were other considerations. I will not pretend otherwise. There always are such things when you are a king or a queen, or a princess.' He smiled sadly. 'But your mother and I wanted your happiness. I still do.'

He fell silent, and Kalila swallowed past the painful lump of emotion in her throat. 'I know,' she whispered.

'I say this now,' Bahir continued in a brisker voice, 'because I am concerned. I did not expect King Zakari to leave you so unattended. I hoped that perhaps you might, if not fall in love with him, then at least have some affection for him before the wedding.'

Kalila tried to smile, and almost managed it. 'That's not quite possible,' she said and Bahir frowned.

'Of course, royal duties are important, sacred. King Zakari must put his country first.' He paused, and Kalila heard— felt—the unspoken *yet*.

And yet. And yet, if Zakari had greeted her in Zaraq instead of Aarif. And yet, if he'd been here when they'd arrived. If he'd even spoken to her...

Would it have kept her from falling in love with Aarif? A few days ago, a week at most, she'd thought she *could* fall in

love with Aarif. The possibility, the wonderful maybe, the
hope of the uncut diamond.

Yet now that possibility had become the present, real, alive,
and diamond-bright.

She loved him. It was so obvious, so overwhelming, she
was amazed she hadn't realised it before. Now, gazing unseeingly at her father, she felt it resonate through her body, vibrate
in her bones.

So this is what love feels like, she thought. *This is what it
feels like to know why you were made, who you are.*

It felt right. It felt whole.

'Kalila?' Bahir prompted her gently. 'It is too late for
regrets now, I know that well. I only speak of this now because
I want you to be happy and I hope—pray—that happiness can
still be found with Zakari.'

Kalila blinked; it took a moment for her father's words to
penetrate. They sank into her slowly, coldly, taking away that
wonderful, resonating warmth of her earlier realisation.

For a moment her love for Aarif had made her strong,
happy, whole. Then truth dawned, stark and unrelenting. It
didn't matter what she felt for Aarif, because she would still
marry Zakari. She must, even if he didn't want to marry her.

Even if...

A new, sudden, impossible thought bloomed in her, buoyed
her spirits. What if Zakari didn't want to marry her? He had
professed so little interest in her so far; what if he would be
grateful for a reprieve?

What if she was free?

Her father was staring at her, Kalila realised, his eyes
narrowed speculatively. She forced herself to smile. 'Thank
you, Father, for your words. I too hope to find happiness.' She
left it at that, although she almost felt as if her father could
hear her thoughts, read her heart.

Happiness that could be found only with Aarif.

She didn't see Aarif for the rest of that day, swept away as she was by preparations for the wedding. Her wedding dress, originally belonging to her mother, had to be tried on before a gaggle of appreciative women, and the resident seamstress came to make last-minute and, Kalila thought, unnecessary alterations.

She was surrounded by people now, chattering, laughing women, and after two weeks of virtual isolation she felt stifled, crowded, needing air and space. And Aarif. Every time she walked down a corridor or by a window, her gaze sought him out. She longed to see him, those dark, knowing eyes, that flickering smile, the scar that swept his cheek and reminded her of the sacrifices he'd made every day of his life, to rectify a mistake that wasn't even really his.

Aarif, however, seemed determined to keep his distance, for she didn't even catch a glimpse of him. The morning before the wedding, she was led to the palace's ancient women's quarters with its private baths for a ceremonial washing. Kalila let herself be carried along by the women's buoyant spirits and happy chattering, even though she felt as if she were separated from it all, isolated in her own bubble of apprehension and hope.

She needed to see Aarif. She needed to talk to him, explain. She needed to tell him she loved him.

Her heart bumped against her ribs and her mouth turned bone-dry at the thought of offering such a private revelation. She remembered his words, so callous and contemptuous, that night in the desert: *you're thinking you've fallen in love with me.*

But I have, she thought now, desperately, yet still clinging to that one shred of hope. *I have*.

The women's baths were something out of an *Arabian Nights* tale: a sunken tub the size of a small swimming pool, fragrant with rose petals and seething with foam. Kalila allowed herself to be undressed and led to the tub, allowed her hair to be washed three times with a heavy clay that felt like mud on her scalp before it was rinsed with rosewater.

The wedding was to be Western in style, so the women

forewent the ceremonial hennaing of Kalila's hands and feet, slipping her instead into a white linen robe before leading her back to her room.

The heavy, cloying scents of perfumes and soap, the high-pitched giggles and provocative murmurs, the entire strangeness of it all made Kalila suddenly feel dizzy, and as they were leaving the baths she took a step back.

'Juhanah…have them go on without me. I need a moment.'

Juhanah's face softened into sympathy and she nodded. 'A moment, then, *ya daanaya*. But then you must come. This is your wedding preparation—' her voice lowered for only Kalila's ears '—even if you don't wish it.'

With her bustling sense of authority, Juhanah rounded up the other women and led them back to Kalila's rooms. Kalila sagged against the cool stone wall and closed her eyes, grateful for the silence and solitude.

I can't do this.

She opened her eyes; had she spoken aloud? She was uncomfortably aware of her still-damp skin, her pounding heart. Tomorrow she would marry Zakari; tomorrow night she would give herself to him.

The thought made bile rise in her throat and she tasted its metallic tang on her tongue.

I can't do this.

Her only hope was to talk to Aarif, yet with each hour slipping towards sunset she realised how unlikely such an opportunity would be. And then it would be too late.

Too late for her, for Aarif, for Zakari. For happiness, for hope. For love.

She swallowed and pushed herself away from the wall, her feet moving in slow, leaden steps back towards her room, and her destiny.

As she came around the latticed corner of the baths her heart seemed to leap into her throat before stopping completely for there, right in front of her, was Aarif.

* * *

Aarif stared at Kalila in both shock and hunger. His eyes roved over her figure clad only in a light robe; he could see the shadowed valley between her breasts, the flat plane of her navel—

He jerked his gaze upwards and strove for a word. A thought.

Yet what could he say? How could he excuse his presence in the women's private bathing quarters, except to admit that he had been lurking, spying like David on Bathsheba?

He'd been wandering the palace for hours, his thoughts in torment, his soul in anguish. He couldn't work; he couldn't even think. His mind—and heart—were controlled by Kalila, by images of her with him as they'd been that night in the desert—and then terrible, painful images of her with Zakari, as his bride, his queen.

She's mine.

But she wasn't, Aarif had told himself again and again. She was most certainly not his; she was forbidden, as forbidden and dangerous as Bathsheba, and he was as drawn to her as David had been.

If he were Zakari, Aarif thought with a sudden, savage bitterness, he wouldn't have let her out of his sight. If he were Zakari, he would cherish her for ever.

But he wasn't.

'Aarif…' Her voice sounded thready, and she stopped, simply staring at him as he was at her, their eyes devouring one another, as intimate and heady as a caress even though neither of them moved or touched.

Aarif opened his mouth, but not a word came out. All he could think of doing was snatching her into his arms, crushing her to him, breathing in the sweet scent of her hair, her skin—

'I'm sorry,' he finally said, his voice rasping. Her eyes widened, and he realised just how many things he had to be sorry for. 'I shouldn't be here. I thought the women had left.'

Her fingers curled around the sash of her robe as if it were a lifeline. 'Were you looking for me?'

'No.' He spoke harshly. He had to. There was no time for
hope now. It was too late; it had always been too late. He swallowed down all the words he wanted to say, the professions,
the promises. Pointless. 'I'm sorry,' he said again, and backed
a step away.

'Aarif…' There was so much hunger and need in that voice,
that one word. His name. So much striving and hope and desperation. If she spoke again, Aarif knew he would break. He
would lose control, and he would take her into his arms and
damn the consequences. To them all.

'I'm sorry,' he said again, and his voice broke; he heard it,
felt it and knew that something inside him was breaking too,
cracking apart and tearing him asunder and there was nothing
he could do about it. Shaking his head, he turned and walked
hurriedly away.

The moon was a pale sickle of silver in the sky when Kalila
crept out of her bedroom. It was well after midnight, and the
palace had settled softly into sleep.

The darkness felt like a living thing, soft and velvety,
wrapping her in anonymity as she crept along the corridor. Her
palms were slick and her heart was beating so loudly she felt
it roaring in her ears, seeming to echo through the endless
hallway as she made her way to Aarif's bedroom.

The idea had come to her that afternoon, when she'd seen
a palace servant tidying a bedroom upstairs. She'd stopped the
young girl and asked her where Prince Aarif's bedroom was,
as she had something to return to him.

The little maid had been shocked at such a question, but
Kalila was too desperate and determined to care. She'd stared
her down, and finally the girl had stammered that the prince's
bedroom was down the hallway, the last door on the left.

'Thank you,' Kalila said coolly, and moved away, her heart
pounding, her face flushed in triumph.

All that remained was waiting…waiting through an endless dinner with a dozen faceless guests, rounds of toasts to Kalila and the still-absent Zakari, meaningless chit-chat with visiting dignitaries. She couldn't even remember what she said as she passed by one important official or royal after another, her eyes resting with the barest interest on Prince Sebastian, heir to the Aristan throne and, it would seem, Zakari's competition.

Aarif kept his distance throughout the whole meal, so she did not even meet his eyes once. She pushed the angry edge of despair this caused away, refused to acknowledge it. Tonight. She still had tonight.

It was all she had.

When the dinner was finally over, there was yet more waiting to be endured as Juhanah and the other women prepared her for bed, giggling and offering knowing smiles and sly winks that simply bounced off Kalila.

'So romantic! Like a fairy tale, Princess. You shan't see the king until your wedding day…but you know how handsome he is!'

Kalila had let the comments, the jokes and sighs, the winks and nods, wash over her. She was beyond it now. All she cared about was seeing Aarif. All she had left, her last desperate throw of the dice, was to find him and see him tonight.

She kept one hand along the wall, guiding her footsteps, as she inched her way down the dark corridor. If someone found her, what would she say? How could she explain?

Kalila could only pray that no one would.

At one point she heard low voices, masculine voices of unknown guests, and she pressed against the wall, grateful for the darkness. The men didn't come down the corridor, but moved on, to another wing of the palace. Kalila breathed a slow, silent sigh of relief.

In the darkness that one hallway seemed to go on for ever, an endless succession of doors like a circle of Dante's Inferno.

She continued to inch forward until finally—finally—she came to the last door on the left. Aarif's door.

Her fingers curled slickly around the doorknob and, breathing a final prayer of supplication and hope, she turned it.

The door swung silently on its hinges; the room, Kalila saw, was swathed in darkness. The windowed doors that led to a terraced balcony were flung open to the night, and she could hear the chirring of cicadas from outside.

Her eyes, already used to the darkness, swept the room and saw within seconds that it was empty. The bed sheets were tousled, but no form lay there. The en suite bathroom, Kalila saw, was also dark.

Disappointment fell on her like a suffocating blanket, extinguishing the faint flickers of hope she'd been sustaining all afternoon, since she'd hatched this plan.

A crazy plan, a pointless one. It hadn't worked.

She stood there for a moment, uncertain, not wanting to leave, unable to bear it. She could wait, she supposed, for Aarif to return, yet what if a servant came? What if he returned and he wasn't alone?

Kalila nibbled at her lower lip and as she stood there, waiting, hesitating, still hoping despite the swamping disappointment. Her choice was made for her.

'Kalila!' Aarif stood in the doorway to the balcony, and even in the darkness Kalila saw the shock, the disapproval etched on his face. Yet she was too relieved and happy to care.

'Aarif!' She stepped in the room and closed the door, leaving them both in the darkness, the moon the only light.

'What are you doing here?'

Kalila swallowed; she couldn't tear her gaze away from Aarif. He wore loose, linen trousers and no shirt; his chest was lean and brown and gloriously bare. She wanted to touch it, to feel his hot skin against hers. She craved that connection, needed that intimacy.

Aarif waited, his body tense, and Kalila swallowed and forced her gaze away from his chest. 'I needed to speak to you.'

Aarif shook his head, his arms folded. 'There is nothing to say.'

'This is our last chance to talk before I am wed,' Kalila said, trying to keep her voice level. 'Don't you think there might be something to say?'

Aarif was silent for a long moment, and then he sighed. He pulled on a shirt discarded on a chair and turned on a table lamp, bathing the room with its simple, masculine furnishings and spartan design in a warm glow. 'Very well. If you feel there is more to say, say it. Then you must go—and quickly, before your presence here is discovered.'

Kalila swallowed again. She'd hoped for a better reception than this. This was like talking to a blank face, a brick wall. How could she convince Aarif to listen? To *hear*?

How could she even know what to say?

'I've been thinking and thinking these last few days,' she began, and was ashamed to hear the telltale wobble in her voice. She lifted her chin, strengthened her spirit. 'I have to believe, Aarif, that there are more choices available to us than you're willing to consider.'

He raised one eyebrow, coldly sceptical. 'Oh?'

'Yes.' Her nails dug into her palms; she longed to wipe that cool, cynical smile off his face, strip his armour so he was as bare and vulnerable as she was. 'I realised today that Zakari has made no effort to contact me,' she said, her voice stilted, awkward. Why were the words so hard to find? 'And it made me wonder if perhaps he has as little interest in marrying me as I have in marrying him.'

She stopped, waited for Aarif to say something, for the light to dawn, the wonderful realisation. *Maybe there's a chance for us after all.* But he did nothing, said nothing, just kept looking at her with that blank, bored indifference.

Kalila wanted to scream. Why was she bothering? Why

was she laying herself open to this, to him, when he looked as if he couldn't wait for her to leave?

Had she been wrong?

'Maybe if we spoke to Zakari,' she forced herself to continue, 'he would realise there is no need to marry me. And…' She couldn't say it. She couldn't ask Aarif to marry her, not when he was like this. The raw humiliation was too much, too deep. 'Aarif, please,' she whispered. 'Don't look at me like that. Like you don't care, when you told me you did. I'm *trying*—' Her voice broke and she gulped back a sob, for she knew if she started to cry, she wouldn't be able to stop. She'd bawl and howl for all her disappointed dreams, and she couldn't afford that now. 'Do you love me?' she finally managed, her voice coming out in a gasp as she struggled to force the tears down, and finally succeeded.

Aarif didn't answer. A muscle beat in his jaw, and something darkened in his eyes. He was a man, Kalila realised, at war with himself, with his very nature. Duty versus desire. Honour versus love.

'Do you?' she asked again, and there was both challenge and need in her voice.

'It doesn't *matter*,' he bit out. He turned away, raking one hand through his hair in frustration. 'Kalila, don't you see? I tried to tell you before. It doesn't matter what I feel, what I want—'

'Why not?' Her voice rose in a cry, and when Aarif swung around, his look a warning, she knew just how dangerous it was for her to be here, to be heard. 'Aarif, why not?' she asked again, her voice quiet. Reasonable. 'Why don't your feelings matter? Who said they couldn't?'

'I did,' he replied flatly. 'I told you before, Kalila. My life is not my own, and it hasn't been since that day…' His throat worked, and he shook his head. 'I will not dishonour my brother by claiming for my own what is rightfully his—'

'You're talking about *me*,' Kalila interjected in a furious whisper. 'Me, a body, a human being with a heart and brain and soul. I'm not a possession—not yours, not Zakari's.'

'You agreed to this marriage—'

'Yes, and I will stand by and say my vows *if need be*. But maybe I don't need to, Aarif! Maybe Zakari would be relieved to find a way out of marriage to me, and still save the alliance between our countries. Why is it not possible? Or are you too afraid to hope, to believe that there could be something good for us? For you?'

Aarif didn't speak, he just shook his head, his eyes stormy and dark. Kalila took a step forward, her hands held out in supplication.

'You warned me that night—the night we were as one—that I thought I was in love with you. And perhaps then I fooled myself with fairy tales, because I wanted to believe. I wanted to be rescued. But I don't want that any more, Aarif, and I know you well enough to know you aren't something out of a fairy tale and you aren't going to rescue me. I want to shape my own destiny, my own identity, and the only way I know of doing that is by loving you.'

'No—'

'Yes.' She was strong now, made strong by her love for him. 'I love you. Not like a child, or a silly girl who believes in foolish stories, but as a woman. I love the man you are, a man who believes in honour and duty and sacrifice. A man who can make me smile, and who reads silly mysteries.' Kalila was gratified to see the faintest flicker of a smile pass over Aarif like a beneficent shadow, and she continued. 'I love you, and I think you love me. Am I wrong?'

The silence was endless, mortifying. Kalila held his gaze and waited; she had nothing more to lose, and that was almost a good feeling. A strong one.

'No,' Aarif finally said, softly. 'You are not wrong.'

The rush of sweet relief made her dizzy, and she had to reach out to grab the back of a chair to steady herself, give her the strength to continue. 'Then that's not something to take lightly, Aarif. That's not something people find every day, or even ever. And yet you're about to throw it away, without even talking to your brother—'

'Don't you realise,' Aarif cut her off, anguish tearing his voice, 'how impossible your request is? If I tell Zakari I love you, Kalila, he is put in an impossible position. It is worse than what you or I must tell him already, which is that I stole your innocence.'

'It wasn't *stealing*—'

'It was! Whether you think it or not, I was the one who should have turned away that night, I was the one who should have known to stop. But I couldn't.' There was such a hopeless despair in Aarif's voice that Kalila wanted to weep. 'God help me, I couldn't. I wanted you, I needed you, and I pushed everything else aside.' His eyes held hers with bleak honesty as he finished quietly, 'I found something in your arms I've never had anywhere else, and I shall not find it again.'

'It doesn't have to be this way—'

'Our choices have been made for us. "It is written", is it not?' He smiled, but there was no humour or happiness in the gesture, only despair. 'Kalila, take comfort if you can in knowing I love you. But you are better off with Zakari—I destroy everything I go near. At least with him you will be queen.'

'I don't want to be queen!' Her voice echoed through the room, but Kalila was too furious to care. 'I want *you*. Aarif, you cannot live your life as a punishment for what happened before. Zafir is dead, but it is not your fault—'

'Don't.' The word was quiet, lethal. Kalila knew she was treading on treacherous ground, yet this was at the heart of the matter, the poisonous root, and it had to be plucked. There was no future, no healing or happiness, until this terrible memory was made whole.

'It wasn't your fault he died,' she said quietly. 'You were responsible for him, it is true, but you didn't kidnap him. You didn't give yourself a bullet wound, you didn't do any of the things that led to his death. You must let it go.'

Aarif was silent, yet Kalila could feel the energy—the anger—pulsating from him, through the room. 'You think I don't know that?' he finally asked. 'You think I don't remind myself of it every day? Do you think my parents, my brothers and sisters, have not told me the same many times before?' His voice was pitched low, yet it throbbed with a desperate intensity. 'Do you think it *matters*?'

'It should—' Kalila whispered, and he shook his head, the motion savage.

'Do you know what I dream of? That nightmare you once rescued me from? I dream of Zafir. He is calling for me, me, not Kaliq, not anyone else. He's begging me, pleading. "Save me," he says. "Save me, Aarif."' His voice broke on his own name before he hardened his tone once more. 'He looked to me to rescue him. I hear him in my dreams, and his voice grows fainter and fainter, and then I am underwater, and I can hear nothing at all. I can do nothing. I am like a dead man.'

Kalila blinked back yet more tears. She was tired of crying, tired of being sad. She wanted happiness; she wanted it for herself and for Aarif. 'And you live life like a dead man, Aarif, waiting for your judgment. You refuse any joy, any life or love or happiness, and that is not right. No one wants that for you.' He shrugged, unmoved, and Kalila felt a sudden, clean surge of fury that even now, after so much time, so many tears, he was still implacable. Determined to mire himself in his façade of duty, live a shell of a life that no one wanted for him.

'You know what I think?' she demanded in a raw whisper. 'I think you wear your sense of duty like a shackle. Chains that bind you, keep you from trying. It's safe, isn't it? It keeps you from risking—*anything*. I think you've become so used to being numb that you're afraid to live again. To love. And that isn't the action of an honourable man. It's the action of a coward.'

Aarif's breath came out in a hiss, and Kalila wondered if she'd gone too far. She hoped she had. It was the only way to reach him now, to pull him back into the living.

'You don't know anything about it,' Aarif snarled. 'You're willing to throw over everything you've promised simply because you want to grasp a little happiness for yourself! That, Princess, is the act of a selfish woman.'

'Maybe so,' Kalila replied steadily, 'but I told you before, I will still marry Zakari *if he wishes it*. Unlike you, Aarif, I am not willing to prostrate myself on this altar of self-sacrifice for no reason. Needless martyrdom does not appeal to me.'

He shook his head, turning away from her, cutting off the argument. Hopelessness crashed over her. Was this it, then? Her last appeal, that desperate gamble, for nothing?

The minutes ticked by in silence and finally, from a fog of despair, Kalila forced herself to speak. 'If you cannot see the sense in what I am saying, there is nothing to be done.' The words were stiff, and hardly conveyed the ache of loss that left her feeling no more than a hollow shell. 'But at least allow me what you promised, that I shall tell Zakari.' Aarif gave a jerky nod, his back still to her. 'I will tell Zakari that I am not…innocent,' Kalila continued, amazed at how steady her voice sounded. She felt ready to break apart. 'But I will not tell him that you were my lover. I'll say it was someone from university, a long time ago—'

'A lie?' Aarif interjected, whirling around, his voice incredulous and cold.

'Sometimes a lie serves better than the truth,' Kalila returned, her head held high. 'What purpose would it serve to tell Zakari about us, except perhaps to allow you to feel punished by your damnable duty?' Aarif jerked as if she'd hit him, but Kalila ploughed on. 'It certainly doesn't do him any favours, Aarif, or me, or my marriage to him. It doesn't help the stability of your family, or your country. All it does is make you feel like you've sacrificed something else, something that balances these scales that haunt you. But you'll never make up for what happened all those years ago, you will never make it right. You can only forgive yourself, and allow yourself to be forgiven by others, and you refuse to do that.'

'You don't—'

'Know?' Kalila finished. 'But I do know, and I understand you better than perhaps you want me to. I thought you loved honour, but now I wonder if it is just a shield, a mask. A way to protect yourself because it's easier. I thought you loved me, but if you really did you'd be willing to take a risk.'

'I *can't*—' Aarif burst out, and there was such trembling anguish in his voice that Kalila stilled, her self-righteous anger trickling coldly away. 'Kalila, I can't. I cannot betray my brother—my family, myself—further. And I can't believe you would love me if I did.'

'No,' Kalila said slowly, 'I wouldn't, if that's what it was. But it's not betrayal, Aarif. It's honesty.'

He shook his head, and there was such despair in that movement that Kalila's heart ached. Yet she knew she couldn't rescue him; you couldn't rescue anyone. She'd wanted to be rescued from her marriage to Zakari, but she knew now it wasn't possible. You could only forge one destiny, one identity, and that was your own.

She took a step closer to him, and then another, until they were only a whisper, a breath apart. Standing on her tiptoes, she traced his cheek, his scar, with her fingers. 'I love you,' she whispered.

Aarif made a choking sound and then, suddenly, she was gathered in his arms, and he was kissing her with a hungry intensity as if he planned to never let her go, even as they both knew it would be the last time they touched.

His hands tangled in her hair and he drew her to him, her body pressed against every intimate contour of his, and yet still he wanted to be closer, kissing her as he did with an urgency and passion that left Kalila breathless and yet wanting more.

She returned the kiss, imbued it with all the love and hope and sorrow she felt, and when it felt as if it could go on for ever she was the one who stepped away, before Aarif could thrust her from him as she knew he would make himself do.

'Goodbye,' she whispered, her voice cracking on the word, and then she fled back into the hallway and the darkness.

CHAPTER TEN

AARIF was awake to see the morning dawn. He'd been awake most of the night, until at least in the grey half-light before sunrise when he'd fallen into an uneasy sleep, and once more the old nightmare had returned.

'Aarif...Aarif...help me...'

Aarif thrashed among his twisted sheets, Zafir's voice haunting him as it always did, an endless, unfulfilled supplication.

'Aarif...'

He moaned aloud, felt himself slip under the sea, the salty water filling his mouth, his lungs—

'Aarif.'

There was no cry this time, no desperate rending of the air. Instead the voice was quiet, gentle. Forgiving. Aarif broke free from the water, climbing to the surface, and found that the sea was still. Calm.

Lying in his bed, he felt the dream recede from his consciousness like a wave from the shore, slowly slipping away until there was nothing left but silence and peace.

Zafir was gone. He was no longer crying out, no longer pleading for help, and Aarif knew he would not hear his brother's desperate voice again.

The realisation was a blessing tinged with sorrow, and

Aarif felt a sense of relief, of release. The dream was gone, and he was no longer afraid.

He opened his eyes to see the first pink finger of dawn creep across the sky, and took a deep, shuddering, healing breath.

It was finished.

Aarif swung his legs over the side of the bed and padded to the window. Outside the desert shimmered in the morning light, and the air was still fresh and cool.

Today was Kalila's wedding day. He pictured her in her bedroom, lying in her bed—had she suffered a sleepless night as he had? Had she had bad dreams?

Yet she, he knew, was responsible for the banishing of his own nightmare. He felt, for the first time in over twenty years, at peace with himself. Forgiven.

That, he thought, was Kalila's gift to him.

What would his gift to her be?

I thought you loved me, but if you really did you'd be willing to take the risk.

If he loved her. Of course he loved her; he loved her spirit and her sense of humour, her honesty and her honour. He loved the way her eyes reflected her every thought and feeling, like a mirror to her soul. He loved her with every fibre of his being, heart, mind, body, and soul. And he knew then that Kalila was right; you couldn't throw that kind of love away.

You needed to take a risk.

Kalila awoke to the same dawn, the soft pink light streaking across the sky in pale fingers. Her body ached and her eyes felt dry and gritty; she'd barely slept at all.

As she lay in bed she heard the palace stirring to life around her: the cheerful twitter of sparrows in the garden, the whistling of a kitchen servant gone outside for an errand.

Today was her wedding day. Strange, she thought distantly, how it failed to affect her now. She felt dull, leaden, lifeless.

The life had drained out of her last night, when Aarif had let her walk away.

Had she thought he wouldn't? Had she actually believed that Aarif might confront Zakari, insist on making her his bride? Kalila's mouth twisted in a grim smile. It seemed incredible now, and so it was.

Aarif didn't love her, or at least not enough. And that was all that mattered.

Although now, she supposed, it didn't matter at all; what mattered was her marriage, and the life marked out for her as Queen of Calista, King Zakari's bride.

A brisk knock sounded on the door, and before Kalila could bid someone to enter Juhanah peeked her head around.

'Good morning, Princess.'

'You're awake early,' Kalila said, trying to summon a smile and failing.

'And so are you. Today is a busy day.'

'Yes.' Kalila knew she sounded completely unenthused, but she knew she could be honest with Juhanah. Later she would need her energy to present the charade of a loving, happy wife. Now she leaned back against the pillows and closed her eyes.

'Kalila.' Juhanah perched on the edge of the bed, one plump hand resting gently on Kalila's arm. 'You must not torture yourself like this.'

Kalila opened her eyes. 'I can't help it, Juhanah.' She lowered her voice to a whisper, conscious even now of who could be listening. 'I don't want to marry him.'

'No, and I am not surprised,' Juhanah replied with a sad little smile. 'You have not even seen him! He has not courted or wooed you, there have been no flowers, no jewels, not even a letter or message.'

Kalila shook her head, managing a wry smile. 'That wouldn't have made a difference.'

'No? You think not?' Juhanah arched one eyebrow, clearly sceptical. 'If you knew your bridegroom was eager to meet you—to *bed* you—then you would not have looked to Aarif for attention.'

'I understand what you are saying,' Kalila said quietly, wanting—needing—to be honest, 'but it wasn't like that. I never expected to fall in love with Aarif. There was very little to love about him at first, you know. But even if Zakari were here, dancing attendance on me, it would have happened.' She thought of Aarif's words: *it is written*. Perhaps it was. 'I could not have kept myself from it, Juhanah, even if I tried, which I confess I did not.'

Juhanah regarded her quietly for a moment, her lips pursed. 'Well,' she said at last, 'it is finished now. Today you will be a bride, a wife, and there is no place for Aarif.' There was a note of warning, even censure, in Juhanah's voice that made Kalila blush. What if her nurse knew the truth of that night apart? Or had she already guessed it?

'I know that, Juhanah. I doubt Aarif and I will even speak in private together again.' How would they deal with one another? she wondered. How would she survive seeing him every day, pretending he was no more than an honoured brother? How would he cope with seeing her as Zakari's wife, holding Zakari's children, when the only children she wanted were—?

Kalila let out a sudden, choked cry as the enormity of Aarif's decision last night hit her with a hammer blow. He'd exiled her for the rest of her life, forced her into a prison of unhappiness that she would never escape.

'Kalila,' Juhanah said gently, her hand tightening on Kalila's arm, 'you must let it go. Let him go. Your future is with Zakari, and by God's grace you can still love him as a wife should.'

The thought was anathema, yet Kalila knew Juhanah was right. Zakari was innocent, if negligent; she could still try to be a good wife to him. It was the only hope she had, thin thread that it was.

'Yes, you're right,' she managed at last. 'I know it, Juhanah. It's just so very hard right now.'

'Of course it is,' Juhanah soothed. 'I shall fetch your breakfast. Take a moment to compose yourself, *ya daanaya*, for the other women will be here soon and you will not be left alone all day.'

Juhanah spoke the truth, Kalila soon realised, for after breakfast her room was filled with a flurry of women, servants and siblings and guests, who were eager to help in the preparations. Kalila felt like a spectator, a ghost; she let herself be dressed, her mother's antique white gown sliding easily over her slight curves—had she lost weight? She let her hair be teased into a high cluster of shiny curls. She let her face be painted, and pearl drops fastened in her ears, a magnificent Calistan diamond necklace around her throat.

The sun was high in the sky, the palace courtyard filled with spectators and guests, luxurious black sedans and sports convertibles as everyone began to assemble for the wedding of the decade.

The wedding was in less than an hour, and Zakari still wasn't here.

Kalila choked down some lunch, although her stomach seethed with nerves. She felt awkward and stiff in her wedding gown, unused to the endless yards of pearl-encrusted satin, the veil's comb that dug into her scalp. She felt hot and uncomfortable, and almost desperately she searched for some kind of happiness or hope to carry her through the rest of the day.

'Come, they are waiting downstairs,' Juhanah said. The room had finally emptied out of people and Kalila was alone, blessedly alone. 'You must be ready.'

Kalila swallowed. It was time. Time to face her destiny, her duty. 'Is King Zakari here yet?' she asked, her voice dry and papery.

Juhanah shrugged, but then Kalila heard the answer to her question in the hectic whirring of a helicopter above the palace. She moved to the window, and saw the helicopter with the

Calistan royal insignia descend to the helipad. It was Zakari, she knew it was, and in a moment she would see him—

Then she saw another figure striding towards the landed helicopter, a figure that was familiar and beloved. Aarif. Aarif was going to meet Zakari, and suddenly Kalila knew that he was going to tell him everything. He wouldn't be able to keep from being honest, no matter what the cost to either of them.

Kalila closed her eyes, unable to bear the sight.

'Come, Princess,' Juhanah murmured, pulling her away from the window. 'There is nothing for you to see. You will see your husband as you walk down the aisle. That is as it should be.'

Kalila nodded, and let herself be led away. Her mind and body was numb, blessedly numb, as Juhanah led her through the palace corridors to a sitting room Kalila had never seen before.

'You will wait here,' Juhanah said, 'until it is time. A servant will knock on the door when it is time to go out.'

Kalila nodded. The wedding ceremony, she knew, was in the formal reception hall of the palace, an ornate room with marble pillars and a frescoed ceiling. She'd seen the servants setting up chairs there yesterday, row upon endless row.

It was tradition, borrowed from the Greeks, for the groom to hand the bride her bouquet, and distantly Kalila wondered if Zakari would remember her flowers. But of course he wouldn't have to; someone would hand him a tasteful bouquet of roses or some such and he would give them to her with a smile as if he'd chosen them himself...

False. It was all going to be false.

The minutes ticked by in agonising slowness. Juhanah stood by the door, stout and grim-faced. Kalila was grateful that they were alone, at least; the other women had taken their seats as guests. She couldn't have borne any more chatter or gossip, winks or sly looks. It was all meant in fun, she knew, but it made her feel sick.

'What's taking so long?' she cried out in frustration after

a quarter of an hour had gone by. It was past time for the ceremony to begin, and by now she just wanted it to be over.

'I don't know,' Juhanah said. She opened the door and poked her head out. 'I can't see anyone—'

'I'll go, then,' Kalila said. She felt frantic from the inactivity, the endless waiting.

'No! You cannot be seen.'

'I don't care—'

'Propriety, Kalila, is important now,' Juhanah said sharply. 'I'll go.'

Juhanah slipped out, and Kalila let out a sigh of frustration, pacing the small room like a caged animal, needing to be free.

She caught sight of her reflection in the mirror, and for a moment she stopped and stared. Her face was pale beneath the make-up, her eyes wide. Yet the dress was beautiful, her mother's gown, a dress made for a woman in love.

And I had love, Kalila realised with a pang of surprise. She knew what it was like to love and be loved, no matter for how short a time, and that was a wonderful gift. A blessing. She would cling to it for the rest of her life, knowing that Aarif had loved her.

It would have to be enough. It would be enough, she vowed, to see her through this day at least.

Juhanah returned, her eyes clouded with anxiety, her lower lip pulled between her teeth. 'I don't know what is going on,' she said in a low voice. 'There has been some delay…'

'Delay?' Kalila repeated, and heard her voice rise in fear. 'What? Why?'

Juhanah shook her head. 'I don't know. Your father—King Bahir—has been called out of the ceremony. Perhaps King Zakari wishes to discuss…'

'No.' Kalila pressed a fist to her lips. Had Aarif told, and Zakari was furious? Was she going to be shamed in front of everyone, and not just her, but Aarif too? Her heart ached for him, having already endured so much, to suffer this as well.

And yet it could provide freedom, if Zakari refused to go through with the marriage. A pointless freedom, useless without Aarif.

Just as that thought was unfurling within her a sharp knock sounded on the door, and Juhanah conversed rapidly with a servant. She turned back to Kalila, her expression resolute yet still filled with apprehension. 'It is time.'

Time. There had been so much time, and now there was none. Now it was mere minutes—seconds—before she came face to face with Zakari, without ever having spoken to him even, and pledged her life. Said her vows.

Kalila walked down the palace corridor, heard the rustle of her gown on the stone floor, felt the relentless drumming of her heart. Her hands were cold and damp and she resisted the impulse to wipe them on the sides of her gown.

Ahead of her the reception hall loomed, its wide doors thrown open, garlanded with lilies.

Kalila moved to stand on the threshold and saw a sea of faces turn expectantly to face her. Her gaze went past the rows of guests to the man standing at the end of the aisle, tall and broad-shouldered, with short, dark hair like Aarif's, his back to her.

Kalila swallowed and she felt Juhanah give her a little nudge in the small of her back. Her legs felt as if they were made of cotton wool, and her vision swam.

Think of Aarif. Think of his love.

She could do this.

She had to.

Slowly she made herself move. One foot in front of the other. The crowd had fallen to a hush, and Kalila saw people smiling. She tried to smile back, but the smile trembled on her lips and slipped right off. She was so close to tears; she felt them at the backs of her lids, in her throat…

She swallowed them down, blinked them back, and moved on.

The aisle was endless. The papery rustling of the stiff folds of her gown was loud in her ears, loud in the expectant hush of that room. She wished Zakari would turn around, so she could see the expression on his face, except perhaps she didn't want to. Perhaps that would be worse.

Another step, and then another—she was almost there.

And then he did turn around, and Kalila nearly stumbled, the room and its hundreds of guests swimming before her eyes, for Zakari was not standing there at all.

Aarif was.

Kalila was dimly conscious of the ripple of speculative murmurs through the crowd, but it was nothing compared to the shock vibrating through her whole being. She stood there, rooted to the spot, her mind unable to catch up, wondering if it was some kind of trick...

Aarif was close enough to touch, and he reached out and curled his hand around her elbow, steadying her, bringing her closer.

When she was close enough so that she alone could hear him speak, he whispered, 'Do you still want me?'

Kalila stared at him, saw the need and hope and love in his eyes, and could only nod. The tears were close again.

'Kalila?' Aarif demanded, his voice still pitched low, and she knew what he needed to hear.

'I love you.'

He smiled then, and Kalila saw the sheen of tears in his own eyes. 'And I love you. More than life.'

Aarif handed her a bouquet of flowers, and Kalila's fingers closed around it automatically. She looked down and saw the delicate, curling petals of a bouquet of irises. Her favourite, just as she'd told Aarif. He'd remembered.

Someone cleared his throat, and Kalila realised there was a man standing next to Aarif, also tall and broad-shouldered, smiling faintly. Zakari.

She smiled back, feeling strange, light-headed, and yet absurdly, wonderfully happy, and the ceremony began.

Kalila was barely conscious of the words being spoken, the vows being said. Her mind was still thrumming with awareness of Aarif, the realisation that she was actually marrying him.

It wasn't until the ceremony was over, and they were walking back down the aisle, that she realised this was real. *He* was real.

Out in the corridor, she turned to him, breathless. 'Tell me—'

'Later.' Aarif pulled her into his arms and kissed her, a kiss that had no secrecy or danger or shame, only love, as pure and brilliant as the finest diamond.

Kalila surrendered herself to the kiss, to the love that flowed between them and through her veins, bubbling up into wondrous joy.

Finally she pulled away, laughing, her hair starting to come undone from its artful cluster in curly tendrils. 'Tell me,' she commanded, 'how you came to be standing there instead of your brother.'

Light danced in Aarif's eyes. 'Are you glad?'

'You know I am!'

Aarif laughed, and it was a sound Kalila loved to hear. She hadn't heard it many times before, and certainly not with such joyous unrestraint.

Aarif pulled her away from the guests pouring out of the reception hall, into a quiet antechamber.

His face had turned serious again, his eyes dark. 'Last night I couldn't sleep. All I could do was think of everything you'd said to me, every accusation and judgment, and realise they were all true.'

'Aarif—' Kalila began, but he held up a hand to stop her.

'Wait. Let me say this, for God knows I should have said it yesterday, and spared us both a sleepless night.' He smiled wryly before his expression sobered once more. 'Kalila, you told me I was trying to balance the scales, and though I'd never thought of that before I realised you were right. That's exactly what I was doing. For the last twenty-one years I've been trying to atone for Zafir's death, even though no one expected me to. It was something I expected of myself, even though I doomed myself to failure from the start. And happiness— love—they were things I didn't even dare dream of.' He shook his head. 'But it's amazing how a prison can become safe. Comfortable, even. And the more I withdrew from life, the less appealing the kinds of risks and dangers living create became to me...all without me even realising it. All I could see was that in loving you, I'd betrayed Zakari. And that night we had together—as right as it felt to have you in my arms—was a betrayal, of a kind. But I realised last night that to allow your marriage to Zakari to go forward without even a word of protest was another betrayal. A betrayal of you, and myself, and what we have shared.'

Kalila thought of Aarif striding so resolutely towards the helicopter. 'So what did you tell Zakari?'

'I told him what happened between us, and that I loved you. I asked for his forgiveness and said that I wanted to marry you.'

'He must have been surprised,' Kalila said weakly, unable to even imagine such a conversation.

'He was, but he was also happy...for me.' Aarif shook his head in wonder. 'My brother is a good man.' He paused, his expression becoming shadowed. 'I told him if he still wished to marry you, I would be forced to stand aside. I do not think you would love me if I had not said that.'

'I know,' Kalila whispered, her throat aching with unshed tears. 'I feel the same.'

'But I also told him that we loved each other, and I would do everything in my power to make you happy and bring honour to both Calista and Zaraq.'

'And what did he say?' Kalila could not even imagine the king's reaction.

Aarif smiled wryly. 'He was shocked, to be sure. But then he laughed, and told me he could tell that I loved you, for he'd never seen me so happy before, and who was he to stand in the way of such love.'

Kalila shook her head in amazement. 'He is indeed a good man.'

'Yes, he is,' Aarif agreed. 'And so is your father. Zakari called him out of the ceremony to explain the situation, and he didn't even look flustered, or very surprised. He graciously agreed, saying that the alliance between our countries would still stand.'

'He told me he wanted my happiness.'

'And does he have it?' Aarif asked. He brought her hand to his lips, kissing her fingers. 'You're happy with this slow-witted husband of yours, who wasn't able to understand his own nature until his wife told him?'

'Very happy,' Kalila whispered, and Aarif kissed her again.

A knock sounded on the door, and Kalila heard a rueful voice exclaim, 'Enough already! The reception—and all your guests—are waiting!'

Laughing, Aarif led her from the chamber to another of the palace's great halls, where guests circulated amidst servants bearing trays of champagne.

As they entered the room a spontaneous round of applause burst forth, and Kalila flushed in both embarrassment and pride. Granted, she thought, it was a bit unusual to have a change of grooms on the day of the wedding, but she was too happy to care if anyone was shocked, and from the looks on people's faces they only wished her and Aarif every joy.

After a round of toasts, Zakari approached them, smiling wryly. 'May I offer my felicitations to the bride?' he said, sketching a slight bow before them.

'Yes, of course, thank you,' Kalila murmured. She glanced up at him, saw that he was as handsome and charming as she'd remembered as a girl, and yet he wasn't Aarif.

'Kalila, you must be an extraordinary woman indeed to have brought my brother to his senses at last. I have never seen him so carefree, so happy.'

'She is extraordinary,' Aarif murmured, his arm around Kalila's waist, drawing her close. 'I am most blessed.'

'I hope one day to be similarly blessed,' Zakari said, and then added with a devilish grin, 'although not today it seems. Brother, a moment of your time before you retire with your bride?' Zakari raised his eyebrows, and with a little nod of assent Kalila watched them draw aside.

'I meant what I said,' Zakari said in a low voice, his hand heavy on Aarif's shoulder. 'I am happy for you both, and I wish you every blessing.'

'Thank you,' Aarif said, his own voice choked, for his brother's blessing made his cup wondrously overflow. 'You are a good man, Zakari.'

'And so are you, brother,' Zakari returned, 'though you have not always thought you are.' Aarif nodded, and found himself overcome with emotion. He was grateful when Zakari switched the conversation to business.

'It is just as well things have happened as they did, for I must leave again tonight. I have heard a rumour that King Aegeus had an affair with a palace maid—years ago, you understand, but there might be something in it.'

'A clue to the missing diamond?' Aarif asked, and Zakari nodded.

'Yes.' Zakari's voice hardened. 'I will find that diamond, Aarif. No matter what happens.' Aarif nodded. He'd never understood the driving determination his brother had to find the diamond, yet he accepted it. Everyone had their own memories, shadows, and ghosts.

Yet thanks to Kalila, his had been released. 'God be with you in your journey.' He clapped his brother's shoulder and Zakari returned the gesture.

'Now you should steal your bride away while there is time. Otherwise you'll be carousing with your guests all evening, and that is no way to spend a wedding night.'

'No indeed.' Aarif grinned, and, taking leave of his brother, he turned back to Kalila.

Kalila suddenly found her mouth was dry, her mind uncertain. She wanted nothing more than to be alone with Aarif, yet now that the moment had come she found herself strangely nervous.

'Come,' Aarif murmured, and he drew her away from the crowd. He led her upstairs, not to his bedroom, but to another room, in its own wing, separate from the rest of the palace.

'Consider this the Calistan honeymoon suite,' he said as he threw open the door. Kalila stepped inside, her surprised gaze taking in the huge bedroom with its lavish four-poster bed piled high with pillows, the wide windows thrown open to the night. Someone had come before them and lit candles, so the room was full of soft, flickering shadows. She saw champagne chilling in a bucket, two fluted glasses waiting to be filled.

It was, she thought, like something out of a fantasy or a fairy tale, something she would have dreamed as a girl.

Yet it was real. The fairy tale was real.

'This is a bit different from a tent in the desert,' she managed, and Aarif smiled, drawing her to him.

'Yes…and I'm not sure which I prefer.'

'This is more comfortable at least,' Kalila joked, and Aarif touched his finger to her chin, tilting her head so she met his eyes.

'*Ayni*, are you afraid?' he asked.

'Not afraid,' Kalila said a bit shakily. 'Just…uncertain. It's hard to believe this is real. That it's…*all right.*'

Aarif laughed softly. 'It is a miracle, is it not? There is no shame here, no secrecy or fear. There is only you and me… and our love.'

He drew her into his arms, his kiss soft yet filled with promise, and Kalila felt her fears melt away. Aarif loved her, and she loved him; it *was* real. Not a fairy tale, but something much better.

She had found herself in love; they had found each other. Smiling, the candlelight creating dancing shadows around them, she reached for Aarif and led him to their marriage bed.

* * * * *

*Read on for our exclusive interview
with Kate Hewitt!*

We chatted to Kate Hewitt about the world of THE ROYAL HOUSE OF KAREDES. *Here are her insights!*

Would you prefer to live on Aristo or Calista? What appeals to you most about either island?

Definitely Calista! I like the exotic remoteness of it, without too much of the glitz.

What did you enjoy about writing about The Royal House of Karedes?

I really enjoyed exploring the ready-made world of Calista and the royal family, while still being able to flesh out the story for myself. The best of both worlds!

How did you find writing as part of a continuity?

It was tricky at first, because you had to consider everyone else's stories, but I really got into it and had a great time.

When you are writing, what is your typical day?

My children are all in school for the first time so I am now trying to write three or so hours every morning, as opposed to at night, which is what I did before. I usually find my time disappears, however, with errands and chores and so forth, so I end up writing at night, too.

Where do you get your inspiration for the characters that you write?

From the depths of my subconscious, which is fed by all the people I see. (Living in New York City, there is plenty of opportunity for people watching!)

What did you like most about your hero and heroine in this continuity?

I liked how star-crossed my lovers were—their situation seemed truly hopeless, and yet love prevailed—of course!

What would be the best and worst things about being part of a royal dynasty?

The wealth and luxury would be the best; having to conform to expected standards and being watched all the time the worst. I like being a commoner!

Are diamonds really a girl's best friend?

Only if you want to be lonely.

The Greek Billionaire's Innocent Princess

CHANTELLE SHAW

Chantelle Shaw lives on the Kent coast, five minutes from the sea, and does much of her thinking about the characters in her books while walking on the beach. She's been an avid reader from an early age. Her school friends used to hide their books when she visited—but Chantelle would retreat into her own world and still writes stories in her head all the time. Chantelle has been blissfully married to her own tall, dark and very patient hero for over twenty years and has six children. She began to read Mills & Boon novels as a teenager and throughout the years of being a stay-at-home mum to her brood found romantic fiction helped her to stay sane! She enjoys reading and writing about strong-willed, feisty women, and even stronger-willed sexy heroes. Chantelle is at her happiest when writing. She is particularly inspired while cooking dinner, which unfortunately results in a lot of culinary disasters! She also loves gardening, walking and eating chocolate (followed by more walking!). Catch up with Chantelle's latest news on her website, www.chantelleshaw.com.

For my husband, Adrian,
with love and thanks for all of your support

CHAPTER ONE

NIKOS ANGELAKI stood at the edge of the ballroom and surveyed the five hundred or so guests who were dancing or sipping champagne beneath the ornate chandeliers. The men were uniform in black tuxedos, while the women—dressed in couture gowns and flaunting a spectacular array of diamonds and precious gems—flitted about the dance floor like gaudy butterflies. He flicked back the cuff of his dinner jacket, glanced at his Rolex, and then began to make his way across the room—aware of the interested glances he received as he passed. At thirty-two he was used to the attention his looks and the rumours of his wealth attracted. An attractive blonde in a daringly low-cut dress caught his attention, and his gaze lingered on her fleetingly before he stepped into the lobby.

It was the first time he had attended the royal ball or visited the Aristan palace, and he was impressed by the elegant splendour of the rooms where the silk-covered walls were lined with priceless works of art. The ruling family of the House of Karedes was one of the wealthiest families in Europe, and the guest-list included members of the aristocracy and heads of state—grand people who had no idea that the Prince Regent's honoured guest tonight had grown up in the slums of Athens.

Nikos wondered cynically if the butler who had escorted him to the state drawing room to greet Prince Sebastian would have been quite so obsequious if he'd known that Nikos's mother had once worked as a lowly kitchen maid at the palace. However, that was something he hadn't even revealed to Sebastian, despite the close friendship that had developed between them.

He strode across the hall, pushed open a door, and found himself in the banqueting suite, which was empty, apart from a waitress at the far end of the room who—unlike the other palace staff who seemed to be rushed off their feet tonight—was idly folding napkins.

The guests had eaten earlier, but Nikos's delayed flight had meant that he had missed the buffet supper, and as he glanced at the mouth-watering selection of canapés he was aware of a hollow feeling in his stomach. Business first, he told himself firmly. It was evening in Aristo, but early afternoon on America's east coast and he had arranged to call a client in New York. He strolled towards the waitress who had her back to him and was still oblivious to his presence.

'Can you tell me if there is somewhere I can be uninterrupted? I need to make an urgent business call.'

The deep, gravelly voice was so innately sensual that the tiny hairs on Kitty's body stood on end, and she turned her head, her heart crashing in her chest when she stared up at the man who had come silently into the room. She had recognised him instantly when he had walked into the ballroom earlier in the evening—Nikos Angelaki, billionaire shipping magnate, notorious playboy, and in recent months one of her brother's closest confidants. Sebastian had explained that he had met Nikos at a business function in Greece, and since then the two men had discovered a mutual liking for poker and the roulette wheel in the nightclubs of Aristo and Athens.

The photographs Kitty had seen of him in the tabloids had triggered her interest, but nothing had prepared her for the impact of Nikos in the flesh. He was suave, sophisticated and spine-tinglingly sexy. Taller than average; his tapered black trousers emphasised his long legs and taut thighs, while his impeccably tailored dinner jacket cloaked formidably broad shoulders. But it was his face that captured her attention. Handsome was a barely adequate description of the chiselled perfection of his features: the slanting, razor-sharp cheekbones and square chin, the heavy brows arched above midnight-dark eyes, and a wide, sensual mouth.

In the silence that stretched between them Kitty sensed his arrogance and devil-may-care confidence, and she felt an unbidden and shockingly intense tug of sexual awareness that sent a quiver down her spine. He was gorgeous, but she suddenly realised that she was staring at him, and she blushed.

'There is a small sitting room through there,' she mumbled, indicating the door at the far end of the room.

'Thank you.'

His eyes skimmed over her, making a brief inspection of her unexciting black cocktail dress, and Kitty wished fervently that she had bought a new outfit for the ball—something slinky and low-cut that would have made him look at her with male appreciation, rather than dismiss her without a second glance.

But she had never been very interested in clothes, preferring her research work for Aristo's museum to shopping, and it had only been when she had flicked through her list of preparations for the ball and seen the words 'buy dress' that she'd realised she had nothing suitable to wear to the palace's most prestigious social event.

She lacked the confidence to wear sexy outfits, anyway, she acknowledged dismally. And she certainly wouldn't stand a chance with a man like Nikos. He had given no sign that he recognised her, but palace protocol dictated that she should make the first introduction. Immediately she felt tongue-tied by the crippling shyness that had afflicted her since childhood.

Not for the first time she wished she shared her sister Princess Elissa's self-confidence and sparkling personality. Liss always made socialising look so easy.

She was Princess Katarina Karedes, fourth in line to the throne of Aristo, Kitty reminded herself. She had been trained practically from birth to deal with social situations, but she had never found meeting new people easy, and she was still steeling herself to offer her hand to Nikos in formal greeting when he spoke again.

'I've a feeling that you are needed to serve champagne in the ballroom. I understand from Prince Sebastian that a number of the catering staff have been taken ill, and I noticed that many of the guests have empty glasses.' He gave her a faint, dismissive smile, as if he expected her to immediately scuttle off, and turned his attention to his phone.

Kitty gaped at him, overwhelmed by his powerful personality, and taken aback by his suggestion that she was needed to serve drinks. She was aware of the problem with the caterers she had booked to work alongside the palace staff, and, having spent the past month planning every detail of the ball like a military operation, she found it annoying that so many of the waiters had succumbed to a virulent sickness virus. Anxious to ensure that the evening ran smoothly she had come to the banqueting room to check over the buffet table, but the head butler had assured her that everything was under control, and she was sure it was not necessary for her to take on the role of waitress.

Usually she had little to do with the royal ball, but this year, with Queen Tia mourning the death of the king, Sebastian had asked her to oversee the arrangements. Seb had enough on his mind, Kitty thought ruefully. After their father's unexpected death Sebastian should have immediately become the new king. But the shocking discovery that the Aristan half of the Stefani diamond, which was set in the Aristan Crown, was a fake, and that the real diamond was missing, had thrown the plans for his coronation into disarray. By royal tradition Sebastian could not be crowned if he did not have the jewel, and until it was found he could only assume the title of Prince Regent.

Lost in her thoughts, Kitty suddenly realised that Nikos Angelaki was watching her with unconcealed impatience. He moved away and began to punch numbers into his phone. 'My client is expecting my call,' he said as he walked towards the door leading to the sitting room. 'And you had better get back to work.' He paused, and looked back at her. 'Actually, you could bring me some champagne—and while you're about it something from the buffet. The *dolmathakia* looks good, and perhaps some bread and olives.'

He was a guest, Kitty reminded herself, and her duty as hostess of the ball was to ensure that the guests enjoyed the evening. But his haughty tone rankled. It was usual for people she did not know to address her as Your Highness, but Nikos was either unaware or unimpressed that he should use her royal title. Throughout her life Kitty had been treated with a deference suited to her royal status. She did not expect to be fawned over, but Nikos had spoken to her as if she were a lackey. Didn't he know who she was?

'You want *me* to serve you?' she queried, taken aback by his arrogant demand.

Her sharp tone caught Nikos's attention and he glanced across the room, his eyes narrowing when he noted the waitress's mutinous expression. He had paid scant attention to her when he had first walked into the room, and had formed a vague impression of a dumpy, rather plain girl in a badly fitting dress. But now, as he studied her more closely, he realised that she was far from uninteresting.

She was unfashionably curvaceous, he mused idly, allowing his gaze to roam over the swell of her hips that flared below her neat waist. Her voluptuous breasts straining beneath her dress would make a generous handful. A vivid mental picture came into his mind of her wearing a strapless, low-cut couture gown that displayed her breasts like plump, round peaches. In his imagination he saw himself slowly removing the gown, drawing it down and feasting his eyes on her nakedness, and he felt his body tighten with unbidden sexual awareness.

She wasn't his type, he reminded himself irritably. He liked tall, elegant blondes, and she was a short, curvy brunette. Her heavy-rimmed glasses were unflattering, but he noted that her skin was smooth and tinted a pale olive-gold, her slanting cheekbones highlighted by a flush of rose-pink, and her mouth was wide, her lips full and lush and eminently kissable.

Hell! He'd obviously been celibate for too long, he thought sardonically. He was a self-confessed workaholic, and under his leadership Petridis Angelaki Shipping's profits had soared. He worked hard and played hard, but recently he hadn't played enough. It was time he redressed the balance—but he doubted Prince Sebastian would be pleased if he seduced a member of the palace staff.

'If it's not too much trouble,' he drawled sarcastically. 'It is your job, after all.'

Kitty thought of the hours she'd spent organising the party, and felt a spurt of temper. She'd been run ragged for weeks, anxious to ensure the ball was a success for Sebastian's sake, but her duties didn't include acting as a personal attendant to one of her brother's friends. Twin spots of colour burned on her cheeks, and she put her hands on her hips.

'The idea of the buffet table is that guests can help themselves,' she informed Nikos tightly.

She saw him frown as his eyes trailed over her, and it suddenly struck her that her high-necked, long-sleeved black dress—which she had bought two seasons ago in the hope that the starkly simple style would make her look slimmer—was almost identical to the uniform that the female serving staff were wearing. *Her job!* Understanding slowly dawned. Could it be that Nikos Angelaki had no idea of her identity? They had never met, and, unlike Liss, who was often pictured in the tabloids, she was rarely recognised by the paparazzi. Nikos clearly believed she was one of the palace staff, and she didn't know whether to be amused or insulted by the mistake.

She opened her mouth to tell him that she was Princess Katarina, not a lowly servant, but something held her back. It was humiliating that he had mistaken her for a waitress. She wished now that she had made more effort with her appearance instead of blithely assuming that no one would take much notice of her. She was acting as the Prince Regent's consort tonight, and people *had* noticed her, but for all the wrong reasons.

During the evening she had overheard various unflattering comments from the guests that she was the Plain Jane Princess who had missed out on her sister's looks: *'...twenty-six...oh, no, not married...must be hard to be in the shadow of lovely Liss. Apparently Princess Katarina is the brainy one, but she doesn't share Princess Elissa's beauty.'*

Kitty wondered how Nikos would react when she told him she was a princess. Would he share the general consensus of the guests that she was the ugly duckling of the family? It didn't help that he was so stunningly good-looking. She could feel her heart thudding erratically as she absorbed the masculine beauty of his face, and she was startled by a fierce longing to run her fingers through the lock of silky black hair that had fallen forwards onto his brow.

She was terrified that he could somehow read her mind, but she could not tear her eyes from his, and she sensed something indefinable pass between them that made her skin prickle and her breasts tingle. To her horror she felt her nipples swell beneath her dress and she hastily crossed her arms over her chest, her cheeks burning.

Nikos recognised the flare of sexual awareness in the waitress's eyes and was infuriated by his own body's involuntary reaction to it. He did not have time to waste dealing with a stroppy domestic, even though the chemistry between them was tangible. 'I suggest you look up the word "servant",' he said coldly. 'You'll find it means "someone who is paid to serve". I'm sure Prince Sebastian is a fair employer who pays you a generous wage, and I would be grateful if you could do as I've asked without further argument.'

He should walk through into the private sitting room and make his call—but for reasons he couldn't explain, he hesitated. He could not dismiss the ridiculous urge to pull the girl into his arms and kiss her senseless. Not a girl, he corrected himself, his eyes drawn once again to the firm swell of her breasts. She was very much a woman, with a gorgeous hourglass figure that might not be 'in' with the fashion police but was incredibly sexy. He felt a fierce tug of sexual hunger in his groin and inhaled sharply, his nostrils flaring. 'What is your name?' he demanded harshly.

'It's…Rina.' The words spilled from Kitty's lips, and the moment they were out it was too late to retract them. She didn't understand what had prompted her to withhold her true identity, but she knew that Nikos had previously met Liss at a party in Paris and, although it was stupid, she could not bear the idea of him comparing her with her beautiful, glamorous sister. 'I'm new here,' she mumbled, assuring herself that she had only lied to save him the embarrassment of learning that he had mistaken a member of the royal family for a servant.

'I see.' Nikos strolled back across the room towards her and Kitty felt her pulse-rate quicken with every step he took. He swamped her senses and she was tempted to turn and flee, but when he halted inches from her she saw the gleam of sexual curiosity in his eyes and shock held her immobile. Surely she was wrong? Nikos had dated some of the world's most beautiful women and it was rumoured that he had been having a white-hot affair with the stunning Hollywood star, Shannon Marsh, for months. It was inconceivable that he could be attracted to a frump like her—wasn't it? She licked her suddenly dry lips and was startled when the expression in his eyes hardened to a predatory gleam that caused her heart to pound.

'Something tells me you have a lot to learn, Rina.'

The mockery in his voice was mixed with a blatant sensual message that sent a quiver of excitement down Kitty's spine. She had led a sheltered life at the palace, and at twenty-six was painfully aware of her sexual inexperience, but the feral heat in Nikos's eyes was unmistakable, even to a novice like her.

'I'd better go…and bring you some champagne, Mr Angelaki,' she said breathlessly, jerking away from him before she gave in to the temptation to close the space between them and press her soft body against the muscled hardness of his. Dangerous thoughts; and instinct warned her he was a man who was way out of her league.

'Yes, you better had.' Nikos laughed softly, self-derisively; breaking the web of sexual tension that curvy little waitress had somehow woven around him. 'Out of interest, how do you know my name?'

'I've seen your photograph, and read about you in the newspapers,' Kitty admitted, although she did not add that she regularly scanned the tabloids for articles about him or that she was rarely disappointed by his absence in the gossip columns. Nikos Angelaki's luck at the roulette table was as legendary as his business acumen. He was a gambler and a risk-taker, a highflier who was frequently snapped by the paparazzi driving around Athens in his Lamborghini with a seemingly inexhaustible supply of beautiful women at his side. 'You have a reputation as a millionaire playboy with a different blonde on your arm almost every week,' she said stiffly.

Nikos shrugged carelessly. 'You shouldn't believe all you read in the papers, Rina. Some of my "blondes" have lasted much longer than a week, and a few have even made it to a month,' he added sardonically. 'But I think my private life is nobody's business but my own—don't you?'

'Absolutely,' Kitty replied tightly, stung by his rebuke. 'It's no concern of mine that you change your women as often as other men change their socks.'

An ominous pause followed her defiant statement, and then Nikos threw back his head and laughed. 'I wonder if Prince Sebastian is aware that he has a rebel among his staff?' he drawled, moving before Kitty had time to react, and capturing her chin between his strong fingers. 'If you're not careful that sassy mouth could get you into a lot of trouble, Rina.'

She was trapped by his closeness, and the heat from his body mingled with the sensual tang of his aftershave stole around her and held her prisoner. The gleam in his eyes sent a tremor through her, and for a few electrifying seconds she thought he was going to lower his head and kiss her. She held her breath, torn between fear and fascination, and felt a crushing sense of disappointment when he abruptly released her. Of course he hadn't intended to kiss her; stupid of her to have thought it.

Nikos wondered if she knew how easily he could read her mind—or how tempted he was to accept her unspoken invitation and crush her soft mouth beneath his. It took every ounce of his will power to step away from her and retrace his steps back across the room. 'Go back to the ballroom before I decide to tell the prince of your reluctance to do the job you are employed to do,' he said tersely. 'And, Rina—' he paused in the doorway of the sitting room '—don't forget my champagne, will you?'

His arrogance was breathtaking. It was on Kitty's lips to tell him that under Aristo's ancient laws his lack of respect for a member of the royal family was a serious offence. He was lucky she did not call for the palace guard, and have him thrown out, she thought angrily. She was renowned for her calm and peaceable nature, but she was infuriated by his insolence.

But it was her own idiotic fault that he believed she was a waitress, and, uttering a most unprincesslike curse, she swung on her heels and marched out of the banqueting hall.

CHAPTER TWO

KITTY spent the rest of the evening carefully avoiding Nikos Angelaki, but she could not forget him, or the electricity that had fizzed between them when they had been alone together. No man had ever looked at her the way Nikos had done—with a raw, sexual hunger in his eyes that had evoked a wild longing deep inside her and left her wishing that he had swept her into his arms and made passionate love to her on the banqueting table.

Unable to dismiss her shocking fantasy from her mind, she had been too embarrassed to face him again with the food and champagne he had requested, and had asked one of the staff to serve him. Later, she had hovered behind a pillar, and watched him partner a steady stream of beautiful women on the dance floor. If it hadn't been for her stupid lie she could have asked Sebastian to introduce them, and maybe he would have asked her to dance. But if she revealed her identity to him now she would look a complete idiot in front of Nikos, and her brother.

She wouldn't know what to say to him anyway, she acknowledged bleakly. She was hopeless with men. The few fledgling romances she'd had at university had been disastrous and she knew her family despaired of her ever finding a husband. Kitty sighed, weighted down by the familiar feeling that she was a failure. Her dress was uncomfortably tight and tendrils of her hair had come loose and curled about her hot face. She wished the ball were over. She'd spent so long fretting over it and she was glad it was a success but she longed for the quiet solitude of the palace library and her books.

The king had shared her fascination with the history of the Adamas Kingdom, and she treasured her memories of the evenings they had spent together researching their ancestors. Nothing was the same without her father, she thought bleakly. One day soon Sebastian would be crowned King and she would give him her full support, but she missed King Aegeus desperately.

Grief surged through her and she bit her lip, knowing that she must control it as Queen Tia managed to do when she was in public. She was tired of the party, and she stepped through the French doors leading onto the terrace. The night air was warm and heavy with the perfume of jasmine and honeysuckle, and the silence was blissful after the hubbub of voices in the ballroom, but her peace did not last long.

'Well, well. Kitty Karedes! I didn't realise it was you. I saw a woman slip furtively out of the ballroom, and assumed she was meeting a lover, but, unless the ice-princess has thawed considerably since we last met, that's not likely, is it?'

'Vasilis! I won't lie and say it's a pleasure to see you. But the idea of you sneaking out to spy on lovers is wholly believable,' Kitty replied contemptuously. She glanced at Vasilis Sarondakos, felt the familiar wave of revulsion sweep over her and turned her back on him, hoping he would get the message and leave her alone. But Vasilis was not renowned for his sensitivity.

The Sarondakos family were leading members of Aristo's aristocracy, and Vasilis's father, Constantine, had been a close friend of the late king. At eighteen, Kitty had been painfully naïve, and had never had a boyfriend. With her father's encouragement she had gone on a date with Vasilis, but she had been deeply traumatised when he had subjected her to a drunken assault. His taunts that her voluptuous body was designed for sex had been devastating, but she had been too ashamed to tell her family what had happened, believing Vasilis's assertion that because she had worn a low-cut dress she had been—in his words—'gagging for it'.

The memory of his hot, alcohol-fuelled breath on her skin and his sweaty hands tearing her dress and touching her breasts still haunted her, and when her father had suggested a couple of years ago that he would be pleased if she married the son of his dear friend, Constantine Sarondakos, he had been taken aback by her fierce refusal.

'So, still no sign of a husband on the horizon, then, Kitty?' Vasilis taunted, coming to stand so close to her that she found herself trapped between him and the low stone wall that encircled the terrace. 'You should have married me while you had the chance.'

'I'd sooner swallow poison.' Kitty tried to edge away from him and tension knotted her stomach when he leaned closer still and rested his hands on the wall on either side of her, effectively caging her in. Five hundred guests were packed into the ballroom less than six feet away, including her three over-protective brothers. She had nothing to fear from Vasilis but she detested his cocky smile and the way he was looking at her as if he was mentally undressing her.

'Is that so?' Vasilis gave a sneering laugh. 'Perhaps you shouldn't be so hasty, my prim little princess. I was talking to Sebastian just the other day and he confided his concern that you'll end up on the shelf; a lonely spinster with only her books for company.'

'I'm twenty-six, not ninety-six,' Kitty snapped. 'And I don't believe for a minute that Sebastian would discuss my private affairs with you.'

'He'd have great difficulty; you don't have affairs.' Vasilis laughed again, clearly proud of his wit. 'I bet you're still a virgin, aren't you, Kitty? Of course, a lot of people think you're a lesbian,' he added conversationally. 'Maybe that's why Sebastian would like to see you married. With rumours that the Stefani diamond is a fake, and Sebastian delaying his coronation, the gossip is that your Calistan cousin Zakari is laying claim to the throne. The people of Aristo are already unsettled. The Karedes family don't need another scandal.'

'There is no scandal! Sebastian *is* the rightful king and he will be crowned as soon as possible,' Kitty said fiercely. 'Zakari Al'Farisi is the King of Calista but he has no right to Aristo's crown, or to be the one ruler of the Adamas Islands.' Kitty wasn't sure how Vasilis had heard the news the diamond was a fake, but she certainly wasn't going to confirm the rumour. 'The people of Aristo have nothing to worry about.

'As for me ever marrying you—hell will freeze over first!' Using all her strength, she pushed against Vasilis's arm until she broke free. 'Leave me alone, Vasilis. You sicken me. I never told my family about what happened between us out of respect for the affection my father felt for yours. But now Papa is dead and if you ever come near me again I'll tell my brothers what kind of a man you are, and you will no longer be welcome at the palace.'

'It'll be your word against mine,' Vasilis muttered, but his bravado was short-lived. The Karedeses were a tight-knit family who he knew would close ranks around one of their own. 'Anyway, do you really think I'd want to marry a woman who's as sexually responsive as a lump of ice?' he demanded spitefully. 'You've got some serious hang-ups about sex, Kitty. Maybe you should see a therapist.'

'I don't have any hang-ups…' Kitty ground her teeth in impotent fury as Vasilis grinned and sauntered through the French doors. She stared after him, knowing she should return to the ballroom, but simply unable to face it. Vasilis's cruel jibes played over and over in her head, compounding her misery that she was a hopeless failure.

She was a princess and she was supposed to be beautiful and glamorous. She was supposed to sparkle at social events and impress everyone with her sophistication and wit, but instead of being the belle of the royal ball tonight she had been mistaken for a waitress. She had never been any good at the whole royal thing, she thought drearily—the pomp and ceremony and waving at crowds—and it had been easier to leave the socialising that was a necessary part of royal life to Liss, and bury herself in the library with her books.

Was that going to be her life? she wondered desperately. Was she going to end up a spinster as Vasilis had prophesied— without love or passion, clinging to the memories of the night a gorgeous, sexy Greek tycoon had almost kissed her? Tears blurred her eyes and misted her glasses, and the sound of music and laughter from the ballroom made her feel lonelier than ever.

With a choked cry she raced down the terrace steps, away from the ballroom, and flew across the lawn. Tonight, when she'd stood at the edge of the ballroom and noted how everyone else seemed to be part of a couple she had faced the fact that she was a lonely, virgin princess, stifled by the formality of royal life. Her brothers and sister seemed to be moving on, but she felt as though she were trapped in a time warp. She had been born at the palace and had always loved it, but suddenly it felt like a prison and she was desperate to be free—to escape a life of duty and find out who Kitty Karedes really was.

She ran through the formal gardens, away from the lights spilling from the ballroom. The perimeter wall of the palace grounds was ten feet tall and built of impenetrable stone, but Kitty knew of the secret gate, half overgrown with climbing roses. In the moonlight she easily found the loose brick in the wall, and the hidden key, and seconds later she fled down a narrow path that led into a small cave at the base of the cliff.

Blow Vasilis Sarondakos and his spiteful tongue! she thought as she scrubbed her eyes. She wasn't on the shelf; she didn't have hang-ups about sex, and so what if she was still a virgin at twenty-six? It didn't make her less of a woman! She kicked her shoes off and wandered down to the water's edge, soothed by the gentle lap of the waves on the shore. She knew she would not be disturbed here. This little cove was a private beach, and the only way to it was along the path from the palace—a path that few people outside the family knew about.

Moonlight dappled the sea so that it shimmered like a flat silver pool. No one could see her here. She was completely alone, and impulsively she wrenched open the buttons on the hateful black dress and tugged it down over her hips until it dropped onto the sand. She placed her glasses carefully on a rock and pulled the pins from her hair, shaking her head so that her glossy dark chestnut tresses uncoiled and fell almost to her waist.

With each item of clothing she removed she felt as though she were discarding another hurtful jibe. So what if she didn't have a model-thin figure? Women were meant to have breasts, and she wasn't ashamed of hers. The silver sea beckoned her; she was already relishing the coolness of it on her skin, and in a moment of defiance against the restrictions of her life she unsnapped her bra, dropped it on top of her dress and stepped out of her knickers before running naked into the water with her hair streaming behind her.

Nikos was not sorry that the royal ball was drawing to an end. He had flown to Aristo from Dubai after a week of intense negotiations, and the eighteen-hour days he'd spent in the boardroom were catching up with him. He liked and admired Prince Sebastian, but he was bored of the other guests' endless, inane chit-chat, the gossip about who was sleeping with whom, and the unsubtle hints from a number of women that they were willing to go to bed with him.

Maybe he was simply tired of blondes, he mused as he stepped out onto the terrace, a half-full bottle of champagne in one hand and his dinner jacket looped over his shoulder. All evening he had been frustrated by his inability to dismiss the waitress, Rina, from his mind. He hadn't seen her again after their confrontation in the banqueting hall but he knew he hadn't imagined the chemistry between them. She intrigued him more than any woman had done for a long time, and he had found himself scanning the ballroom for her, irritated by his disappointment that she seemed to have disappeared.

He strolled through the shadowy gardens. The palace was as amazing as his mother had led him to believe many years ago when she had recounted tales of the time she had worked here before he had been born. As a child he had listened in awe to her description of the huge rooms and opulent décor, and as he'd looked around the cramped, run-down apartment block where they had lived it had seemed impossible that such a grand place existed.

He walked to the far end of the garden and was about to turn back when he recalled a distant memory his mother had told him of a gate in the wall, and a path that led from the palace to the beach. With a faint, self-derisive smile on his lips at his curiosity Nikos took one of the Chinese lanterns that illuminated the path and held it aloft as he walked back to the wall. The gate was tucked into a corner, and well disguised by the rose bushes that grew around it. He pushed it, expecting it to be locked, but when it opened he was sufficiently intrigued to follow the path that led from it.

The ground sloped steeply down until it disappeared between an opening in the rocks. Nikos had to duck his head as he entered the cave. It was dry inside, he noted, when he swung the lantern from side to side. Obviously the tide never came up this far. The air smelled faintly of seaweed and through the cave he could see the sea shimmering silver in the moonlight, but as he emerged onto the beach he stopped abruptly, and his heart kicked in his chest. For a moment he wondered if his mind was playing tricks on him, but the woman standing a few feet away from him was undoubtedly real, and her hourglass figure was instantly recognisable— even without her clothes.

Kitty swam right across the bay and back again with clean, strong strokes and then flipped onto her back and stared up at the moon, and the crystal stars that studded the midnight sky. She felt bold and empowered—as unashamedly naked as Eve had been in the Garden of Eden. There was something wickedly sensuous about the silken slide of the water over her bare limbs. She loved swimming and in the water she felt as light and graceful as a water nymph—at peace with her body instead of hating it for not conforming to the model slender form she had tried, through numerous diets and exercise regimes, to acquire.

Vasilis wouldn't be so ready to taunt her about her supposed sexual hang-ups if he could see her now, she thought as she turned onto her front and allowed the waves to carry her back to the shore. The beach was shadowed and mysterious in the moonlight. The huge boulders that stood guard at either end of the cove loomed like faceless giants, but despite the darkness and her short-sightedness Kitty could distinctly make out the figure of a man, and her heart almost leapt from her chest.

Dear God! Had Vasilis followed her? Fear uncoiled in the pit of her stomach, a wave caught her unawares and dragged her under, and she bobbed back to the surface gagging from the salt water she'd swallowed but desperate not to cough and attract the attention of the intruder. It had to be Vasilis. Few of the other guests at the ball were aware of the path leading from the palace to the beach, but Vasilis knew about it and had come here several times with her brothers.

The prospect of meeting her tormentor on the secluded beach sent a shiver of trepidation down Kitty's spine. She had seen the way he'd looked at her on the terrace, his lecherous grin that had changed to anger when she'd made it clear that she wanted nothing to do with him. Vasilis would not have dared lay a finger on her outside the ballroom, but here there was no one to help her—or hear her scream.

Clouds drifted across the moon, blotting out its brilliant gleam and plunging the beach into pitch blackness, and, seizing her chance, Kitty tore up the sand and crouched behind a rock. Her breath came in shallow gasps and her heart was pounding when the figure strolled down towards the water's edge.

'Hello, Rina,' he drawled. 'This is the second time tonight I've caught you playing hooky. Shouldn't you be busy at work at the ball?'

For a few seconds shock rendered Kitty speechless. *'You!'* she spluttered at last as the clouds above them parted and moonlight danced across Nikos Angelaki's sculpted features. Attack seemed the best form of defence and although her nakedness forced her to remain behind the rock her voice was sharp when she snapped, 'Do you know you're trespassing? This is a private beach.'

'Indeed it is. It belongs to the royal family, and I have express permission from Prince Sebastian to be here,' Nikos replied coolly. 'The only trespasser is you—unless the prince has suddenly opened up the beach for use by the palace staff. Do you have permission to be here, Rina?'

Kitty stared at him wordlessly, not knowing how to answer without revealing her true identity. She was agonisingly aware that she was naked, and she wished a hole would appear at her feet and swallow her up. 'The party hasn't finished yet. What are you doing here?' she mumbled in a voice thick with embarrassment.

In the pearly light cast by the moon she saw Nikos shrug.

'It was hot in the ballroom, and I decided to walk down to the beach for some fresh air. I could hardly believe my eyes when I came through the cave and caught sight of you.'

'You should have said something. I believed I was alone,' Kitty said miserably, burning up with mortification when she recalled how she had stripped out of her clothes. She prayed Nikos had arrived after she had run into the sea, but he swiftly shattered her tenuous hope.

'I was afraid I'd startle you,' he drawled. His voice dipped and the amusement in his tone was mixed with something else. 'Besides, what red-blooded male would have spoken out and risked spoiling the show? I was so careful not to make a sound that I barely drew breath.' He paused for a heartbeat and then said quietly, 'Watching you slowly reveal your body was the most erotic experience I've ever had.'

In a corner of her mind Kitty registered that the teasing note had disappeared from his voice, and the undisguised sensuality in his deep tone sent a quiver of reaction down her spine. But the idea that she had unwittingly revealed her curvy figure, which she so despised, to him, made her want to weep with shame. 'You are disgusting!' she choked. 'I can just about swallow the line that you didn't want to scare me, but if you were a gentleman you'd have shut your eyes.'

Nikos's rich laughter swirled around the empty beach. 'Ah, but I have never professed to be a gentleman, Rina. I am a pirate, an opportunist who answers to no one, and I do what I please.' His voice lowered to a sexy growl, 'And I promise you, *agape,* you pleased me very much.'

Kitty did not know how to react to that startling statement, and she hugged her arms around herself and peeped warily over the top of the rock.

She was as tempting as a siren from Greek mythology, Nikos owned as he stared at bare shoulders and her mass of dark hair that fell in damp tendrils down her back. But he was not about to admit that he'd been so turned on when he had watched her remove her clothes that he'd almost embarrassed himself.

When he had first seen her, he had assumed that she must have come down to the beach for an assignation with a lover. But no one else had appeared, and if he was honest he'd been so stunned by the sight of her stepping out of her dress and running down to the sea that he had been struck dumb.

Before his eyes Rina had emerged from her cocoon of drab clothes, and he had been riveted by her beauty. Pale fingers of moonlight had illuminated every dip and curve of her body, and tinted her satiny skin with silver brushstrokes. He had held his breath when she'd released her hair and it had tumbled down her back like a river of pure silk, and exhaled sharply when she had unfastened her bra and bared the creamy mounds of her full breasts to his hungry gaze.

His arousal had been instant and uncomfortably hard and his urgency to pillow himself between her soft thighs was still so acute that he was glad of the all concealing dark. It didn't seem to matter how much he tried to rationalise his reaction to her or remind himself that he liked slim, graceful blondes—and preferably the comfort of a large bed when he made love.

Rina had intrigued him in the banqueting hall earlier, when he had recognised the sizzling chemistry between them. Now, he desired her with a stark, primitive hunger that sent his blood thundering through his veins. He wanted to make love to her here on the sand, beneath the stars, and with a passion that was as wild and elemental as the untamed beach.

CHAPTER THREE

DESPITE the warmth of the night air Kitty was shivering—as much from the shock of Nikos's sudden appearance on the beach as from her swim. Her hair was hanging in wet coils and her skin was covered in goose-bumps but she reassured herself that her nipples had hardened into tight, tingling peaks because she was cold, *not* because of her overwhelming awareness of the sexiest man she had ever met.

She gritted her teeth to prevent them from chattering, and wished he would go back to the palace. Her dress was somewhere on the other side of the beach, but she would rather stay behind her rock all night and risk hypothermia than parade naked in front of him. She had already done so once, she acknowledged, blushing furiously again at the memory, but she had been unaware of his presence in the cave. No way was she going to make an exhibition of herself again.

'Here, put this on while I go and find your clothes.' Nikos stepped closer and dropped his jacket over the rock, and Kitty seized it gratefully and slipped it on. It was immense on her; the arms were several inches too long and to her relief the hem of the jacket reached to her mid-thighs. The silk lining felt deliciously sensuous against her skin; still warm from the heat of Nikos's body and carrying the faint musk of his aftershave. She burrowed deeper into the folds and inhaled deeply. She had been short-sighted for most of her life, but, as if to compensate for her poor vision, her other senses were particularly acute and she could detect his clean, male scent.

Molten heat stole through her veins as she imagined him wrapping his arms around her rather than his jacket. She remembered the fantasy she'd had earlier of him making love to her on the banqueting table, and pictured with shocking clarity him stripping out of his own clothes and tumbling her down on the sand. What was the matter with her? Scarlet-cheeked, she lifted her eyes to his, and caught her breath at the flash of fire she glimpsed before his lashes fell and hid his expression. But she had seen the desire in his gaze, and despite her inexperience she had recognised his need and found that it evoked an answering ache inside her.

She shivered again, and this time her whole body trembled—with reaction to Nikos rather than cold. She saw him tense, saw his eyes narrow, and knew that the wildfire awareness between them was terrifyingly real. Incredible though it seemed, Nikos Angelaki—playboy and serial womaniser—found her attractive. For the first time ever in her twenty-six years she felt as though she was a desirable woman, and she wanted to savour the moment—certain that any second now he would blink and realise that she was too short, too plump and too plain to hold his attention for long.

'You had better wait in the cave, you'll be warmer there,' he said, suddenly breaking the silence. His voice sounded so harsh that Kitty wondered what had angered him. He turned and strode away, and Kitty hesitated, her heart hammering, before she stepped from behind her rock and hurried up the beach. Almost instantly he reappeared at her side and caught hold of her arm to swing her round to him. 'I assume you need these,' he murmured as he unfolded her glasses and placed them on her nose.

'Thank you.' Kitty stared transfixed at his features, which

were now sharply defined rather than blurred. Moonbeams high-lighted the angles and planes of his incredible bone-structure, and she could not tear her eyes from the firm line of his mouth.

She heard him draw a sharp breath, and she gasped when he slid his hand beneath her chin and tilted her face to his. 'Hasn't anyone ever told you it's dangerous to swim in the sea alone?' he demanded impatiently. 'You could have got into trouble in the current, and no one would have known.' His eyes dropped to her small frame enveloped by his jacket, and he tried unsuccessfully to dismiss the image of her running naked across the sand. 'Tell me, do you often swim naked in the moonlight?'

'No, of course not,' Kitty replied quickly, squirming. It was not entirely the truth, she acknowledged silently. She loathed the sight of her body in a bikini and often came to swim alone in the dark when no one would see her. 'I know this is a private beach, and I thought I would be undisturbed here,' she said pointedly. 'Like you, I came down for some fresh air, but the sea looked so inviting that I was overcome with a mad impulse to…strip off and dive in.'

'Is that so?' Nikos's voice was no longer harsh, but velvet soft, stroking over Kitty's skin so that each tiny hair on her body stood on end. The chemistry that had been simmering between them since he had appeared on the beach was at combustion point, and her head spun with a dizzying mixture of trepidation and breathless excitement.

'What are you doing?' she mumbled when he removed her glasses and put them back in his jacket pocket.

'Following my own mad impulse,' he growled, ignoring her shocked gasp when he suddenly jerked her up against his chest. 'The same impulse we both felt in the banqueting hall. Don't deny it, Rina,' he warned silkily when she frantically shook her head from side to side. 'I saw what was in your mind.'

Recalling her shamefully erotic fantasy, which had

involved him sliding his hand beneath her skirt, and touching her where no man had ever touched her before, Kitty prayed he hadn't. But Nikos was lowering his head towards her, and it seemed to her shell-shocked brain as if everything were happening in slow motion. She tensed, torn between wanting to pull out of his arms and race back to the palace, and another, shocking need to stay and allow him to fulfil the determined intent in his dark gaze.

She moistened her suddenly dry lips with the tip of her tongue—and, watching her, Nikos felt his stomach muscles clench. This had been building since she had stood up to him earlier in the evening. He hadn't felt such a searing sexual attraction to a woman for a long time, and he dipped his head slowly, savouring the anticipation, and exploring the shape of her lips with his tongue before he claimed her mouth with a hunger he could no longer control.

Until the split second before Nikos slanted his mouth over hers, Kitty hadn't really believed he would kiss her, but her little gasp of shock was smothered beneath the pressure of his lips firmly coaxing hers apart. He was totally in control and he let her know it with the determined sweep of his tongue as he probed between her lips, demanding access to the moistness within. And she was powerless to stop him; lost from the moment he'd first touched her and caught up in a maelstrom of emotions as she felt the piercing sweetness of intense sexual desire for the first time in her life.

Nikos slid his hand round to Kitty's nape, tangled his fingers in her hair and tugged gently, angling her head so that he could deepen the kiss. Her response was instant and had a devastating affect on his libido so that he closed his other arm around her waist and dragged her hard up against the solid length of his arousal straining urgently beneath his trousers.

Rina was small and soft, and through his jacket he could feel the outline of her ripe curves that had proved such an unbearable temptation when she had stripped in the moonlight. She smelled of the sea; tasted of it too, he noted when he moved his mouth to her throat and stroked his tongue along her collarbone. He was used to women who wore designer clothes and drenched their skin in expensive perfumes, but there was something earthy, almost pagan, about this woman that struck a chord deep inside him. She was naturally sensual and totally in tune with her femininity, and instinct told him she would be a generous and adventurous lover.

His eyes were drawn to the deep valley of her cleavage and with a tortured groan he claimed her mouth once more, crushing her soft lips beneath his while he slid his hand into the front of his jacket and stroked his fingers lightly over one of her full, firm breasts.

He must have startled her because her whole body jerked with reaction, and, sensing her hesitation, he withdrew his hand, feeling a sharp tug of regret that he was denied the pleasure of caressing the erect point of her nipple. *Theos,* she was a sorceress; a sea-witch enticing him to forget everything but his desperation to sink his swollen shaft deep within her and possess her, but he could feel the sudden tension that gripped her, and calling on all his will power, he tore his mouth from hers and stared down at her, fighting for breath. 'This is madness,' he grated harshly. 'If either of us had any sense we should return to the palace. But my sanity seems to have deserted me, Rina, so the choice is yours. Will you end this now and go back? Or stay and drink champagne with me in the moonlight?'

It felt like a defining moment in her life, but Nikos had only asked her to drink champagne with him, Kitty reassured herself as she snatched oxygen into her lungs and tried to control the frantic thudding of her heart. He was watching her intently, waiting for her answer, and she gave a little shiver.

No man had ever asked her to drink champagne on a beach in the moonlight; no man had ever kissed her the way Nikos had, or stirred the passion that had been locked deep inside her for so long.

After a life spent adhering to duty and protocol Nikos Angelaki was like a breath of fresh air. He was dark and sexy and dangerous to know, but he made her feel daring—and the heat in his eyes made her feel desirable for the first time in her life.

She swallowed and forced herself to meet his gaze, feeling as though she were about to cast herself over the edge of a precipice. 'I love champagne,' she whispered shyly, shocked by her temerity.

He made no reply, and for a few agonising seconds she thought he had changed his mind and was going to send her away. But then he relaxed, and his slow smile stole her breath.

'Come, then,' he said, holding out his hand. His fingers closed around hers and even that tiny gesture was wonderfully new. She was twenty-six and she had never walked along a beach hand in hand with a lover, she thought despairingly. She didn't know where the years had gone, but it seemed as though one minute she had been a child and suddenly she was a grown woman who had been so absorbed with her studies and her work for the museum that romance and boyfriends had bypassed her.

She had taken on her share of royal commitments uncomplainingly because that was how she had been brought up: dutiful, obedient, always conscious of her position and grateful for the privileges that came with being a member of the royal family. But Nikos did not know she was a princess; he thought she was a waitress called Rina, and for a few hours she could be normal—just a woman who had met a man and was free to respond to the chemistry that smouldered between them.

The cave was illuminated by a lamp that he must have

brought from the garden. The pale beam of light that spilled from it highlighted the sculpted beauty of his face, and Kitty felt a fluttering sensation in her chest as her eyes focused on the sensual curve of his mouth. She hovered uncertainly while he dropped down onto the dry sand, the common sense for which she was famed telling her to go—now—before she did something she would later regret. But her feet seemed to be melded to the floor of the cave, and when he patted the sand next to him she walked slowly forwards.

He held out a bottle of champagne. 'Here, have some. You're shivering again. It's a pity it isn't brandy, but I'm afraid you'll have to make do with vintage Bollinger.' He stretched out so that his lean, hard body was spread temptingly before her. His white silk shirt was open at the throat revealing the tanned column of his throat and a mass of dark body hair that she'd noticed also covered his forearms. He was so *male,* so overwhelmingly virile, Kitty thought shakily as she sank onto her knees beside him and took the bottle.

'It doesn't seem right to drink champagne from the bottle,' she murmured. 'It's very…decadent.'

'Decadent?' Nikos's low rumble of laughter echoed around the cave. 'What a curious mix of contradictions you are, Rina. You sound as prim as a Victorian governess, and yet you're happy to go skinny-dipping in the moonlight. Do I need to remind you that you are naked beneath my jacket?'

He couldn't remember the last time he had seen a woman blush, Nikos mused idly. The sexually confident women he dated were sophisticated game-players long past the first flush of virginal innocence. The thought caused him to frown as he watched Kitty take a sip of champagne. She seemed to be a curious mixture: shy one minute and eagerly responsive to him the next. When he had first kissed her he'd gained the impression that it was a new experience for her, but after her initial hesitation she had parted her mouth beneath his and kissed him back with such fiery passion that he had dismissed the idea.

He didn't need to remind himself that she was wearing nothing, he acknowledged grimly when she handed him the champagne bottle and he took a long draught. The dinner jacket was far too big for her and fastened so low that he could see the rounded contours of her breasts. He did not know what crazy impulse had made him ask her to stay, and he was already regretting it. He never made rash decisions. Even when he gambled he carefully weighed up the odds before he threw the dice. But for some reason Rina disturbed his cool, logical brain—and disturbed other areas of his body too. He wanted to kiss her again and never stop, but instead he forced himself to relax and tried to ignore the temptation of tasting champagne from her lips.

'So, Rina,' he queried lightly, 'what made you decide to become a waitress?'

Oh, Lord—how did she answer that? 'I...um, I need to work,' Kitty mumbled awkwardly, thinking that now might be a good time to bid him goodnight. 'Like most people, I have to earn a living, and I'm not trained to do anything else.' She thought of the years she'd spent studying for her degree, and her absorbing work at Aristo's museum, and tried to imagine what life would be like if she hadn't had the benefit of an excellent education, and really did have to work in some menial job. She had little idea of life outside her gilded cage, and although she supported various charities she couldn't imagine what it must be like to be poor. The only experience she'd had of life in the real world was when she had worked as a volunteer at Aristo's hospital, but, although she had found the work rewarding, her father had disapproved—citing concerns for her safety—and forbidden her from going.

'Have you always lived on Aristo?'

That was easier to answer, and Kitty nodded. 'I was born

here, and I never want to live anywhere else. Aristo is the most beautiful place on earth.'

Nikos laughed. 'Have you visited many other places, then—on a waitress's pay?'

'Well...no,' Kitty faltered. She could hardly tell him that she had spent a year travelling around Europe and had visited Paris, Rome, cosmopolitan London, Venice and Florence, followed by six months at an exclusive finishing school in Switzerland. She had been a guest at royal palaces and country mansions, had wandered around fabulous art galleries and been taken on tours of all the famous sights, but nowhere compared to Aristo, the jewel of the Mediterranean. 'Aristo is my home and I love it here,' she told Nikos firmly.

Her passion for the island intrigued him, and he wondered why she felt so strongly about it. Was it the place or people that held her heart? 'Do you have a family here?' he asked curiously.

What would he say if she revealed that her family had ruled Aristo for generations? Kitty felt as though she were falling deeper and deeper into a mire. She wasn't lying exactly, she told herself. She just wasn't telling the whole truth. 'I have a mother, sister, brothers...' She faltered, thinking of the person who was missing from the list, and her heart contracted. 'My father died a few months ago.'

'I'm sorry.'

It wasn't a throwaway remark—Kitty heard the note of compassion in Nikos's voice, and tears, sudden and unbidden, stung her eyes. 'I miss him so much,' she admitted thickly. 'Sometimes I see his face in my mind, hear his voice, and I can't believe he isn't here any more.' She brushed her hand across her wet eyes, and was startled when Nikos captured her fingers in one of his strong hands and traced his thumb pad down her cheek, following the damp trail.

'I'm sorry.' She didn't want to cry in front of him. Her grief was a private matter that she shared with no one, not even her family. She had been especially close to the king, and he had called her his gentle dove, but she had been taught never to display her emotions. One of the golden rules of the royal family was to exert self-control at all times. Embarrassed by her weakness, she tried to draw away from Nikos but he curled his arm around her shoulders and tugged her towards him.

'Don't be sorry,' he said quietly. 'I know how devastating it is to lose a parent. My mother died many years ago, but I will never forget her. You won't forget your father, Rina, but the memories will become easier, and eventually you will think of him without the sadness you feel now.'

He smoothed her hair back from her face, and Kitty closed her eyes, soothed by the rhythmic stroking of his fingers. She felt his warm breath on her face and when she lifted her lashes she drowned in the depths of his midnight-dark gaze. He was so strong, so *alive,* and she wanted to absorb some of his strength because she felt weak and lost and achingly lonely inside.

Tentatively she rested her hand on his chest and felt the steady thud of his heart beneath her fingertips. It was utterly silent in the cave, as if they were cut off from the outside world and were the only two people in the universe. She could hear the sound of Nikos breathing—no longer steady but quicker, like his heartbeat; and she lifted her eyes to his face and stared at him, mesmerised by his masculine beauty.

Nikos knew he should move and break the spell that had been cast on him in the witching hour, but his muscles were locked. In the lamplight the tears that spiked Rina's lashes glittered like tiny diamonds and the shadow of pain in her eyes moved him. It was more than fifteen years since his mother had died. He had been sixteen, a boy suddenly forced to be a man, but he still remembered the pain in his gut, the feeling that his insides had been ripped out, and the dull acceptance that the only person who had ever loved him had gone.

Rina's loss was clearly still raw, the unspoken plea in her

eyes asked for comfort, and that was all Nikos intended to give when he lowered his head and brushed his mouth softly over hers. For a moment she did not respond, but neither did she pull away and he tasted her again, delicately, offering her the warmth of his body and silently letting her know that he understood the agony of grief. Even when she parted her mouth beneath his and tilted her head back a fraction for him to deepen the kiss he was sure he was in control. But her lips were so beguilingly soft and the temptation to dip his tongue between them and drink the lingering nectar of champagne became overwhelming.

Slowly he tightened his arm around her and slid his hand into her hair. It felt like silk against his skin and his heart began to pound with a thudding drumbeat of desire as he tangled his fingers in the chestnut strands and drew her closer still so that her breasts pushed against the wall of his chest.

Kitty couldn't pinpoint the exact moment when Nikos's kiss changed from a gentle caress that soothed her fragile emotions to one of hungry passion that stirred her soul and sent molten heat flooding through her veins. All she knew was that the pressure of his mouth increased and slid over hers with increasing urgency, and his tongue no longer traced the shape of her lips but thrust between them with a fierce demand that made her tremble.

The voice in her head warned her that she was heading into dangerous waters and she should pull back now, before she was swept away. But she did not want to move out of his arms and feel cold and alone again. She wanted him to hold her even closer so that she could absorb the warmth of his body, and she curled her hands around his neck and pressed herself against him, making no protest when he drew her down so that they were stretched out on the sand.

Now they were lying hip to hip, and the unmistakable evidence of Nikos's arousal jutting against her thighs caused her muscles to tense. This was wrong, very wrong, and it had to stop—now. But when he found her mouth once more in a slow, drugging kiss, she could not help but respond. Just a few more minutes in his arms, and then she would draw away from him, she promised herself. Surely it wasn't too much to ask— a few passionate kisses with the sexiest man she had ever met before she returned to her lonely life. But now she no longer felt relaxed, she was aware of a restless ache deep in her pelvis, and when he lifted his mouth from hers she gave a little murmur of protest.

'*Theos*, Rina!' Nikos's ragged voice echoed harshly in the cloistered quiet of the cave. 'This is insanity. You should leave while I still have some measure of control.' He stared down at her, his blood thundering in his veins when he saw the dazed passion in her eyes, and said slowly, 'Because if you do not, I can't guarantee that I will be able to stop.'

CHAPTER FOUR

NIKOS'S words were an unwelcome intrusion, slicing through the fog that clouded Kitty's brain. She didn't want to think, she wanted to feel and touch and lose herself in the world of sensory pleasure that his kisses evoked. She felt as though she were standing on the threshold of some new and wonderful place and Nikos was giving her the choice of stepping through the door, or closing it and turning back. Her mind flew to the royal ball and the loneliness she'd felt as she'd watched the couples on the dance floor. Everyone seemed to have a partner except her. All her friends were getting married and starting families but she had never even had a proper boyfriend. She recalled Vasilis Sarondakos's cruel taunts that she would end up a virgin spinster, and despair tugged her heart. She didn't want to be alone any more, and the flames of desire in Nikos's eyes told her that tonight she didn't have to be.

Tentatively she touched his face, and traced her finger across his mouth. She could hardly believe she was lying in the dark cave with the sexiest man she had ever met, and that sense of unreality numbed her to everything but her longing for him to kiss her again. Her innate shyness trapped her tongue, but the silent message in her eyes was enough for Nikos, and his chest heaved as he drew a harsh breath. The flare of feral hunger in his dark gaze sent a frisson of trepidation through Kitty, but then she forgot everything but the feel and touch and taste of him as he kissed her with an unrestrained hunger that warned her she had opened Pandora's box and had better be prepared for the consequences.

The feel of Nikos's hands brushing lightly against her skin as he unfastened the buttons on his jacket caused Kitty's heart to jerk frantically beneath her ribs, and doubt flooded through her. The memory of Vasilis roughly pawing her breasts filled her mind, and she tensed, her breath coming in sharp little gasps of panic. But Nikos was not rough, and the glitter of male appreciation in his eyes as he slowly pushed the edges of the jacket apart and revealed the pouting fullness of her breasts sent a shiver of another kind through Kitty. Her panic gradually receded as he gently cupped each breast in his palms and felt their weight and softness.

He muttered something indistinct beneath his breath and colour flared briefly along his cheekbones. 'Beautiful,' he said thickly, and stroked his fingertip across one nipple in a feather-light caress. The sensation was so exquisite that Kitty gasped and then closed her eyes and felt the pleasure build when he brushed his thumb pad lightly over the crest of her other breast.

Nikos guided her hands to the front of his shirt and aided her in freeing the buttons. Hands shaking, Kitty pushed the material aside to reveal his broad, muscular chest; olive-gold satin covered with whorls of dark hair that arrowed down over his taut abdomen. He drew her to him and she caught her breath at that very first contact of a hard male chest pressed against the softness of her breasts. It felt so good, so right, and so very seductive that she burrowed closer still, loving the strength of his arms around her as he found her mouth once more and kissed her until she was breathless.

Nikos had convinced himself that he was in control and that he would only allow things to go so far before he called a halt.

He had occasionally had one-night stands: brief, mutually satisfying encounters with sexually confident women who, like him, wanted to answer a basic need without the complication of emotions. But those occasions had always been on his terms and, although the sex had invariably been enjoyable, he had never been driven by uncontrollable desire. For reasons he did not understand Rina was different. The raging need he felt to make love to her had never happened before and he was shocked to realise that he couldn't fight it.

Perhaps it was because she was so amazingly responsive and so unguarded in her pleasure when he caressed her? Frustrated by his inability to resist her, he gave her a hard, almost angry kiss, but she responded with such sweet passion that he gave up battling with himself and eased the pressure of his lips until the kiss evolved into a sensual tasting that became increasingly erotic. When she was utterly pliant in his arms he trailed his mouth lower, following the path of his hands to her breasts and drew lazy circles with his tongue around one nipple until it hardened to a taut peak.

The sensation of Nikos's mouth on her breast was indescribable, and when he drew her nipple fully into his mouth Kitty instinctively arched her back. She curled her fingers into his hair and gave a soft cry, shifting her hips restlessly beneath him as the tugging sensation on her breast became unbearably exquisite.

'Nikos…' His name left her lips as a whimpered plea and she tossed her head from side to side when he transferred his mouth to her other swollen crest and metered the same delicious torture.

He growled something she did not catch, but his intention became clear when he unfastened the last button of his jacket and spread the material to reveal the faint curve of her stomach and the triangle of dark curls clustered at the junction between her thighs. He moved so that he was kneeling above her, and

Kitty blushed when he trailed his eyes deliberately down her body. The knowledge that he had watched her undress earlier was no help. She had been unaware of his presence, and even beneath the bright moon she must have been partly in shadow. Now she was completely exposed to him. No man had ever seen her body before, and desperate shyness, combined with her insecurities about her figure, caused her to try and shield herself with her hands.

It was time to end this craziness, Nikos acknowledged, trying to ignore the stomach-dipping sense of disappointment that clawed at his insides. He couldn't quite comprehend how they had got to this point. He'd had no intention of actually having sex with the waitress he'd met only hours before, but she was so sexy she would tempt a saint, let alone a mortal man who was burning up with sexual frustration.

But Rina had tensed, he could sense her uncertainty, and it would be unfair of him to try and persuade her to take their passion to its ultimate conclusion—even though he was certain that with patience and restraint he could arouse her to a level where she would willingly make love with him. Another moment and he would refasten the jacket and bring them both back down to reality, he told himself. He took a deep breath, nostrils flaring as he fought for control, but he could not resist stroking his hand lightly over her stomach, and then lower.

Her thighs were silky smooth, and he caught her faint gasp when he brushed his fingers through her silky curls. 'Why do you want to hide yourself from me?' he murmured huskily. 'You have a beautiful body, Rina. I'm sure you can be in no doubt that I'm massively turned on by you,' he added self-de-risively, knowing that she could hardly miss the throbbing hardness of his erection pressed against her thigh.

'Are you?' her breathy little voice whispered in the silent cave and Nikos stiffened, thinking that she was taunting him.

But there was no hint of teasing in the big brown eyes that were focused on him. She reminded him of a timid deer that was poised for flight, and yet, with gentle handling, might stay and allow him closer.

'What do you think?' he said quietly as he took her hand and laid it over the bulge beneath his trousers. He watched her eyes widen, her pupils hugely dilated, and could not resist lowering his head and kissing her softly swollen mouth. The feel of her lips parting beneath his threatened to shatter his self-control, and, tempted beyond bearing, he slid his hand between her legs and delicately probed the tightly closed edge of her femininity. Her whole body jerked with reaction, and he thought for a moment that she would reject him, but then she slowly relaxed, and his blood thundered in his veins when he gently parted her and discovered the unmistakable evidence of her arousal.

Kitty's heart was beating so fast that she was sure it would burst through her chest as she felt Nikos part her, and she caught her breath when he slowly inserted a finger between her silken folds. She could feel the betraying dampness between her legs and was embarrassed that he would know she was aroused, but he gave a low growl of satisfaction and eased deeper inside her while his thumb pad found the tight little nub of her clitoris and tenderly stroked across it with devastating effect.

'Oh...' The shock of experiencing her first intimate male caress caused Kitty to cry out. The feel of Nikos's finger moving inside her was bliss, rapture beyond anything she had ever imagined, and she trembled as intense sensations rippled through her. To her untutored body it seemed impossible that there could be more, that she wasn't already at the peak, but the ache deep inside her was growing ever more demanding, and following an instinct as old as time she tried clumsily to pull him down on top of her.

'Wait, *agape.*' His voice was hoarse, as if he too was no longer in control of himself and was driven by a deeply in-grained, basic need that could no longer be denied. Kitty did not know how he divested himself of his clothes without her being aware of it, but suddenly he was naked and he spread the edges of his jacket that she was still wearing wide open and came down on her, the rough hairs that covered his thighs and abdomen feeling slightly abrasive against her skin. She felt the jutting length of his penis press into her belly—so shockingly rigid and alien to her that her eyes flew open and she stared up at him as he loomed over her, and swallowed at the hard gleam in his eyes.

What on earth was she doing? Was she really going to allow Nikos—a man she had never met until tonight—to make love to her? A tremor ran through her. She shouldn't be here, should never have allowed the fiery attraction between them to burst into flame. Nikos was a notorious playboy and she was a princess from the royal house of Karedes—yet even knowing that it was wrong, she acknowledged with searing honesty that she didn't want Nikos to stop.

'I bet you're still a virgin.' Vasilis's sneering voice echoed in her head, and rebellion flared in her heart. She was twenty-six, and it was time she became a woman, but out of fairness to Nikos she knew she must confess her inexperience.

'Nikos,' she whispered faintly, 'I think I should tell you…' But the rest of her words were lost beneath his mouth as he claimed her lips in a searing, soul-shattering kiss that disman-tled the last of her doubts and fears.

'Tell me what?' he muttered. 'You're not on the Pill—is that it? Don't worry. I'll take care of it.' The sensual smoki-ness of his voice wrapped around Kitty like a cocoon, and she was only dimly conscious of him reaching into his jacket pocket and donning protection with a swift efficiency that spoke of plenty of practice. Then he came down on her once more, settled his hard, muscular body between her thighs, and she could feel the pulsing thickness of his shaft press impatiently against her opening.

This was it, the moment she had wondered about all of her adult life, and she still couldn't quite believe that it was going to happen. Her heart was galloping, her breath coming in short, shallow pants, and suddenly her nerve deserted her and she tried to bring her legs together. But she was too late, Nikos was already surging forwards, and he gently but firmly pushed her thighs apart and entered her with one deep, powerful thrust that brought a shocked cry from Kitty's lips.

'Theos!' He stilled instantly and stared down at her, his brows lowering in a harsh frown. 'Your first time? How can it be?' Nikos demanded in stunned incomprehension. He began to withdraw from her, but now that Kitty was over the first shock of penetration her muscles were stretching around him and the brief pain was fading. She loved the new and wondrous sensation of having him fill her completely, and the restless ache inside her was once again clamouring to be assuaged.

'Don't stop…please.' She clung to his shoulders, urging him down again, and, sensing his indecision, she wrapped her legs around him, inviting him to push into her once more. It was an invitation he couldn't refuse and with a muttered imprecation he surged forward, taking it slower this time, but the power of each ensuing thrust was no less intense and Kitty arched beneath him and gave herself up to the pleasure of feeling him move within her.

Deeper, harder, Nikos was aware that he was losing control, and he slipped his hands under her and cupped her bottom, lifting her so that he could plunge deeper still, setting a rhythm that was fast and frantic as he took them both to the edge.

The burning ache in her pelvis was unbearable now, and Kitty felt as if something inside her were being stretched until it could be stretched no more and it would snap at any second.

'Please…' She couldn't stand it any longer. It had to happen, *now*. She curled her fingers into the sweat-dampened hair at Nikos's nape and clung to him while he drove into her again and again, taking her higher and increasing her excitement with every stroke.

And suddenly, when she was trembling and desperate, he gave one more devastating thrust, and the dam burst. A tidal wave of pleasure swept through her as her muscles contracted in pulse after pulse of exquisite sensation, and the ripples radiated out until every inch of her body was suffused in ecstasy. Almost simultaneously she heard the low groan that seemed to be ripped from his throat and felt the great shudders that tore through him as he reached his own release. He slumped on top of her and she felt his heart slamming in his chest.

In a protective gesture as old as womankind she crossed her arms over his back and cradled him on her breasts, holding him tight for those few moments while he was at his most vulnerable. Tears filled her eyes and tenderness swamped her heart. He had just given her the most incredible experience of her life and in the aftermath she felt as though their souls as well as their bodies had been as one. It seemed impossible that he did not feel it too. But too soon he raised himself onto his elbows and stared down at her, the gleam in his eyes no longer caused by passion, but anger, as he demanded, 'Why the *hell* didn't you tell me you were a virgin?'

Kitty took one look at Nikos's grim expression and swiftly dismissed the idea that the intense passion they had just shared had meant anything more to him than a physical release of lust. This feeling that their souls had meshed and were now inextricably entwined was an illusion brought on by the intensity of her first sexual experience, and the coldness in his eyes warned her he did not share her fantasy.

Now that the heat of passion was cooling she felt faintly

sick, and her limbs were trembling uncontrollably with shocked reaction to what had happened, but pride dictated that she hide her emotional turmoil from Nikos.

'It was my business,' she murmured lightly, striving to sound as though giving him her virginity was no big deal.

Nikos was not appeased. 'But now you have made it my business,' he said harshly. 'I am not in the habit of seducing virgins. If you had told me, I would have stopped.'

'But I didn't want you to stop,' Kitty admitted quietly, silently acknowledging the truth of her statement. The strength of passion he had aroused in her had been a revelation, and for those few wild moments she had forgotten everything but her need for fulfilment. It was only now that the self-recriminations were queuing up in her head.

Nikos had rolled off her and was now watching her intently, his eyes narrowed and suspicious on her face. Intuitively she knew what was bothering him. He was a playboy with a well-publicised aversion to commitment. She guessed he was wondering what she might want from him, and was doubtless determined to impress on her that he would give her nothing. Perhaps he feared that she would turn clingy and emotional? He wasn't to know that she would rather die than allow him to see how much he affected her.

Feeling acutely self-conscious now, she tugged the edges of his jacket together, flushing beneath his sardonic look that said it was a little too late for modesty. 'If you want the honest truth, my virginity had become something of a hindrance,' she told him, hoping she sounded confident and convincing, rather than perilously close to tears. 'I wanted my first time to be an enjoyable experience, but I wanted a man, not some clumsy, inexperienced boy. Your reputation as an expert lover was a temptation I couldn't resist, and I certainly wasn't disappointed—' her voice faltered slightly '—but I apologise if my performance and experience were less than you'd expected.'

'Don't be ridiculous. I wasn't disappointed, as I'm sure—despite your inexperience—you must have noticed,' he responded dryly, remembering the shattering intensity of his release. 'You were amazing, *agape*.'

Nikos shifted onto his back and stared up at the shadows flickering on the roof of the cave. The stark shock of discovering that he was her first lover was fading, and he acknowledged that it had been the best sex he'd had for a long time. He glanced at Rina lying beside him and slowly relaxed, relieved that she had made no attempt to cuddle up to him. It seemed that he had no need to worry. She had been a virgin but she understood the rules. He hadn't intended to see her again after tonight, but if she could be trusted not to make demands on him then he saw no reason why they shouldn't meet up occasionally when he came to Aristo.

'I also have a confession to make,' he said lazily as he rolled onto his side once more and wound a lock of her still-damp hair around his finger.

Kitty's heart shuddered to a standstill. 'Are you married?'

He gave a snort of disgust. '*Theos*—no!' Nikos's face hardened, and he suddenly seemed so remote that Kitty wondered despairingly what utter madness had led her to have sex for the first time in her life with this man who was a stranger to her. 'I'm divorced,' he told her with a grim smile that did not reach his eyes, 'and, since I evicted my ex-wife from my life, resolutely single.'

Nikos felt the familiar black hatred surge through him as his mind dwelled on the woman he had once believed he had loved, his bitterness mixed with fury with himself that he had been such a damnable fool. Never again, he thought savagely. Greta's terrible deceit had taught him a hard lesson, but he had learned it well. Never trust any woman or invest emotion in them, because, as he had found out in the cruellest way imaginable, they weren't worth it.

He jerked his thoughts from the past and realised that Rina was staring at him. His eyes narrowed on her startled expression. 'If you're harbouring any romantic illusions about me, then I suggest you forget them fast, *agape*. I value my freedom above everything.'

Kitty was silent for a moment, trying to assimilate the knowledge that he had been married. It was the first real thing she had learned about him, and she couldn't help feeling shocked and—even more ridiculous—crushingly disappointed. She couldn't picture him married—it didn't fit with his image. She wondered what his wife had been like. Stunningly beautiful, of course, she brooded. Probably a glamorous model like the women he was frequently photographed in the papers with.

She was curious about the reasons why the marriage had ended. Nikos had been unable to hide the bitter note in his voice when he had spoken of his ex-wife. Whatever had happened in his past had clearly had a huge impact on him and his relationships since his divorce, because his affairs were numerous and short-lived, and a few of his ex-lovers who had sold their story to the tabloids had stated that he had a heart of granite.

She glanced up to find him watching her, the expression in his dark eyes unfathomable. Inside she felt in turmoil, but she managed a careless shrug. 'Lucky I stopped believing in fairy tales long ago, then. I have no illusions about the kind of man you are, Nikos. But I'm still curious to hear your confession.'

The brief tension between them passed, she saw Nikos visibly relax and his seductive smile sent a quiver of reaction through her. 'I didn't have permission from the Prince Regent to come down to the beach, either,' he drawled.

'Then how did you know about the path from the palace?' Kitty asked, confused.

'My mother told me about it when I was a child. I was

walking in the gardens tonight when I suddenly remembered her saying that there was a secret path to the beach, and I decided to look for it, not knowing for sure if the story was true, or simply a rumour she had heard when she—' He broke off abruptly, and then, in answer to Kitty's bewildered stare, added, 'When she lived here on Aristo.'

There was no particular reason why he should not tell Rina that his mother had been a servant at the palace, Nikos conceded. If anything, it was rather ironic that he had been drawn to a member of the palace staff rather than one of the sophisticated guests at the ball. Perhaps he had a secret desire to return to his roots, he thought dryly. But his personal life was his own, and for all he knew Rina might decide to sell her story of how she had met him to the tabloids. MY SEX SESSION ON THE SAND WITH GREEK TYCOON might be a headline grabber, but a revelation that Nikos Angelaki was the illegitimate child of a palace servant would sell even better, and he refused to have his mother's reputation smeared in some sleazy rag.

'I thought you are Greek?' Kitty murmured, eager to learn more about him.

'My mother was born and grew up on Aristo. She came from around the bay, at a place called Varna.'

Kitty knew every part of Aristo, and she frowned as she thought of the tiny fishing village where Nikos had said his mother had lived. There were a few big estates on the hills above Varna, and she supposed his family owned one of them. 'I know you said your mother died some years ago, but do you visit her family often?'

'No.' Nikos's jaw hardened as he thought of the relatives he had never met—his mother's family who had thrown her out when she had fallen pregnant with him. None of them were left now. According to the private detective he had employed to trace them, his grandmother had died years ago, and his grandfather had passed away at the ripe age of eighty-six—without ever knowing that he had a grandson, and taking the identity of Nikos's father with him to the grave.

Nikos's mother had steadfastly refused to tell him the name of the man who had made her pregnant and then abandoned her—revealing only that he had been a Greek fisherman. It wasn't a lot to go on, Nikos acknowledged grimly. Realistically he accepted that there was no chance he would ever know who had sired him, but that didn't stop him wondering whose blood ran through his veins.

'My mother's family are all dead,' he told Kitty, his tone warning her that he did not want to continue the discussion. He rolled onto his back once more, suddenly feeling dog-tired. God knew how many hours it had been since he had boarded a plane at Dubai International Airport, but jet lag was catching up with him and his eyelids felt heavy. He wouldn't go to sleep, he promised himself. He would just rest his eyes for a couple of minutes…

Kitty listened to the rhythmic sound of Nikos breathing and carefully inched away from him. He looked curiously vulnerable in sleep and she longed to brush the lock of black hair back from his brow. He was so gorgeous; she could sit and look at him for ever, but what would happen when he woke up? Her face burned as she imagined them casually pulling on their clothes and strolling back to the palace. She supposed he would bid her goodnight—maybe even kiss her again? She had been trained in the rules of etiquette but she had no knowledge of the rules of lovers.

Would Nikos ask to see her again or ask for her phone number? *At what point would she tell him that she was Princess Katarina, his best friend's sister—and not a waitress called Rina?*

She should never have lied to him, she thought desperately. But when she had met him at the ball and allowed him to think she was a servant she'd had no idea that they would be lovers before the night was out. The enormity of what she had done struck her with the force of a tidal wave and she held her hand against her mouth to hold back her cry of despair. She had to go now, before Nikos woke up.

Heart racing, she scrambled to her feet and groped for her glasses. Nikos had placed her clothes on a rock and she quickly slipped off his jacket and folded it neatly next to him before she dragged her dress over her head, not daring to waste precious time fumbling with her underwear.

She realised that her shoes must still be down by the shore, but Nikos could stir at any minute, and so she ran barefoot to the back of the cave, out through the narrow hole in the rocks and up the path leading back to the palace. Heart pounding, she fled through the dark, thankful that she knew every twist and turn and half expecting to hear Nikos coming after her. But there was no sound of his footfall and she flew across the garden and into the palace through the now empty kitchens.

The party was over and the guests had gone. The caterers had left, and the palace staff had all retired for the night. No one saw her on her way up to her bedroom but her heart felt as though it would burst when she locked her door and staggered over to the mirror to stare at the reflection of the woman she barely recognised as herself, with her swollen mouth and her hair tumbling in wild disarray over her shoulders.

What had she done? She must have been out of her mind. Nikos had invited her to drink champagne with him but she'd barely had a sip and couldn't blame alcohol for her appalling behaviour. Kitty buried her face in her hands, as if she could somehow blot out the memories of the wild passion she had shared with Nikos in the cave. God knew what he must think of her. But it couldn't be any worse than her opinion of herself. She was just thankful she was never likely to see him again. She could never risk him discovering her true identity. It was far better that he believed he'd had a one-night stand with a lowly domestic assistant called Rina—and for her to forget she had ever met him.

CHAPTER FIVE

In the days following the royal ball Kitty did her best to banish Nikos from her mind—but failed hopelessly. Every time she closed her eyes she saw his face, and at night she dreamed she was in his arms, their bodies intimately entwined.

Sexual frustration was a new and unwelcome experience, but soon another reason kept her awake until the early hours. Her period was late—and she had always been as regular as clockwork. As the days passed with no sign that would put her mind at rest she acknowledged that it was no good trying to ignore her fears. But buying a pregnancy-test kit was no simple task for a member of the ruling family of Aristo. She was one of the lesser-known royals, but she couldn't just waltz into a chemist and brazenly buy a kit.

Eventually she drove into the centre of Ellos, Aristo's thriving capital city, and, hiding behind large sunglasses and an oversized sunhat, bought a kit from a busy outlet before swiftly leaving the shop, terrified that someone had recognised her. The test result was horribly predictable, and at the same time utterly shocking, and two weeks after the royal ball she stood in her bathroom and stared numbly at the blue line that had appeared on the pregnancy kit, wondering if the churning sensation in her stomach was caused by fear, or whether it was the first physical indication that she was expecting Nikos's baby. How could it be possible? she thought despairingly. Nikos had used protection. She felt as though she were caught in a nightmare from which there was no escape, and she wanted to bury her head under the duvet and wait for morning to come. But this wasn't a bad dream, this was real, and she had to face the fact that she was an unmarried, pregnant princess.

She was still in a state of shocked disbelief when Sebastian found her in the library later that morning. 'Ah, there you are, Kitty.' He stared at her closely. 'Are you okay? You've been looking pale for the past few days and Mama is concerned about you.'

'I'm fine,' Kitty said quickly. She swung away from Sebastian's sharp glance but not before he'd glimpsed the sheen of tears in her eyes.

'Hey, Kitty-Kat, what's the matter?'

'Nothing.' Her brother's gentle concern and his use of her childhood nickname tore at Kitty's frayed emotions, and she dropped her head in her hands, great sobs racking her as the dam holding back her fears burst.

'*Kitty!* What the hell is it?' Sebastian's voice was harsh with anxiety as he walked round the desk and put his arm around her shoulders. 'Come on, you can tell me. Whatever it is it can't be *that* bad,' he coaxed softly. 'And you know I'll always help you.'

Sebastian had always been her protector, but even he couldn't sort out this problem. There was no way of lessening the impact of her announcement so she said starkly, 'I'm pregnant.'

For a few seconds the silent library seemed to echo with Sebastian's shock before he exploded into speech. '*What*? What do you mean?' he demanded, staring at her as if she had suddenly grown another head. 'I don't understand.'

For some reason his stunned incomprehension caused the truth to finally sink into Kitty's brain and she took a deep, shuddering breath. 'It's quite simple. I'm going to have a baby.'

Once again Sebastian was rendered speechless, but finally he straightened up, his jaw rigid as he asked with deadly softness, 'Whose baby?'

Nikos's arrogantly handsome face filtered into Kitty's mind. 'I can't tell you that,' she whispered miserably.

'Don't be ridiculous—' Sebastian broke off and frowned. 'Are you saying you *don't* know? That the father could be one of several partners? *Theos*, Kitty, do you have a whole secret life that I know nothing about?'

'*No*…of course not,' she cried, more tears falling at the flare of disappointment in Sebastian's eyes. 'I know who the baby's father is—it could only be one person,' she said thickly. 'But it was an accident, a mistake and he…he won't be pleased. I've decided not to tell him.'

'I don't give a damn if he's pleased or not,' Sebastian growled, swinging away from her and raking his hand through his hair. 'It's you I'm concerned about. Kitty…' He broke off and closed his eyes briefly at the sight of her tear-streaked face. 'You are a royal princess of the House of Karedes. You are fourth in line to the throne, and you cannot be a single mother.'

Kitty bit her lip. It was no wonder Sebastian looked devastated. On the night of the ball Vasilis Sarondakos had taunted her that the royal family could not afford to be tainted by another scandal. No member of the ruling family of Aristo had ever given birth to an illegitimate child, and the implications could rock the House of Karedes to its foundations.

But her choices were limited; in fact they were non-existent. She was pregnant, and *not* having her baby was absolutely not a consideration. Involving Nikos was another matter. He was Sebastian's closest friend, she thought despairingly, her heart cracking at her brother's shattered expression. How much worse would Sebastian feel if she revealed that she had been seduced by a man he trusted implicitly?

And she had lied to Nikos. She had allowed him to believe

she was a waitress called Rina. How would he react if she revealed that, not only was she a royal princess, but that during their brief, sexual pairing she had conceived his child?

If you're harbouring any romantic illusions about me, then I suggest you forget them fast, he'd warned her immediately after he'd made love to her. *I value my freedom above everything.*

This was her problem and she would have to deal with it alone. She would have to retire from public duties and live quietly somewhere away from the palace. Financially she had the security of an annuity from her father, and when her child was older her qualifications would hopefully enable her to resume her career as a researcher at the museum. She took a deep breath and felt a sense of calm replace her earlier panic. Everything would be okay; she would cope. But she had no intention of ever revealing the identity of her baby's father—even to her family.

'Sebastian, I'm sorry but I can't tell you.' Kitty jumped to her feet and the colour drained from her face as a wave of dizziness swept over her. 'You'll have to excuse me. I'm not feeling very well,' she muttered as she hurried towards the door.

'What about Mama?' Sebastian's voice stopped her. 'She'll have to be told about this—and coming so soon after Papa's death it will break her heart. *Theos*, Kitty, what a mess,' he muttered grimly.

His stark words filled Kitty with guilt and shame. 'I will speak to Mama and the rest of the family. Just give me a few days to…to come to terms with things myself. Please, Seb.'

Sebastian hesitated, his gaze locked with her tear-filled eyes, and then he nodded abruptly. 'But if I ever find out who the father is, I swear I'll tear him limb from limb,' he vowed savagely. 'You deserve better than this, Kitty.'

A week later Kitty stood on the palace balcony, waving to the crowds who had gathered for the Day of Independence celebration that marked the day the Adamas Islands had gained independence from British rule. Queen Tia, still consumed with grief for her husband, had a chest infection and had been advised by her doctors not to attend. Prince Alex and his wife Maria were in America, and Prince Andreas was with his new wife Holly in her native Australia. Liss had other royal duties elsewhere to deal with and so Kitty had assured Sebastian that she would act as his consort—aware that once she was a single mother she would no longer appear at state occasions.

Saturday was a beautiful June day typical of early summer in Aristo. Warm sunshine bathed the crowds who had followed the carnival procession through the streets, and as they flocked into the palace courtyard Kitty smiled and tried to ignore the discomfort of her heavy silk state gown and the ornate diamond tiara on her brow that had given her a headache.

'I don't think I've ever seen such a huge crowd of well-wishers. Hundreds of people have come to show their support for you, Sebastian,' she commented as she stepped off the balcony, into the drawing room, peeling off her white gloves as she walked and handing them to a footman. Her brother was chatting with a guest but at the sound of her voice he swung round—and as Kitty caught sight of his companion her heart stopped beating. If was as if someone had pressed the mute button. The voices of the people around her faded, and she was conscious of the fractured sound of her breathing and a peculiar rushing sound in her ears.

'Nikos, I don't think you actually met my sister at the ball a few weeks ago. This is Princess Katarina…' Sebastian fell silent, plainly bemused by Nikos Angelaki's coldly furious expression and Kitty's sudden pallor. The tense silence between them caused a ripple to run through the room, and Kitty felt the curious stares of the assembled guests, but her wide, shocked eyes were locked on Nikos's face.

He was the first to speak. 'Oh, we met, my friend,' he

drawled in an icy tone that sent a shiver down Kitty's spine. His eyes narrowed, and Kitty could feel the aggression that emanated from him. 'But it seems that Princess Katarina likes to play games, and regrettably she neglected to properly introduce herself—didn't you, *Rina?*'

Shock surged like a foaming torrent through Nikos's blood, and with it a black rage that threatened to choke him. The woman who had come in from the balcony and was staring at him fearfully was instantly recognisable when she had spent the past three weeks lodged in his brain—and yet, dressed in her royal robes and tiara, she was someone he did not know.

She had lied to him that night on the beach. How she had lied! He closed his eyes briefly and tried to get a grip on the savage anger that made him want to shake her and demand an explanation as to *why* she had pretended to be a servant, instead of telling him at the start that she was Princess Katarina Karedes.

Had she found the pretence amusing? Fury burned corrosively in his gut. And why the *hell* had she slept with him? Not slept, he corrected himself grimly. She hadn't slept in his arms, she'd had sex with him—and even then she had lied by omission when she had failed to warn him she was a virgin. But he had slept. Overcome with exhaustion, and physically sated after making love to her, he had felt more relaxed than he had done in years and had been unable to fight the tiredness that had settled on him. When he had stirred again he'd discovered that an hour had passed, and Rina had disappeared.

Memories of the wild passion they had shared filled his mind. And another memory, of the private conversation he'd had with Sebastian when he had first arrived at the palace today, caused his heart to crash in his chest. Sebastian had been tense and grim-faced, and at first Nikos had assumed his friend was uptight about the fact that he had still not located the Stefani diamond. But the prince had wanted to confide in him about another matter, and had sworn him to secrecy before revealing that another scandal was about to rock the House of Karedes. His sister, Princess Katarina, had been seduced by some unknown man, and was pregnant.

Theos, no! It could not be true. He stared at Rina—unable to think of her as Princess Katarina—and tried to decipher the truth from her pale face. Not again, not to him. Not after the tragedy of his past that he would never forget for as long as he lived. But he knew instantly that this was no cruel trick. It was entirely possible that Rina had conceived his baby, and from the frown forming on Sebastian's brow it was clear that his friendship with the prince was about to be blown to pieces.

Kitty could not tear her eyes from Nikos's face, and the glittering fury in his dark gaze filled her with trepidation. He could not possibly guess her secret, she assured herself. But her hand moved instinctively to her stomach and she saw his eyes narrow as he witnessed the betraying gesture.

Sebastian was speaking, but his words did not register in Kitty's brain as she watched his concerned expression change to one of dawning comprehension followed by stunned fury. The rushing sound in her ears grew louder, as if she were standing at the edge of a waterfall. And then she was falling, and a great dark nothingness rushed up to meet her.

Kitty slowly opened her eyes and stared up at the fresco of cherubs that adorned the ceiling. For a moment she felt disorientated, but then her brain clicked into gear—and her memory returned with a vengeance. She turned her head to look around and realised that she was in the small ante-room leading from the formal drawing room. She recalled the blanket of black nothingness that had enveloped her, and understood. She must have fainted, for the first time in her life, and someone had carried her in here and placed her on the sofa. That someone was now silhouetted against the bright sunlight streaming in through the window, and even though she could not discern his features she was conscious of the waves of anger emanating from him.

Nikos! She swung her legs off the sofa and jerked upright, and then gasped as a wave of nausea swept over her. To be sick in front of him would be the ultimate humiliation, and she gritted her teeth and waited while the room righted itself and her head stopped spinning.

'There is a glass of water on the table next to you. I suggest you drink some,' he said in a terse voice. Kitty reached for the glass and lifted it to her lips. Her hands were shaking so much that she could barely take a sip, but the water was ice-cold and refreshing, and gradually the sickness passed. She stood up and risked a furtive glance across the room, and could not restrain a startled cry when she saw the livid bruise on Nikos's jaw.

'What happened to your face?'

'Sebastian,' he informed her shortly.

Kitty shook her head disbelievingly. 'He *hit* you?' She recalled the expression of shocked understanding she'd seen on her brother's face just before she had slipped into unconsciousness, and a heavy dread filled her.

'After the news he's just given me I don't blame him,' Nikos said, still in that cold, clipped voice that could not disguise his fury. 'In case you're worried, I did not retaliate. Sebastian was defending your honour, and to be honest I would have thought less of him if he hadn't taken a swing at me.' He paused, and in the tense silence the ticking clock and the sound of Kitty's heartbeat both sounded over-loud to her ears.

'But all things considered, it was a rather dramatic way to learn that I am going to be a father,' he drawled—sarcasm his only outlet for the murderous rage burning inside him, because if he lost control and vented his fury at the top of his voice he would alert the palace guards standing on duty outside the door. 'With you passing out, and the Prince Regent giving a good impression of a prize knuckle-fighter in front of a hundred or so dignitaries and members of the press, the story is likely to make the newspaper headlines worldwide.'

Nikos sucked in a harsh breath and swung round to stare blindly out of the window. Below, in the courtyard, the crowds were dispersing and streaming through the palace gates, many clutching flags bearing the national colours of Aristo and the coat of arms of the House of Karedes. He felt a deepening sense of unreality, a feeling that his life was about to change irrevocably, but he knew he must bring his anger under control and establish the real facts.

'Is it true?' His voice rasped in his throat, and he had to force himself to turn away from the window. 'Are you really pregnant, or are you playing another peculiar game of charades?'

'It's true,' Kitty choked, forcing the words past her numb lips. 'I did a test, and yesterday my doctor confirmed it.'

She did not know how she had expected Nikos to react. She hadn't dared picture a scenario in which she told him she had conceived his child, let alone imagined what he would say. He was clearly shocked, and she could understand that he might be angry, but the icy rage in his eyes shook her.

'And is the child mine, as Sebastian seems to think?'

His harsh tone triggered a flare of anger inside Kitty, and she flushed. 'Of course it's yours. I was a virgin when I met you and I haven't leapt into bed with half a dozen lovers since then. I didn't want to involve you. I don't even understand *how* I can be pregnant,' she added, dropping her eyes from his cold stare. 'You used protection.'

'It failed,' Nikos said bluntly. 'I discovered when I woke up that there was a slim chance I could have made you pregnant. When I realised you had left the cave I searched for you, fearing you may have gone for another swim and got into trouble in the current. It was only when I saw your clothes had gone that I faced the fact that you had run out on me.

'If you had stayed I would have told you there was a possibility you could have conceived, and insisted we kept in contact until we knew either way,' he finished curtly.

Nikos drew a ragged breath, recalling his concern in the days after he had had sex with Rina in the cave that a faulty contraceptive could have resulted in a child. When he had tried to trace her, and found that she seemed to have disappeared from the planet, his concern had turned to a gut-wrenching fear he could not dismiss, despite telling himself that history could not repeat itself.

Now he knew that it could.

Memories of the past that he had ruthlessly suppressed for so long surged into his mind. Five years ago his lover had fallen pregnant with his child. During his relationship with Greta he had confided that he felt as though a part of his identity was missing because he did not know who his father was, and he had vowed he would not abandon a woman if she fell pregnant with his child. Soon after, when Greta had revealed she was expecting his baby, he had immediately proposed. But his desire to marry the Danish model had not only been for the sake of the child.

He had loved her, Nikos acknowledged grimly. After his mother's death, work had become his obsession and he had never allowed any of his lovers to get too close. But Greta had been different. Their affair had been Nikos's longest relationship, and he had finally admitted that the beautiful blonde had got beneath his guard and captured his heart.

After his initial shock he had been glad about the baby, knowing that his child would be his only blood relation in the world. But a month after he and Greta had married, tragedy had occurred. To his dying day he would never forget her phone call from Denmark, where she had gone for a modelling assignment, telling him that she had miscarried.

Nikos stared blindly out of the palace window, remembering the sorrow that had swamped him. It had been a bitter blow, but he had dealt with his grief privately, and done his best to comfort Greta—unaware that her tears had been an act. In the months that had followed she had appeared to recover well, and quickly returned to modelling. But it had not been long before cracks appeared in their relationship. Greta loved to party, and had accused him of being a boring Greek husband. And she had been adamant that she wanted to concentrate on her career when Nikos had suggested they should try for another child.

Her open use of cocaine, and her revelation that she had hidden her habit before their marriage, had led to a series of increasingly bitter rows, and it had been during one of her drug-fuelled rages that Greta had screamed the truth at him. She had never wanted a baby—but when she had fallen pregnant, and Nikos had proposed, she had seized her chance to marry a multimillionaire. She had waited until after the wedding, but on her trip to Denmark she hadn't miscarried their child—she had chosen to terminate her pregnancy.

Nikos swallowed the bile in his throat, and forced his mind away from his ex-wife. Greta was in the past. The newspaper reports two years ago of her death from a drug overdose had elicited no sympathy from him. From the moment he'd learned how she had callously deprived him of his child his heart had frozen over, and, although he was a living, breathing man, inside he was emotionless and cold.

But he did not feel dead inside now. For the first time in five years something stirred within him, and he stared at the woman who had sworn she was carrying his baby, his heart pounding. Fate had given him another chance, another child— and he would move heaven and earth to ensure that the tiny speck of life created from his seed would have a chance of life.

CHAPTER SIX

KITTY stared numbly at Nikos, shaken by the bleakness in his eyes. He looked *devastated* by the news that she was expecting his baby. His jaw was rigid, his skin stretched so taut over his sharp cheekbones that he looked as though he had been carved from marble—cold and hard and utterly unforgiving.

The idea of fatherhood definitely did not appeal to him—that much was clear, she brooded bitterly. The tiny flame of hope that had lurked deep in her subconscious was snuffed out and pride made her voice strong. 'Don't look so worried, Nikos. I don't want anything from you. This is my problem, and I'll deal with it. You needn't be involved.'

Something flared in his eyes, an emotion Kitty could not define but that made her feel as though her legs were about to give way, and she sank weakly back down on the sofa.

'Deal with it?' he said in a dangerous tone. 'You are talking about a human life. In what way were you planning to deal with it?'

'I meant that I will take care of the baby, financially and in every other way,' Kitty faltered. 'What do you think I meant?' Her eyes widened as the implication of his words hit her, and sickness surged through her. 'You can't possibly think...' She took a shaky breath, but when she spoke her voice was fierce. 'I am having this baby, and as far as I'm concerned there is no viable alternative I would *ever* consider. But as I said before, you don't have to be involved.'

Nikos felt some of the terrible tension that had gripped him lessen. She had sounded convincing, but Rina, or Katarina as he now knew her, was an accomplished actress—he had evidence of that. 'But I am involved,' he said implacably, his eyes locked with hers. 'You are carrying my child, and I have a responsibility towards both of you that I fully intend to honour.'

He thought again of how she had deceived him, and was swamped by another wave of bitter anger. 'When were you going to tell me? Or weren't you going to bother? It would have been difficult, I suppose, when you had lied about your identity,' he added scathingly.

Kitty flushed and hung her head. 'I haven't known what to do these past few weeks,' she admitted huskily.

Nikos gave her a savage glance. 'While you were trying to decide, I was doing my best to find you. I made enquiries at the palace, but when I was told there was no employee here called Rina I contacted all the catering companies on Aristo. I'm sure you won't be surprised to hear that nobody had ever heard of you,' he drawled acidly. He paused, his dark brows lowered in a slashing frown. 'So tell me, *Rina*, do you often masquerade as a servant, or did you deliberately set out to make a fool of me?'

'I didn't…' Kitty bit her lip when she caught the glittering anger in his eyes. 'You have every right to be angry,' she admitted honestly.

'Well, that's good to know—' his voice dripped with sarcasm '—because I'm *livid—Your Highness*. Hell!' He swung away from her and raked a hand through his hair, 'I don't even know your name. Are you Rina, or Katarina?'

'I'm Kitty,' Kitty said quickly. 'It was my father's nickname for me when I was a little girl, and it stuck.' She risked another glance at him and felt her stomach dip. He was even more gorgeous than she remembered. In a pale grey suit and blue shirt he looked remote and forbidding, every inch the sophisticated, urbane businessman who was at the top of his game. He had been in her mind constantly since he had made love to her on the night of the ball, and now she could not prevent herself from staring at him and greedily absorbing his stunning looks.

'I didn't trick you intentionally. You mistook me for a servant at the ball and it seemed easier to go along with it. Be honest, would you have believed me if I'd told you my real identity?' she demanded when he glared at her. 'Everyone at the ball compared me unfavourably with my sister Liss, and they were right, I didn't look like a glamorous princess, I looked like the frumpy waitress you believed me to be. When we met on the beach later that night I was amazed when you said you found me attractive. You made me feel beautiful, even though I know I'm not,' she said bleakly, 'and I wanted to carry on being sexy Rina, rather than drab Kitty.'

'And having fooled me that you were Rina the waitress, you decided that it was a good opportunity to lose your virginity to an experienced man rather than a fumbling boy?' Nikos reminded her of her words when he had discovered her innocence, no hint of softening on his hard face. 'You are an heir to the crown of Aristo—*what the hell were you thinking of*?' he exploded furiously.

'It was a moment of madness,' Kitty defended herself. She moved her hand instinctively to her stomach, thinking of the tiny life that was growing inside her. 'I never dreamed that it would have such catastrophic consequences.'

'But it did, and now we must deal with those consequences,' Nikos told her bluntly. He paused and in the tense silence Kitty felt the same sickening dread that had filled her when, despite her fear of heights, she had volunteered to do a bungee jump for charity and had crouched at the top of the platform one hundred and fifty feet above the ground, preparing to launch herself over the edge.

'The only possible solution is for us to marry.'

There was no other alternative, Nikos acknowledged silently as he watched Kitty's mouth fall open in an expression of utter shock. He had vowed never to marry again, but if he wanted this child—and he did, unquestionably—then he would have to sacrifice his freedom and take a woman who had proved herself to be untrustworthy as his bride. 'It may not be ideal,' he snapped when Kitty shook her head frantically. 'Believe me, the situation is not what I would have chosen, either. But I have promised Sebastian that I will do my duty by you.'

The room suddenly seemed to be spinning—or was it her? Kitty collapsed back against the cushions. 'The idea is ridiculous,' she said faintly, repelled by the word 'duty'.

'Are you saying you have a better suggestion?' Nikos strolled over to the sofa and stared down at her, his eyebrows raised in an expression of haughty arrogance. 'I'm intrigued, Your Highness. What are you intending to do? I'd like to make it crystal clear, by the way, that no child of mine will be born illegitimately,' he added harshly when she stared at him in numb silence. 'And I should point out that Sebastian looked mightily relieved when I assured him of my intention to marry you as soon as it can be arranged. He has enough problems at the moment without worrying about you.'

'He doesn't need to worry about me. I can take care of myself,' Kitty muttered stubbornly, knowing in her heart that Sebastian's concern was not simply for her, but for the damaging effect her unplanned pregnancy might have on the monarchy. The situation was unprecedented. The people of Aristo were ardent royalists, but they would be dismayed to hear that a member of the royal family was pregnant and unmarried, and, as Nikos had said, this was a difficult enough time for Sebastian, the would-be-King who was waiting to be crowned.

But marry Nikos? Marry a man who was furious with her for lying to him, and who was staring at her with scathing contempt, as if she were the lowest life-form on the planet? It wasn't just ridiculous, it was utter madness and she absolutely would not agree to it. Since she was a little girl she had clung to the belief that she would one day fall in love and be loved in return, and she could not bear to see the fairy tale turn to ashes before her eyes. 'How can we marry?' she asked huskily. 'We don't love each other.'

Nikos spared her a derisive glance. 'What is love other than an illusion found in books and films?' he said sardonically. 'Too often people mistake *lust* for love, but it's not an error I'm ever likely to make. I am suggesting a marriage of convenience purely for the sake of our child.

'I have never known the identity of my father,' he revealed harshly. 'My mother would never tell me his name, but I have always wondered if I look like him or if we share similar traits.' He stared down at Kitty, his eyes suddenly blazing. 'I won't allow my child to suffer the trauma of not knowing his bloodline.'

Kitty was startled by the raw emotion in his voice, and even more shocked by the realisation that he was deadly serious. 'Nikos, let's be sensible about this,' she said desperately. 'I'm only three weeks pregnant and it would be madness to rush into marriage, and…and then find that it had been needless.' Her voice faltered when she imagined losing her baby. Already she had formed an emotional bond with the tiny new life that she and Nikos had unwittingly created, but she had to be prosaic. There was no history of miscarriages in her family but no one could foretell the future.

'There are plenty of other options open to us,' she went on when his jaw tightened. 'If you really want to play a part in the baby's life we could come to an arrangement about access and so on. You could visit the palace regularly…' She could feel his dark eyes boring into her and faltered. 'What I'm trying to say is that there is no need for either of us to make rash decisions. I'm not a poorly paid waitress, I have financial security and a supportive family here on Aristo, and I will manage to bring up this child perfectly well on my own.'

Nikos's blood had frozen at the word access, and it hit him suddenly that if he wasn't careful things could go very wrong. From the sound of it Kitty was determined to bring up their child on her own, but he was equally determined to be part of his baby's life. He was going to be a proper father, not some semi-stranger who visited the palace occasionally according to the rules of his visitation rights. Kitty had stated that she did not need him, and she certainly had the means to bring up a child without his help. Somehow he was going to have to convince her that he was indispensable—and he was prepared to use emotional blackmail to persuade her to marry him.

'So, are you going to tell your mother, while she is unwell and still grief-stricken by the death of the king, that you refuse to marry the father of your baby—and that you don't care that your actions will bring shame on the royal family?' he asked Kitty harshly. 'Sebastian is speaking to the queen now. He was anxious that she should learn of your pregnancy from him, rather than overhear the gossip among the servants which is inevitable after the scene in the drawing room.' His dark eyes bored into Kitty remorselessly when she gave a cry of distress. 'We can only hope that none of the guests or members of the press who were at the reception today actually guessed that you are pregnant. If we marry quickly no one need know that it's a shotgun wedding.'

He watched Kitty twisting her hands in the folds of her blue satin gown that the Queen and princesses customarily wore on formal state occasions. The floor-length dress disguised her shape, but beneath the stiff material he could picture the rounded fullness of her breasts and the dip and curve of her waist and hips, and he felt the familiar tug of sexual frustration that had plagued him since the night of the ball. He felt a sudden urge to pull the pins from her hair and run his fingers through the rich chestnut silk, and when she lifted her head he noted that her eyes were a deep, dark brown, velvet soft and fringed by impossibly long, thick lashes.

'Where are your glasses? Or were they part of your costume for your little theatrical performance the night we met?' he queried mockingly, forcing himself to move away from the temptation of her lush pink mouth. He was infuriated that he still wanted her despite the evidence that she had lied to him. The whole 'Rina the waitress' charade was still beyond his comprehension and he hated the idea that she had played him for a fool, but he couldn't forget the wild passion they had shared in the cave, and he was aware from the familiar tightening in his gut that his body was impatient for a repeat performance.

'I'm wearing my contact lenses today,' Kitty told him stiffly, 'and I've already explained that I didn't deliberately set out to trick you. Circumstances just...happened.' Her voice wavered as she tried to imagine her mother's shock and concern at the news of her pregnancy. Queen Tia would want her to marry Nikos, she acknowledged heavily, and Sebastian would be in favour of a quick solution to the embarrassing problem of her pregnancy. But how could she go through with it, and marry a man who had made it clear that he did not believe in love and would never care for her?

'Make no mistake, Kitty,' Nikos said quietly as he watched the play of emotions on her face. 'If you think I will simply walk away and allow you to bring up our child on your own, be warned, I will fight you for custody. Even if it means sacrificing my friendship with Sebastian I will have no compunction about dragging you and the rest of the royal family through the courts, and the fallout is likely to be extremely damaging to the monarchy.'

There was no doubt that Nikos was deadly serious, and a shiver ran through Kitty when she met his hard stare. The first time she had met him she had detected a ruthless side to him that he hid beneath a veneer of seductive charm. There was no sign of that charm now. He had called himself a pirate, and she realised with terrifying certainty that if she chose to do battle with him, she would lose.

'I am utterly determined that my child will live in Greece with me,' he said curtly. 'It's up to you if you want to take an active role in his upbringing.'

'What do you mean—an active role in his upbringing? It's my baby! And why do you think it's a boy? There's just as much chance it's a girl,' Kitty said shakily, still reeling from Nikos's assertion that he wanted their child to live in Greece. 'You can't possibly expect me to leave Aristo. I've lived here all my life.'

On the night of the ball the palace had seemed stifling, and she had felt a restless longing to escape the confines of royal life. Now that life seemed safe and reassuring and she wanted it to remain unchanged. But of course her life would change, she was going to be a mother, and in her heart she knew she could not remain at the palace and bring up her child without its father. 'If we were to marry, why couldn't you live here at the palace too?' she asked Nikos faintly.

'My business is based in Athens, and I need to be there,' he explained coolly. 'Naturally, as my wife, you will live with me, and although we will retain strong ties with Aristo and the royal family, our child, boy or girl,' he said pointedly, 'will grow up in Greece. I've discussed it with Sebastian and he is in complete agreement,' he added, as if that settled the matter.

Kitty shivered at the grim finality of his words. Sebastian had agreed, and, although her brother would never force her into marrying Nikos, she knew realistically that she had no option. She felt as though prison bars were closing around her.

The room suddenly seemed claustrophobic and she stumbled to her feet and hurried across to the door. For the sake of her child, and the royal family, she would have to marry Nikos, but the prospect of being trapped in a loveless union with a man whose scathing opinion of marriage was well known, and who was furious with her for making a fool of him, filled her with despair.

'I need some time to think,' she muttered, every muscle in her body tensing when Nikos moved with the speed and grace of a big cat to stand in front of her.

'Far from being the poorly educated waitress you led me to believe at the ball, I have learned from Sebastian that you are a brilliant academic, and I have no doubt that you understand the gravity of the situation,' he said harshly. 'You have to make a decision *now*. Sebastian and your mother know that I am at this moment asking you to marry me, and we are expected to go immediately to the queen's private quarters and tell them your answer.

'As I see it, neither of us has any option,' he continued when she made no reply, and, although her mind screamed in silent rejection of his words, Kitty acknowledged with a leaden heart that he was right.

Warily she lifted her eyes to him, and even in the midst of her turmoil heat flared inside her when she studied his hard-boned, handsome face. It seemed a lifetime ago that they had made love in the cave, and when she focused on the cruel line of his mouth it seemed impossible that he had once kissed her with fierce passion. His aura of power was tangible, and she suddenly felt weak and drained. Everything was stacked in his favour, and she did not have the strength to fight him.

'When?' She forced the word past her numb lips, barely able to believe that she was contemplating agreeing to his offer. 'I suppose the wedding will have to be in the next few months?' Before she grew big with his child and everyone guessed the real reason for their marriage.

'Sooner than that,' Nikos corrected her. 'Sebastian has pencilled the eleventh of July into his diary, and cancelled all other state events.'

Kitty did a hurried mental calculation. 'That's three weeks from now!' Panic engulfed her and she shook her head wildly. 'I can't go through with it, Nikos.'

'Yes, you can,' he told her grimly, the cold determination in his eyes freezing her blood, 'because to be frank, Kitty, you have no choice.'

CHAPTER SEVEN

THE following three weeks passed in a blur, and Kitty felt increasingly detached from her life and the preparations for the wedding that were going on around her. She could almost believe she was caught up in a dream, and fully expected to wake up and find that she had never met a man called Nikos Angelaki, let alone become pregnant with his baby. But when she opened her eyes on the morning of her wedding and saw her bridal gown hanging against the wardrobe she was forced to make a reality check. This was real; in a few hours from now she would be his wife, and for the sake of the child developing inside her she could not escape the fate that awaited her.

'I told you all brides look beautiful on their wedding day,' Liss said later as she smoothed a crease from the full skirt of Kitty's white silk wedding dress. 'You look breathtaking. The dress shows off your figure perfectly. Don't you dare go back to wearing those ghastly, shapeless sweatshirts you're so fond of! Not that Nikos will allow you to,' Liss added breezily. 'He leads a hectic social life and I bet he'll insist on buying you loads of gorgeous, sexy clothes for all the parties you'll be going to in Greece.'

Kitty felt a heavy weight settle around her heart as she contemplated her future life away from Aristo. 'You know I don't like parties,' she said dismally. 'In a few months from now I'll be huge, and I definitely won't look sexy—just fat. I've already gained weight, especially on my bust. Do you think I'm showing too much cleavage?' she asked worriedly, studying the dress's exquisite bodice, beaded with tiny pearls and crystals, and the firm swell of her breasts that appeared in imminent danger of spilling over the sweetheart neckline.

'Nikos's eyes will be on stalks,' Liss assured her cheerfully. 'I'm glad you decided to wear your hair down. It's a much softer style than when you pull it back off your face.'

'I suppose so, but it's not very practical.' Kitty's silky, dark chestnut hair was naturally wavy and it rippled down her back almost to her waist. At Liss's persuasion she had left it loose, and instead of a tiara and veil she had chosen a circlet of white roses for her headdress. Her sister had insisted on doing her make-up, but had kept it light, emphasising her brown eyes with a taupe shadow and adding a rose-pink gloss to her lips.

The finished effect was startling, and Kitty couldn't quite believe the woman in the mirror was her. Because of one night, and a few moments of uncharacteristic madness, her life had changed for ever. Her hand moved instinctively to her stomach, and she took a deep breath. She was marrying Nikos for the same reason that he was marrying her—for the sake of the child they had created—and there was no point in feeling emotional or fooled by the romance of the occasion.

'You're not supposed to look *practical*,' Liss argued, casting her eyes heavenwards. 'This is your wedding day, you're about to marry one of the sexiest men on the planet, *and* he sent you these… Gaea,' she called to the maid, 'bring in the flowers Mr Angelaki sent.'

The maid hurried out to the corridor and reappeared carrying an exquisite bouquet of pink and white rosebuds mixed with delicate fronds of gypsophila, which she handed to Kitty.

'I know you keep telling me this is a marriage of convenience, but there's obviously something between you and

Nikos,' Liss said archly. 'I saw the glances he kept giving you at dinner last night—as if he couldn't wait to take you to bed.' Her eyes gleamed with amusement when Kitty blushed scarlet. 'And he phoned me from New York a few days ago to ask my advice on your favourite flowers.'

'Did he?' Kitty strove to sound casual and told herself not to read too much into Liss's words, but her heart gave a little lurch when she buried her face in the blooms and inhaled their delicate perfume. No man had ever sent her flowers before, and the fact that Nikos had gone to some effort to ensure she had a bridal bouquet filled her with hope that this marriage was not as doomed to failure as she'd convinced herself. The roses were a talisman of hope, and tears glistened in her eyes when she stared at her reflection again and saw that Liss wasn't lying, and that by some miracle she really did look beautiful.

'Thank you for helping me with my dress,' she murmured. 'You know I'm hopeless with clothes, but thanks to your advice, and the designer's skill, my wedding dress is everything I could have hoped for.'

'No problem.' Liss shrugged her shoulders and gave a cursory glance in the mirror at her pale pink silk bridesmaid dress. 'I can't wait for everyone's reaction when they see you,' she said with a wide smile, 'especially Nikos's.'

Her smile faded when she glimpsed Kitty's over-bright eyes. 'I hope it works out for you,' Liss said softly. 'I know the baby was unplanned, and you've been pushed into getting married. I detect that Nikos is just as high-handed and determined to have his own way as Sebastian, and between the two of them, and the queen's stipulation that duty comes before everything, I bet you didn't stand a chance of refusing. But you must know that Seb and Mama and the rest of the family have your best interests at heart, and I'm sure that marrying Nikos is the right thing for you to do.'

'I hope so,' Kitty replied, unable to disguise the tremor in her voice. In the three weeks since their engagement had been announced to the media Nikos had only visited the palace twice before he had flown to America, and on both occasions they had spent no time alone. He had been polite and charming, and had completely won over Queen Tia, but to Kitty he had seemed remote and unapproachable and she hadn't known how to talk to him. Even when he had phoned from the States, their conversations had been limited to how she was feeling in the first stages of her pregnancy, and whether she was eating enough.

She had been able to reassure him on that point, Kitty thought gloomily. Apart from a couple of mornings when she'd felt nauseous, she was fit and healthy and had an appetite like a horse. Her mother said she was obviously one of those women who looked pregnant from early on, and that she was blooming, but she wasn't sure what Nikos's reaction would be to her body that was already filling out with his child.

More to the point, was he even going to see her body? she wondered. The wild passion they had shared in the cave seemed like a distant dream, and if it weren't for the fact that she was carrying his child she could almost believe she had imagined the pleasure of his mouth on hers and the touch of his hands on her breasts.

Would Nikos expect her to share his bed tonight—their wedding night? Kitty stared at her reflection as her face flooded with colour, and beneath her dress her breasts suddenly felt full and heavy. They had not discussed that aspect of their marriage, but Nikos was a supremely virile male and she guessed he would not want to live a life without sex. But he had given no indication, either on the day he had asked her to marry him, or the occasions she had seen him since, that he still desired her.

There had been virtually no physical contact between them since the one time he had made love to her. Even when they had posed for the official photographs to mark their engage-ment, Nikos had pressed his lips lightly to her hand, but hadn't kissed her properly on the mouth as she had longed for him to do. And when a member of the press had asked if he was in love, he had replied with some flippant remark that had made the journalists laugh but had emphasised to Kitty that she meant nothing to him.

Liss glanced at the clock. 'We'd better go. Are you ready?'

Was she? How ready could you be when you were about to leap into the unknown? Kitty took a deep breath and nodded. 'As ready as I'll ever be,' she murmured. Her heart was beating painfully fast when she walked over to the door, and as she turned and glanced around the room that had been her bedroom for twenty-six years she felt a sharp pang of sadness that after today the palace would no longer be her home. From now on home would be Athens, with Nikos, and she could only pray that her decision to marry him was the right one.

The private chapel in the grounds of the palace was packed with guests. When Kitty stepped through the arched doorway a murmur of excited voices seemed to echo around the nave, heads turned and she was conscious of the faint gasp that rippled through the crowd as they caught sight of her in her bridal gown. But her eyes were fixed straight ahead, on the tall, broad-shouldered man in a charcoal-grey suit who was standing at the altar.

Nikos must have known from the reaction of the guests that she had arrived, but he remained unmoving and did not even give a cursory glance over his shoulder towards his bride. His lack of curiosity, and his obvious reluctance to face the woman he felt obliged to marry, hit Kitty as painfully as if he had physi-cally struck her, and trepidation knotted in her stomach. For a moment blind panic swept through her, and she could not restrain a shiver as she faced the reality of what she was about to do.

'Are you all right?' Sebastian whispered as he linked his arm with hers and stared down at her paper-white face. '*Theos,* Kitty, you're not going to faint, are you?'

The deep, pure notes of the organ music swirled up to the roof of the chapel and seemed to resound through Kitty's body. She stumbled, and for a few seconds the urge to turn and flee from the church, from Nikos, and the loveless future that awaited her, was overwhelming. But then she saw the anxiety in her brother's eyes, and the lesson that had been ingrained in her throughout her life—that adherence to duty was paramount—came to her rescue. She gripped her bouquet of roses and forced a smile for Sebastian, trying to disguise the fact that she felt as cold as if she had been carved from ice. 'I'm fine,' she assured him.

The journey down the aisle seemed to take for ever and when she finally reached Nikos's side she lifted her eyes warily to him and met his expressionless gaze. He made his responses in a cool, clear tone devoid of any emotion, but the constriction in Kitty's throat meant that her voice emerged as little more than a whisper, and she felt a deep sense of sadness that they had both lied when they had vowed to love and honour each other until death parted them. Tears stung her eyes when he slid a plain gold band onto her finger, and she could not stifle a shocked gasp when he followed her wedding ring with a spectacular diamond cluster that sparkled like teardrops in the sunlight that streamed down on them through the high windows.

When the priest murmured that Nikos could kiss his bride, Kitty turned her head, expecting a perfunctory brush of his lips, but as she lifted her face to him she was startled by the sudden blaze of heat in his eyes. Her heart thudded erratically in her chest when he drew her into his arms and she felt his strong, hard body pressed against hers. To her amazement he was no longer cold and remote, and she made no attempt to deny him when he lowered his head and claimed her mouth with undisguised hunger.

She had been starved of him for so long that she was unable to control her response to him. She kissed him back with equal fervour, welcoming the masterful sweep of his tongue between her lips and feeling a quiver of sexual excitement run through her at his low growl of frustration when the priest's polite cough reminded them that their display of passion was being watched by two hundred guests.

Their marriage was one of convenience, and a far cry from the love match she had dreamed of, Kitty acknowledged when they walked together back down the aisle and stepped out of the chapel into the bright sunshine. But for better or worse she was Nikos Angelaki's, wife and it was time she banished her romantic fantasies and accepted that she had married a man who would never love her but, for now at least it seemed, desired her.

'You look beautiful in your wedding dress,' he startled her by saying later at the reception, when the wedding lunch, speeches and champagne toasts were finally finished, and she had told him that she was going to get changed before they left for Athens. 'Don't take too long, *agape*. It will be another hour at least before we make it onto the helicopter and early evening by the time we land in Athens, and I am impatient to be alone with my bride.'

The sultry gleam in Nikos's eyes filled Kitty with nervous apprehension, and she hurried up to her room to change into her going-away outfit, desperate to spend a few minutes away from his disturbing presence. The jade silk skirt and close-fitting jacket had been Liss's choice that made the most of her curvy figure, and suited her colouring. As she studied her re-flection she wondered if Nikos would approve when he dis-covered that she was wearing nothing beneath her suit other than a black lace bra and matching French knickers. From the sound of it he wanted their marriage to be a proper one, and she could not deny that the sexual chemistry between them was as strong as it had been on the night of the royal ball. But despite her desperate awareness of him, she felt nervous at the prospect of sharing his bed when she barely knew him. For her, the intimacy of making love was a big issue, but she had a feeling that Nikos regarded sex as the single benefit of their enforced marriage.

Lost in her thoughts she walked back down the corridor, but as she turned the corner she cannoned into Vasilis Sarondakos, and her heart sank.

'You hardly look the joyful bride,' he said mockingly. 'What's the matter, Kitty? Are you afraid that if you leave your husband alone for too long his attention will stray—towards your sister perhaps?'

Vasilis was drunk. His speech was slurred, and Kitty wrinkled her nose when she caught a waft of alcohol on his breath. She had been dismayed to find his name on the guest list, but he was an old family friend, and she'd reminded herself that after today she would probably never see him again. She attempted to push past him, but he grabbed her arm and shoved her up against the wall. *'Let go of me!'* She tried to jerk free of his hold but Vasilis tightened his grip and laughed.

'You have every reason to worry,' he taunted. 'Liss was blessed with more than her fair share of good looks, and Nikos is a notorious playboy.'

'Shut up, Vasilis!' Kitty couldn't quite banish her envy of her sister's beauty, and she despised herself. 'There's nothing going on between Liss and Nikos. He married me, didn't he?'

'Ah, but the reason for your hasty trip down the aisle isn't as secret as you might wish,' Vasilis said with a sly wink. 'But I've got to hand it to Angelaki—he's even more of a ruthless social climber than I realised, and he struck gold with you. Who else would have set out to deliberately seduce a naïve, virgin princess, impregnate her with his child and then marry her pronto to spare embarrassment to the royal family? I'm surprised Sebastian hasn't knighted him for services above and beyond the call of duty,' Vasilis finished bitterly.

'Don't be ridiculous,' Kitty said faintly, reeling from Vasilis's shocking statement. How on earth did he know about her pregnancy? 'What do you mean when you say Nikos is a social climber?' she demanded. 'He's a multimillionaire who heads his own hugely successful company.'

'A company that he inherited after he seduced another gullible woman,' Vasilis said sneeringly. 'It's not only Hollywood starlets who sleep their way to the top. Nikos Angelaki was the illegitimate son of a peasant woman. He grew up in the slums of Athens, and as a teenager he was already involved with the criminal underworld.' Vasilis paused when he saw Kitty's shocked expression, and gave an unpleasant smile. 'I take it your new husband hasn't told you about his past? Ask him about the tattoo on his shoulder if you don't believe me.

'Somehow, Nikos met a millionairess, Larissa Petridis, daughter of the shipping magnate Stamos Petridis,' Vasilis continued. 'Larissa had inherited her father's company after his death. She was a spinster with a penchant for good-looking young men. Rumour has it that she quickly became besotted with charming, handsome Nikos, despite the fact that he was twenty years younger than her. Nikos seized his chance to escape a life of poverty and he became her lover, and when Larissa died a few years later she left Petridis Shipping to him. Not a bad prize for being a stud to a lonely older woman, was it?' Vasilis jeered.

Kitty felt dizzy as Vasilis's poisonous words swirled in her mind, but she was determined not to reveal her shock at his revelations by fainting, and she pressed her back against the wall for support. 'I don't believe you,' she muttered. 'How do you know so much about Nikos?'

'I hired someone to make a few enquiries,' Vasilis said without a flicker of shame. 'I like to discover the skeletons in people's closets. You never know when the information might come in useful. I'll show you the report my private eye filed on Angelaki if you like. It makes interesting reading. Almost as interesting as this week's edition of *Glamorous* magazine,' Vasilis added, grinning at Kitty's puzzled expression.

'Is there anything to *read* in a downmarket publication devoted entirely to celebrity gossip?' she queried coldly.

'Not much,' Vasilis admitted, 'but there are plenty of pictures showing what your new husband was getting up to in the three weeks prior to your wedding.'

'Nikos was in the US, working hard to tie up a business deal,' Kitty said sharply.

'Well, he was certainly working hard, but in the bedroom rather than the boardroom. Face it, Kitty,' Vasilis said nastily. 'You're not Angelaki's type—which I guess is why he spent the last weeks with his mistress, Shannon Marsh…here's the evidence.' He withdrew a copy of the glossy magazine from his jacket pocket and flipped it open to a double page spread of photographs showing Nikos and a stunning, tanned blonde.

In the photos Nikos looked bronzed and gorgeous with a lock of his dark hair falling across his brow. He was relaxed and laughing with his beautiful companion and the obvious familiarity between them tore at Kitty's heart even more than the images of Shannon pressing her naked breasts against Nikos's muscular chest.

She snatched the magazine from Vasilis and scanned the short paragraph beneath the photos, paling when her own name leapt from the page together with the speculation that, while Nikos was about to marry a European princess, he was still clearly smitten with his American lover.

'I told you that you should have married me.' Vasilis swayed unsteadily. 'I wouldn't have humiliated you on your wedding day. As it is, many of the guests here today have probably read this over their breakfast this morning, and there's fevered speculation among them about the real reason why Nikos hurried you down the aisle.'

A wave of nausea swept over Kitty at Vasilis's words and her fragile self-confidence shattered. The wedding guests hadn't stared at her in the chapel because she'd been transformed into a beautiful bride—they had been comparing her to Shannon Marsh, whose stunning figure was revealed in all its lissom glory in a magazine that had worldwide circulation.

And what about Nikos, and his apparent eagerness to take her to bed—how could he possibly desire her when he had Shannon waiting for him in America? She would be a poor consolation prize, Kitty thought miserably.

She jerked out of Vasilis's hold, and felt no sympathy when he stumbled drunkenly. She was shocked to realise that her whole body was shaking with reaction. The tension wouldn't be good for the baby, and the knowledge forced her to take a ragged breath. The baby was the only thing that mattered, the only reason she had married Nikos, and from now on she would concentrate all her energies on the tiny scrap of life growing inside her.

'Angelaki only married you for the kudos of having a royal bride.'

Vasilis's spiteful taunt followed Kitty as she walked slowly back down the stairs, but she did not pause or look back. She knew exactly why Nikos had made her his wife. He wanted his child. But he had told her once that he valued his freedom above everything, and the magazine photos were clear evidence that he had no intention of taking his marriage vows seriously.

CHAPTER EIGHT

KITTY had been taught from an early age that members of the royal family never displayed their emotions in public, and the training proved invaluable for the remainder of the reception. Somehow she managed to smile at the well-wishers who crowded onto the palace lawn where Nikos's helicopter was waiting, and she was confident she had fooled Sebastian and the queen that she was happy to be leaving Aristo for her new life in Greece.

As soon as the helicopter took off she closed her eyes and feigned sleep, unable to face Nikos. She reminded herself that in the days before their wedding he had been free to do as he chose—even if that meant cavorting on a public beach with his half-naked lover—but she felt deeply humiliated that he had flaunted his affair so openly.

As for Vasilis's story about Nikos's past—she did not know what to think. Knowing Vasilis's warped personality as she did, it was entirely likely that he had employed an investigator to dig up any dirt on Nikos, and she supposed the facts would be easy to verify. She did not care if Nikos came from a poor background, but the idea that he had acquired his wealth and success because he had played on the emotions of a rich older woman filled her with dismay.

Her thoughts tormented her as the helicopter flew over the

sea, and her heart ached as Aristo faded to a tiny speck in the distance. Nikos had been speaking to the pilot, but now he came and sat down next to her, and despite everything she had learned of him her senses quivered at his nearness. She felt his gaze on her and squeezed her eyes tightly shut. Tension gripped her but after a few moments she heard him sigh, and when she peeped at him she saw he was engrossed in his newspaper.

Nikos lived in the heart of Athens in an imposing tower block that loomed high above the busy city streets. It was a far cry from the peace and tranquillity of Aristo, and Kitty felt a pang of homesickness when his chauffeur-driven limousine turned into the underground car park beneath his apartment.

'When I am at work my driver, Stavros, will take you to wherever you wish to go. He is a trained bodyguard and you are not to leave the apartment without him,' Nikos told her when they stepped into the lift.

'I didn't have a bodyguard on Aristo and I won't need one here,' Kitty argued, startled.

'It's different on Aristo. All the members of the royal family are well loved by the Aristan people, and no one would ever harm you there. But here in Athens you are already something of a talking point,' Nikos said tersely. 'People, especially the press, are fascinated by the idea of having a princess in their midst. You can't have missed the paparazzi who tailed us from the airport. Your photograph will be on the front pages of all tomorrow's papers, and unfortunately that level of interest isn't always healthy.'

Kitty frowned. 'What do you mean?'

'I mean that there are some individuals who resent my wealth, and yours,' he told her grimly. 'I don't wish to scare you, Kitty, but you have to be aware of the possibility of kidnap—a possibility that is reduced to zero if you do as you are told and always stay close to Stavros.'

He had instructed Stavros to tail her every move, but not

only to ensure her safety, Nikos brooded. Kitty had insisted she wanted the baby, but he was taking no chances—he would know her whereabouts every minute of the day.

The expression on Nikos's face warned Kitty to say no more on the subject of a bodyguard, but her heart sank. She had thought she would have more freedom here in Athens, away from the stiff protocol of palace life, but it seemed that she had swapped one prison for another, and she was to have her own personal jailer.

The lift halted at the top floor, and Nikos took her by surprise when he swept her into his arms and carried her into his apartment. 'Now you are truly my bride,' he murmured, frowning slightly when he noted how she had stiffened at his touch.

His words settled like concrete in Kitty's stomach as she wondered if he was intending to carry her on into his bedroom and make her his wife in the time-honoured fashion. She could not forget the magazine pictures of him and Shannon Marsh, and she wriggled in his arms so that he was forced to set her on her feet. 'I'm too heavy for you,' she muttered. 'I'll break your back.'

'I think that is unlikely, *agape,*' he drawled, his eyes narrowing when she refused to meet his gaze. It was the first time she had visited his home, and it was perhaps natural that she seemed tense, Nikos told himself. And of course she wasn't merely visiting, this would be her home too now, and it must seem very different from what she was used to. His penthouse apartment was luxurious but it was not a royal palace.

They would both have to make adjustments, he acknowledged. He liked his space, and since his divorce had never invited any of his lovers to spend a night at the apartment. Now Kitty would be living here; but she was his wife, not his mistress, and he could not expect their relationship to only be confined to the bedroom. Presumably they would eat breakfast together every morning, and dine together when he returned home in the evening, and he wasn't sure how he felt about sharing his private domain. He had been alone for so long that it had become his way of life, but in a few months from now the baby would be here, and he felt a fierce jolt of excitement as he imagined life with his child.

He would be a good father, he vowed silently. His child would want for nothing, especially his love. But for the sake of the child he would have to help Kitty settle in Athens so that she was not tempted to flee back to Aristo. He glanced at her, his eyes narrowing on the firm swell of her breasts outlined beneath her silk jacket. The matching skirt moulded her delightfully round bottom, and as he imagined tugging the jade silk over her hips he felt himself harden, and he was fiercely tempted to lead her down the hall to the master bedroom and demonstrate that from now on the only place she would ever want to be was in Athens—in his bed.

His heartbeat quickened and he placed his hand on her shoulder, stroking back her long chestnut hair that felt like silk against his skin. He wanted to brush her hair to one side and press his lips to the pulse beating at the base of her throat, but once again he was aware of her sudden tension and he dropped his hand back to his side.

He did not know what was wrong with her, and, quite frankly, he wasn't in the mood to play games. When he had kissed her in the church her eager response had been a satisfactory indication that she shared his impatience to consummate their marriage. But since then she had cooled considerably, and her edginess puzzled him. Maybe she just needed time to adjust? Marriage, impending motherhood and moving from Aristo to Athens were all momentous changes to her life, and he guessed that she had found the wedding a strain. Even though they had planned to keep it low-key, the marriage of a member of the royal family was a significant event and it had seemed as though half the population of Aristo had been invited to the wedding.

Curbing his impatience to take her to bed, he moved away from her. 'I'll give you a guided tour of the apartment, and perhaps you'll start to feel more at home.'

'Thank you.' Kitty followed Nikos down the hall, her heart sinking as she glanced around. His apartment was ultra-modern and minimalist with white marble floors and pale walls teamed with black leather sofas and silver furnishings. It was a typical bachelor pad designed for a busy executive and not the sort of place she could imagine bringing up a baby. She remembered the shabby but comfortable palace nursery where she had spent her childhood: toys strewn across the floor and the vast bookshelf stuffed with her beloved fairy tales. Tears welled in her eyes when she recalled how her father had visited the nursery every evening to read to her, even if he'd had to interrupt important meetings to do so. She couldn't imagine Nikos doing the same for their child, and she could not picture them living here together, playing happy families.

'There will be no need for you to spend much time in here,' he informed her when he ushered her into the gleaming, stainless-steel kitchen. 'My butler and cook, Sotiri, takes care of everything on the domestic front. I'll introduce you to him later.'

He continued on down the hall, past the elegant dining room, and three generous-sized bedrooms, one of which Kitty supposed would be a nursery when the baby was born. At the far end of the corridor Nikos flung open the remaining door—and Kitty came to an abrupt halt in the doorway.

The master bedroom overlooked the Acropolis which, now that dusk had fallen, was illuminated by spotlights and gleamed gold against the indigo sky. It was a breathtaking sight, but Kitty's attention was riveted by the enormous bed that dominated the room, with its leather headboard and black silk sheets. Floor-to-ceiling mirrors covered the length of one wall, reflecting the bed—and its occupants, she realised, her heart lurching when she spied the bottle of champagne cooling in an ice bucket. It was a room designed for seduction, and she wondered how many other women Nikos had brought here and whether they had paused to admire the view before they had joined him on that huge bed.

She stared at him, her heart hammering in her chest as she wondered if he was anticipating taking *her* to bed *right* now.

'The maid unpacked the trunks sent over from the palace and put your belongings in your dressing room. Come, I'll show you.' Nikos walked over to a door at the far end of the master bedroom, and Kitty hurried after him, grateful for the reprieve. The dressing room was spacious, fitted with oak wardrobes, a matching dressing table, and a large sofa, while another door led to the en suite bathroom. Slowly some of her panic receded when she realised that she would have a measure of privacy.

Nikos had opened the wardrobes and was studying their meagre contents with a frown. 'This can't be all your clothes. Why didn't you send everything over from Aristo?'

'That *is* everything,' Kitty said tightly. 'I've never taken much interest in fashion.'

'Well, I suggest you start.' He flicked impatiently through the hangers. 'I appreciate that you are still in mourning for your father, but your entire wardrobe seems to consist of black outfits.'

'They're not mourning clothes. I wear black because it makes me look slimmer.' Kitty could feel the stain of hot colour flood her cheeks at his scathing expression.

'Black doesn't suit you,' he stated bluntly, 'and I can see we need to go shopping. I do a lot of socialising, and my diary is already filling up with invitations from people who are all eager to meet my princess bride.'

Kitty's heart sank at his words, and she couldn't help thinking that the 'people' Nikos had mentioned were likely to be disappointed when they met her and discovered that she was not the glamorous, sophisticated royal they expected.

Nikos strolled over to her, and the butterflies in her stomach leapt into life once more when he took her hand in his and led her firmly through the connecting door, into the master bedroom. 'I approve of the outfit you are wearing now,' he murmured, his voice so deep and sensuous that Kitty could not prevent the tremor that ran through her, and she caught her breath when he slid his hand over her shoulder and down the front of her jacket.

'Liss chose it for me,' she mumbled.

He laughed softly, 'In that case it's a pity your sister did not choose all your clothes.'

At his words Kitty felt a familiar stab of jealousy. Liss was beautiful and glamorous, and she had exquisite taste in clothes. If she had been at the royal ball six weeks ago, Nikos would almost certainly have noticed her, and he would never have walked down to the beach and made love to a waitress called Rina.

All her old insecurities came flooding back. She hadn't needed Vasilis to tell her that she wasn't Nikos's type. She was only too aware that she did not have a model's figure like Liss, or Shannon Marsh, and she could not bear the idea of him comparing her plump curves with his American mistress's gorgeous, toned body.

Nikos had discarded his jacket, and her mouth went dry when he began to casually unbutton his shirt.

'I want to sleep alone tonight,' she told him baldly, her heart jerking painfully beneath her ribs. 'It's been a long day and I'm exhausted.' She felt as though she had been on an emotional roller coaster and now her limbs were trembling with reaction.

Nikos had stilled at her startling announcement, and now his brows rose quizzically. 'In that case why didn't you sleep on the journey here? Your rather childish pretence to be asleep didn't fool me for a second,' he added.

The note of impatience in his voice triggered Kitty's

temper. It was all right for him. He had got his own way on everything. *Her* life had been turned upside down, but their marriage was barely going to have any impact on him at all.

'You're right; I did pretend to be asleep—so that I wouldn't have to talk to you,' she said wildly. 'And the very idea of going to bed with you makes me feel ill.'

Nikos's jaw tightened as he sought to control his anger. He had no patience for feminine wiles—or tantrums. 'That's not the impression you gave me when I kissed you in the church,' he said silkily. 'What has caused your sudden change of heart, I wonder?'

Kitty blushed as she remembered how she had responded to him. She had been blissfully unaware then that he had spent the days before their wedding with his American mistress. Nikos had ceased unbuttoning his shirt but it was open to the waist and her eyes were drawn to his broad, golden-skinned chest. He was so gorgeous, and she was so very ordinary, she thought miserably. The idea of undressing in front of him and exposing her body made her cringe.

'What's the real issue here, Kitty?' he demanded, frustrated by his inability to understand her.

It was clear from the determined set of his jaw that he was prepared to wait all night if necessary for an explanation. Kitty hesitated for a moment and then muttered, 'At the reception, when I went to change out of my wedding dress, I met someone—a family friend...' Her voice faltered at the idea of calling loathsome Vasilis Sarondakos a friend. 'I learned something about *you*,' she revealed hesitantly, 'facts about your background that I was unaware of, such as that you had grown up in poverty and been in trouble with the law.'

In the tense silence that stretched between them Kitty felt increasingly awkward, and she blurted out the doubts that Vasilis had planted in her mind. 'I also learned of the rumours that you owe your business success to a wealthy heiress, Larissa Petridis, who bequeathed you her father's shipping company when she died because you had been her toy-boy lover.'

'Who was this friend, I wonder?' Nikos drawled in a dangerously soft tone. His brows arched in an expression of arrogant amusement but the hard gleam in his eyes warned Kitty that he was furious, and she took an involuntary step backwards. 'At least have the decency to name the individual who has gone to such trouble to stab me in the back.'

Kitty hesitated. 'It was a friend of Sebastian's—Vasilis Sarondakos.'

Nikos gave a harsh laugh. 'Sarondakos is no friend of your brother's. Sebastian only included him on the guest list because King Aegeus was good friends with Vasilis's father.'

That was the reason she had never told anyone about Vasilis's assault on her, Kitty thought bleakly. Vasilis had played on his family's royal connections for too long, but had he been lying about Nikos?

'Are the rumours true?' she asked in a choked voice.

'The details of my background are no secret.' Nikos gave a careless shrug. He appeared relaxed but Kitty sensed his simmering anger, and she took another step backwards until her legs hit the end of the bed and she had nowhere else to go.

'I grew up in the slums, in conditions you cannot imagine,' he told her harshly. 'How could *you* know—a princess who has spent her whole life in a royal palace enjoying the trappings of wealth and luxury? My mother worked all the hours she could to feed and clothe me, but she was young and poorly educated, forced to struggle alone after the man who had seduced her—my father—abandoned her, and her family disowned her when they learned she was pregnant.'

Nikos's face hardened. 'You have no idea what it is like to be hungry, to roam the streets like a stray dog and steal food to survive. I am not ashamed of my background, and the hunger in my belly fuelled my determination to make a better life for me and my mother. But it's true that there was a time in my late teens when I was drawn to the street gangs, and if it had not been for Larissa Petridis I could easily be in prison right now rather than the head of a multimillion pound company.'

Kitty stared at Nikos with wide, troubled eyes. 'So you did seduce a rich older woman and became her lover in the hope of inheriting her company?'

'My relationship with Larissa is not open for discussion,' Nikos said coldly. 'I admit I inherited Petridis Shipping from Larissa, but although she was an amazing person, she was an appalling businesswoman and when I took over the company it was on the verge of bankruptcy. I worked long and hard to turn it around, and I take all the credit for the fact that Petridis Angelaki Shipping has recently announced record profits.'

While he had been speaking Nikos had moved closer, and now Kitty realised that she was trapped between him and the bed. She could feel the anger emanating from him and, heart thumping, she edged sideways and gave a cry of alarm when his hand shot out and gripped her chin. *'Let me go.'*

'What's the matter, Kitty?' Nikos demanded grimly. 'Are you afraid you'll get your hands dirty if you touch me now you know I'm of peasant stock rather than a blue-blooded aristocrat?'

'Of course I don't think that,' she denied instantly. She didn't care about his social status, or where he came from— it was where he had been for the weeks leading up to their wedding and the woman he had spent his time with that bothered her.

'We should never have married,' she said wildly, her stomach churning at the images in her mind of him making love to Shannon. 'I should never have allowed myself to be talked into it…I want an annulment.'

'Because you think I'm not good enough for you?' he queried furiously. 'I know you are a princess but I had no idea that you are also a spoilt, over-indulged snob.'

'That's not the reason,' she snapped, stung by his scathing tone. She reached into her handbag for the magazine that Vasilis had given her, all the anger and misery that had been building inside her for the past few hours exploding in a torrent of emotion. 'You've made a fool of me, Nikos—not just here in Greece, but everywhere. *Glamorous* magazine has a worldwide circulation and everyone, including most of the guests at our wedding, will have seen *these*…' She hurled the magazine at him, open at the page of the damning photos. 'Everyone must have been laughing at me behind my back— fat, frumpy Kitty whose new husband spent the weeks preceding the wedding flaunting his affair with his beautiful blonde mistress.

'No wonder there's widespread speculation about the real reason you married me. Most people will have put two and two together and realised I'm pregnant. Like me, everyone who has seen those pictures will know you never had any intention of being a faithful husband.'

Kitty took a deep, shuddering breath, shocked to realise that her whole body was trembling and her heart was beating so hard that she could feel it slamming beneath her ribs. It couldn't be good for the baby. She placed a hand protectively on her stomach and her fury drained away as a wave of nausea swept over her. She could hear a peculiar rushing noise in her ears and suddenly strong hands were on her shoulders, forcing her to sit down on the bed, and her head was pushed down towards her knees so that her blood rushed to her brain.

'Take a deep breath…and another.' Nikos's voice sounded harsh with impatience, and silly tears welled in Kitty's eyes and slid down her cheeks when he continued savagely, 'If you carry on like this you could lose the baby.'

'Maybe you'd be relieved if I did,' Kitty whispered. 'At least then we could end this façade of a marriage.'

He swore long and hard and leaned down so that his face

was level with hers. 'Accuse me of whatever else you like,' he said grittily, 'but never that. Our child was conceived by accident but I do not regret it, even if you do.'

'I don't—of course I don't,' she denied quickly, scrubbing her wet face with the back of her hand. 'And I know you want the baby—just as I know it's the only reason you married me.'

Nikos stared at her, his expression unfathomable. 'You almost passed out. I'm going to call the doctor.'

Kitty shook her head frantically. 'I don't need a doctor. I'm fine now, I was just upset—that's all.'

'About the photos?' Nikos glanced down at the copy of the magazine in his hands. 'Where did you get this? I'm surprised you read this sort of trash.'

'I don't usually. Vasilis gave it to me.' Kitty flushed beneath Nikos's hard stare. She felt horribly embarrassed by her loss of temper, and wished he would go away and leave her alone, but the determined gleam in his eyes warned her he was not going to let the matter drop. 'I knew you had flown to America after I'd agreed to marry you, but I would have preferred you to have been honest about your reasons for going,' she said stiffly. 'Obviously you didn't go on business, but to see your mistress, and you didn't even bother to be discreet about it,' she added bitterly. 'You've made me a laughing stock, Nikos, and I'll never forgive you.'

When he made no reply she lifted her head to find him studying the magazine photos intently—and probably comparing her to the gorgeous Shannon, she thought bleakly. He looked at her, and his dark eyes seemed to bore into her skull, as if he could divine her thoughts.

'It's true that I went to the US with the express intention of seeing Shannon,' he said steadily. 'We had enjoyed a relationship for several months before I met you. It was a casual affair; we both lead busy lives and we met up whenever we happened to be in the same country. But I owed it to her to end it face to face rather than by a long-distance phone call.'

Kitty's heart jerked at the words 'end it' but the photos still haunted her. 'In those pictures you and Shannon are rather more than *face to face*,' she said sarcastically. 'The two of you are practically naked and superglued together. I don't *care*— you understand,' she insisted sharply. 'I just hate the idea that our wedding guests felt sorry for me—Princess Plump who couldn't hold onto her man even before the trip down the aisle.'

'*Theos*, Kitty, why do you have such a low opinion of yourself?' Nikos growled impatiently. 'You have a fantastic body and you know damn well I can't keep my hands off you. If I'd had a better hold on my self-control the night we met, we might not be in this mess now,' he added tersely. 'These pictures are *old*.' He waved the magazine at her. 'They were taken several months ago, soon after Shannon and I had met, and at the height of our affair. When I visited her three weeks ago to tell her I was getting married, we met in New York. We were nowhere near the Caribbean beach shown in the photos.'

'But the article gives the impression that the pictures were taken recently,' Kitty said faintly, her head reeling.

Nikos shrugged. 'Of course. Publications like this print rubbish all the time, and unfortunately there's nothing to stop them from digging out archive photos. The written piece is careful not to suggest that it is actually referring to the pictures above it. I'll contact my lawyers and see if we can get an apology from the magazine, but to be honest I've learned to ignore the paparazzi and I suggest you do the same.'

That was easy for him to say—he hadn't been made to feel an idiot. But it seemed pointless to say so, and Kitty suddenly felt so drained that she could barely think straight. She could not bring herself to look at Nikos, and she gave a little start of surprise when he hunkered down beside her and slid his hand beneath her chin to tilt her face to his.

'I married you today with every intention of being a faithful husband,' he said with a quiet intensity that shook her. 'I admit I did not live the life of a monk before I met you, but now there is the baby to consider, and I will do my duty towards you and our child. Shannon is in my past,' he continued as Kitty tried to ignore the dull feeling inside her at his emphasis on the word 'duty'. 'You are my future, Kitty.'

His hand lay on her thigh, and seemed to burn her flesh through her silk skirt. He looked devastatingly sexy with his dark hair falling over his brow, and she was seriously tempted to place her hand on his bare chest and run her fingers through the dark hairs that arrowed down his flat abdomen and disappeared beneath the waistband of his trousers.

She knew he wanted to take her to bed, could see the feral hunger in his eyes and hear the sudden quickening of his breath. But did he want to make love to her because he desired her, or because he believed it was his right to have sex with his wife whom he had only married out of *duty*?

'But we're not like most newly married couples,' Kitty said carefully. 'We married because I'm pregnant, and I feel that we should wait a while before we—' she could feel her face burning beneath his sardonic stare '—before we have relations.'

'Can I take it that by "have relations" you mean, have sex?'

'We barely know each other,' Kitty snapped, stung by the mockery in his tone. In her agitation she jumped up from the bed, and he straightened up so that he towered over her.

'Agreed, but we will get to know each other a lot quicker if we share a bed,' Nikos said tersely.

'That isn't the "getting to know" I mean.' Kitty bit her lip, aware from his grim expression that Nikos's desire was rapidly turning to anger. 'In a few months from now we will be parents. Surely we should spend some time before the baby comes learning about each other's thoughts and feelings? There has to be more to our relationship than just sex.'

The flame that had warmed his eyes died, and now they were dark and icy cold. 'Actually there doesn't,' he told her harshly. 'Sexual awareness drew us together in the first place, and the child that was created as a result of our passion is the only other link between us.'

He saw the flash of hurt in her eyes, and for a fleeting second something tugged at his heart, but he instantly dismissed it. Kitty's suggestion of sharing their thoughts and feelings was his idea of hell. His thoughts were his own; he'd learned long ago, when he was growing up on the streets, to keep his own counsel and trust no one—and that lesson had been brutally reinforced by his ex-wife.

'We know we are sexually compatible,' he continued in a coldly clinical tone, 'and I believe that is as good a basis for marriage as any. The chemistry between us burns as fiercely now as it did on the night of the ball,' he insisted when she shook her head. 'But perhaps this will convince you.'

'Nikos…' He moved before she had time to react, and her cry of protest was lost when he snaked his arm around her waist and lowered his head to claim her mouth in a searing kiss. His lips were firm, moving over hers with fierce urgency, while his tongue probed the stubborn line of her mouth with an implacable determination to force her response.

And it was growing harder and harder to resist him. Crushed against his chest, Kitty could feel the heat that emanated from him, and smell his clean, male scent—a mixture of soap and aftershave and another, more subtle scent of male pheromones—that inflamed her senses. When he had kissed her in the church she had wanted him to never stop, and now she felt that same sense of being swept away to a place where nothing but Nikos and the mastery of his touch mattered. Her mind and body were locked in a battle where caution waged against the sensations he was arousing in her and she could feel her resolve slipping away.

He slid his hand beneath her hair and cupped her nape, angling her head so that he could deepen the kiss to something so flagrantly erotic that Kitty's will crumbled and she sagged against him, parting her mouth beneath his. She was barely aware of him unfastening her jacket and sliding it over her shoulders. And then somehow they were on the bed and he had removed her bra, and she gasped when he cupped her breasts in his palms and stroked his fingers lightly across her nipples, so that they swelled to tight, tingling peaks.

He was her husband; they were tied together because of the child they had created during a brief passionate encounter, and maybe he was right, maybe sex would be a start to them building a relationship. She was so confused by what she wanted, but the solid ridge of his arousal nudging her thigh drove the uncertainty from her mind and replaced it with piercing desire that caused molten heat to flood between her legs. She gave up trying to fight him and the dictates of her treacherous body, and curled her arms around his neck, but instead of responding to the tentative foray of her tongue into his mouth, Nikos lifted his head and stared down at her, his dark eyes glittering.

'Yes, the chemistry is still there, isn't it, *agape*?' he drawled, his mouth curving into a mocking smile when she blinked at him dazedly. To her shocked disbelief he rolled off her and sauntered out of the room, leaving her lying half naked on the bed. He returned almost instantly with what looked like a pile of laundry in his hands.

'Sheets,' he told her. 'You'll need them if you're going to make up a bed on the sofa in your dressing room.' He paused and his eyes trailed an insolent path over her flushed cheeks and bare breasts where her nipples were still jutting provocatively. 'Unless you've changed your mind about wanting to sleep alone, of course?'

'I…' Kitty's tongue seemed to have cleaved to the roof of

her mouth, and she felt sick with humiliation that she had succumbed so easily to his potent charm.

'Still not sure, I see.' Nikos laughed softly as he walked over to the bed, dropped the sheets into her lap and scooped her up into his arms, blithely ignoring her sharp cry of protest as her battered pride finally woke up. 'We both know that I could make love to you for the rest of the night, and you would be willing and responsive in my arms,' he told her with breathtaking arrogance that made her want to hit him, 'but I don't want a reluctant bride. I have never taken a woman against her will in my life, and I don't intend to start with you, *agape.*'

He strode though the connecting doors into her dressing room and dumped her unceremoniously on the sofa. 'You know where to find me when you've admitted the truth to yourself.'

'The truth being that I find you irresistible, I suppose?' Kitty said grittily as she clutched the sheets to her breasts. She hated him, and hated herself more for her pathetic inability to resist him. 'You'll be waiting a long time.'

In reply he dropped a brief, stinging kiss on her lips that left her aching for more. 'I don't think so,' he said confidently. 'The sofa pulls out to a bed, by the way, and it's extremely comfortable. Sleep well, Kitty—' he turned back in the doorway and gave her another mocking smile as he murmured '—if you can.'

CHAPTER NINE

THE sofa bed was as comfortable as Nikos had promised, but Kitty tossed and turned beneath the sheets for most of the night as she fought the urge to bury her face in the pillows and cry. Nikos was so in control, and he made her feel so stupid. She didn't even know now why she had made such a fuss about sleeping with him; it was just some deeply in-grained instinct for self-protection that warned her against giving herself to a man who might be her husband, but was a man she knew very little about.

Eventually she fell into a fitful doze and when she woke sunlight was streaming through the blinds. She took her time showering and drying her hair, but she could not put off facing Nikos for ever, and, spurred on by hunger, and the knowledge that she must eat for the baby, she ventured out of her room.

She found him sitting at the breakfast table on the terrace, engrossed in his newspaper. Dressed in pale jeans and a cream shirt that contrasted with his bronzed skin, he was impossibly handsome, and Kitty halted in the living room while she tried to control her desperate awareness of him.

He stood up when she stepped onto the terrace, and pulled out a chair for her. She had steeled herself for a sarcastic enquiry about how she had slept, and she knew from the dark shadows beneath her eyes that he would guess she'd barely slept at all, but to her relief he made no comment about the previous night.

'There is fruit and yoghurt and fresh rolls, but if you would like something cooked I'll tell Sotiri,' he greeted her.

'This will be fine,' Kitty mumbled, glancing at the dish of mixed summer berries and the creamy yoghurt, 'but no coffee, thank you. I haven't been able to drink it since I fell pregnant.'

'Have you suffered much from morning sickness?'

'Not really—I've felt nauseous a few times, but unfortunately it hasn't affected my appetite. I'm already bursting out of most of my clothes.' She broke off, blushing furiously when Nikos's gaze hovered on her blouse that was too tight and was gaping over her breasts. 'No doubt I'll get a lot bigger yet,' she muttered dismally as she resisted pouring honey onto her yoghurt.

Nikos's eyes narrowed at her rueful tone, and he voiced the question that had been gnawing away at him. 'How do you feel about this baby, Kitty?'

'I don't know,' she replied slowly. 'To be honest, it all seems to be part of a dream and I keep thinking that one day soon I'll wake up and find I'm at the palace on Aristo with nothing to think about other than my research work for the museum.'

'Is that what you wish?'

'I would be lying if I didn't say that part of me wishes I was back there,' she admitted. 'Aristo was my home for my whole life and it was a wrench to leave and come to somewhere new. I don't know Athens at all, and from what I've seen it looks big and busy, and I'll probably spend my whole time getting lost.'

Nikos caught the wistful note in her voice, and for the first time he appreciated just how hard it must have been for her to leave the island she loved. 'I will do my best to help you settle here,' he murmured. 'I haven't arranged a honeymoon, but I've taken some time off work so that I can show you around the city.' He paused, aware that for the first time in his life he felt awkward about how to treat a woman. Kitty was not any woman, she was his wife, and in a few months she would be the mother of his child. 'I was thinking about what you said last night,' he said quietly. 'And for the baby's sake I think you are right to suggest that we should get to know each other better, and to become... friends.'

Friends! Kitty gave a little start of shock. If she was honest she could not imagine being friends with Nikos. He was too remote, too forbidding, and way too sexy for her to believe they could establish a comfortable, friendly relationship. But wasn't this what she wanted? she reminded herself—an opportunity to learn more about the man behind the mask.

'As for your pregnancy feeling unreal, it may seem more real after we have seen the obstetrician,' Nikos continued. 'He has suggested an early scan to determine the date the baby is due.'

'That's not hard to work out. There is only one possible date that I could have conceived...' Once again hot colour flooded Kitty's cheeks and she dared not meet Nikos's gaze as she recalled the passion they had shared in the cave on the night of the royal ball. He could have no idea why she had refused to consummate their marriage last night, and no comprehension of her shyness in front of him or her insecurities about her body. But if he felt impatient he hid it well, and the unexpected warmth of his smile stole her breath.

'So what would you like to do today? I could show you the best places to shop in Athens. Ermou Street has some excellent boutiques.'

'If we are going to get to know each other better, then the first thing you should understand is that I hate shopping,' Kitty said firmly. 'But I would like to explore Athens. Have you always lived in the city?'

'Yes.' His smile faded. 'But the streets where I grew up are not on the tourist trail, and I'm sure you don't want a tour of the slums.'

Was he ashamed of his background? Kitty wondered. 'You aren't responsible for the circumstances of your birth,' she murmured. 'And you must be proud of all you have achieved. You are one of Greece's most successful businessmen.'

Nikos shrugged, but her words stayed in his mind. His success was phenomenal, but he had never stopped to consider his achievements. He had always been focused on the next deal, planning his next move up the corporate ladder. But he supposed he was proud—the boy from the gutter who had clawed his way to the top. He had never had anyone to share his success with before, but Kitty made him feel good about himself, and he realised suddenly that his new wife might appear quiet and shy, but she was deeply perceptive.

He relaxed back in his seat and smiled at her again, noting how the sun made her hair gleam like raw silk. 'If it's not to be shopping, where would you like to go?'

'The Parthenon, the Temple of Zeus, the National Gardens.' Kitty listed the famous landmarks. 'You are a native Athenian, so I guess you know those places well.'

'I certainly do, *agape*.' He had never thought of himself as a native Athenian; he had always felt rootless and incomplete because he had no knowledge of who had fathered him. But it came to Nikos then that he was proud of his city and he wanted to show it to Kitty, and one day to their child who would be born here. 'Let's play tourists, then,' he said as he stood and held out his hand to her. 'I understand that you miss Aristo, but I will make you fall in love with Athens.'

Would Nikos also make her fall in love with him? Kitty brooded three days later as they walked around the National Archaeological Museum. He had been an enthusiastic guide showing her around the sights of the city, and during the days that they had spent together he had revealed some of the real Nikos Angelaki. She now knew that he kept his body in shape by playing squash and working out at the gym; that he liked sushi, and preferred to eat out with a few close friends rather than attend the lavish parties he was regularly invited to.

Stavros, his chauffer, and Sotiri, his butler, were clearly devoted to him, and Kitty was impressed that he engendered such loyalty from his staff. For such a wealthy and successful man, he appreciated the simple things in life—good food, good friends—and she had discovered a shared interest in contemporary films and authors, which had led to several long and interesting discussions when she had forgotten her shyness and chatted to him animatedly.

Away from the apartment at least, they seemed to be developing the friendship he had suggested, and even though she knew he was making an effort for the future, when they would be parents to their child, she clung to the nuggets of himself that he was willing to share. But back at the apartment the tension between them returned, brought about by the fierce sexual awareness that smouldered like a sleeping volcano between them and seemed in danger of erupting at any moment.

It was a situation she had brought on herself, Kitty admitted, thinking of the previous night when yet again she had been unable to sleep and had stared at the door connecting her room to his, wondering if she would ever have the courage to walk through it and end the deadlock. But she could not throw off her wariness. She was not afraid of the physical intimacy of sex, but she feared that if she gave herself totally to Nikos he would have a power over her that she was not ready to award him.

'Where to next?' His voice echoed faintly in the vast, marble-floored museum and broke into her thoughts. 'Shall we carry on into the Sculptures Collection, or do you want to rest now? You look tired today, and for the baby's sake you don't want to overdo things.'

The only reason she was tired was because she had spent the night fantasising about him making love to her, Kitty acknowledged silently, blushing beneath Nikos's piercing gaze and praying he could not read her mind as he seemed able to do.

'I'd like to carry on,' she told him. 'Isn't it incredible to think that some of these pieces date back to the seventh century BC? We have a few ancient sculptures from the time of the Roman and Byzantine Empires in Aristo's museum, but the collection here in Greece is the most important in the world, and I can't tell you how thrilled I am to see it.'

'I'm glad you find something in Athens thrilling, *agape*,' Nikos taunted softly, feeling a mixture of amusement and impatience when Kitty blushed again. She was staring at him with her big, wary eyes; reminding him of a nervous deer poised to dash away should he venture too near.

At first, when she had refused to sleep with him, he had thought she was playing some sort of game. He had met women who used sex as a weapon and had no compunction about withholding it as a form of blackmail to get what they wanted, and he had cynically assumed that Kitty was no different. But he had learned these past few days that his wife *was* different. He had never met anyone like her before, but he was growing more and more convinced that her sweet, shy nature was not an act.

'If you are bored, we could go—and I'll come back another time,' she said anxiously.

'I'm not at all bored, *agape*. Your knowledge of your subject is quite astounding and you make a far more fascinating guide than the guidebook.' He was surprised to realise that he was speaking the truth. He enjoyed talking to Kitty and hearing about her work as a researcher at Aristo's Museum of History. She was fiercely intelligent and her passion for her work made her interesting.

He did not often have meaningful conversations with

women, Nikos owned. His ex-lovers had invariably been models or socialites who talked predominantly about themselves or the latest gossip in the tabloids, and he had allowed them to witter on, and made suitable responses, during the necessary few dinner dates before he took them to bed.

With Kitty he could not give in to the urgent clamouring of his body and sweep her off to bed. He did not understand why she was holding back. He knew that she wanted him, and had had as little sleep as him for the past few nights, but he was not going to jump on her like some callow youth at the mercy of his hormones. He was determined to wait until she gave some indication that she had resolved the issues that clearly bothered her—and so he'd had no choice but to talk to her, and to his amazement he had discovered that he liked her as a person and would value her friendship.

'Actually, there's something in the next room that I want to show you,' she told him as they walked past the exhibits. 'This little figurine was sculpted round about five hundred and forty BC, and she was found about twenty years ago on Aristo—in the little fishing village, Varna. I remember you said that your mother's family came from there, and I thought you would be interested to see a little piece of your heritage.'

'My heritage?' Nikos frowned. 'I never knew my family in Varna. My grandparents cut off all contact with my mother when she fell pregnant with me and I don't suppose they even knew of my existence.'

'But even so, you have roots on Aristo,' Kitty insisted. 'I was thinking that it might be nice to trace your family tree. I can trace my ancestors back for generations, but one day our child will want to know about your side of the family.'

'You won't get far tracing my father. My mother took his identity with her to her grave,' Nikos said harshly.

'That must be strange,' Kitty said softly. 'I imagine you feel as though a part of you is missing. But to my mind that is even more reason to research your mother's side—so that we can give our child as complete a history as possible.'

She wandered off to look at the next exhibit, leaving Nikos staring after her. She was almost too perceptive, he brooded. Not knowing the identity of his father had always haunted him and Kitty had touched a nerve when she had guessed that he felt a part of him was missing. His child would make him feel whole, but he was unnerved by the realisation that Kitty probably guessed how much his baby meant to him.

The paparazzi were waiting for them when they walked out of the museum—a group of four or five sitting astride motor-scooters, who started snapping photographs despite Nikos's angry demand to stop.

'Someone must have recognised the car and tipped them off,' Stavros growled after he had opened the rear door for them to scramble inside, and then leapt into the driver's seat, pulling away from the kerb with a squeal of tyres.

'Then it's time to change the car,' Nikos replied tersely as he glanced out of the back window at the press-pack following close behind. He was used to a certain amount of media attention, but his marriage to a princess had been headline news around the world. Pictures showing him and Kitty together were selling for big money, and the photographers were growing increasingly aggressive as they fought for the shot that could make them a fortune. 'See if you can lose them, Stavros.'

'Aren't we going back to the apartment now?' Kitty queried, glancing at Nikos's shuttered expression.

'I'm afraid you are not going to like where we are going next,' he replied dryly, aware that the camaraderie between them was about to be blown to pieces. 'But the matter of your wardrobe has to be addressed, *agape,* and we are going shopping.'

Stavros was a skilled driver who seemed to know every

back street in Athens. Eventually he lost the bikers and drew up in Kolonaki—an affluent district of the city famed for its designer boutiques. For the next couple of hours Kitty trailed around the shops while Nikos selected armfuls of outfits that she could tell from the bright colours and overtly sexy styles were not going to suit her.

'Try them on,' he bade her, the steely glint in his eyes warning her that arguing would be useless. The head saleswoman was clearly overawed by him and whisked them off to a private room so that Kitty could change in comfort. But when she stepped out from behind the curtain in a tight-fitting dress that left nothing to the imagination, she halted abruptly at the sight of Nikos sitting comfortably on the sofa, waiting for her.

'What are you doing?' she muttered beneath her breath, supremely conscious of the saleswoman nearby, and the fact that her breasts were in danger of spilling out of the dress. She had enjoyed his company at the museum, but shopping was a torture he had instigated, and she glared at him crossly.

'Giving my advice on what suits you,' he replied blandly. 'And having seen the clothes you brought from Aristo, believe me, you need help.' He trailed a deliberate path over her shapely figure, his dark eyes scorching her, and to Kitty's horror she felt her nipples harden.

'Very nice.' Nikos felt a shaft of desire surge through him as he pictured unlacing the ribbons that held the front of the dress together and releasing her magnificent breasts. He shifted slightly in his chair. 'We'll definitely take this one,' he told the saleswoman, his eyes still focused intently on Kitty as sexual tension crackled between them. She could feel her face grow hot, and her blush deepened when he gave her a mocking smile. 'Go and try on the next one,' he ordered. 'I haven't got all day.'

By the time they left the boutique, followed by three of the shop staff laden with bags, Kitty was flustered and furious. 'I hope you enjoyed humiliating me,' she muttered as they fought a path through the crowd who had gathered to see one of Greece's richest tycoons, and his royal bride.

'How did I humiliate you?' Nikos demanded impatiently.

'By making me try on all those things and parade around in front of you as if you owned me.' Kitty had felt excruciatingly self-conscious and convinced that he must have been comparing her voluptuous curves with his numerous skinny, blonde ex-lovers. 'None of the outfits you insisted on buying suited me, and it was a waste of money. They'll just sit at the back of the wardrobe because I'll never wear them.'

'Oh, but you will, *agape.*' He put a protective arm around her shoulder as someone in the crowd jostled her. Startled, Kitty glanced up and her eyes clashed with his mocking gaze. 'In fact you'll wear the red silk evening dress tonight. We've been invited to a party in aid of one of the charities I support, and all eyes will be on my wife.'

Kitty's horrified protest died on her lips when they emerged from the shop and were half blinded by the flash of a dozen cameras. The paparazzi had caught up with them. But fortunately Stavros was there and used his massive frame to shoulder a path to the car where he wrenched open the door so that Nikos could bundle Kitty inside.

'Why are they so interested?' Kitty cried as the car accelerated away and she watched the photographers weaving dangerously in and out of the traffic on their motor-scooters, in hot pursuit. 'It's not as if I've done anything to warrant such attention. I haven't done something wonderful for charity, or saved a life. I'm just drab, boring Kitty Karedes, who happens by an accident of birth to be a princess.'

'You are Kitty Angelaki now,' Nikos reminded her, 'and you are neither drab nor boring. But I agree that people seem to be increasingly celebrity obsessed.'

'The people on Aristo aren't,' Kitty muttered. 'Nothing

like this ever happened to me there. I even used to ride around the island on my bike and the most attention anyone ever paid me was a smile or a wave.' She leaned her head back against the leather seat and placed her hand protectively on her stomach, more shaken than she cared to admit by the overwhelming media fascination with her. She felt desperately homesick for the peace and tranquillity of the palace, and the freedom that she had taken for granted on Aristo. Of course she'd had her royal duties to perform, but attending the opening of a new wing of the hospital had attracted only mild interest from the Aristan press and she wasn't used to being in the constant glare of the media spotlight.

She wished she could go home, back to where she felt safe. But home was now Nikos's elegant but characterless apartment that felt more like a five-star hotel than a comfortable bolt hole, and her misery was compounded by the news that tonight Nikos was taking her to a party where she would meet many of his sophisticated friends.

Sotiri greeted them when they walked into the apartment. 'Some boxes have arrived from Aristo for you, Miss Kitty,' he said, throwing open the door to the living room where four huge trunks were stacked.

'My books…' Kitty forgot the horrors of the shopping trip as she tore open one of the boxes and smiled at the sight of the dozens of books packed inside.

'*Theos*! Are *all* these crates full of books?' Nikos picked up a battered hardback. 'Where are you going to put them all? The apartment is spacious, but it's not big enough to house an entire library.'

'They're the books that I use for my research work, and I need them here,' Kitty said stubbornly.

'Well, there's no room for them in my study. I'll ask Sotiri to move the boxes into one of the spare bedrooms, and I suppose we can turn it into an office for you if you intend to carry on working—although I doubt you'll have much free time, and of course financially there is no need for you to work.'

'I definitely want to carry on writing my book about the early history of the Adamas Islands, and I'd like to continue with my advisory work for Aristo's museum, certainly until the baby is born,' Kitty said slowly. 'If you are at your office all day, what else will I do?'

'I assumed you would want to get involved in charity work. A friend of mine, Melina Demakis, is a well-known social hostess in Athens who organises lunches and other fund-raising activities for a number of charities. I'll ask her to contact you.'

Kitty's heart sank at the prospect of filling her days lunching with wealthy and no doubt well-meaning doyennes of worthy organisations, and 'doing her bit' for charity. There had to be something more worthwhile she could do with her life, she thought heavily. 'I was thinking perhaps that I could volunteer to help out at the local hospital—visiting patients and maybe working a few hours in the coffee shop like I used to do at the hospital on Aristo.'

'You mean where you were once subjected to a vicious attack by a mentally ill patient? Sebastian told me that your father forbid you to go back there after the incident,' Nikos said in a scathing tone that showed what he thought of her idea.

'It wasn't a vicious attack. The patient lashed out and caught my cheek, but he didn't know what he was doing, poor man. My father was always rather overprotective,' Kitty added ruefully.

'As I am,' Nikos replied. 'How could you possibly work at a hospital with the paparazzi tailing your every move as they did today? You would be a hindrance rather than a help.'

'The paparazzi wouldn't know my whereabouts if I didn't draw attention to myself by turning up in a limousine, with a bodyguard at my side.'

'Well, you are certainly not stepping foot outside this apartment without Stavros,' Nikos said tersely. 'You are pregnant, Kitty, and I won't allow you to put yourself and our child in danger.'

'I have no intention of putting me or the baby in any sort of danger. But what do you mean by "won't allow"?' Kitty saw red as the empathy she had felt with him at the museum evaporated. 'Since when did you have authority over me?' she demanded furiously.

'Since you became my wife—and, more importantly, since you conceived my baby,' he replied in a tone that brooked no further argument. He glanced at his watch and strolled down the hall. 'I have an hour's work to do in my study. I suggest you start preparing for the party. From past experience I know how long it takes women to get ready.'

That final reference to his previous women—with emphasis on the plural—was the final straw, and Kitty was seriously tempted to fling the porcelain figurine of Aphrodite that stood on the hall dresser at his head. But Nikos had disappeared into his study, and after a few minutes she trailed down the hall and through the master bedroom to her dressing room, carried on into the en suite and ran herself a bath, hoping that a long soak in fragrant bubbles would relieve her growing tension at the prospect of socialising with a hoard of people she had never met before.

An hour later she stood in front of the mirror and studied her reflection with dismay. The floor-length evening gown made from rich ruby-red satin had a strapless, tight-fitting bodice, and an even tighter fitting skirt that clung to her hips and bottom and flared out from mid-thigh, with a side split that at least enabled her to walk. It was the most daringly sexy dress she had ever seen, let alone possessed—and it made her look like a tart, she decided grimly as she turned sideways to the mirror and sucked in her stomach. Any woman who wore this dress would attract attention. But that was the last thing she wanted to do at tonight's party.

If she had realised how much of her body was displayed by the plunging neckline she would have sneaked it back on the rail in the shop, Kitty thought fiercely as she tugged the zip down and stepped out of the dress.

The black evening dress she'd brought from Aristo was not unattractive, and at least it didn't make her look as if she walked the streets for a living. Even better, it would draw no attention at all, and with luck she could slink into a corner and remain there for the evening.

She swept her hair up into a knot on top of her head, exchanged the four-inch stilettos that matched the red dress for black two-inch kitten heels, and walked through the connecting door just as Nikos emerged from his bathroom.

He was devastating in a black tuxedo and a white silk shirt, his bow tie as yet unfastened and hanging open at his throat. He looked every inch the urbane, sophisticated, billionaire tycoon, with a raw sex appeal that would make every woman at the party go weak at the knees. Kitty felt a fierce tug of sexual awareness that made her heart race and her breath catch in her throat. But from the expression on his face, he was clearly not impressed by her appearance, and his brows lowered in a slashing frown as he walked towards her.

'Not quite what I had in mind, *agape*,' he drawled as his eyes slid down from her severe hairstyle to her prim, plain dress. 'I thought we had decided that you would wear the red dress?'

'No, you decided I would wear the red dress,' Kitty snapped. 'But I refuse to go out looking like a hooker you've picked up from some bar.'

'You prefer to go out looking as though you are on your way to a funeral?' His brows rose, and Kitty itched to wipe the arrogant expression from his face. 'You have five minutes to change,' he said in a dangerously soft voice. 'You are my wife, Kitty, and I expect you to dress accordingly, not wear something that makes you resemble a maiden aunt.'

Kitty's temper had been simmering since their argument about her working at the hospital, and it ignited at his heavy-handedness.

'I feel more comfortable wearing clothes of my choice,' she began, and then emitted a startled cry when his hands shot out and wrenched the front of her dress open so that the buttons running from neck to waist pinged in all directions.

'What do you think you're doing? *How dare you?*' She was breathing hard, her chest heaving so that Nikos's attention was drawn to her breasts, which were barely contained in a semi-transparent black bra.

'I dare, Kitty *mou*,' he drawled, his voice no longer sharp with annoyance but thick with sexual desire that caused an answering shiver of awareness to run down her spine, 'because you are my wife.' With deft fingers he tugged the pins from her hair so that it fell down her back in a river of silk. 'You now have two minutes to exchange dresses, or risk me removing what is left of this one,' he warned her silkily. 'And if I strip you completely I think it's a safe bet that we won't be going anywhere but my bed tonight.'

The determined gleam in his eyes told Kitty that he meant it too. A dignified retreat seemed her only option, and, head held high, she swung round and marched into her room, venting her temper by slamming the connecting door, and grinding her teeth when she heard his mocking laughter through the thin walls.

She hated him, she told her reflection, tears of mortification stinging her eyes as she stepped out of her ruined dress and squeezed herself into the red ball-gown. He was the most arrogant, overbearing man she had ever met—and it was a bitter irony that he was the only man who had ever made her ache with desire.

Because she wanted him, she acknowledged with reluctant honesty. She had wanted him that night in the cave, and she wanted him now. It was not fear of the physical act of making love with him that had made her sleep in another room, but the fear of giving herself to him, body and soul, and receiving nothing in return.

She could very easily fall in love with him, she thought bleakly as she ran a brush through her hair so that it fell around her shoulders like a curtain of silk. But she would be a fool to lose her heart to him, because his was carved from ice, and he had made it clear that it would never melt.

The connecting door swung open, and for a second her eyes clashed with Nikos's unfathomable gaze reflected in the mirror. Quickly she lowered her lashes, praying he had not guessed her thoughts, but her heart was hammering when he came to stand behind her.

'I knew the dress would suit you. You look stunning.'

Kitty had spent her whole adult life longing to be told she looked attractive, but Nikos's coolly delivered compliment left her feeling strangely deflated. He was just being polite, she decided. He was probably thinking that her bottom looked huge, and regretting on insisting that she should wear the dress.

'It's really not my style,' she muttered, her cheeks burning when his eyes slid over her and lingered on her voluptuous breasts that were thrusting provocatively above the tight-fitting bodice. 'I want to wear something else, Nikos—another of the dresses we bought today.' Preferably one that was less eye-catching.

'Don't be ridiculous.' He could not hide the impatience in his voice. 'And don't keep looking down at the floor.' He swung her round and caught her chin between his fingers, tilting her face to his. 'A dress like this needs to be worn with confidence.' From his jacket he extracted a narrow velvet box, which he opened to reveal an exquisite ruby and diamond pendant suspended on a gold chain. He smiled when Kitty gave an audible gasp. 'This matches the dress perfectly,' he murmured as he fastened it around her neck.

His hands were warm against her skin, but Kitty shivered as he swung her back round to face the mirror. Once again her eyes locked with his and she felt the familiar, prickling tension between them. The pulse at the base of her throat was plainly visible, beating erratically beneath her skin, and she caught her breath when he lowered his head and brushed his mouth along her collarbone.

'Time to go, Kitty *mou.*' His voice was deep and husky, and sent another shiver of acute awareness down her spine. 'Have pity on me tonight,' he murmured, his mouth curving into a self-derisive smile as he stepped away from her. 'Every time I look at you I will be imagining you wearing nothing but the necklace.'

She swallowed hard at the feral hunger in his eyes. 'You shouldn't say things like that.'

He shrugged. 'Why not, when it's the truth? And before much longer the image in my head will be reality. My patience is wearing thin, *agape,*' he warned her silkily, and turned and walked out of the room, leaving Kitty staring after him, her heart thumping.

CHAPTER TEN

THE charity gala was being held at an exclusive five-star hotel in the heart of Athens. As the car drew up outside the front steps and Kitty glanced out of the window at the blinding flashbulbs from the paparazzi's cameras she felt the familiar sick dread in the pit of her stomach. Some of her tension must have shown on her face because Nikos frowned as he leaned towards her.

'Relax, *agape*. You look as though you are about to be thrown to the lions rather than attend a party where you are the star guest.'

'I'd rather be thrown into a lions' den,' Kitty muttered.

'You're not still worried about your dress, are you?' Now there was an edge of impatience in Nikos's voice. 'I told you, you look stunning, and all eyes will be on you.'

'I don't *want* everyone to notice me. I've always been hopeless at socialising,' Kitty admitted miserably.

'But you must have regularly attended parties and functions at the palace.'

'Yes, but I never enjoyed it. Liss was always the party girl, and she has the looks and confidence to walk into a room full of strangers. I just get tongue-tied and never know what to say to people. I'm afraid you're going to find me a big disappointment, Nikos,' she finished gloomily.

'I did not realise you found socialising such an ordeal,' he murmured, taken aback by her revelation. 'But I assure you I will not find you a disappointment, Kitty. And I will be by your side constantly to introduce you to people. Have you ever thought that they might be nervous about meeting you?' he queried.

'Why would anyone feel nervous about meeting me?' Kitty demanded, startled.

'Because you are a princess. I think a lot of people could feel overawed by your royal status, not to mention the fact that you are intelligent and highly educated. Think about it,' Nikos murmured as Stavros opened the car door and he stepped out, turning back to assist Kitty in alighting from the car.

She was so shocked by the idea that people might be unnerved by meeting her that she barely noticed the press pack jostling around them, and she gave a shocked gasp when Nikos put his arm around her waist and dipped his head to kiss her full on the mouth. His lips were warm and firm and she responded to him without conscious thought, her eyes wide with confusion when he broke the kiss after a disappointingly short time.

'Why did you do that?' she mumbled as he drew her hand through his arm and escorted her up the steps and into the hotel.

'We are newly-weds, Kitty *mou*,' he reminded her, his eyes gleaming with amusement and something else that made her stomach dip. 'I thought it was about time we gave the paparazzi something to photograph.'

The moment they walked into the ballroom, they were the centre of attention—Athens's most famous billionaire shipping magnate and his princess bride. Glancing around at the female guests in their couture gowns and spectacular jewellery, Kitty reluctantly had to admit that she would have stuck out like a sore thumb in her drab black dress. But there was no chance of her slinking into a quiet corner in the daring red gown, and Nikos stayed true to his word and did not leave her side.

Instead he moved seamlessly from one group of guests to the next, introducing Kitty, and initiating conversation on topics he knew she was interested in so that she had something to say.

To her utter amazement she realised that Nikos had been right and that many of the people she met were not actually stiff and unfriendly as she had thought, but that they felt awkward in the presence of royalty and did not know quite how to treat her. Anxious to put them at their ease, she forgot her shyness and chatted to them, and to her surprise she discovered halfway through the evening that she was enjoying herself.

This really wasn't so bad, she mused later as she strolled over to the bar and asked the waiter for a fruit juice. Seeing that her confidence had soared, Nikos had left her for a few minutes to go and talk to one of his business associates, but Kitty was not alone for long.

'Princess Katarina? My name is Darius Christakis. I'm a lecturer at the university of Athens.'

She had noticed the man looking at her several times during the evening, and now, as he held out his hand to her, Kitty smiled and returned his greeting.

'Mr Christakis.'

He was very good-looking, she mused, and he was attracting interested glances from several women around the room. But he appeared to only have eyes for her, and she was startled when faint colour flared in his face.

'Darius, please.'

'And I'm Kitty,' she murmured, wanting to put him at his ease. 'The whole royal title thing is a bit of a mouthful, don't you think?'

'Actually, I think you are amazing.' The young man's flush deepened. 'I studied your paper on The Crusades during the twelfth century and the impact on Greece and the surrounding Mediterranean islands, and to be honest it was one of the most fascinating pieces I've ever read.' Darius grinned sheepishly. 'I must admit I imagined you to look like a learned scholar with glasses and a tweed skirt, but instead I find that you are gorgeous—if you don't mind my saying so,' he added, raking a hand distractedly through his hair.

'I don't mind,' Kitty said with a laugh, her self-confidence boosted by his description of her. If only he knew that a few weeks ago she *had* been a frumpy scholar, more interested in her books than her looks, but as she saw the undisguised admiration in Darius's eyes she felt a spurt of gratitude to Nikos who had transformed her from drab to, apparently, gorgeous.

'I was wondering if you would consider being a guest speaker at the university?' Darius continued. 'Your work at the museum on Aristo is well known and my students would really enjoy meeting you.'

Kitty's heart lurched at the idea of public speaking. But it would be on her specialist subject, and she would enjoy visiting Athens's university. On a sudden rush of confidence she nodded to Darius. 'I'd love to.'

'Great.' He beamed at her. 'Maybe we could get together soon to discuss your visit?'

'I'm afraid my wife will need to consult her diary before she makes any commitments.' Nikos materialised at Kitty's side, his dark brows drawn into a frown as he slid his arm possessively around her waist and clamped her so hard against him that she could barely breathe.

'Nikos, this is Darius Christakis…' Kitty began, breaking off at the look of open hostility in Nikos' eyes as he glared at the younger man.

'I see that your companions are waiting for you, Mr Christakis,' he said in a dangerously soft tone. 'You'd better go back to them.'

'Right.' The younger man backed away, gave Kitty a brief, nervous smile and shot off across the room.

'That was incredibly rude of you.' She rounded on Nikos the moment the other man was out of earshot. 'He only wanted to talk about a paper I'd written.'

'He wanted to dive into the front of your dress, *agape*,' Nikos drawled sardonically, his eyes glinting as he stared at Kitty's angry face. 'I've noticed the way he's been looking at you all night.'

'Nonsense…' She paused, blushing when she recalled how Darius had called her gorgeous. 'Anyway, it was you who insisted I should wear this dress.'

'A decision I am now regretting,' Nikos murmured as he led her onto the dance floor and drew her into his arms. 'You are attracting too much male attention, and I have discovered that I am very possessive. In future you can wear something beige and baggy to hide your delectable body from everyone but me.'

He was teasing her, surely, Kitty thought, her eyes widening when she realised that the expression in his dark gaze was deadly serious. 'Are you…*jealous*, Nikos?' She blushed scarlet as the words left her lips, certain that he would deny it. Instead his eyes narrowed and he tightened his arms around her so that her pelvis came into direct contact with the shockingly hard ridge of his arousal.

'It is not an emotion I am familiar with, Kitty *mou*,' he murmured dulcetly, 'but if you so much as look at another man for the hour or so remaining until we can leave, I will demonstrate in front of everyone here just how possessive I am of my wife—and how very impatient I am to make love to her.'

'Nikos!' Kitty could not hold back her shocked cry, or restrain the quiver of white-hot sexual awareness that ripped through her. This had been building for the past few days, she acknowledged numbly as she stared at him and saw the sensual gleam beneath his heavy lids. The drumbeat of desire that she had tried so hard to ignore was now thudding deep inside her, sending her blood coursing through her veins.

They were moving in time with the music, their bodies locked together so that she could feel every muscle and sinew of his hard thighs pressed against her softer flesh.

'You take my breath away tonight—my lady in red,' he murmured, his voice so low and husky in her ear that it seemed to reverberate right through her. She could feel the faint abrasion of his cheek against her face and knew that if she turned her head a fraction their mouths would meet. Her heartbeat quickened when he slid his hand into her hair, and when he exerted gentle pressure she lifted her face to him and felt his breath warm her skin before his lips claimed hers in a deep, slow kiss—a sensual tasting that she was powerless to resist.

The other guests on the dance floor faded away and the music of the band seemed distant. Nothing existed but Nikos: the strength of his arms holding her close against his chest, and the languorous drift of his mouth moving over hers in a drugging kiss that seemed to last a lifetime. Kitty responded to him helplessly, her wariness and insecurities forgotten as the fire inside her flamed into urgent life, and she murmured her protest when at last he lifted his head.

'Time to go home,' he growled as he whisked her off the dance floor and headed determinedly in the direction of their host.

It was on the tip of Kitty's tongue to tell him that it would be impolite to leave halfway through the party, but her brain seemed to have stopped functioning, and her body was burning up. In the car on the way back across town she tried to remind herself of the reasons why she had held out against making love with Nikos—but he no longer seemed the remote stranger he had been on their wedding day. He had been a kind and charming companion for the past few days when he had shown her around Athens, and she had found herself falling under his spell. As for her worries that he could not really be attracted to her when he had previously dated beautiful blonde models—he had only had eyes for her tonight, and his self-confessed jealousy when she had chatted to the university lecturer had made her feel like a desirable woman.

She was a mass of confused emotions when the lift whisked them up to the apartment and she dared not look at Nikos even though she knew he was staring at her with his dark, brooding gaze. The tension between them was tangible, and she gasped when the lift doors opened and he suddenly scooped her into his arms as if she weighed nothing.

'What are you doing?' She clutched his shoulders and looked into his face, her heart pounding when she saw the determined glint in his eyes.

'What I wanted to do when we first arrived here on our wedding day,' he told her as he strode down the hall and into the master bedroom, where the blinds were drawn and the room was bathed in a soft apricot glow from the bedside lamps. 'And what we both want now,' he added as he set her on her feet. 'Your body has been sending out signals all night, *agape*.' And for the past few days if she had but known it, Nikos brooded, recalling every shy smile she had given him, the way she often moistened her lips with the tip of her pink tongue in an unconscious invitation and the way she stared at him with her big brown eyes when she thought he wouldn't notice. For the past few nights he had lain awake aching with frustration, fighting the temptation to walk through the connecting door and snatch her into his arms.

'I want you to be my wife in every sense, Kitty,' he said deeply, running his finger lightly down her cheek and noting how her pupils had dilated so that her eyes seemed too big for her delicate face. 'I want to recapture the passion we once shared, and I dare you to deny that you want that too.

'Your body has already given you away, *agape*,' he growled when she made no reply. Following his gaze, she looked down and saw the stiff peaks of her nipples straining against her silk dress, and she caught her breath when he cupped her breasts and caressed them, brushing his fingers across their swollen crests so that sensation pierced her. Her dress was an intolerable barrier. She was desperate to feel his hands on her naked flesh, and suddenly nothing else mattered except that he should appease the desire that was flooding through her in an unstoppable torrent.

But she did not know what to say—how to tell him that she was ready to be his wife. Actions seemed easier than words. Her heart was thudding painfully beneath her ribs as, eyes locked with his, she reached behind her and drew the zip of her dress down from her neck to her waist. For a second he did not react, and tension screamed between them before he brought his mouth down on hers in a kiss of utter possession that told her clearer than any words that she had made her decision and there would be no going back.

The bodice of Kitty's dress was boned, meaning that she hadn't needed to wear a bra. As Nikos drew the red silk down lower and lower her breasts emerged like plump peaches and spilled into his hands. Instantly he felt his body stir, and for a second he was tempted to rip the dress from her body, throw her down on the bed and take her hard and fast. But with formidable will power he curbed his impatience. He could sense her lingering uncertainty, and he knew he must take it slow and arouse her fully until she ached as he ached with hot sexual frustration that clamoured for release.

He pushed her dress down over her hips and tugged it down her thighs until it slithered to the floor. Through the lacy panel of her knickers he could see the dark shadow of silky hair that shielded her femininity, and he heard her swift indrawn breath when he hooked his fingers into the waistband and stripped her completely.

When he had made love to her that first and only time in the cave she had been half hidden in shadow. But now her body was exposed in all its voluptuous glory and he feasted his eyes on her, gently moving her hands down when she tried to cover her breasts. 'Why do you want to hide yourself from me?' he queried softly. 'You are beautiful, Kitty, and I have never wanted any woman the way I want you.'

Kitty trembled at his words, and watched, wide eyed, as he deftly removed his own clothes, dropping his shirt and trousers carelessly to the floor to reveal his hard, muscular chest and thighs. His silk boxers could not disguise the jutting length of his erection, and she snatched a sharp little breath when he stepped out of them and stood before her, his awesome arousal sending a flicker of trepidation through her.

But then he caught her to him and crushed her soft, pliant body against the hardness of his as he slanted his mouth over hers and kissed her until she could think of nothing but him and her desperate need for him to touch her between her legs and soothe the throbbing ache that began low in her stomach. His tongue delved between her lips, taking the kiss to a deeper level, and she responded mindlessly, matching his fierce passion until he groaned and lifted her onto the bed, coming down beside her with one thigh across her hip to anchor her to the sheets.

'You have magnificent breasts, Kitty *mou*.' There was no hint of teasing in his low tone, just raw, feral need that sent an answering shaft of desire through her and made her arch her back when he traced his mouth down from her lips to the deep valley of her cleavage. The flick of his tongue across one dusky, swollen nipple and then its twin was so exquisite that she cried out and dug her fingers into his thick black hair to hold him to her breasts. His soft laughter feathered her skin, and when he took each stiff crest in turn into his mouth and sucked hard she twisted her hips restlessly and felt damp heat flood between her legs.

'Nikos…' The last shadows in her mind were blown away when he slid his hand over her stomach to her thighs and rested there, tantalisingly close to where she longed for him to touch her. She held her breath when he gently parted her, and when he slid his finger into her and caressed her with rhythmic strokes she spread her legs a little wider so that he could continue his erotic foreplay.

She could feel the solid length of his erection pushing against her thigh, and a tremor of shock ran through her when he took her hand and placed it on his arousal. He was so hard and powerful, and any second now she was going to have to take him inside her. She had done so once before, she reminded herself as panic fluttered in her stomach. But then he moved over her, slid his hand beneath her bottom to lift her slightly, and there was no time for doubt because he eased forwards and entered her with one sure thrust that made her gasp as he filled her.

For a moment he stilled and stared down at her, his dark eyes burning into hers. Then he began to move; firm, steady strokes as he drove into her, setting a pagan rhythm that echoed the drumbeat of her heart and sent her blood thundering through her veins. She could feel the tension inside her spiral with each exquisite thrust, and now he moved faster, harder, taking them inexorably towards the edge. Kitty felt as though she was losing her grip on reality, lost to sensation and the pleasure that was building and building. She clung to his shoulders and anchored there while the storm raged. Little ripples were starting deep inside her and radiating out as her climax hovered tantalisingly close. Desperation made her sob his name, and she pleaded with him to never, ever stop. And suddenly she was there, suspended for timeless seconds while he withdrew almost fully, and then with his next powerful thrust the dam broke and she was racked by spasm after spasm of intense sensation that dragged a sharp, animal cry from her throat.

Still he continued to move, each thrust more forceful and urgent than the last. But the feel of her vaginal muscles tightening around him, squeezing him, shattered his formidable control, and with a harsh groan Nikos spilled his seed inside her, his big body shuddering with the power of his release and his chest heaving as he dragged oxygen into his lungs.

In the aftermath Kitty lay still, and stared dazedly at the ceiling. His head lay on her breasts and she crossed her arms around his back, swamped by the same feeling she'd had in the cave when she had lost her virginity to him: that their souls were inextricably linked. It was an illusion of course, she told herself firmly, brought about by the intensity of the passion they had just shared. For Nikos it was simply good sex—a fact that he emphasised when he rolled off her and stretched his lean body out on the silk sheets, tucking his arms behind his head as if he were a sultan who had just enjoyed the services of his favourite concubine.

'You see, *agape,*' he murmured lazily. 'Our sexual compatibility is not in doubt.' He drew a ragged breath, waiting for his heartbeat to slow and wondering why he had felt so reluctant to withdraw from her. He would have liked to pillow his head on her breasts and simply lie with her. But the curious feeling of closeness that had swamped him in the aftermath of their lovemaking wasn't real, he assured himself. It was just good sex that he hadn't wanted to end. Fantastic sex; the best he'd had in a long time. Perhaps ever, his mind taunted him. It didn't mean anything. He had married Kitty because he wanted his child, and the fact that sex with her was dynamite was an added bonus that left his body satisfied and his heart untouched.

Kitty's skin had quickly cooled without the heat and welcome weight of Nikos's body pressing down on her, and she longed to curl up against him and lay her head on his chest. But now that he no longer filled her she sensed a distance between them far greater than the width of the bed. For her own self-protection it was vital she rebuilt her defences against him. She did not know what he expected now that he had made love to her. He seemed suddenly remote, lost in his thoughts, and she wanted to escape to the privacy of her own room, but when she sat up and swung her legs over the side of the bed he reached out and curled his arm around her waist.

'Where are you going?'

'I thought I would sleep in my room.'

His eyes narrowed on her flushed face and he sensed the tension that once more gripped her. 'It's too late to run away now, *agape*. You are mine, and from now on you will sleep with me. Besides,' he murmured as he drew her back down and moved over her, 'I intend to make love to you several times during the night and it would be most inconvenient if I had to trek backwards and forwards to fetch you.'

Beneath his teasing tone was a wealth of sensual promise that caused a tugging sensation low in Kitty's stomach. 'Several times?' she murmured faintly.

'Certainly, *agape*,' he assured her, 'starting now.'

Kitty watched their reflection in the wall of mirrors; Nikos's dark head bent to her breast, and she inhaled sharply when he painted moist circles around one areola with his tongue and then drew her nipple into his mouth. She ran her fingers through his hair, and then paused when she noticed for the first time the tattoo of a scorpion on his shoulder.

'What is this?' she asked, remembering how Vasilis had said that Nikos had once been part of the criminal underworld.

He followed her gaze to his reflection in the mirror, and his face hardened. 'A reminder of my past—it is the mark of the street gang I used to belong to when I was a youth. Stavros and Sotiri were members of the same gang, and we used to make money from illegal bare-knuckle boxing in back-street clubs.'

'Dear God!' She could not keep the shock from her voice. 'How old were you?'

He shrugged. 'Fifteen—but as I was bigger than most of

my opponents, none of the sharks who organised the fights cared too much.'

'You mean you fought men, even though you were not much more than a boy?' Kitty felt sick and her horror must have shown in her eyes because Nikos grimaced.

'Many things in my past are not pretty, *agape*. I had a tough childhood—but our child will not have to fight to survive,' he vowed fiercely, placing a hand on her stomach as if to protect the tiny life she carried. 'I grew up knowing hunger and deprivation, and there were many times when my mother had no money to pay the rent and we were evicted onto the streets. But even though life was hard I never doubted her love for me. She worked herself quite literally to death to feed and care for me.'

The words were torn from his throat. Words he had never spoken to anyone before, and he wondered why he felt this urge to unburden the memories of his past to Kitty. Her brown eyes were gentle and velvet soft, and she made no comment, simply waited patiently for him to continue.

'My mother was terrified I would fall into a life of crime,' he admitted grimly, 'but when I was sixteen she was offered a job as housekeeper for Larissa Petridis, and I was allowed to live with her in the staff quarters of the Petridis mansion. Stamos Petridis had died some years before and had left Petridis Shipping to his only daughter. Larissa had never married and had no children of her own but she took an interest in me. She offered to pay to send me to college, and, although it hurt my pride, I accepted, knowing that if I gained a degree I could get a good job and support my mother as she had supported me.'

He rolled onto his back, his jaw rigid as the memories he had pushed away for so long returned to haunt him. 'My mother died of cancer before I graduated. *Theos*, she was only in her early thirties,' he grated, his voice cracking, 'but the hardships she had suffered during her life had taken their toll, and when she became ill she had no strength to fight the disease. For a while I was crazy with grief but Larissa persuaded me to make something of my life. She offered me a position within her company and I quickly demonstrated a flair for business—although there was some gossip that my rise to top management was because I was Larissa's lover.

'The rumours were unfounded,' he told Kitty. 'I looked upon Larissa as a surrogate mother, and she treated me like the son she had never had—although it amused her to allow the media to think there was something between us. Larissa was what you might call a character,' he added dryly.

'When she died suddenly I was as shocked as anyone when I learned that she had made me her sole beneficiary. I took charge of the company, and I've worked hard to make it successful.'

He broke off, his eyes dark and tortured, and Kitty's heart turned over. 'I'm sure Larissa would have been proud of you,' she said softly. She had heard the affection in his voice when he spoke of the woman who had befriended him—yet Larissa had died only a few short years after his mother and once again he had been left alone. No wonder he seemed so hard and ruthless. His father had abandoned him before he had been born, and he had lost the only two people he had loved. She wanted to weep for the lonely boy he had once been, and the man who had built an impenetrable wall around his heart. Acting on instinct, and uncaring that she might reveal too much of herself to him, she cupped his face in her hands and brought her mouth to his in a kiss that offered comfort and understanding and a tenderness that shook Nikos to his core.

Passion built swiftly between them and he moved over her and entered her, taking them both to the heights of pleasure. It was just good sex; he repeated the mantra in his head as he drove into her and felt his pleasure build and build until it was intolerable and he could hold back no longer. Sexual alchemy was a potent force that held them both in its thrall, but that was *all* it was, he assured himself as her soft cries shattered the last remnants of his control.

But afterwards, as he lay with his head on her breasts, he felt more relaxed than he could ever remember. And later, when he lay beside her and she curled up against him, he slept peacefully for the first time in years.

CHAPTER ELEVEN

SUNLIGHT slanting through the blinds roused Kitty from a deep sleep. She stretched, and rolled over, smiling at the sight of the cup of camomile tea that Nikos had placed on her bedside table. She was now into the second month of her pregnancy and often woke feeling nauseous. The herbal tea was the only thing that seemed to settle her stomach, and Nikos made it for her every morning, and would not allow her out of bed until she had drunk it.

She had seen a new side to him these past couple of weeks, she mused. He still seemed remote sometimes, and he worked long hours, driven, she guessed, by the demons of his impoverished childhood. But most nights he came home in time for them to eat dinner together, even though he often carried on working in his study for a few hours afterwards. She looked forward to their shared meals. Face it, Nikos coming home was the highlight of her day, she admitted wryly. She enjoyed their conversations about her work and his, or their lively discussions about events in the news. She was as passionate about politics as she was about history, and in Nikos she had found someone who was happy to challenge her views and state his own. He made her feel alive in a way no other man ever had—and when he swept her off to bed every night and made love to her with skilled passion, he gave her body more pleasure than she had believed was possible.

Since the night of the charity gala that had ended with them consummating their marriage they had attended numerous parties and social events, and she was slowly beginning to find it less nerve-racking when she walked into a room full of strangers. Unlike on Aristo where she had managed to avoid the limelight, people in Athens seemed fascinated by her royal status and wherever she went she was the focus of avid interest from Nikos's wide circle of friends and business associates.

But it was difficult not to attract attention when Nikos insisted on her wearing the glamorous gowns that now filled her wardrobe. The clothes she had brought from Aristo had mysteriously disappeared, and been replaced by elegant daywear, and exotic, overtly sexy cocktail dresses and ball-gowns that she would never have chosen for herself. Some-times she wondered if he was trying to turn her into a woman more like the sophisticated models he had dated before he had married her, but her insecurities about her body were gradu-ally fading and her self-confidence growing as she blossomed beneath his attention and his undisguised desire for her.

She could hear the sounds of the shower and knew that he would emerge from the en suite dressed in one of his designer suits that he wore for work. He would look as gorgeous as ever, but a glance in the mirror revealed that her hair looked like a bush and her face was a peculiar shade of green. The nausea was bad again this morning. Yesterday she had actually been sick, but fortunately not until after Nikos had gone.

She sat up slowly, praying the feeling would pass. She couldn't bear the idea of throwing up while he was around. It would be so undignified, she thought miserably, but her body cared nothing for dignity, and with a gasp she shot off the bed and raced through the connecting door to her dressing room and bathroom.

Nikos found her there five minutes later, and, ignoring her terse plea to go away and leave her alone, he remained with her while she lost the contents of her stomach, and then wiped her face with a damp cloth as if she were a helpless child.

'Are you feeling any better?' he asked quietly when she sat on the edge of the bath, ashen-faced and utterly spent. For some reason the concern in his voice angered her. He wasn't asking because he cared about her; he was only worried about the baby. She caught sight of her reflection in the mirror, and tears stung her eyes when she saw her sallow skin and her hair hanging limp and lustreless on her shoulders. She looked disgusting, and she felt embarrassed about him seeing her at her most vulnerable and unattractive.

'I *hate* feeling like this,' she admitted miserably.

Nikos stiffened at her words. 'It is a natural side effect of pregnancy. The doctor said the sickness should lessen in a few more weeks.'

He made her sound as though she was making a huge fuss over something trivial, and Kitty glared at him. 'Well, he would say that, he's a man, and he's never had to go through this.' Any more than Nikos had. The unspoken words hung in the air. 'You have no idea how revolting I feel right now,' she told him tightly. 'It's okay for you. Your body isn't going to change out of all recognition and blow up like a balloon, and you don't have to worry that whatever you eat for dinner is likely to bounce back up before breakfast.'

'True,' he said in a clipped tone, his dark eyes focused intently on her as if he was determined to read her mind. 'But it will be worth it in the end—when the baby is here.'

'I suppose,' Kitty muttered. Now she was ashamed of her silly outburst, and for some reason she wanted to cry, but not in front of him. Hormones had a lot to answer for, she thought heavily. 'I'm fine now,' she assured him. 'Go to work, Nikos.'

He hesitated. 'If it was any other day I would cancel my

engagements and stay home. But I have a series of important meetings scheduled.'

She was desperate for him to go so that she could shower and wash her hair, try and make herself look vaguely human. 'I don't need you here,' she told him edgily. 'The nausea is passing, and in a while I'll eat something.' When he still did not move she cast around her mind for something to convince him she was perfectly all right. 'I thought I might look into some charities that I could support. You said you have a friend who organises fund-raising events,' she prompted him.

'Yes, Melina Demakis. I'll find you her number. But I don't want you to take on too much. Your main priority should be caring for your health, and that of the baby.'

'I realise that, and I will take care of myself.' Kitty thought of the lonely hours she had spent in the apartment since he had returned to work. 'You're at your office all day, and I can't just sit around for the next seven months until the baby comes.'

He stared at her for a moment more and then nodded. 'All right—come with me now and I'll give you Melina's contact details.'

Nikos's office was decorated in the same minimalist style as the rest of the apartment, pale walls and black furniture, a couple of modern prints in silver frames on the walls. The only personal item in the room was a small framed photograph on his desk.

'My mother,' he said when Kitty glanced curiously at the picture of a woman with dark hair and a gentle smile. 'That was taken when I was a child. I found it among her things after she died. It's the only photo I have of her,' he added, taking the picture from Kitty and staring down at it.

'She was very pretty,' she murmured, 'and she looks kind.'

'She was.'

Kitty was startled by the flare of pain in his eyes, but it was quickly hidden behind the sweep of his thick lashes. He set the photo down without further comment and flipped open the address book on his desk. 'Melina's details are here. I'm afraid I must go, I'm running late, and I may not be back for dinner. But Sotiri will cook for you, so make sure you eat— for the baby's sake.'

His concern for his child was indisputable, Kitty thought when he had gone. Naturally she wanted to do what was best for the baby, but sometimes Nikos made her feel more like an incubator than an expectant mother.

By late morning she was feeling more like her usual self, and when she had showered and dressed, and eaten a huge breakfast, the day stretched before her. She had phoned Melina Demakis and spoken at length about possible charities she might like to support, and had arranged to meet the older woman and several of her committee members the following week. It seemed that she was destined to spend her life attending fund-raising events, and because of her royal status she was likely to bring attention to the organisations she supported, but it seemed an empty existence, and she wished she could do something more worthwhile.

She flicked idly through the daily newspaper, pausing when a familiar name caught her attention. She had met Father Thomaso a few years ago when she had opened a hospice on Aristo that he had raised funds for. Now in his late sixties, the priest was at an age when he could have retired, but instead he was living in Athens and had set up a charity to help underprivileged young people.

In the article Father Thomaso spoke movingly of the problems facing the very poor, especially children and teenagers—many of whom were immigrants who had come to Athens for a better life and had ended up living in slums or rough on the streets. He had opened a youth centre to provide a place of safety for children and adolescents, and was asking for financial and practical support.

Deeply touched by the case stories she had read, Kitty

picked up the phone, and when she set it down again twenty minutes later she had arranged to visit the Father and his youth centre to see what she could do to help.

Later that day Kitty stared worriedly out of the taxi window at the volume of traffic on the road. She had stayed at the youth centre for much longer than she had planned, and a glance at her watch told her that she was going to be seriously late to meet Stavros at the National Archaeological Museum.

Up until now her plan had worked well—although she didn't feel comfortable about tricking Stavros, or deceiving Nikos. She wasn't really deceiving him, she told herself. She had actually phoned his office to tell him she was going to visit the youth centre run by Father Thomaso, but his secretary had said he was in a meeting and had given instructions not to be disturbed unless there was an emergency.

She could have left a message, Kitty acknowledged. But it had seemed easier to keep her plans to herself. Nikos had forbidden her from working as a volunteer at the local hospital, and she was sure he would not allow her to visit a notoriously rough area of the city to work with disadvantaged youths.

It was that word 'allow' that infuriated her, she brooded as the taxi crept along at snail's pace. She understood his concerns for the baby, but she was an adult who could make her own decisions. After her phone call to Father Thomaso she had been determined to visit the youth centre and meet some of the young people he was trying to support. But she knew that Stavros would immediately report back to Nikos, and so she had asked him to take her to the museum, knowing that he could be persuaded to wait in the car for her rather than be dragged around the exhibit rooms.

Once Stavros had left her, she had slipped out of a side door and hailed a taxi to take her across town. The hours she had spent with Father Thomaso had convinced her that she had finally found something worthwhile to do with her empty days while Nikos was at work. But she knew she could not continue to deceive Nikos. On the journey back across town she wondered how she could convince him that she would come to no harm working at the youth centre—but when the taxi finally drew up outside the museum her heart sank at the sight of him standing, grim-faced, with Stavros.

Okay, she shouldn't have gone behind his back, she owned when she stepped out of the taxi. She owed him an apology and an explanation, but she hadn't broken any laws, and there was no reason why he should be looking at her with such icy fury that her blood ran cold.

'Stavros is in no way to blame,' she said quietly when she reached him. 'I sent him away, but I can explain.'

'Can you?' Nikos ground out, struggling to control the anger that had surged through him when he had seen her in the taxi and realised she had deliberately tricked her bodyguard. When Stavros had phoned him and explained that Kitty had disappeared from the museum, he had broken off his board meeting and raced across town, breaking every speed limit. Thoughts of kidnap had filled him with dread, but now a new fear churned in his gut. Where had she been? And why had she needed to go off in secret? He glanced round at Stavros and the security staff from the museum who had searched for her, and caught hold of Kitty's arm in a bruising grip that made her wince. 'We can't talk here,' he bit out tersely as he marched her over to his car and yanked open the door. 'Get in.'

Kitty knew better than to argue. His fury was palpable, and she quickly slid into her seat and stared straight ahead when he walked round the car and got in next to her. His silence during the journey back to the apartment shredded her nerves, and when she preceded him down the hall she was tempted to make a run for it and lock herself in her bathroom. She walked into the living room with him close behind her, and he immediately crossed to the bar, poured whisky into a glass and gulped it down. His tension was so fierce that even from a few feet away Kitty could feel it, and she felt a frisson of real fear when he strode towards her.

'Where have you been all day, Kitty?' His hand shot out and gripped her chin, holding her so tight that she was sure he would crush her jaw.

'Nikos…you're hurting me.' Tears filled her eyes, and she swayed, feeling sick. She suddenly remembered that she had missed lunch. She had been busy talking to one of the boys at the youth club who had run away from home after his abusive stepfather had beaten him. Time had passed as she had sat with Yanni and tried to comfort him, but now her blood sugars were low and she was afraid she was going to faint. 'Let go of me and I'll tell you,' she pleaded. 'For pity's sake, Nikos! You're scaring me, and this level of tension can't be good for the baby.'

'You mean there is still a baby?' he growled savagely. He flung her from him, and she stumbled, but he stood staring at her, his eyes so dark and bitter that she shook her head in bewilderment.

'Of course there's still a baby. Why wouldn't there be?' she faltered.

'You tell me, Kitty. This morning you told me how much you hate being pregnant, and then later you gave Stavros the slip and went off without telling anyone where you were going. But maybe you didn't want anyone to know,' he snarled. 'Maybe you went to a private clinic and dealt with the problem of your pregnancy.'

Either she was crazy, or he was. 'What clinic?' she demanded desperately. 'There isn't a problem with my pregnancy. I don't understand what you mean, Nikos.' She kept replaying his words in her head, and slowly, slowly, they made an appalling kind of sense. *Dealt with the problem of your pregnancy!* Her knees sagged and she dropped down onto the sofa. 'You can't mean…you can't think…' She felt as though an iron band were tightening around her chest, squeezing the oxygen from her lungs. 'You can't think that I would—' she could hardly bring herself to utter the words '—get rid of the baby?'

'Why not?' His eyes were black and dead. 'It's what my first wife did.'

'No.' What he was telling her was too terrible to comprehend, and she closed her eyes, feeling utterly incapable of dealing with the pain that ravaged his face. 'You must be wrong,' she said jerkily. 'Surely your wife wouldn't have done that…*I* wouldn't do that,' she said in a stronger voice as she got unsteadily to her feet and crossed the room towards him. He stood immovable and grim-faced, and she saw him tense in rejection when she came close. But she did not care. Nothing mattered except that he should understand their child was safe.

She took his hand and held it over her stomach, and stared up at him, her eyes locked with his. 'Our baby is here inside me, and only fate will decide if it will be born safe and well in seven months' time. But I will do my best to nurture and protect it, and I would never, ever do anything to harm it. Please, Nikos, you must believe me,' she said shakily when he remained still and cold as a marble statue. 'I didn't say I hated being pregnant this morning.' Colour stained her pale face as she remembered how she had been ill in front of him. 'I meant that I hated being sick while you were there. I was… embarrassed for you to see me like that. Morning sickness isn't very glamorous,' she muttered.

At last he moved, as if blood once more ran in his veins rather than ice. 'You could not help being sick,' he said harshly. He stared at his hand on her stomach, and curved his fingers slightly as if he could somehow cradle the child within her. Slowly he lifted his eyes to her face and felt a jolt of shock when he saw her tears falling in a silent stream down her cheeks. 'I thought—' He broke off. 'You were so miserable this morning, and you seemed to resent being pregnant. When I learned from Stavros that you had disappeared, and then realised the lengths you had taken to get away from him, I believed there could only be one reason why you would make such an elaborate deceit. My past experience coloured my judgement, and I jumped to the wrong conclusion,' he said stiffly. He took his hand from her stomach and swung away to stare bleakly out over the city. 'Forgive me.'

His tone told her that he did not care whether she did or not.

Kitty stared at his rigid shoulders, and bit her lip, wondering if she dared voice the questions circling in her head. 'Did your first wife really…?'

'Abort my child?' He finished the question for her, his voice now flat and utterly devoid of emotion. 'Yes.' He had never spoken of it before, but he suddenly found the words spilling from him. 'I had told Greta of my family history and she knew I would never abandon my child as my father had done. I don't know if Greta's pregnancy was a genuine mistake, or if she missed her contraceptive Pill deliberately, but when I learned she was expecting my baby I immediately offered to marry her.

'I was devastated when she told me soon after our marriage that she had suffered a miscarriage,' he continued grimly. 'She knew I wanted the child, but I discovered later that she had set her sights on marrying a millionaire, and once she had achieved her goal the child was no longer necessary. When our marriage crumbled because of her drug addiction, and she knew I intended to divorce her, she wanted to hurt me, and she told me that she had had an abortion.'

No wonder his heart was buried beneath impenetrable layers of granite, Kitty thought, aching with sadness for him. She wanted to wrap her arms around him and simply hold

him, but she knew he would reject her, and now she understood why. His trust and faith in humanity had not just been
shattered, but utterly and cruelly destroyed beyond repair.

'Where is Greta now?' she asked huskily.

'She died two years ago as a result of her drug habit.'

There was not a shred of pity in his voice. He had stated
that he had married his first wife after she conceived his baby,
but Kitty knew instinctively that it had been more than that.
Had he loved her? She was startled by how much the idea hurt,
and she pushed her ridiculous jealousy away. If he had cared
for Greta, then her betrayal must have been doubly agonising.

She understood now why he wanted his child so desperately. He had lost his only blood relative when he was a vulnerable teenager, and later suffered the most terrible betrayal
by his first wife. The baby inside her meant everything to him,
and she knew then that whatever happened between them in
the future—even if they ended up rowing constantly—she
could never separate him from his child.

But she could not contemplate a time when she might want
to end their marriage. She loved him, Kitty admitted silently.
From the very beginning she had been drawn to him by more
than just the sexual chemistry that burned between them. She
had thought he was cold and heartless, but how could he be
anything else after the pain he had suffered in his life? She
wished she could go to him and tell him that she would always
be there for him. But he did not want her love, and she did
not want to burden him with it or make him feel guilty that
he could never love her in return.

She was at a loss to know what to say to him, and even
though he was standing only a few feet away the distance
between them seemed unbridgeable. Tiredness rolled over
her in a wave, and with it a feeling of defeat. After all he had
suffered he would never lower his guard and feel normal
emotions like trust and caring. When they had married he'd

told her bluntly that he would never love her, and she had accepted it. But it hadn't stopped her secretly hoping that over time their physical relationship would develop into something more. Now she knew there was no hope of that ever happening. His emotional scars ran too deep and she could not blame him for refusing to risk being hurt again.

Nikos was staring unseeingly out of the window, lost in his bitter memories, but he suddenly swung round and pierced her with a sharp stare. 'So, where did you go today?'

Kitty took a deep breath, ashamed of her stupid deceit now that she knew how badly he had been deceived in the past. 'I went to visit a youth centre for underprivileged children and teenagers. I read about it in the newspaper, and remembered the priest who runs it, Father Thomaso, from Aristo.

'I know I should have told you, Nikos, but I was afraid you would stop me. You have no idea what terrible lives some of those children have had,' she said urgently. 'I've spent my whole life as a pampered princess, and I want to do something useful and meaningful. I know I can give money, but what the children really need is someone to listen to them, someone to care—'

She broke off, not encouraged by his frown, and fully expecting him to accuse her of putting the baby at risk, but his reaction surprised her.

'Actually I know only too well from my own childhood experiences what their lives are like,' he said quietly, staring at her intently as he tried to understand her. She was a princess from one of the wealthiest families in Europe, yet despite her privileged upbringing she wanted to help the poor and desperate who lived on the streets. None of the women he had ever dated in his past had had a social conscience, and he didn't know quite what to make of her.

'I told you that I inherited Petridis Shipping from Larissa.' He broke the silence that had fallen between them. 'But I did not want Larissa's personal fortune, I was determined to make my own, and so I put her money into a charitable fund which provides financial support to a number of causes, including, as it happens, the youth centre you visited today. I have never met Father Thomaso, but I know of his work and I have already organised for Larissa's charitable fund to make a significant donation to his centre.'

Something flared in his eyes, a new respect for her that lifted her heart. 'I don't think you should take on too many commitments while you are pregnant, and after the baby is born you will be busy. But I am looking for someone to become president of the charitable fund I've set up. The position is yours, if you want it.'

He walked over to her when she eagerly nodded her head, and slid his hand beneath her chin, tilting her face to him. 'We married for the sake of our child, and if I'm honest I believed you were as shallow as the women I dated before I met you,' he said bluntly. 'But you constantly surprise me, Kitty,' he finished, his frustration that he did not understand her tangible. He was shocked that he had revealed so much of himself to her, but to his surprise he realised that he did not regret telling her about his past. After Greta, he had believed he would never trust anyone, but when he looked into Kitty's soft, brown eyes he felt… *healed.*

He looked down at her pale face and frowned when she swayed unsteadily on her feet. 'What's wrong?' he demanded sharply. 'Are you ill?'

'I forgot lunch,' she admitted sheepishly. 'And now I feel sick again and I don't think I can manage dinner.'

'Kitty! Do you think you could worry about other people a bit less, and yourself a bit more?' he growled, ignoring her startled gasp as he swung her into his arms and strode down the hall.

'I'm sorry,' she mumbled, trying to resist the urge to press her face into his neck and breathe in his tantalising male scent. 'I know you're concerned for the baby.'

'Actually, *agape,* I am concerned about you.' She looked drained and infinitely fragile, and something indefinable tugged at his heart, but he forced it away and reminded himself that she was the mother of his child and so of course he cared about her welfare.

He stopped off at the kitchen and stood over her until she had forced down a banana and a glass of milk. Then he carried her to the bedroom—as if she were as light as a feather rather than a well-built, pregnant woman, Kitty mused sleepily as he removed her clothes and slipped a nightdress over her head before he helped her into bed. She was asleep within seconds of her head touching the pillow, but Nikos lay awake long into the night, his thoughts preoccupied—not by his past, but his future with the woman lying beside him.

CHAPTER TWELVE

KITTY smoothed a crease from the skirt of her elegant cream linen suit, and skimmed through her notes one last time. Around her, the hotel banqueting room was filled with guests who were attending the lunch in support of the youth centre Father Thomaso had set up—and in her role as patron of the charity, she was about to give a speech outlining the aims of the centre and asking for donations.

Beside her, Nikos smiled and rested his hand lightly on her thigh. 'Are you nervous, *agape?* There must be several hundred people here today.'

Kitty took a deep breath, and squared her shoulders. 'I'm fine,' she said confidently, ignoring the few butterflies in her stomach. She knew that once she walked onto the stage, and began to talk about the centre and the lives of the children it aimed to support, her nerves would disappear.

It seemed hard to believe that only a short while ago she had been so crippled by shyness that any type of socialising had been an ordeal. Since she had married Nikos and moved to Athens she felt as though she had emerged from a shell. She was no longer drab, dumpy Kitty Karedes. She knew she looked good in the clothes he bought her, and the admiration in his eyes made her feel more confident about her curvy figure.

'Are you sure? You look a little flushed,' Nikos murmured, his eyes glinting wickedly as his hand inched higher up her skirt.

'Will you behave—at least until later, when we're alone?' Kitty choked, amusement and desire mingling as she prised his hand from her leg. 'You have an insatiable appetite, Nikos.'

'Only for you, Kitty *mou*,' he drawled lazily. The sensual promise in his eyes caused the familiar weakness in Kitty's limbs, and she wished they were back home at the apartment and he would spend the rest of the afternoon making love to her. But first she had a speech to give, and then they were going to the hospital for her first antenatal scan. Up on stage the event organiser announced her name, and she gathered up her notes.

'Wish me luck,' she murmured, and gave a startled gasp when he leaned towards her and claimed her mouth in a slow, sweet kiss.

'You don't need luck—you're a brilliant speaker.' He paused and then said quietly, 'I am very proud of you, *agape*.'

She blushed and gave one of her soft smiles that tugged at Nikos's insides before she walked up the room, and when she stepped onto the stage he joined the other guests and applauded her, feeling a mixture of pride and frustration that just lately she seemed to dominate his thoughts to the exclusion of anything else.

Ever since the day she had visited Father Thomaso's youth centre, and the explosive confrontation that had followed, which had led him to telling her about his past, a fragile bond had developed between them. The last few weeks had been… good, he admitted, refusing to dwell on the fact that he had cut back significantly on his working hours so that he could spend time with her. It was important that they established a friendly relationship before the baby was born, but he was surprised and faintly dismayed by how much he enjoyed her company.

Kitty was no longer the wary and reserved person she had been when he had first brought her to Athens, and since he had appointed her as head of the Larissa Petridis Foundation her confidence had soared. She took her charity work seriously and the media had dubbed her the Caring Princess. She had become something of a celebrity in Athens, and even he was privately amazed by her transformation from a shy, reluctant royal to a graceful and breathtakingly beautiful princess.

Without him being aware of her doing it, she had encouraged him to talk about the issues that still haunted him, in particular his feeling that he had failed to protect his first child. Thanks to Kitty he was slowly coming to terms with his past, and he was looking forward to the future when he would be a father. But although he trusted her in a way he had never believed he would trust any human being, he couldn't shake off the feeling that she was holding back from him, particularly when he made love to her, and that in turn made him reluctant to lower his guard.

The press were waiting for them when they emerged from the hotel. Kitty did not enjoy their constant attention, but she dealt with it with quiet dignity, smiling and standing with Nikos's arm around her waist while the photographers jostled to take pictures.

'At least it will bring the youth centre to everyone's notice,' she murmured when they finally made it to the car and Stavros sped off. But she was glad they had lost the paparazzi by the time they reached the hospital. The scan was a private matter for her and Nikos and she didn't want to share the experience with the rest of the world.

Inside the private hospital they walked along plush carpeted corridors to the obstetrician's office. 'Dr Antoniadis is the best in Greece,' Nikos had told her when he had made the appointment. 'He will oversee your care and personally deliver the baby.' Nothing, it seemed, was too good for Nikos's child.

Dr Antoniadis carried out some basic checks on Kitty and then chatted to them both about the type of birth she hoped to have.

'Painless, hopefully,' she quipped, feeling a sudden rush of nerves when she thought about the technicalities of giving birth. To her surprise, Nikos reached across and clasped her hand.

'I will be with you every minute of your labour,' he promised. And for some reason the strength in his voice and the firmness of his fingers gripping hers made Kitty want to cry. Fortunately a nurse appeared and led her off to change into a hospital gown, ready for the scan, and then, when she lay on the bed in the scanning room and someone smeared cold jelly over her, she was more concerned with the size of her stomach, which was already discernibly rounded, to give much thought to anything else.

'You won't see much at this early stage,' the technician explained as a fuzzy grey blur appeared on the screen. 'We really just want to check the heartbeat—and there it is. Can you see it? That little pulse there is your baby.'

Kitty stared at the screen, at the indistinct blob of cells and the tiny but plainly visible speck that was beating rhythmically, and emotion flooded through her. In that moment her pregnancy became real. It was no longer something vague: a line on a pregnancy kit and nausea in the mornings. A human life was developing inside her: her child—hers and Nikos's. She blinked to dispel the moisture that had welled in her eyes, and turned to him. And more tears gathered when she saw his face. He was leaning forward slightly in his chair, staring intently at the grainy image, and she could see the tension in his shoulders, the absolute stillness, as if he were afraid that if he moved the picture on the screen would disappear.

'Nikos.' Her voice was choked, and he stirred then and gripped her hand, lifted it to his mouth and pressed his lips to her fingers.

'We will give our child everything,' he said rawly.

She knew he was thinking about his own childhood when he had had so little. 'Of course we will,' she assured him softly. 'But a child needs more than material things. A child needs love, perhaps more than anything—and we will love it—he or she,' she added with a smile as she pictured a little boy with dark hair and flashing eyes, or a girl with pink cheeks—probably chubby cheeks if the baby took after her, she thought ruefully.

Afterwards they strolled around the park next to the hospital, where the late afternoon sunshine filtered through the leaves of the cypress trees and made patterns of gold on the paths.

'What do you hope it is—a boy or a girl?' she asked curiously.

'I don't know.' Nikos looked startled for a moment, as if it was the first time he had considered that the baby would be one or the other. 'I don't mind,' he said seriously, echoing her own thoughts, and she glanced at him and shared the unspoken message that what really mattered was that their child would be healthy and born safely.

'It's exciting, isn't it—to think that in a few months from now the baby will actually be here?' Kitty felt her heart flip as she imagined cradling her child in her arms. Since the scan she couldn't stop smiling. Her pregnancy had been unplanned and a huge shock, but she did not regret it, and she couldn't wait to be a mother.

'Yes, it's exciting.' Nikos returned her smile and slipped his hand into hers as they walked. Their child would form a bond between them that would last a lifetime, Kitty realised, loving the new closeness she sensed was developing between them.

'Tell me about your childhood,' he said suddenly. 'I've told you about mine, but yours must have been very different, growing up in a palace with the other members of the royal family.'

'Well, I certainly never wanted for anything,' she murmured. 'The palace was an amazing place to grow up, although of course when I was a child I didn't realise how privileged I was. But it wasn't just material things. There were five of us children, so I was never lonely. And although my parents were busy much of the time with state affairs, they always had time for us.

'I was especially close to my father,' she revealed with a soft smile as she remembered the late king. 'I adored him. When I was a little girl he used to come to the nursery every night and read stories from my favourite book—*Russian Fairy Tales and Fables.*' Kitty's smile faded and she felt the familiar pang of sadness that she would never see her father again, or hear his deep, rumbling tones. 'He used to tell me that I would grow up to be a beautiful princess like in the fairy tales, and that one day I would marry a handsome prince.'

But in fairy tales the prince always fell in love with the princess—which just went to show the difference between fantasy fiction and real life, she thought bleakly as she stared at Nikos's sculpted features and saw the inherent toughness in the hard line of his jaw.

'I wish I still had the book,' she said wistfully. 'Unfortunately it was lost in a fire that destroyed part of the palace nursery a few years ago. It's out of print now, and the few copies that exist are owned by private collectors, so I don't suppose I'll ever be able to read it to our child.'

'We'll buy new books, and toys—everything the baby needs,' Nikos murmured, thinking of his own childhood that had lacked even basic necessities such as food, let alone toys and books. Kitty had said that a child needed love more than material possessions, and maybe she was right. He knew without doubt that he would love his child, but what kind of father would he be when he had never had a role model? He felt singularly inadequate for the job, especially when Kitty would surely compare his efforts at fatherhood with her own father, whom she had obviously idolised.

Her life had turned out vastly different from the life she must have imagined as a child, he brooded. Instead of meeting a prince with an aristocratic lineage she had been forced to marry a commoner who had no idea who had fathered him. And she missed Aristo and the royal palace—she never said so, but he knew she didn't enjoy living in the apartment in the centre of a busy city, and that when he was at work she often visited Athens' famous National Gardens.

'Maybe we should start looking at houses,' he startled Kitty by saying. 'Somewhere in the suburbs, with a garden for the baby to play in when it's older. Would you like that?'

'It would be nice,' she replied slowly. 'But you like the apartment. It's your bachelor pad.'

'Mmm, but I am not a bachelor any more, and I want what is best for our child—I'll contact some estate agents,' Nikos said decisively. 'But moving takes time, and for now I was thinking that we could turn your dressing room into a nursery so that we are close to the baby if it wakes during the night—unless you're planning on sleeping in there again yourself?'

Kitty blushed at the teasing glint in his eyes, knowing that he was remembering her first few nights at the apartment when she had refused to share his bed. 'You might prefer us to sleep apart when I'm nine months pregnant and the size of a whale,' she murmured, voicing the fear that had been niggling away at her that he would no longer find her attractive when she was heavily pregnant. 'Really, Nikos, I'm sure I'm going to be *huge*. I've already gained weight.'

'I know,' he growled as he leaned against a tree and drew her into his arms. 'Your breasts are bigger—and I am definitely a breast man,' he muttered, deftly unbuttoning her jacket so that he could caress her full curves that were straining beneath her silk blouse. He ran his finger lightly down her cheek and saw the betraying quiver that ran through her. 'You look tired, *agape.*'

'Oh!' Kitty's face fell. She did not want to be told she looked tired; she wanted Nikos to tell her she looked gorgeous and sexy and that he was impatient to take her to bed. 'Well, I'm not. I feel fine.'

'What a pity.' His mouth curved into an amused smile when she stared at him in confusion. 'I was thinking that you should spend the rest of the afternoon lying down—and to prevent you from feeling bored, I would lie with you and…entertain you.'

Kitty couldn't restrain the little shiver of excitement that ran through her, and she felt a delicious tingle of anticipation at the sultry gleam in Nikos's eyes. 'In that case, we'd better go home,' she whispered against his mouth, and gave a low murmur of approval when he claimed her lips in a hungry kiss that demanded her eager response.

Fortunately it was not far back to the apartment, although Nikos was so impatient that he had already removed her jacket and unfastened her blouse by the time the lift reached the top floor.

'You mustn't keep carrying me,' she protested when he swept her into his arms and raced down the hall. 'I'm no lightweight, Nikos.'

He laughed, and the sound rumbled in his big chest as he lowered her to her feet in the bedroom. 'I like carrying you. You fit into my arms,' he murmured, tugging her blouse over her shoulders and reaching round to unsnap her bra.

Her breasts were getting huge, and her nipples were bigger and darker, Kitty noted dismally when she glanced down. She looked so different from the skinny, flat-chested blonde models Nikos had dated in the past, and some of her old insecurity about her shape returned. Sunshine was pouring through the windows, and she was unnerved at the thought of taking off her clothes and standing stark naked in the brilliant light, when before they had only ever made love in the soft glow from the bedside lamps.

'I'll shut the blinds,' she murmured, inching away from him and crossing her arms over her breasts.

His brows rose quizzically and he paused in the act of removing his shirt. 'Why? We're on the top floor and not overlooked by anyone,' he said, the amusement in his voice fading when he tried to prise her arms open and she stubbornly resisted. 'What's the matter, Kitty? Why don't you like me seeing your body? Don't think I haven't noticed that you hide beneath the sheets whenever you can.'

His strength easily outmatched hers, and Kitty hung her head when he drew her arms down to her sides. 'I'm fat,' she burst out miserably. 'And it's not all due to being pregnant. I've always had curves, and I've never liked my body—not since—' She broke off and stared determinedly at the carpet.

Frowning, Nikos put a finger under her chin and tilted her face up. 'Not since what, *agape?*'

She shrugged awkwardly, sure that Nikos must be growing impatient with her. But when she looked at him she saw nothing but concern in his dark eyes, and she felt a sudden urge to confide in him.

'It's stupid, really,' she muttered. 'I went on a date years ago. My first date as it happens. My father had always been very protective, and I was ridiculously naïve. Anyway, my father persuaded me to go on a date with the son of one of his friends—I think Papa probably arranged it because he'd realised I was never going to find a boyfriend when I spent all my time in the library,' she told Nikos wryly.

'The evening was a disaster, culminating in my "date" assaulting me in the back of his car.'

'What do you mean by *assaulted*? Were you raped?' Nikos was shocked by the savage anger that coursed through him, and the surge of protectiveness that made him want to pull Kitty into his arms and simply hold her.

'No, no,' she assured him quickly. 'To be honest, I think he was too drunk. But he ripped my dress and…and touched me, and when I tried to stop him, he accused me of leading him on. He made me feel ashamed of my body, and I suppose I let the incident grow huge in my mind.

'When I met you, and we made love in the cave, I was pretending to be somebody else, and I forgot all my inhibitions…' She trailed off and stared at Nikos, and then said rather desperately, 'I really would be happier if we shut the blinds.'

He shook his head, and reached for her, drawing her gently against him so that her breasts were crushed against his chest while he threaded his fingers through her hair. 'Who was this friend of the family who violated you and shattered your self-confidence?' he demanded.

Kitty hesitated. 'Vasilis Sarondakos.'

'*Theos*! Sarondakos again! Pray for his sake that I never run into him, because my fist is itching to meet his face,' Nikos said grimly. 'But there are more subtle methods of retribution. I happen to know that Vasilis has spent the fortune he inherited from his grandfather and is desperately looking for a backer for his business venture. Wouldn't it be a pity if he failed to get the cash he needs?' he murmured with a cold gleam in his eyes that warned Kitty he would be a dangerous opponent in the boardroom. 'I'll call in a few favours with my banking friends.' He smiled at her, warmth replacing the icy anger that he felt for Vasilis.

'Forget Sarondakos and his spite, *agape*. You should be proud of your gorgeous body, not want to hide it away. Do you feel dirty or ashamed when I make love to you?' he asked softly.

Slowly, Kitty shook her head, afraid that if she admitted she felt nothing but desperate, searing desire when she was in his arms he would realise the effect he had on her.

He was stroking her hair, soothing the tension from her, and her heart missed a beat when he eased her away from him a fraction and cradled her breasts in his hands. 'I want to see the sunlight gild your body when I make love to you,' he said, his voice as soft and sensuous as crushed velvet. 'I want to watch your eyes darken when I touch you like this.' He brushed his thumb pads over her nipples and then rolled the taut peaks between his fingers, sending exquisite sensation shooting through her. 'And I want to see all of you, Kitty, every last delectable inch.'

Her skirt fluttered to the floor, and she heard him inhale sharply as his gaze roamed over her gossamer-fine stockings and stiletto heels, and the tiny scrap of white lace that covered her femininity. Her thick chestnut hair had fallen forwards, and he pushed it back over her shoulders and cupped her breasts again, his eyes gleaming hotly beneath his heavy lids.

'*Theos*, how can you doubt what you do to me?' he demanded rawly as his restraint gave way and he hauled her into his arms so that the throbbing force of his arousal pushed insistently between her thighs. He claimed her mouth in a fierce, hungry kiss, and somehow managed to strip out of his clothes and push her backwards onto the bed without taking his lips from hers.

In the sunlight his hair gleamed like black satin as he moved down her body, pausing to take each swollen nipple into his mouth while he dipped his hand between her thighs. She was wet and ready for him and arched her hips in mute supplication as he caressed her. He withdrew his finger and pushed her legs wider apart and she thought he would take her immediately, and her breathing quickened. Instead she gave a shocked cry when he bent his head and placed his mouth over her femininity, his tongue taking the place of his finger as he thrust it into her damp opening.

'Nikos...no!' Frantic with embarrassment she gripped his hair and tried to drag his head up, but he did not cease his intimate caress and soon she forgot everything but the molten heat of her desire and her spiralling need for his full possession. Just when she thought she could withstand no more, and teetered on the edge of orgasm, he moved over her and entered her with one forceful thrust, his erection so powerful that he had to pause while her muscles stretched to accommodate him. And then he moved again, quick and hard, each sure stroke building her pleasure until it was unbearable and she could feel the first spasms pulsate deep in her pelvis.

She almost cried out as wave after wave of sensation ripped through her, but some deep-held instinct for self-protection made her stifle her moans, and she closed her eyes so that he would not see the depth of her emotions as they climaxed simultaneously. He was the love of her life, she thought when they lay together while their breathing gradually slowed. After the incredible passion they had just shared it seemed impossible that he did not feel something for her, some small glimmer of affection that would give hope to her starving heart.

But when he rolled off her and gave a languorous stretch, his satisfied smile was that of a man who had just enjoyed fantastic sex that had left his body sated and his emotions untouched. He got up from the bed, and her eyes were drawn helplessly to him, her stomach dipping as she absorbed the masculine beauty of his lean, hard body, gleaming like bronze in the afternoon sunlight. She thought he was heading for the en suite, but he carried on out of the bedroom, returning minutes later with a slim velvet box in his hands.

'I bought you a present,' he murmured as he rejoined her on the bed.

'Another one?' she protested faintly, thinking of the numerous dresses, exotic underwear, and fabulous jewellery he had given her over the past few weeks. If he only knew it, she would swap all of them for the words she longed to hear from him. But she knew he would never say them. She was his wife, and the mother of his child, but she was not the love of his life, and she never would be. It was just a pity her aching heart could not accept that fact.

'Aren't you going to open it?'

Quickly she flipped open the box and stared at the necklace made up of dozens of square-cut diamonds that glittered like teardrops on the black velvet cushion. It was breathtaking, and, from her knowledge of jewellery from the Royal Collection on Aristo, mind-bogglingly expensive.

He was waiting for her to say something, but for some reason she wanted to cry and she bit down hard on her lip, her eyes blurring so that the diamonds seemed to fracture into a thousand sparkling shards. 'It's beautiful,' she choked, 'but you've already given me so much.' And yet of the things that mattered, so little. 'You don't have to keep buying me presents, Nikos.'

He lifted the necklace from the box and fastened it around her neck so that it lay cold against her skin. 'I like to buy you gifts,' he said with a shrug. 'I want you to know that I appreciate you.'

'Do you?' she asked cautiously, her heart trembling with fragile hope.

'Certainly.' His mouth curved into a sensual smile as he leaned back on the pillows to admire the diamonds at her throat. They had cost him the earth, but they were worth every penny when they were displayed in all their shimmering glory on her naked skin. 'Our marriage was not what either of us would have chosen,' he stated coolly, 'but we both acknowledge the responsibility we have towards the baby we created during a moment of madness. I think we have become friends as well as lovers, haven't we, Kitty? And I believe that our companionable relationship, based on mutual respect and trust, is the greatest gift we can give our child.'

Was that the reason he had made the effort to spend time with her—to befriend her and make her trust him? Was it all for the baby's sake? Of course it was, she acknowledged painfully. Their child would grow up in a harmonious environment with two parents who were polite and courteous towards each other as all good friends were. It should be enough. It would have to be enough. But it wasn't, and the loveless future that stretched before her suddenly seemed very bleak.

CHAPTER THIRTEEN

NIKOS felt the last spasms slowly drain from his body, and rested his head on Kitty's breasts. Her skin was velvet soft beneath his cheek and he inhaled the delicate, floral scent of her perfume. He was tempted to remain lying on top of her, their bodies joined, but after a few moments he rolled over and stared up at the ceiling, feeling the familiar frustration that, although sex with her seemed to get better and better, the distance he sensed between them was growing wider.

He did not like clingy women, he reminded himself irritably. He should be pleased that Kitty no longer cuddled up to him after sex and instead moved to her side of the bed as soon as their passion was spent, but perversely he wished that she were not quite so unmoved by their physical intimacy.

He propped up on one elbow as she swung her legs over the side of the bed. At least she was no longer shy about her body, and did not rush to cover up, he mused as he studied her voluptuous breasts and delightfully round bottom, and felt himself harden again. He knew he should have no complaints about their marriage. They got on well out of bed, and their sex life was amazing. So why did he feel as though something was missing—something elusive, that he did not understand, but seemed to be the cause of the curious flatness he felt inside?

She had been brushing her hair, and now it rippled down

her back like a river of silk. 'I thought we could host a dinner party next week,' she murmured as she set down the brush and turned to face him. 'We've been invited to several recently, and it's time we returned the compliment.'

'Fine—but it can't be next week,' he replied, thinking of the meeting that had been arranged at the last minute. 'I'm flying to New York on Sunday night and I'll be away until the following weekend.'

Kitty felt a stab of disappointment, and her voice was unwittingly sharp when she spoke. 'This is the first I've heard of your business trip.' She paused, and then added, 'I assume it is for business?' Shannon Marsh lived in New York. Was he planning on a reunion to catch up on old times? She instantly dismissed the idea. She trusted Nikos; he had married her because he wanted his child, and for the same reason he would remain faithful to her.

But she did not want him to go away. They had been getting on well recently, better than she had ever dared hope at the start of their marriage, and she was afraid that while he was away he might revert back to the old, cold Nikos. She wished he would suggest that she accompanied him to America, but maybe he thought she was too busy with her charity work? She hesitated, feeling a rush of nerves, and then murmured, 'Perhaps I could come with you?'

'Not this time, I'm afraid.'

His smile was meant to take the sting out of the words, but when all was said and done it was still a rejection, Kitty thought miserably.

'I'll be busy all week, and you'll get bored.' He saw the flare of hurt in her eyes and briefly contemplated changing his mind. But these were important negotiations, and she would be a distraction. If he was honest, the real reason he didn't want her with him was because he wanted some time to himself, Nikos acknowledged. She was in his mind a lot lately, more than he was comfortable with, and he needed to prove to himself that he could walk away from her any time he liked.

'Well—' Kitty dredged up a smile and tried to act as if it was no big deal '—another time, maybe?' But she was so hurt that she couldn't help being cool with him for the rest of the weekend, and he either didn't notice, or didn't care, because he made no comment when she turned away from him in bed on Saturday night, and, instead of pulling her into his arms as she longed for him to do, he rolled over and fell asleep, unaware that she wept silent tears into her pillow.

She had to stop this, Kitty told herself at the beginning of the following week—after she had bade Nikos a frosty goodbye and he had shrugged carelessly and walked out of the apartment without a backward glance. She had to stop longing for what he could never give her, and make the most of what she had—a charming, attentive, extremely virile husband who she knew was determined to make their marriage work.

But the days without him dragged, and although she kept herself busy with her work for the foundation she missed him desperately. He phoned every evening, but their conversations were stilted. The distance between them had nothing to do with the fact that they were miles apart; there was a subtle change in their relationship, and she was afraid she was losing the tenuous closeness she had sensed had grown between them.

But what was she expecting from him? she asked herself towards the end of the week, when his absence sat like a dull weight in her chest. She knew his history, and understood how terribly he had been damaged by his past. It was possible that he would never fully recover, yet she was still waiting for him to act like a knight in shining armour from the fairy tales she used to read, and go down on bended knee to proclaim his undying love for her.

Unlike him she had enjoyed a blissfully happy childhood

surrounded by love from her parents, brothers and sister. It was easy for her to love when she had never known pain and rejection. But instead of telling him honestly how she felt about him, she hugged her love for him to herself like a miser, and hid her emotions behind her pride.

Perhaps it was time to dismiss her pride and ignore that little voice in her head that whispered that in love stories the hero had to admit his love first. This wasn't a story, this was real life—and Nikos's life had been far from a fairy tale. The worst he could do would be to tell her that he would never love her in return, she told herself, feeling a flutter of fear in her stomach at that very likely prospect. Since he had married her he had shown her kindness and respect, and his faith in her ability to head the charitable foundation he had set up in honour of the woman who had befriended him had been a huge boost to her self-confidence.

Lost in her thoughts, she did not notice that Sotiri had come out onto the terrace with her breakfast until he halted by the table and gave a low whistle.

'Anastasia!'

Kitty followed his gaze to the portrait of Nikos's mother that had been delivered to the apartment that morning and was now propped on a chair. 'Was that her name? I didn't realise you knew her, Sotiri.'

'Sure thing—Nikos and I grew up on the same streets. His mother was a lovely lady; everyone liked her. It broke Nikos's heart when she died,' Sotiri said gruffly. 'Where did you get the painting?'

'I took a copy of the little photo on his desk and sent it to an artist on Aristo who has painted all the recent portraits of the royal family,' Kitty explained. 'Nikos had told me that the photo was his only memento of his mother, and I thought it would be nice to have a proper painting of her. The artist has done a good job and caught her likeness perfectly,' she murmured as she studied the painting. 'I was planning to give it to Nikos when he arrives home on Sunday—which I also happen to know is his birthday, although he hasn't mentioned it. Do you think he'll like it, Sotiri?' she queried, doubts forming when he continued to stare at the picture with a curious expression on his face.

He turned to her and gave her an intent glance. 'I think he'll be speechless, Miss Kitty.' He hesitated and then said quietly, 'He does have a heart, you know; he just keeps it well hidden.'

Kitty spent the whole of Sunday torn between excitement because Nikos would soon be home and dread because he might not like the painting, or her reason for giving it to him. She had learned from his secretary that his flight was due to land in Athens late in the afternoon. Sotiri had prepared a special dinner, and had left it ready for her to serve, and she set the table, added candles and flowers and placed the wrapped portrait on his chair.

After a long debate over what to wear she chose a simple gold silk gown, which was cleverly cut to disguise the pregnancy weight she'd gained on her hips and stomach, and had a low-cut neckline that she knew Nikos would approve of. She left her hair loose, the way he liked it, put on the diamond necklace that had been his last gift to her, and sprayed perfume to her pulse points, and then paced the apartment impatiently, her heart thudding.

But he didn't come home. As the evening ticked by her tension grew, and finally, when it seemed unlikely that his flight would be this late, she phoned his mobile.

'Angelaki,' he answered just as she was about to cut the call, and she frowned at the background sounds of music and female voices.

'Nikos, I was expecting you home hours ago.'

'Were you?' He sounded dismissive and vaguely surprised. 'I don't remember saying what time I would be home.'

'No, but I thought…' She trailed off. 'Are you back in Athens? Where are you?'

'The casino—I bumped into a couple of friends at the airport.' A woman laughed close to the phone. No doubt she was some blonde bimbo who was hanging onto his arm, waiting for him to finish his call to his wife, Kitty thought furiously. 'Don't wait up for me, *agape*. I could be a while.'

'Fine.' Her hands were shaking when she ended the call, and tears burned her eyes. She had spent the whole week looking forward to him coming home, but he couldn't have emphasised more clearly that he hadn't given her a second thought while he had been away, and was in no rush to see her again.

He had never given any indication that he wanted her to be anything more than his convenient sex partner and the mother of his child, she reminded herself bleakly. It was not his fault that she had fallen in love with him, and he would be astonished if he could see her now, with tears and mascara streaking her face as she threw herself on the bed and cried until her heart ached.

Nothing much had changed, Nikos brooded as he glanced around the casino. It was the same old crowd of die-hard bachelors grouped around the roulette table, the same vacuous girls flirting with any rich-looking man under seventy. This had been his way of life for years and he had never questioned whether or not he enjoyed it, he thought as he detached himself from a predatory blonde and walked towards the exit.

He didn't know why he had come here. But that was a lie, he acknowledged, raking a hand through his hair. He had come because he was scared to go home. Him—Nikos Angelaki—the toughest kid on the streets, the most feared adversary in the boardroom. He had known this churning feeling in his gut before; when he'd sat with his mother in the hospital and vowed he would earn the money somehow for her cancer treatment, and she had smiled her soft smile at him and said it was too late. He'd felt that same sickening sensation in his gut when he'd looked at Greta, spaced out on cocaine, and realised she was telling him the truth about his baby.

But this was a different feeling, and it had been gnawing away at him all week while he had been in the States missing Kitty so badly that he had only felt half alive. He had been blind for weeks, or maybe so afraid of what he could see that he had closed his eyes and ignored it. He couldn't ignore it any longer—or avoid her, he brooded as he stepped off the kerb and hailed a taxi. He didn't belong in the nightclubs and casinos; he belonged at home with his wife.

It was almost midnight when he walked into the apartment. He had expected it to be in darkness, and Kitty to have gone to bed, but a light glowed beneath the dining-room door. Frowning, he opened it, and stopped dead. Someone had taken great care with the table—but he doubted Sotiri had arranged the floral centrepiece or hung the birthday banner on the wall.

A faint noise from behind him told him he was no longer alone, and he jerked his head round to see Kitty standing in the doorway. She was wearing a shimmery gold dress that displayed a tantalising amount of her full breasts, and predictably desire surged through him. His gaze moved up to her face. Unusually she was wearing her glasses instead of her contacts, but he could see that her eyes were red-rimmed as if she had been crying.

'How was your trip?' she asked in a curiously flat voice.

'Successful.' He shrugged, unable to drum up much interest in the completion of a deal that a few months ago would have had him buzzing for days. He glanced back at the table. 'If I'd known you had planned for us to have dinner together I would have come home earlier.'

It was a fair point, Kitty admitted silently. But she had been afraid to tell him of her plans for his birthday in case he rejected her. 'It's your birthday,' she murmured, 'and you have a right to spend it how you choose.'

He gave a faint laugh. 'I'd forgotten it was my birthday until I walked in and saw the banner. The last birthday I celebrated was my sixteenth, before my mother died.' He looked at the wrapped parcel. 'How did you know it was today?'

'I looked in your passport.' Kitty tried to imagine him at sixteen: a boy on the threshold of manhood who less than a year later had been left without a single relative in the world. She groped for courage and smiled at him. 'Are you going to open your present?' she asked softly.

Nikos did not know what he was expecting, or why his heart was jerking unevenly in his chest. He couldn't actually remember having a surprise birthday present in his life, and he didn't know how to react. Kitty was watching him, and after a moment's hesitation he ripped off the paper and stared in stunned silence at the portrait, feeling an unfamiliar stinging sensation behind his eyelids.

'Do you like it?' Kitty could not bear the taut silence. 'The artist worked from a copy of the photo of your mother. I think he's done a good job, don't you?'

'I...don't know what to say.' His throat felt raw as the emotions he had suppressed for so many years burned a fiery path inside him. It was many long years since the woman captured so perfectly on the canvas had smiled at him and told him that she loved him, but as Nikos stared at the image of his mother he felt his heart crack open.

'Nikos?' His frozen stillness was not the reaction Kitty had hoped for and for a terrible moment she thought he was angry. But then he looked over at her and she saw his wet lashes, and the tension that had gripped her for the past few hours when she had been waiting for him to come home snapped. 'Oh, Nikos—*don't*!'

She flew to him and touched his face with trembling fingers. 'I never meant to upset you.'

'You haven't.' He fought to control the emotions that were coursing through him like a relentless torrent released from a dam. 'It's a wonderful present, Kitty. I can't believe you went to so much trouble.' He looked again at the painting and his eyes ached. 'Why did you?'

'Because I know how much you loved her.' She took a deep breath, her heart beating liked a trapped bird beneath her ribs. 'And because I love *you,* Nikos. With all my heart.'

'Kitty!' He placed the painting carefully on the table and then turned back to her and gripped her upper arms so tightly that his fingers bit into her skin. Was he going to shake her until she retracted her last statement? she wondered, her heart turning over at the hunted expression on his face.

'It's all right,' she assured him gently. 'I know you don't feel the same way about me. I think you loved Greta, and I understand that after what she did you would never want to love anyone again.'

Tears blurred her vision and misted her glasses, and when she took them off she missed the flare of emotion in his eyes. 'I fell in love with you that night in the cave,' she told him, her voice steady and fearless, although inside she was shaking, 'and although I tried hard to deny my feelings, I know I will love you until I die.'

She wished he would say something, even if it was the words of rejection she was expecting, but he continued to stare at her as if he had never really seen her before, and his thoughts were hidden behind his lashes that were still spiked with moisture.

'I have something for you, too.'

It was the last thing she had expected him to say, and she bit her lip when he suddenly released her and strode over to his briefcase. He handed her a square, wrapped package, and she took it with a sinking heart. At least it felt too heavy to be more jewellery, she thought numbly, hoping that she could manage to sound suitably pleased with his gift, when inside her heart was breaking that he hadn't made any response, bar shock, when she had told him how she felt about him.

'Open it, *agape*,' he said quietly. 'I am not good with the words, and I've had so little practice in saying what I need to say. But my gift may explain better.'

Startled by the distinct tremor in his voice she fumbled with the packaging, and as she tore off the paper her heart—time, the universe—seemed to stand still. Even without her glasses she recognised the familiar book from her childhood, and suddenly her heart began to beat very fast.

'*Russian Fairy Tales and Fables*—the book my father used to read to me,' she whispered, her voice sounding as if it came from a long way off. 'I can't believe it. It's the most wonderful present you've ever given me, Nikos. Where on earth did you get it?' And, more importantly—why? she wanted to ask. But she was too afraid of his answer to voice the question.

'One of the reasons I went to New York was to meet the private collector who owned it, and persuade him to part with it.' Nikos stroked her hair back from her face with an unsteady hand, and the emotion that blazed in his eyes made her catch her breath.

'I know how much you miss your father, and how special this book is to you. I want—' he swallowed hard, emotion still clogging his throat '—I want to be a good father to our child, Kitty. A father like you had—who reads stories every night and loves his child unreservedly.' He paused, and felt as though he were about to leap off a precipice, into the unknown. But then he looked into Kitty's soft brown eyes, saw the love there—her love for him—and he felt an arrow pierce his heart. 'But more important than that, I found the book because I didn't know how else to tell you that you are my life, Kitty, and all that I am, everything I have worked for, is meaningless without you.'

Kitty took a ragged little breath, not daring to hope that he meant the words he had uttered in his velvet-soft tone. 'You don't have to pretend…or say things just because you think I want to hear them. I understand how your past must have affected you, and made it impossible for you to ever trust another person…'

Nikos placed his finger lightly across her lips. 'I trust you, Kitty *mou*,' he said, and with the words came an indescribable feeling of release and joy as he had never known before. His wife was honest and open, brave, and heartbreakingly generous. Her love for him shone in her eyes and he felt it wash over him and cleanse him until he felt weak with relief and empowered by the strength of *his* love for *her.*

'I love you, Kitty.' He drew her into his arms—tentatively, as if she were made of finest porcelain and he was afraid she would break—and held her against his chest, feeling their hearts beat in unison. 'I think I probably fell in love with you when I mistook you for a waitress at the palace ball—and, certainly, after I had made love to you in the cave and you then disappeared. I tried everything to find you and if I had I would have hoped to have had a relationship with you.'

'You mean you were going to ask Rina to be your mistress?' Kitty queried, her eyes widening at his tender smile.

'It was all I could have offered, then,' he said, his voice low and aching with regret for the time he had wasted. 'I had vowed never to marry again, and certainly never to fall in love. But then I learned that there was a baby…and within weeks I had broken my first vow, and was fast on my way to breaking the second.'

'Oh, Nikos.' The expression in his eyes told her louder than any words that it was true—unbelievably, miraculously, he loved her. And because she understood how hard it must have been for him to admit his feelings to himself, let alone to her—and allow himself to be vulnerable and open to hurt—she loved him even more. Suddenly words were not enough, and she reached up to cup his face with her hands and brushed her mouth over his, emotion flooding through her when he responded instantly and kissed her with such sweet passion, such *love*, that tears slipped silently down her cheeks.

'Don't cry,' he pleaded as he lifted her and carried her down the hall. 'I never want to make you cry, Kitty *mou*.' But his eyes were wet too when he reached their bedroom and stood her by the bed while he drew down the zip of her gold dress and gently tugged the material until it fell in a shimmering pool at her feet.

'You are so beautiful, so soft and perfectly formed,' he whispered against her mouth as he removed the rest of her clothes, his, and drew her down onto the bed, covering her body with his own. 'After what happened with Greta and the baby I felt frozen inside,' he admitted rawly. 'And to be honest I was glad that nothing ever touched my emotions. I didn't want to care for anyone ever again, and I told myself I was happy dating dozens of women who meant nothing to me.

'I didn't want to marry you, and I certainly didn't expect to fall in love with you, but bit by bit you crept under my guard. You were so generous and giving, and although you had enjoyed a privileged upbringing you cared so much for others who have nothing. Sometimes I think you want to change the world,' he said softly, smiling down at her. 'You changed me, Kitty. You made me feel again, and you made me see that I was being a coward by denying how I felt about you, even though I was sure you could not love me when I had forced you to leave the home you loved, and your family. We will move back to Aristo if you want,' he offered. 'I want you to be happy, Kitty, and I realised during the week I was in the States that I don't care where I live as long as I am with you.'

She shook her head firmly. 'You belong in Athens, Nikos, and I belong with you. But I agree; it doesn't really matter where we are, as long as we're together—you, me, and soon the baby.' She traced her fingers over his jaw and the sensual curve of his mouth, and felt desire flood through her when his body stirred against hers. 'But, Nikos, do you think we could stop talking now?' she whispered against his mouth. 'So that I can show you how much I love you.'

And she did with such passion and generosity and the love that she no longer had to hide from him that Nikos's heart overflowed with the emotions he had denied for so long. And when he moved over her and joined them as one, it seemed to him that their souls as well as their bodies had fused, and he knew that the love they shared would last a lifetime.

* * * * *

*Read on for our exclusive interview
with Chantelle Shaw!*

We chatted to Chantelle Shaw about the world of THE ROYAL HOUSE OF KAREDES. *Here are her insights!*

Would you prefer to live on Aristo or Calista? What appeals to you most about either island?

I think I would prefer to live on Aristo—known as the jewel in the Mediterranean—because it has stunning scenery, fabulous beaches and fantastic shopping and nightlife. Who wouldn't want to live in a millionaire's paradise! But the wildness and beauty of the desert on Calista appeals to my romantic nature.

What did you enjoy about writing about The Royal House of Karedes?

I liked the fact that the stories and characters in The Royal House of Karedes are all interwoven, and yet at the same time I was given the opportunity to make the story line I was given my own. The locations and the fact that the stories were set around a royal dynasty meant lots of Harlequin Presents glamour, which was great fun to write!

How did you find writing as part of a continuity?

It was the first time I have written a continuity book, and rather daunting when some of the other authors are so much more experienced than me. But it was a great honor, and I enjoyed taking part. I can't wait to read all the other books in the series.

When you are writing, what is your typical day?

On a typical day I write from 9:30 a.m. until 3:00 p.m. while my children are at school. In the evening, after sorting out dinner, homework and after-school clubs, I often write for another hour or so, and I try to snatch some time at weekends, especially as my story develops and I want to know what will happen next.

Where do you get your inspiration for the characters that you write?

Inspiration for my characters is difficult to explain. They usually just come into my head and I know exactly what they look like—hair color, etc.—and usually they arrive with a name, but sometimes I look through a name book and one will jump out that I know instinctively is right for my character. I think about the character's background right back to childhood and I make loads of notes that I don't often use in the book but that help me to really know the person I am writing about. I also spend quite a lot of time thinking and researching the character's job, interests and talents.

What did you like most about your hero and heroine in this continuity?

I liked my heroine, Kitty, because she seemed a very real person, and like many of us she was insecure about her body and how she looked. Her lack of confidence made being in the public eye an ordeal for her, but despite her shyness she forced herself to carry out her royal duties. Her gentle demeanor hid a strong will and she also had a deeply compassionate nature. My hero, Nikos, seemed like a ruthless businessman and a playboy, but underneath, his vulnerability made me like him. He had developed a tough shell because he had been hurt by so many things in his past. Not knowing the identity of his father troubled him and made him feel as if he was only half a person—and later he had been devastated when he was cruelly betrayed by his first wife, whom he had loved.

What would be the best—and worst—things about being part of a royal dynasty?

The best thing about being part of a royal dynasty would be the glamorous lifestyle and the opportunities for travel. The worst would be constantly being in the public eye, with your every move scrutinized by the media (Prince William and Kate Middleton spring to mind).

Are diamonds really a girl's best friend?

Well, I have been married to my lovely husband for twenty-six years and I've never owned a diamond. When we got engaged all those years ago he couldn't afford an expensive engagement ring. Something sparkly would be nice—but he is definitely my best friend, and for me love is more important than 'things.'

The Future
King's Love-Child

MELANIE MILBURNE

Melanie Milburne says: 'One of the greatest joys of being a writer is the process of falling in love with the characters and then watching as they fall in love with each other. I am an absolutely hopeless romantic. I fell in love with my husband on our second date and we even had a secret engagement, so you see it must have been destined for me to be a Mills & Boon® author! The other great joy of being a romance writer is hearing from readers. You can hear all about the other things I do when I'm not writing and even drop me a line at: www.melaniemilburne.com.au.'

Dedicated to my beautiful daughter-in-law Dunya, who is one of the most courageous and loving young women I know. We are so delighted to have you as part of the family, it seems like you have been tailor made just for us.

Love you round the world and back. xxx.

CHAPTER ONE

CASSIE was just congratulating herself on getting through two hours of successfully shielding herself behind the Aristo palace's pillars and pot plants, dodging both the press and Prince Regent Sebastian Karedes, when she suddenly came face to face with him.

She swallowed thickly, her heart coming to a clunking stop in her chest as her eyes went to his inscrutable dark brown ones so far above hers. She opened her mouth to speak but her throat was too tight to get a single word out. She felt the slow creep of colour staining her cheeks, and wondered if he had any idea of how much over the last six years she had dreaded this moment.

'Cassie.' His deep voice was like a warm velvet glove stroking along the bare skin of her shivering arms. 'Have you only just arrived? I have not seen you until a few moments ago.'

Cassie moistened her dry-as-parchment lips with the tip of her tongue. 'Um….no,' she said, shifting her gaze sideways. 'I've been here all evening…'

A small silence began to weight the atmosphere, like humidity just before a storm.

'I see.'

Cassie marvelled at how he could inject so much into saying so little. Those two little words contained disdain and distrust, and something else she couldn't quite put her finger on.

'So why are you here?' he asked, his eyes narrowing even further. 'I do not recall seeing your name on the official guest list.'

Cassie swept the point of her tongue across her lips again, trying to keep her gaze averted. 'As part of my…um…parole programme, I took a job at the orphanage,' she said, loathing the shame she could feel staining her face. 'I've been working there for the last eleven months.'

When he didn't respond immediately Cassie felt compelled to bring her gaze back to his, but then wished she hadn't.

A corner of his mouth was lifted in an unmistakably mocking manner. '*You* are looking after children?'

She felt herself bristling. 'Yes,' she clipped out. 'I enjoy every minute of it. I'm here tonight with some of the other carers and educational staff. They insisted I attend.'

Another tight silence began to shred at Cassie's nerves. She would have given just about anything to have avoided coming here this evening. She had felt as if she had been playing a high stakes game of hide and seek all night, the strain of keeping out of the line of Sebastian's deep brown gaze had made her head pound with sickening tension. Even now the hammer blows behind her eyes were making it harder and harder for her to keep her manner cool and unaffected before him. His commanding and totally charismatic presence both drew her and terrified her, but the very last thing she wanted was for him to realise it.

She surreptitiously fondled the smooth pearls of the bracelet around her wrist, the only thing she still had left of her mother's, hoping it would give her the courage and fortitude to get through the next few minutes until she could make good her escape.

'Well, then,' he said as his eyes continued to skewer hers, that sardonic half-smile still in place. 'As the royal patron of the orphanage you now work for, I would have thought you would have made every effort to include yourself in this evening's proceedings rather than hide behind the flower arrangements.'

Cassie's chin came up. 'And have the press hound me for an exclusive photo and interview?' she asked. 'Not until my parole is up. Maybe then I'll think about it.'

His eyes began to burn with brooding intensity. 'I must say I am surprised you haven't already sold your story to the press, Cassie,' he said. 'But perhaps I should warn you before you think about doing so. One word about our...' he paused over the word for an infinitesimal moment '...past involvement, and I will have you thrown back into prison where the majority of the population of Aristo believes you still belong. Have I made myself clear?'

Cassie felt anger run through her like a red-hot tide. 'Perfectly,' she bit out, her eyes flashing with fury. How she hated him at that moment. The injustice she had suffered was bad enough, but to have him threaten her in such a ruthless manner was abominable. But until her parole was up what else could she do but pretend she had nothing to hide? She had learned the hard way that silence was her best defence—her *only* defence.

Sebastian was conscious of the time and the press of the crowd behind them. He had told his bodyguards to give him a few minutes but he knew they would come looking for him soon. His formal duties for the evening were more or less over and the crowd would soon begin to disperse. But he hadn't seen Cassandra Kyriakis for close to six years, and he had to make sure she was not going to be a threat to his future as King of Aristo now she was out of prison. They had parted on such bitter terms; he had been so blisteringly angry at the way she had ended their affair, and her betrayal still rankled even after all this time.

When he had caught sight of her disappearing behind one of the pillars he had thought he must have conjured up her image, so great was the shock and effect on him of seeing her again. It had taken every bit of the thirty-two years of his royal training to keep his reaction hidden. He had formally opened the gala, chatted with the official guests, smiled in all the right places, but all the while wondering how he could capture five minutes in private with her.

But now that he had, he wondered if it had been wise to seek her out. Every pore of his skin was erect with awareness, his nostrils automatically flaring in the primal hunt for her feminine scent, and his groin tightening with an ache so intense he had trouble standing still.

It annoyed him to find his body still hummed with desire for her. He had considered himself over her, and yet one glimpse into that emerald gaze of hers had made him realise there was still a place deep inside him that responded almost involuntarily when he looked at her. It was as if she had secretly planted a tiny fish hook in his chest all those years ago, and every time their eyes met he felt its tiny but still-painful tug.

For all her supermodel beauty there was no escaping the fact she was a sleep-around socialite tart who had wantonly led him on only to dump him, no doubt for the glory of having bedded a prince. He had met plenty of women like her before and since, but he had not seen her rejection and betrayal coming and that irked him more than he wanted to admit. No one had done that to him before. He had never had his pride rubbed in the dust like that, but then that was Cassie for you. She had come along with those amazing green eyes, her long, silky, blonde hair and sensually seductive wiles, and snatched the breath right out of his chest.

His eyes ran over her appraisingly. She was wearing a shell-pink sheath of a dress that clung lovingly to her willowy frame, highlighting the small but perfect globes of her breasts, skimming over the slight, almost boyish hips and the endless legs that had so many times wrapped around his in the throes of their heated passion. Her slender arms were bare, but on her left wrist she wore a pearl bracelet which he had noticed her fiddling with earlier with those slim fingers of hers.

Sebastian had to remind himself Cassandra Kyriakis had killed her father with those very delicate feminine hands. The lesser charge of manslaughter didn't make her any less of a murderess, or at least certainly not according to the press and public's view. But right now she didn't look capable of doing anyone harm. She looked nervous, agitated almost, her bottom lip being savaged by her small white teeth, and her body looked tense and ill at ease.

A little stab of guilt pierced him. His threat had perhaps been a little heavy-handed and ruthless, but he had to be absolutely sure she would keep quiet about their previous relationship. He would make it worth her while, although any dealings he had with her now would have to be conducted under the strictest secrecy. The press were like sniffer dogs when it came to the Karedes royal family and it would be risky even being seen talking to her, but it would be well and truly worth it if he could achieve what he wanted. He knew it just by looking at her. The old adage might have it that revenge was a dish best served cold, but the sort of revenge Sebastian had in mind was going to be hot—blazingly so, for he had a score to settle with her and he knew where it would be settled best.

In his bed.

A palace official approached, and Sebastian exchanged a few words with him, turning back barely thirty seconds later to find Cassie had completely disappeared. He narrowed his gaze and scanned the crowd, looking for a flash of baby-pink chiffon or platinum-blonde hair, but there was none.

'Are you looking for someone in particular, Your Royal Highness?' the junior official asked. 'I can organise security to find them for you if you like.'

Sebastian schooled his features into impassivity. There was only one aide in the palace he could trust with this sort of minefield situation, and this unfortunately was not him. 'No,' he said curtly. 'That will not be necessary.'

The young man gave an obsequious bow and moved away. It was only then that Sebastian saw the tiny bracelet lying on the floor where Cassie had been standing such a short time ago. He bent down and picked it up, his fingers absently stroking over the string of smooth orbs as he scanned the dispersing crowd once more.

As yet another official approached, Sebastian surreptitiously slipped the bracelet into his trouser pocket, inwardly smiling as he let the pearls slide through his fingers, one by one.

Cinderella might have escaped from the ball, but this particular Prince Charming was going to lure her back to him with something even more fitting than a glass slipper.

'Cassie, what's wrong?' Angelica, Cassie's flatmate, asked as soon as she came in. 'You look totally flustered. Is everything all right?'

Cassie closed the door and leaning back against it, pinched the bridge of her nose with two fingers, her eyes squeezed tightly shut in a vain effort to ease the tension about to explode behind her temples. 'No…no, I'm fine, just a headache.' She opened her eyes and, pushing herself away from the door, moved farther into the flat.

'Is Sam OK?'

'Of course he is,' Angelica assured her. 'He was a bit unsettled at first, but I promised him you would be back as soon as you could, and he eventually went to sleep and hasn't stirred since. I just checked him a few moments ago. He's out for the count.'

'That's good,' Cassie said, expelling a tiny breath of relief, although her stomach was still full of fist-like knots.

'You worry too much, Cassie,' Angelica admonished her gently. 'Sam's five years old now. He needs to learn to be away from you occasionally. You can't keep him tied to you for ever, you know.'

'I know. It's just he's never really got over being separated from me when I was in prison,' Cassie said, trying not to think of that harrowing time when Sam's desperate cries had echoed in her head for months after he was wrenched from her arms. She had been allowed to give birth to him inside the high walls of the Aristo prison and keep him with her until he turned three. Of all the suffering she had endured over the years that had been by far the very worst. Relinquishing Sam had felt like having one of her limbs torn off. She still had nightmares about it, waking up in a lather of sweat, in case someone had crept into the flat during the night and stolen her baby son away from her all over again.

'You're the one who hasn't got over it,' Angelica said astutely. 'Put it in the past where it belongs. You're on a roll now, Cassie. Your work at the orphanage is your ticket to a new life off the island once your parole is up. And, speaking of the orphanage, how did the fund-raising event go at the palace? Did you see Prince Sebastian? Is he as handsome as he looks in all the press photos?'

'Um…yes, he is…' Cassie felt her heart give a painful squeeze as she thought of that brooding, dark, all-seeing gaze. She had taken a huge risk leaving the gala so abruptly, but she couldn't have coped with another torturous minute in

Sebastian's company. The air between them had been charged with sexual energy; she had felt it as soon as she looked into his face. She had felt the slow burn of his gaze through the fine layers of her dress, as if he was recalling every intimate inch of her and how he had pleasured her in the past. A shiver travelled the entire length of her spine at the thought of how she had come apart time and time again in his arms. Had he guessed she still felt the same way? *Oh, please, God, don't let him have guessed!*

Her fingers automatically went to her left wrist, her heart giving a sudden lurch of panic when she found it totally bare. 'Oh, no!'

'What's wrong?' Angelica asked. 'You've gone as white as a ghost.'

Cassie swung around and backtracked her way to the front door of the tiny flat with agitated steps. 'I've lost my bracelet,' she said, searching the floor in rising desperation. 'My mother's pearl one. It must have fallen off on the way home. I was sure it was still on my wrist when I was at the palace.'

'Maybe it fell off in the cab,' Angelica suggested. 'You could call up the company and ask them to look for it.'

Cassie turned to look at her friend. 'I didn't take a cab home.'

Angelica's eyes widened. 'You walked home in the dark in *those* shoes?'

No, I ran home in the dark, Cassie felt tempted to confess but instead said, 'I felt like I needed the fresh air. The palace was crowded and…and stuffy.'

'I'll get a torch for you,' Angelica said. 'I'll mind Sam while you retrace your steps, or do you think we should wait until morning when we can both search?'

Cassie shook her head determinedly. 'No, someone might pick it up before then. I'll go a few blocks and see if I can find it. I'm sure it can't be too far away.'

'Make sure you take your mobile with you,' Angelica said. 'You don't know who might be out on the streets at this time of night. And you had better get changed. You are going to stick out like a sore thumb in that dress.'

Cassie quickly checked on Sam on her way to her room to change into a track suit and sneakers. He was sleeping peacefully, his beautiful face so like his father's it made her heart contract again in unbearable pain. Her little son would never be able to run to his daddy and place his arms around his neck; he would never be able to look him in the those deep brown eyes exactly the same shade as his for reassurance, or for the guidance and support she could already see he so desperately needed.

He had been cheated of so much, just as she had, but she was going to do her utmost to make it up to him. As soon as her parole period was up she and Sam would be off the island and begin a new life, a life where no one knew who Cassie was, what she had supposedly done and—even more importantly—whose child she had secretly borne.

CHAPTER TWO

THE cobbled streets were lit with the occasional lamp post but even so Cassie felt the menacing shadows of the night creeping towards her with every step she took. She shone the narrow beam of the torch Angelica had given her around, but so far she had found nothing but the occasional cigarette butt or gum wrapper. It made her think of her father, how he as the town mayor had orchestrated a campaign to clean up the ancient streets of Aristo, even though his own home had contained the most filthy of all secrets.

Cassie gave a little shudder and forced the memories back and continued on her mission, her head down, her steps carefully measured as she went as close to the palace as she dared.

She was no more than three blocks away when she suddenly came up short, her heart thudding in fear as a pair of large male sports shoes were illuminated by her torch. She brought the beam shakily upwards to find Sebastian Karedes, dressed similarly to her in a dark track suit, his eyes unreadable as they meshed with hers.

'Looking for something, Cassie?' he asked.

Cassie had never imagined there would be a time in her life when she would have rather met a mugger on a dark street than the man she had once loved with all her being. She had faced fear before, many times, gut-wrenching fear that most people thankfully never had to face. But this was something else again. Sebastian had the power to destroy her in a way even her father hadn't been able to do. Everything she had fought so long and hard for seemed to be hinged on these next few moments. The tension built in her spine; she could feel it moving up vertebra by vertebra, a vicelike grip that made her stomach crawl with the long spidery legs of apprehension.

'I...I seem to have lost my bracelet,' she said, lowering the torch. 'I thought if I retraced my steps I might find it.'

'You left without saying goodbye,' he said. 'I was hoping for a few more minutes with you in private. There are some things I would like to discuss with you.'

Cassie turned off the torch with her thumb in case the soft light showed the fear on her face. 'I'm not sure it's such a good idea for us to be seen anywhere together, Sebastian,' she said. 'You know what the paparazzi are like. You are about to be crowned as King. It would not do your reputation any favours being seen talking with an ex-prisoner.'

'There is no one about now,' he said. 'We could go back to your place. We would not be disturbed there, I am sure.'

Cassie was glad he couldn't see the way her eyes suddenly flared in panic. Sam was not the deepest of sleepers. He still occasionally wet the bed, which made him wake up distressed and call out for her. 'No,' she said, far too quickly. 'I mean... it's awkward...I...I have a flatmate.'

'A man?'

'No.'

'You have no present lover?'

Cassie felt the fine hairs on the back of her neck start to prickle at the seemingly casually asked question. Unless she turned the torch back on she had no way of reading his expression, and even then there was no guarantee she would be able to decipher what motive lay behind his query. Sebastian was a master of disguising his feelings, if indeed he had any. She had often wondered if his aloofness and slight air of condescension were a guise or an innate part of his personality. She had never quite made up her mind either way. He had been trained from a young age to step up to the throne upon the death of his father, which had occurred only a few months ago. That he was prepared to risk being seen with her was as surprising as it was deeply disturbing.

Cassie knew she was at risk of revealing too much. She could feel it now even under the cloak of darkness. The pulse of her blood was like thunder in her veins, her breasts felt tight and sensitive, and that secret feminine place he had possessed so many times throbbed with a hollow ache that was almost painful.

'I've been seeing someone,' she lied, hoping it would put an end to the undercurrent of attraction she could feel coming towards her.

'The same person you were seeing when you ended our affair?' he asked with bitterness sharpening his tone.

'No...someone else.' *Oh, how easily the second lie followed the first,* she thought.

'How serious is your relationship with this man?' he asked.

'Serious enough.'

'Serious enough to risk your freedom?'

Cassie dropped the torch, but even as she heard it clatter its way over the cobblestones she was unable to move. 'W-what are you suggesting?' she asked in a dry croak.

He bent down and retrieved the torch and, flicking it on, shone it on her face. 'How about we go back to my private quarters and discuss it?' he said.

Cassie blinked against the probe of the torch's beam. 'I am not sure there is anything we have to discuss,' she said, 'or at least nothing of interest to me.'

'On the contrary, I think it will be of the greatest interest to you,' he said, and turned off the torch with a click that sounded portentous in the still night air. 'You see, Cassie, I have something of yours.'

Yes, well, so do I, Cassie thought wryly, once again glad of the mantle of darkness so he couldn't read the apprehension on her face. 'My bracelet?' she asked hopefully. 'Do you have it with you?'

'No, it is at the palace.'

Cassie wondered if he was telling the truth, but she could hardly ask to search him. She gnawed at her lip for a moment. 'Could you have someone send it to me in the post?' she asked.

'Not unless you want to take the risk of it being mislaid or perhaps even stolen,' he said. 'I would prefer to hand it over to you face to face. It looks rather valuable.'

'It is,' Cassie said, her heart sinking as she realised she would have no choice but to accompany him back to the palace. They had met in secret so many times in the past, just the thought of doing so again conjured up so many intimate images. She wondered if Sebastian was revisiting any of them in his own mind.

'Come.' He placed a firm hand at her elbow. 'There is a back entrance to the palace a couple of blocks from here.'

Cassie reluctantly fell into step beside him, her flesh burning under the touch of his hand. They walked in silence, she because she didn't know what to say and he—she assumed—because he was waiting until he had her somewhere secluded to discuss whatever he had planned for her. That there was a plan she was in no doubt. Proud men like Sebastian Karedes did not take rejection on the chin, and her rejection of him had been particularly cruel.

Sebastian led her through a wrought-iron gate where an aide was waiting. They exchanged a brief exchange before the man led the way to a suite of rooms down a long, marbled corridor. The walls were lined with generations of the Karedes family; all their eyes seemed to be following Cassie as she walked soundlessly by Sebastian's side.

The aide opened a door leading into a private lounge. The furniture was modern and, although the palace was centuries old, somehow the mix of old and new worked brilliantly.

'So, Cassie,' Sebastian said once the aide had closed the door on his exit. 'This is like old times, is it not?'

Cassie searched his features for a moment but couldn't read his inscrutable expression. 'I'm not sure what you mean,' she hedged, although her mind had already taken a wild guess.

He reached out and lifted her chin with the blunt end of one of his long fingers. She felt a shiver of reaction cascade like a shower of exploding fireworks down her spine at that jolt of skin-to-skin electricity passing from his body to hers. It had always been this way between them. The air in the room was charged with the electric tension of sexual attraction. She could see it in the dark, brooding intensity of his gaze; she could sense it in the sensual curve of his mouth and, God help her, she could feel it in the core of her body where her intimate muscles were already starting to ache.

'You and I always met in secret, did we not?' he said, looking down at her mouth for a pulsing moment. 'I see no reason to change that now.'

Cassie stepped back out of his light but eminently disturbing hold, her legs almost tripping over themselves in her haste to put some distance between her body and his. 'You are surely not suggesting we resume our illicit affair?' she said in a brittle keep-away-from-me tone.

He gave a little shrug. 'We were good together, Caz,' he said, using the private nickname he had chosen for her all those years ago. 'You know we were.'

Cassie wanted to cover her ears and block out the sensual lure of his deep velvet-toned voice. God, did he have any idea of how he still affected her? How could he possibly think she had forgotten how good they had been together? The moment she had set eyes on him again it had been as if the faint background pulse in her body she had done her best to ignore had suddenly come to fervent life again. It was thumping now beneath her skin, so strong and heavy it made her feel dizzy.

She had been *so* strong for all this time. Now was not the time to fall apart. Not now when she was so close to final freedom. She had just a matter of weeks to go until her parole period was finished. Once that time was up she would leave Aristo with Sam, making a new life for them both. This was not the time to be drawn back into Sebastian Karedes's sensual orbit, no matter how very tempting it was.

Cassie pulled back her shoulders and sent him a glittering glare. 'You seem to be forgetting something, Sebastian. We ended our association six years ago.'

'You ended it, Cassandra. I did not,' he said with an unmistakably embittered edge to his voice.

Cassie lifted her chin even higher. 'I *can* still call you Sebastian, can't I, or would you prefer Your Royal Highness? Should I have bowed or curtsied when I ran into you on the street? How very remiss of me.'

Something moved at the side of his mouth as if her words had pulled on a tight string beneath the skin on his jaw. 'Sebastian will be fine,' he said through tight lips. 'At least while we are alone.'

This time it was Cassie's mouth that went tight. 'I do not intend being alone with you in future,' she said with a deliberately haughty look. 'Please give me back my bracelet. I need to get home.'

His eyes burned into hers. 'You are forgetting yourself,

Cassie,' he said. 'That is not the way to speak to a member of the royal household. I will dismiss you when I see fit, not the other way around.'

'What are you going to do about it, Sebastian?' she asked, throwing him another mocking glare. 'Lock me up in the palace tower and throw away the key? I'm sure I'll institutionalise rather quickly considering where I've spent the last few years, don't you agree?'

He held her gaze for an interminable pause but Cassie was determined not to look away first.

She could *do* this.

She could stand here and fire back at him without breaking down.

She *had* to do this.

His expression was nothing short of contemptuous as he held her look. 'Your anger towards me is rather misplaced, Cassie,' he said. 'You were the one to bring an end to our affair by flaunting a host of lovers in my face. If anyone has a right to be angry it should be me.'

Cassie gave herself a mental kick. He was right. She had told him a parcel of lies in an attempt to get away from the island, never dreaming it would backfire on her the way it had.

'Is that not correct, Cassie?' he prompted again with steely purpose.

She pressed her lips together and lowered her gaze from the searing probe of his. 'Yes...' she said. 'That is correct.'

'Is that who you are rushing off to return to now?' he asked. 'One of your many lovers? No doubt you are keen to make up for lost time, *ne?*'

Cassie now understood what it felt like to be hoist with one's own petard and it wasn't particularly comfortable. 'There is just the one person I care about now,' she answered.

There was a short but tense pause.

'Do you intend to marry this man?' he asked.

Cassie brought her eyes back to his. 'No, I do not.'

She saw the disdain in his gaze as it warred with hers, and, although he didn't say the words out loud, she could hear them ringing in the stiff silence.

Whore.

Slut.

Jailbird.

'I want to see you again,' Sebastian said with a masklike expression. 'Here, tomorrow, for lunch, and do not think about saying no.'

Cassie felt her eyes go wide and struggled to control her escalating panic. 'I-I'm working at the orphanage t-tomorrow,' she stammered. 'We're short staffed as it is. I can't just breeze out for lunch.'

His stance was implacable. It was clear in the months since his father had died Sebastian had become accustomed to having each and every one of his words obeyed. 'I will have my personal secretary notify the head of the orphanage that you have an official appointment at the palace.'

Cassie gave a tight swallow. 'What will the press make of that if they hear about it?' she asked.

'They will not hear about it from me,' he said. 'If on the other hand you get it in your pretty little blonde head to inform them yourself, I have already warned you what will happen if you do.'

She glared at him in fury. 'You think you can blackmail me, don't you?'

He gave her an imperious smile. 'If you want your bracelet back, then, yes, I am sure I can blackmail you to do whatever I want.'

Cassie clenched her hands into fists. 'You bastard,' she ground out bitterly.

'Careful, Cassie,' he warned her silkily. 'I don't think a charge of common assault will go down too well right now with your parole officer, will it?'

Right now Cassie felt as if it would be worth it just to slap that arrogant look off his too-handsome face. 'I am going to ask you one more time,' she said in a cold, hard tone. 'Give me back my bracelet.'

He held up his hands above his head. 'Come and get it,' he said, nodding towards his left-hand trouser pocket.

Cassie felt her heart skip a beat at the challenging glint in his dark eyes. She pulled in a breath, and with a hand that was nowhere near as steady as she would have liked, slipped it tentatively into his pocket. Her belly quivered as she felt the distinctive swell of his body against her searching fingers, but there was no bracelet. She pulled out her hand and sent him a fulminating look.

'Try the other one,' he said with an inscrutable smile. 'I must have forgotten which side I put it.'

Cassie sucked in another furious breath and a little less cautiously this time dug her hand into his right pocket, but before she could locate the circle of pearls his hands came down and held hers against his now pulsing full-on erection. Her eyes flew to his in shock, the erotic feel of him even through the layers of fabric making her heart race out of control.

'How much do you want your bracelet?' he asked, his eyes now almost black with diamond-hard purpose.

She felt him surging against the palm of her hand and her stomach turned over, every pore of her flesh crawling with a desire so overwhelming she was sure he could sense it. 'What exactly are you asking me to do, Sebastian?' she asked in a brittle tone. 'Get down on my knees and service you like the whore you think you can make me?'

His pupils flared, making his eyes even darker, like bottomless pools of ink. 'If anyone has made you a whore it is yourself,' he said. 'I know the game you are playing, Cassie. You deliberately left that bracelet behind this evening, did you not?'

Cassie threw him a withering look. 'That really would have been casting pearls before swine, now, wouldn't it?'

He pulled her hands away from his body, bracketing her wrists either side of her body in a movement so sudden she felt every last breath of air rush out of her chest. 'I must say I like this new hard-to-get game you are intent on playing,' he said, pressing his hardened lower body into the softness of hers. 'It makes me all the more determined to have you.'

Cassie's gaze went to his mouth, her stomach doing a quick flip-flop as she realised his intention. But instead of pulling out of his hold, she pressed herself closer as his mouth came down to hers.

It was an angry kiss, a kiss of built-up resentment and bitterness, but even so she couldn't stop herself from responding to it. His tongue didn't ask for permission to enter her mouth, it demanded it, thrusting between her trembling lips with an intention that was as deeply erotic as it was irresistible. His mouth ground against hers, drawing from her whimpers, not of protest but of pleasure. Her body moulded itself against his, seeking his hardness, thrilling in the feel of his arousal, her heart racing at the thought of the dangerous game they both were playing.

One of his hands slid beneath her track-suit top, his warm palm rediscovering the weight of her bra-less breast. Cassie's belly contracted when he took her nipple between his thumb and index finger, the gentle pinch and pull caress making her breathless with desire.

Her hands went on their own journey of rediscovery, pulling his T-shirt free so she could feel his skin beneath her palms. She felt the heavy thud of his heart against her hand, before she took her hand lower to feel the shape of him through his track pants. She heard him groan as she stroked his length, and she increased the speed and pressure of her caresses.

He lifted his mouth off hers to place it hot and moistly over her breast, sucking on her, not too hard, not too soft, but enough to have her senses spinning madly out of control.

He pulled her hand away from his body and looked down at her with his eyes blazing with desire. 'So it is the same for you as it is for me,' he said. 'Six years has done nothing to change the chemistry between us.'

Cassie wanted to deny it, but her hand was still tingling where she had touched him, so instead she said nothing.

He brought up her chin and pressed a brief hard kiss to her mouth. 'You can have your bracelet back tomorrow,' he said. 'I will give it to you after we have lunch together.'

'That's blackmail.'

Sebastian gave her a nonchalant smile. 'No,' he said. 'That is a promise.'

He watched as her mouth tightened. 'My bracelet is valuable to me, but not enough to lose my self-respect,' she said. 'If I sleep with you again it will be because I want to, not because I have been forced to.'

Sebastian held her fiery look for a moment. It was a sweet salve to his pride to know she still wanted him. He could take her here and now, he could see it in her eyes, the way they kept flicking to his mouth, her tongue sneaking out to her lips to taste where he had been. But he wanted to keep her dangling, just as she had done to him in the past.

'All right,' he said, moving away to the other side of the room where a desk was situated. He unlocked one of the drawers and, taking out her bracelet, came back to where she was standing.

He took her right hand and laid the pearls against the soft

bed of her palm, then gently closed her fingers over them, one by one. 'I think you should have the safety catch repaired before you wear it again,' he said, his eyes meshing with hers.

Cassie swallowed as his eyes burned into hers, their sensual promise heating her blood all over again.

'If you do not turn up tomorrow as arranged, Cassie, I will come to the orphanage and fetch you myself,' he said with a glint of steel in his gaze.

Cassie felt something small and dark scuttle inside her chest cavity. Would he do it? Would he draw such attention to himself or was he calling her bluff? How could she risk it either way? 'I-I will be here,' she said, slipping her eyes out of reach of his.

He touched her briefly on the curve of her cheek with the tip of one finger. 'See you tomorrow, Cassie,' he said, and reached for the bell to summon his aide. 'I am already looking forward to it.'

Within seconds Cassie was being driven home, her chest feeling as if a headstone had been placed inside it, making it hard to pull in a breath. She looked back at the glittering ancient palace as the dark car growled like a panther as it ate up the cobbled streets, and suppressed a little shiver.

Until tomorrow…

CHAPTER THREE

SAM'S little hand suddenly clutched at the front of Cassie's uniform, his eyes huge in his stricken face. 'You're c-coming back again, aren't you, Mummy?'

Cassie squatted down to his level and looked deep into his troubled gaze. 'Yes, sweetie, of course I am.'

His expression was still white with worry. 'You're not g-going to be locked away like before, are you?'

Cassie suppressed a frown as she hugged him close. She had always tried to be as honest with him as possible without distressing him with details too difficult for him to understand. After all, it seemed pointless pretending the fifteen-foot-high barbed wire and concrete enclosure of the Aristo prison was some sort of luxury accommodation, but she had never gone into the sordid details of why she had had to be housed there. But it made her wonder who had been talking to him about her past and why. He was only just five years old. Apart from her flatmate and close friend, Angelica, he was with her all the time at the orphanage. But it was clear someone had said something to him, or perhaps he had overheard some staff members talking.

'Baby, that was a long time ago and it's never going to happen again, I promise you with all my heart,' she said, holding him gently by his thin little shoulders. 'I am never going to be separated from you again. *Never.*'

Sam's chin wobbled slightly and his stammer continued in spite of his effort to control it. 'I heard Spiro t-talking to one of the carers,' he said. 'He said you k-killed my grandfather, and that you said it was an accident, but no one believed you.'

Cassie bit down on her bottom lip. She had naively hoped this conversation was several years away, but the gardener at the orphanage had never liked her since she had spurned his advances a few months ago. But that he would discuss her past with one of the children's carers was reprehensible to say the least. She loved her job. She *needed* her job. It wasn't just the money—the wage was hardly what anyone would call lucrative; it was the fact that for once in her life she was able to give something back to those in need. She had misspent her youth, wasted so many precious years being seen at the right parties with the right people, turning into a glamorous coat hanger for the 'right' clothes, mouthing the vacuous words that marked her as a shallow socialite looking for a good time.

The more her prestige-conscious and controlling father had protested, the more outrageous she had become. Cassie hadn't needed the prison psychologist to tell her why she had behaved the way she had. She had known it from the very first time she had realised what her birthday represented. It was certainly not a date to be celebrated, but she hadn't realised the sick irony of it until she had faced the judge and jury.

Cassandra Kyriakis had not just killed her father, but on the day she had come into the world she had taken her mother's life as well.

Cassie hugged Sam close to her chest, breathing in the small-child scent of him, her heart swelling with overwhelming love. 'We'll talk about this when I get back and Mummy will explain everything. I won't be away long, my precious,' she said. 'I'm just having a quick lunch with…with a friend.'

Sam eased back in her hold to look up at her. 'Who with, Mummy? Have I met them?' he asked.

Cassie shook her head and gently ruffled the black silk of his hair. 'No, you have never met him,' she said, her heart aching at the thought of her little boy never knowing his father. She had never known her mother and often wondered if her life would have been different for her if she had.

'He's a very important person on Aristo,' she added. 'He is soon to be the king.'

Sam's eyes were like wide black pools. 'Can I give you a picture to take for him to hang at his palace?' he said. 'Do you think he would like that?'

She smiled at him tenderly, her heart squeezing again. 'You know something, sweetie, I think he would.'

He scampered over to his little wooden desk and brought back a coloured drawing of a dog and a cat and something she thought looked like a horse. 'If he likes it I can do another one and you can give it to him the next time you see him,' he said with a shy smile.

'That's a great idea,' Cassie said and, folding the picture neatly, put it in her handbag. She didn't like to tell her little son she didn't intend seeing Sebastian again. Instead she got to her feet and, holding his hand, led him back to Sophie, one of the chief carers at the orphanage. She bent down and gave him another quick hug and kiss, and, while Sophie cleverly distracted him with a puzzle she had set out, Cassie quietly slipped out.

The palace was no less intimidating in the daylight than it had been the night before. With commanding views over most of the island, including the resort and Bay of Apollonia and the casino and the Port of Messaria, the royal residence was much more than a landmark. Every time Cassie had seen those twinkling lights from the prison on the western end of the island she had thought of the richness of Aristo as a kingdom and how Sebastian's father, King Aegeus, had built it up to be the wealthy paradise it was today.

It was only as Cassie came up to the imposing front gates that she realised Sebastian hadn't given her instructions on how to gain access. But she need not have worried, for waiting at the entrance was the aide, Stefanos, who had been present the previous evening. After a quick word to the guards on duty he led her through the palace, using a similar route to the night before, but this time taking her to a sitting room overlooking the formal gardens of the palace.

'The Prince Regent will be with you shortly,' Stefanos informed her and closed the door firmly on his exit.

Cassie let out her breath in a ragged stream and looked to where a small dining table with two chairs had been assembled in front of one of the large windows.

The door opened behind her and she turned to see Sebastian enter the room. He was wearing charcoal-grey trousers and a white open-necked shirt, the cuffs rolled back casually past his wrists. It didn't seem to matter what he wore, he still had an imposing air about him, an aura of authority and command that only added to his breathtakingly handsome features.

'I am glad you decided to come,' he said into the silence.

'I figured the orphanage is not quite ready for an impromptu visit from royalty,' Cassie said, thinking on her feet. 'The press attention might have upset the children.'

He frowned as he came closer. 'Seeing you at the gala last night was a shock,' he said, looking down at her. 'A big shock.'

'Did you think I had escaped from prison and had come to

gatecrash your party?' she asked, not quite able to subdue the bitterness in her tone.

He gave her a long and studied look. 'No, Cassie, I did not think that. It was just that I wish I had been told you had been released.'

'You could have made your own enquiries,' she pointed out and, with another embittered look, tacked on, 'discreetly, of course.'

A two-beat silence passed.

'You are very bitter,' he observed.

'I've lost almost six years of my life,' she bit out. 'Do you know what that feels like, Sebastian? The world is suddenly a different place. I feel like I don't belong anywhere any more.'

'You killed your father, Cassie,' he reminded her. 'I am not sure what led you to do that, but the laws of this island dictate you must pay for that in some way. There are many people on Aristo who feel you have been given a very lenient sentence.'

'Yes, well, they didn't know my father, did they?' she shot back without thinking.

His frown deepened. 'Your father was well respected in all quarters. What are you saying...that he was not the private man we all knew in public?'

Cassie wished she could have pulled her words back. She had revealed far more than she had intended to. She had told no one of her father's behaviour over the years. Who would believe her if she had? It was a secret, a dirty secret that she alone had lived with. Shame had always kept her silent and it would continue to do so. Besides, she hadn't done herself any favours behaving like a spoilt brat for most of her life. Her father had played on that for all it was worth, publicly tearing his hair out over her behaviour to all his well-connected friends and colleagues.

Cassie quickly averted her gaze, and, shuffling in her bag,

drew out the picture Sam had drawn in a desperate attempt to change the subject. 'Um…I almost forgot to give you this,' she said, handing it to him with fingers that made the paper give a betraying rattle. 'One of the…er…orphans drew it for you. He insisted I give it to you.'

He took the picture and gently unfolded it, his eyes taking in the childish strokes of pencil and brightly coloured crayons. 'It is very…nice,' he said and brought his gaze back to hers. 'You said this child is without parents?'

Cassie looked at him blankly for a moment.

'Um…well…I…he's…'

'The child is a boy?'

'Yes.'

'And an orphan.' He looked back at the drawing, his brows moving together over his eyes. 'How old is he?' he asked, looking back at her again.

Cassie felt as if his eyes were burning a pathway to her soul. 'He's…five or thereabouts,' she said, shifting her gaze once more.

'Too young to be all alone in the world,' Sebastian said with deep compassion in his tone. 'Do you know anything of his background, where he came from, who his parents were or what happened to them?'

The hole Cassie had dug for herself was getting bigger by the moment. She could feel the fast pace of panic throughout her body, making her heart thump unevenly and her skin break out in fine beads of perspiration, some of which were even now beginning to trickle down between her shoulder blades.

'Cassie?'

'Um…' She brushed a strand of hair off her face as she returned her eyes to his, the stutter of her heart painful in her chest. 'I'm not sure of the details of every individual child's

background. All I know is the children at the Aristo orphanage are there because they don't have anywhere else to go.'

Sebastian laid the picture on a sideboard as if it were a priceless work of art. 'I am very touched that a small abandoned child
would take the time to do this for me,' he said in a tone that was
gravel-rough. 'I have lived with nothing but privilege all my life
so it is hard for me to imagine what it must be like to have no
one you can turn to, especially when one is so young.'

Damn right it is, Cassie silently agreed.

He turned and looked directly at her. 'I would like to meet
this child,' he said. 'I would like to thank him personally.'

Cassie felt as if her eyes were going to pop out of her head
and land on the carpeted floor at his feet. She looked at him
in abject horror, her mouth opening and closing like a stranded
fish, her heart going so hard and fast it felt as if it were going
to come through the wall of her chest. 'I—I'm not sure that
can be arranged,' she stammered.

He gave her a frowning look. 'I fail to see why not. After all,
I am now the royal patron of the orphanage. It is only reasonable and fair that I give my support in ways other than financial.'

'Y-yes, but showing preference for one child over another
is not to be advised,' Cassie said, relieved she could think of
something reasonably plausible on the spot. 'The child who
sent you this drawing is one of many who long to be noticed.
You would be doing more harm than good singling any one
of them out over another.'

His gaze was still unwavering on hers. 'What if I were to
invite all the children to a special party at the palace?' he suggested. 'That way no one will feel left out.'

'Um…I…I…' she choked as her self-made petard gave her
another sharp poke.

'At the gala it occurred to me that the most important people were not at the event—the children themselves,' he went

on. 'I had a word to my events secretary about arranging something last night.'

Cassie was still trying to get her voice to cooperate. 'Um…is that such a good idea?' she asked. 'The kids might be a little intimidated by the palace… I mean, royal protocol is off-putting enough for adults…'

'My father had a hands-off approach when it came to the organisations he put his name to,' he said. 'I intend to do things differently, and what better place to start than the orphanage right on the palace doorstep?'

'It's hardly on the doorstep,' Cassie said. 'It's practically attached to the prison.'

He rubbed at his jaw for a moment. 'Yes, that is true. But that is something I would like to discuss with you over lunch.' He pulled out one of the chairs next to the small dining table. 'Would you care to sit down?'

'Thank you,' Cassie said, immensely glad of the seat as her legs were still trembling out of control.

She watched as he took his own seat, his longs legs brushing against hers under the table. She drew in a quick, unsteady breath and moved her legs back, but she could still sense the heat and strength of his in close proximity to hers.

Sebastian rang a small bell, and within seconds the aide appeared pushing a trolley with several covered dishes as well as iced water and a bottle of chilled white wine.

Cassie sat fidgeting with the neck of her uniform as the aide served them both the light lunch of char-grilled octopus and a Greek salad and fresh crusty rolls.

'Would you care for some wine, Dhespinis Kyriakis?'

'No…thank you,' she said. 'Water will be fine. Thank you.'

'Thank you, Stefanos,' Sebastian said once his wine and Cassie's water had been poured. 'Has a date been confirmed for the event we discussed?'

'Yes, Your Highness,' Stefanos said and handed Sebastian a slip of paper. 'Your diary has been cleared.'

Sebastian glanced down at the date on the paper before he folded it and slipped it into the breast pocket of his shirt. 'That was very efficient of you, Stefanos,' he said. 'Well done.'

The aide bowed respectfully and left the room, closing the door softly but firmly behind him.

Sebastian picked up his glass of wine, twirling it in his hand for a moment as he centred his gaze on Cassie. 'You do not drink alcohol any more, Cassie?' he asked.

Cassie looked at the tiny condensation bubbles clinging to the outside of his crystal glass and wondered if she would ever be able to look at alcohol again without feeling shame. In the past she had done so many things while inebriated she would never have done normally. She cringed at the thought of how she had come across to so many people, Sebastian included. She had always been the life of the party, laughing and care-free as drink after drink had been consumed. Her worries had lessened with every mouthful and, even though the head-aches the next morning had been unpleasant, she had been prepared to put up with some discomfort for the temporary reprieve the consumption of alcohol had given her.

She was suddenly conscious of the stretching silence and Sebastian's steady dark gaze on her. 'I lost my taste for alcohol while I was in prison,' she said quietly. 'I haven't touched it since.'

'That is probably a good thing,' he said. 'I don't drink as much as I did when I was young. I guess we have grown up, *ne?* A glass of wine at lunch or dinner is plenty.'

'Do you ever see any of the gang we used to hang around with?' Cassie asked once they had commenced eating the de-licious salad.

'The brat-pack?' he asked with a ghost of a wistful smile.

Cassie nodded, thinking of the hip crowd and the hangers-on they had associated with six years ago. She could almost guarantee she had been the only one to end up with a criminal record. The others were like Sebastian, out to have fun until family duty called. Not like she, who had been looking for something to take her mind off what she couldn't quite face...

'I see a few of them, of course, do business occasionally with them,' Sebastian said, and then smiled. 'I do not see so much of Odessa Tsoulis. Last I heard she had married a billionaire from Texas.'

Cassie felt a small smile tug at her mouth. 'She was rather intent on landing herself a rich husband, if I recall.'

'Yes, indeed,' Sebastian said with a small laugh. 'She was good fun. I liked her. She was very no-nonsense if you know what I mean. What you saw was what you got.'

'Unlike me.' Cassie wasn't sure why she had said it, much less how she was going to deal with it now it was said. She looked away from his suddenly penetrating gaze, and, picking up her fork with a tiny rattle against the plate, resumed eating, but with little appetite.

'Tell me about it, Cassie,' he pressed her gently. 'Tell me what happened that night.'

Cassie stared at one of the octopus curls on her plate and wished herself a thousand miles away. Why couldn't he leave the past where it belonged? What good did it do to haul over the ice-cold coals of regret? She couldn't change anything. That had been the problem in the first place.

She couldn't change anything.

'I'd rather not talk about it,' she said, and put her fork down with another little clatter against the edge of the plate.

'Did you have an argument or something?' he asked.

'Or something,' she said with a curl of her lip. 'I said leave it, Sebastian. It's done with. I don't like being reminded of it.'

'It must have been terrifying for you to be carted off to prison like that,' he said, clearly determined to keep pressing her.

Cassie gave him a resentful look. 'I didn't happen to see you in the crowd to offer me your support.'

His expression darkened. 'Would you have accepted my support if I had offered it?' he asked. 'You told me never to contact you again, remember? In any case I went abroad for several months after you ended our affair. I didn't hear much about what was going on and no one in my family thought to tell me because they didn't even know of our involvement. By the time I got back my father had already warned Lissa never to contact you and had packed her off to university in Paris before she could utter a single word of protest.'

'So when you did get back you let me rot in prison because you didn't want your father to find out we'd had an affair,' she said bitterly.

'Wrong!' He was only a decibel or two away from shouting the word at her. 'Cassie, why can't you see this from my point of view?'

Cassie got up from the table, pushing in her chair with such force it sent a shock wave through his wineglass, the alcohol spilling over the edges and onto the crisp white tablecloth. 'Oh, I can see this from your point of view, all right,' she snipped at him. 'A few months ago I was just yet another nameless person locked away in prison. Someone from your past you didn't dare speak about, much less step forward and defend. Now you find I am one of the key players at the orphanage you want to support, so you think it might be timely to pour oil over troubled waters to mollify me enough to maintain your reputation in case I spill all to the press about our little clandestine affair.'

'I care nothing for my reputation,' he ground out with a flintlike flash of his dark eyes. 'It is my family I am concerned about. I owe it to the generations of Karedes who have gone before me to act in a manner fitting for a future king.'

She rolled her eyes at him. 'So I guess that's why we aren't having lunch where everyone can see us, right, Sebastian? To maintain your family's honour.'

His brow was still deeply furrowed. 'I was thinking of your safety. I told you last night there are still many people in the community who think you should have got life in prison.'

'I did get life!' Cassie said, closer to tears than she had been in years. 'Do you think this is ever going to go away? I am marked for life as the daughter who killed her father. I see the way people look at me. They even cross to the other side of the road rather than look me in the eye. Don't tell me I haven't already been punished enough. Just don't tell me.'

He stepped towards her but she moved away, holding up a hand like a barrier to ward him off. 'Please…' She was close to begging and hated herself for it. 'Give me a moment…*please*…'

Sebastian clenched his hands to stop them reaching for her. He wanted to comfort her, to tell her things would improve now she was free, but he wasn't sure she wanted to hear such platitudes from him. In any case, he wasn't entirely sure they held any truth. But he'd also wanted to tell her how deeply shocked he had been to hear of her father's death and the charge of murder she had been landed with. He could not believe his Caz could have done such a thing. But then he hadn't thought her capable of the black-hearted deceit she had informed him of the day prior to her father's death.

She had gone from his bed to one of her many lovers, probably laughing about him behind his back the whole time. His gut still churned thinking about it, even after all this time. She wasn't the person he had fallen in love with. He realised in hindsight the person he had loved was a fantasy he had constructed in his head. He had been a fool not to see her for what she was. She had acted the part of the devoted lover so easily and he had fallen for it. She was like a chameleon, changing constantly to fit in with the company or each situation she found herself in.

But who was Cassandra Kyriakis now? She had spent five years in prison and another eleven months on parole, an experience any young woman would find life-changing, hopefully even reforming in some way. In any case, her days of living off her father's wealth were long gone. Theo's estate had been divided up between distant relatives, leaving Cassie virtually penniless. While her father had been alive, Cassie had spent his money as if entitled to every euro of it.

Each time Sebastian had dared to bring up the subject of her taking a career or job of her own she had laughed in his face, telling him she was having a perfectly fine time living the life of a socialite.

Cassie appeared to enjoy her work at the orphanage now, but what would happen when her parole period was up? Sebastian had had enough trouble adjusting to living constantly in the public eye, but how much worse would it be for Cassie with the shame of her father's death hanging over her?

CHAPTER FOUR

CASSIE composed herself with an effort and resumed her seat at the table as if nothing had happened. She picked up her glass of water and drank several mouthfuls, conscious of Sebastian looking at her with a frown beetling his brows.

She set her glass back down. 'You said you had something to discuss with me over lunch about the orphanage,' she reminded him coolly, and pointedly looked at her watch, making it clear she was on a strict time line, and, more to the point, he was not important enough to her to adjust it to accommodate him.

He came back to the table and sat down, his expression still brooding. 'You switch it on and off like magic, don't you, Cassie?' he said.

She sent him an indifferent look without answering.

'Damn it, Cassie, for once in your life show me you're human,' he growled at her. 'You never let anyone get close to you.'

Cassie clenched her hands into hard fists of tension in her lap and glared at him across the table. 'What do you want me to do, Sebastian? Weep and wail and gnash my teeth? Would that make you feel better? To think I'm an emotional wreck, crippled by guilt and unable to resume my place in the world?'

His eyes travelled over her face, pausing for a moment on

the tight line of her mouth before locking on her flinty gaze. 'I am not sure what I want from you, to tell you the truth,' he said heavily.

'Perhaps that's why you invited me here,' Cassie went on in the same resentful and embittered tone, 'to have a gawk at me, a real-life prisoner. I guess not too many prince regents get the opportunity to have a private meeting with an ex-criminal.'

His mouth tightened. 'It's not like that at all, Cassie,' he said.

'Then what is it like, Sebastian?' she asked. 'Why am I here?'

He held her feisty look, his dark gaze sombre. 'I wanted to see you again. To make sure you are all right.' He released a breath in a small sigh and added, 'I guess to see if you had changed.'

Cassie cocked one eyebrow at him. 'And what is your verdict?'

He surveyed her features for several seconds, each one seeming like an eternity to Cassie under his ever-tightening scrutiny.

'It's hard to say,' he said at last. 'You look the same, you even sound the same, but something tells me you are very different.'

'The correction services people will be very glad to hear that,' she quipped without humour. 'What a waste of public money if my incarceration hadn't had some effect on my rebellious character.'

His eyes held hers for another moment or two. 'You still don't like yourself, though, do you, Cassie?'

Cassie forced herself to keep her gaze trained on his, but it cost her dearly. She felt her defences crumbling and hoped she could hold herself together until she was alone. 'I am quite at home with who I am,' she said. 'Like a lot of people, I have things I don't like about myself, but no one's perfect.'

'What don't you like about yourself?'

She chewed on her bottom lip and then, realising he was

watching her, quickly released it. 'I don't like my…er…feet,' she said, suddenly stuck for an answer. 'I have ugly feet.'

His mouth tilted in a smile. 'You have beautiful feet, *agape mou,*' he said. 'How can you think they are not?'

'I think they're too big,' she said. 'I would like dainty feet like my mother had. I found a pair of her shoes one day but I could barely get my big toe in. She was so beautiful, so petite and elegant.'

'I saw one or two photographs of her in your father's office when I accompanied my father one time,' he said. 'She was indeed very lovely, but you are exactly like her.'

Cassie picked up her water glass so she could break his gaze. 'I sometimes wonder if we would have got on…you know…if she had lived.'

'I am sure you would have enjoyed a close relationship,' he said. 'There is something about a mother's love. My mother is much softer than my father ever was. He ruled with an iron fist but my mother was an expert in shaping our behaviour with positive attention and positive and loving feedback.'

'She must have taken your father's death very hard,' Cassie said and, biting her lip again, added, 'I am sorry I didn't express my condolences to you before now. I should have said something last night.'

'Do not trouble yourself,' he said. 'It was a dreadful shock, yes, especially as it happened on the night of my mother's sixtieth birthday party.'

'Yes, I heard about that,' she said, looking up at him again. 'A heart attack, wasn't it?'

He gave a grim nod. 'All my life I have been groomed for the position of taking my father's place when he died. I have developed a strong sense of duty as a result. This island is my home. The people who live here are my people. The only thing

I am having trouble with now is I did not expect the responsibility to be passed on quite so soon.'

'Yes…yes, of course,' she said softly.

'But enough about that for now,' he said with a stiff smile that didn't quite involve his eyes. 'I wanted to talk to you about the orphanage. It seems an odd position for it to be located next to the prison, don't you think?'

'It is, but there's never been any problem as far as I know,' Cassie said. 'And with the prison having its own crèche it makes it easier for female prisoners with babies and young children to have them on site with them.'

A frown wrinkled his forehead. 'You mean there are some women who have children in prison with them while they serve their sentence?'

Cassie kept her eyes on his even though she could feel her face heating. 'Yes…but only until the child is three years old. After that they are usually fostered out until the mother's sentence comes to an end.'

'But is prison really the best place for an infant or toddler?' he asked, still with a frown in place.

'The best place for any small child is with its mother,' Cassie said. 'The child hasn't done anything wrong. Why should it be separated from its mother at such a young and vulnerable age?'

'Is that what happened to the little boy who drew me that picture?'

Cassie lowered her eyes and reached for her water glass again. 'I told you I'm not familiar with every child's circumstances, but, yes, it could well be that he has been taken away from his mother and that he had nowhere else to go. Relatives are not always well placed to take on someone else's child, especially a child whose mother is serving time in prison.'

A small silence fell into the space between them. Cassie

could hear it ringing in her ears, her heart thudding so loudly she could feel the blood tingling in her fingertips where she was holding on to her glass. She forced herself to relax, making her shoulders soften from their stiffly held position, taking a moment to concentrate on breathing evenly and deeply to establish some semblance of calm.

'I am uncomfortable with the notion of an infant under three being housed along with violent criminals,' he said. 'The same arrangement would not for a moment be considered in a male prison.'

'Yes, that is true, but there are very good reasons for that,' Cassie said. 'For one, almost ninety per cent of female prisoners are jailed for non-violent crimes. They are far more commonly in for drug abuse or drug-related offences to feed their habit. They are very often the victims of childhood abuse and fall into the no-win cycle of drugs to help them cope with the devastation of their lives. Also, people now recognise the important bonding that goes on with an infant and its mother.'

'You grew close to some of those women?' he asked, appearing genuinely interested.

'It is hard not to in such a confined place,' Cassie said, thinking of the lifelong friends she had made, including Angelica. 'The loss of dignity hits hard, not to mention the loss of freedom. Counting the days off the calendar can be a very lonely task unless you have someone to talk to.'

'Will you be able to move on from this?' he asked softly.

'I would like to think so,' she said with a small measure of carefully nurtured confidence. 'Once my parole is up I want to leave Aristo and start afresh.'

'What will you do?'

'I am a bit limited given my criminal record,' Cassie said. 'Not many employers want an ex-prisoner on their books. But I would like to study. I wasted my time at school so the thought of doing my leaving certificate again is tempting. After that, who knows? As long as it brings in enough money to put food on the table for us…I mean, for me, I'll be happy.'

'I heard your father did not leave you well provided for.'

Cassie gave him a twisted look. 'No, funny that, don't you think? He left everything he owned to some distant cousins twice removed. He must have known I was going to push him down the stairs that night.'

'What happened, Cassie?' he asked again, looking at her intently.

Cassie dropped her gaze from his. 'We argued,' she said in a flat emotionless tone. 'I hardly remember what we argued about now—it all seems so muddled and foggy in my head. He was shouting at me, I was shouting back at him and then…' She closed her eyes tight, mentally skipping over that distressing scene until she felt she had control again. She reopened her eyes and carried on as if discussing the weekend weather. 'Suddenly he was lying at the foot of the staircase with a head wound.'

'What did you do?'

'I panicked,' she said, frowning as she forced herself to re-member what had happened next. 'I tried to get him to stand up. I thought he was putting it on just to scare me but he…' she swallowed '…he didn't…he didn't wake up…'

'So the police came and arrested you?'

She shook her head. 'Not at first. They treated it as an ac-cidental death, but a few weeks later one of the neighbours came forward and testified to hearing us arguing that night. Apparently that was enough to set the ball rolling. Within a few hours I was handcuffed and dragged off to give a state-ment. I pleaded guilty to manslaughter early the following day.' *Because I didn't have the strength to fight after being hounded and questioned for hours by the police and no one would believe me if I told them the truth in any case,* Cassie added silently. The interview room had been full of her father's cronies. What chance had she had to clear her name?

'It must have been terrifying for you,' Sebastian said, his voice sounding as if it had been dragged over something rough. 'You were only eighteen years old.'

'It is over now,' she said. 'I have many regrets over how things were handled, but the police were only doing their job. My father was a high-profile man. People wanted their scape-goat and I was it.'

'What are you saying, Cassie? That you were forced into confessing to a crime you did not commit?' he asked with a heavy frown.

Here's your chance, Cassie thought. *Tell him what it was like. Tell him everything.* She even got as far as opening her mouth but the words wouldn't come out. If she told him about her father she would have to tell him about Sam. What if Sebastian and his family decided she was not a good enough mother for a royal prince? Sam had already been wrenched out of her arms when he was little more than a baby; he would be devastated to have it happen again, even though he was close to school age. If he was taken away from her a second time her devastation would be complete. The only reason she had survived the hell of the last six years had been because of her love for her little boy. To have come this far and lose him at the last hurdle was unthinkable.

'Cassie?'

'No,' she said, addressing his left shoulder rather than his all-seeing gaze. 'No, of course I wasn't forced. I understood what was going on and agreed to accept the lesser charge of manslaughter.'

'Did you have good legal representation?' he asked.

Cassie thought of the sleazy lawyer she had been assigned.

During each of the long drawn-out weeks of the trial he had looked at her as if she had been sitting there naked, his snake-like eyes sliding all over her, reminding her so much of that last altercation with her father she would have agreed to a charge of murder if it had meant she could be free of the lawyer's loathsome presence all the sooner.

'I had a lawyer,' she said tonelessly. 'We didn't exactly hit it off, but beggars can't be choosers, right?'

Sebastian felt another knifelike twist of guilt assail him at her tone. He knew there was a lot she wasn't telling him, but he could read between the lines enough to know a competent lawyer should have been able to get her off given her age at the time. What if she had acted in self-defence? Surely she shouldn't have been punished under those circumstances?

But then he thought of the rumours that had been going round at the time of Theo Kyriakis's death. Rumours of Theo's increasing despair over his wayward daughter's drug and alcohol problems. Sebastian knew about Cassie's drinking but he had never seen her using or acting under the influence of drugs. That didn't mean she hadn't been using them, of course. Drug addicts were notoriously adept at keeping secrets. She could easily have popped any number of pills when he wasn't with her. Their time together had been limited in any case. Keeping their relationship a secret had been his idea; he hadn't wanted the interference of his overbearing father, not to mention the ever-present paparazzi.

Once Sebastian had found out about Cassie's betrayal he'd had good reason to be glad their relationship had been such a closely guarded secret. It had been bad enough imagining her laughing at him, let alone the whole population of Aristo. But even so, sometimes he wondered if he had done the right thing.

He had never mentioned it to anyone, but Theo Kyriakis had often struck Sebastian as a little too suave and smooth talking for his liking. He couldn't quite put his finger on it, but there had been something about the man he hadn't warmed to as others—including his father—had done. For instance, if Theo had been such a loving and concerned father, why on earth had his will been written in such a way unless he had known Cassie was going to kill him, as she had hinted at only moments ago? It didn't make sense. What made even less sense was why the lawyer defending her hadn't pointed that out at the time.

'How are you managing for money now?' Sebastian asked.

A glitter of pride flashed in her gaze as it met his. 'I'm fine. I have what I need for…for myself.'

Sebastian wondered if she was telling the truth. There was something about her that suggested she was more than a little uncomfortable in his presence. She never used to shift her gaze and gnaw at her bottom lip in that restive manner. But then perhaps her time in prison had made her wary of people. It was understandable considering what he had heard about life in prison. He didn't like to think about what she must have suffered. There was no secret about the violence and rivalry behind bars, even in women's prisons. Drug use was rife, vicious hierarchies existed and corruption amongst guards was commonplace. No wonder she was edgy and unable to relax even for a moment.

She looked at her watch and got to her feet. 'I have to go,' she said. 'My lunch hour is almost up.'

He intercepted her before she had even picked up her purse off the floor. 'No, Cassie,' he said, placing one of his hands over her forearm. 'I have not finished talking to you yet.'

Cassie looked down at his tanned fingers lying across her bare arm and gave an involuntary shiver. Those hands had taught her so much about passion. They had explored every contour of her body. And for close to six years she had dreamt

of how it would feel to have them touch her again. The way
he had touched and kissed her last night had made her all the
more vulnerable to him. She didn't have the courage to look
at his face, for she was sure he would see the longing there in
her eyes. She ached with it; it was like a taut thread in her body,
tightening unbearably every time she was near him, pulling
her inexorably closer to him.

'Look at me, Cassie,' he said into the thrumming silence.

She swallowed and slowly brought her eyes to his. 'I really
have to go, Sebastian,' she said. 'Some of the younger children have naps after lunch and I always read to them. They
will become agitated if I'm not there.' She took a tiny swallow
and added, 'I don't like letting them down.'

'I told my secretary to inform the director you would not
be back until three at the latest.'

She narrowed her eyes at him. *You did what?*

His fingers moved down her arm to encircle her wrist,
bringing her closer to his hard, tall frame. 'I cleared my diary
so we could have this time together.'

'You had no right to interfere like that!' Cassie said, tugging at his hold to no avail. She felt herself climb yet another
unstable rung on the ladder of her panic. She could see her
little son's worried face at the window, waiting for her. She
could hear the nervous staccato of his speech as he asked
Sophie or Kara where his mummy was. She could even see
the puddle on the floor and his wet pants, which would
distress Sam even though he couldn't help it during times of
acute stress.

'Why all the fuss?' Sebastian asked, still holding her firmly. 'Surely you have earned a couple of hours off?'

Cassie tried to prise off his fingers but he placed his other
hand over hers, a move she had no hope of counteracting. She
gulped in a ragged breath as she brought her eyes to his. His

dark eyes became even darker as they centred on her mouth, the touch of his fingers going from firm and restraining to gentle and tantalisingly sensual. The drugging movement of his thumb on the underside of her wrist caused the slow but inexorable melt of her bones and what was left of her resistance. The blood in her veins became hectic under the rapid-fire beat of her heart. Her stomach felt hollow, her legs felt weak and her breathing became shallow and uneven as his warm breath skated over the surface of her lips as his head came down...

The first brushlike stroke of his mouth on hers was tentative, even a little hesitant, a bit like a goose feather, so soft she wondered if she had imagined it. The second was firmer, with a hint of growing urgency, but the third tasted of desire hot and strong, rocking Cassie to the core. She opened her mouth to the searching glide of his tongue, her insides turning to jelly when that deliciously erotic contact was made. The kiss became more urgent, more passionate, more out of control and she was swept away with it. It felt so wonderful to be held in his arms again, to have his hands at her waist, holding her trembling body against the heat and strength of his. He was hard and getting harder as every second passed, the hollow ache in her body echoing the pounding of his blood against her.

His hands moved from her waist to the small of her back, bringing her closer to his surging heat. Cassie felt her body moisten and her stomach did another dip and dive at the thought of how it had felt with him deep inside her in the past, the rocking motion of their bodies bringing them to the ultimate moment in human pleasure. It was like a craving he had started within her and no one else could ever satisfy it but him. The thought of sharing her body with anyone else was abhorrent to her and had been from the first time she had experienced pleasure in his arms. She had resigned herself to a lifetime of celibacy, never dreaming that one day he would come back into her life and want her again.

He lifted his mouth off hers, his eyes blazing as they locked on hers. 'I want you and I intend to have you again even if it is only for one night. Think about it, Cassie. One night to remember for the rest of our lives.'

'This can't happen, Sebastian,' she whispered hoarsely even as she felt her body sway towards him. 'You know it can't. We were worlds apart before. Now we live in different universes.'

He traced the outline of her cupid's bow with the tip of his index finger. 'My head is telling me that but not the rest of me. Why do you do this to me, Cassie? Have you cast a spell on me?'

'Please don't make this any harder than it already is,' she pleaded with him. 'Let me go, Sebastian, before we do something we will not just remember, but quite possibly regret for the rest of our lives.'

He cupped her face in his hands, locking her gaze with his. 'No one needs to know about it but us.'

Cassie's heart gave another head-spinning lurch. 'You're really serious about this…'

His thumbs began caressing the twin curves of her cheeks, his eyes so dark she couldn't see his pupils. 'I want you, Caz. I still want you. As soon as I saw you at the gala last night I knew I would not rest until I had you again. After we kissed…well, that confirmed to me that you felt the same.'

'Sebastian…' She tried to inject some implacability to her tone but she wasn't sure she quite pulled it off. 'There are lots of things in life people want but it doesn't mean they can have them. This will never work between us. You're the Prince Regent of Aristo and I am…well, you know what I am… everyone knows what I am…'

'What does it matter what you are or what you have done?'

he asked. 'This is about here and now, not the future. I cannot offer you marriage, you know that, and, if what you said in the past is true, you don't want me to. I am offering you an affair to satisfy our needs, that is all.'

Cassie dipped out of his hold and put some distance between them. 'This is crazy, Sebastian.' She rubbed at her upper arms as if warding off a chill. 'You kept our relationship a secret last time but only just. The threat of exposure was constant. How much worse will it be now? Everyone watches your every move. The paparazzi are like ants at a picnic. The guards you surround yourself with could so easily be bribed for a price on your comings and goings. You are no longer in a position to control your public life, let alone your private one.'

'I have ways and means to keep some aspects of my life absolutely private,' he countered. 'I have chosen my personal staff very carefully. They would not betray me. I am absolutely sure of it.'

'This…this thing between us is just about sex,' she said in rising frustration. 'Do you have any idea how that makes me feel?'

He gave her an ironic look. 'Feelings, Cassie?' he said. 'What is this? What happened to the I-just-want-to-have-fun-without-strings Cassie Kyriakis of the past, hmm?'

She never existed in the first place, Cassie said to herself and dearly wished she could say it out loud. She had constructed a fantasy to keep people from seeing the real Cassie. Who would want the real deal? Even her father, her only living relative, had not been able to look at her without hatred and disgust glittering in his eyes.

'I want different things now,' she said, trying to control the slight wobble in her voice. 'I have spent a long time thinking about where I went wrong. I don't want to make the same mistakes this time around.'

A glint of resentment lit his gaze as it pinned hers. 'So you consider your involvement with me back then as a mistake?'

Cassie thought of her little son. *Their* little son. How could she regret the one good thing, the *only* good thing that had come out of their short-lived and secret relationship? Sam was everything to her. He was her saviour, her reason for living. She could never, not in a million years, regret anything to do with how he was conceived. 'No…' she said at the end of an expelled breath. 'I went into our relationship with my eyes wide open.'

'Not to mention your legs.'

She flinched as if he had struck her. 'I beg your pardon?'

'Come on, Cassie,' he said with a derisive look. 'You were no blushing virgin when you leapt into my bed.'

She ground her teeth as she fought to contain her temper. 'That's a rather sexist thing to say. You had plenty of experience yourself, if I remember correctly.'

'But still not enough for you,' he said with a cutting edge to his tone. 'You had God knows how many other men lining up to pleasure you. You gave me a list of names, remember?'

Each and every lie she had ever told seemed determined to backfire on her one way or the other. The only thing she could do was to paper over her previous lies with more lies and hope to God he never discovered the truth. 'I am not particularly proud of my behaviour back then,' she said stiffly, 'but you never gave me any indication you were developing more serious feelings for me. I thought we wanted the same things—fun without strings.'

'It started that way, yes, but you had a rather bewitching way about you, Cassie, that made me want more,' he said. 'I was going to tell you but you got in first with your announcement that you wanted out.'

Cassie stared at him, her heart sinking at the thought of

what she had inadvertently thrown away. Why hadn't he given her some clue earlier? She had never for a moment suspected he was falling for her. He had been very passionate and attentive, yes, but as for showing any sign of developing stronger feelings... Oh, dear God! What cruel twist of fate had led them to this torturous impasse?

The silence stretched and stretched to the point of agony.

'Aren't you going to ask me, Cassie?' Sebastian said.

She shook herself out of her frozen state. 'Ask you w-what?'

His top lip curled sardonically. 'The question women always ask in situations such as this.'

Cassie pressed her lips together as she struggled with her see-sawing emotions. 'OK, then...' She took an unsteady breath and asked him even though she knew it would not help her to know, but rather would only make it a thousand times worse. 'Do you still have feelings for me?'

He stood looking at her for a long time before answering. Cassie wondered if he was still making up his mind. But in the end she wasn't all that surprised by his answer—heart-wrenchingly disappointed, yes, but not a bit surprised.

'I do not love you,' he said. 'Do not mistake physical desire for more noble feelings. There is nothing noble or indeed proper about what I feel for you now, Cassie. I want an affair with you to get you out of my system before I take up the reins of duty. I will be expected to marry and to marry well. I believe someone has already been earmarked as a potential bride.'

Cassie felt as if he had plunged a serrated fishing knife deep into her chest. She wanted to bend over double to counteract the pain but only pride kept her upright and rigid. 'Oh, really?' she said in a disinterested tone. 'That certainly takes the legwork out for you, doesn't it? Just think—no hours wasted flirting, no money thrown away on flowers and meals at exclusive restaurants. Lucky you.'

His eyes were dark slits of brooding anger. 'This is not over, Cassie,' he said. 'Not by a long shot. I would not have brought you here if I did not believe you want the same thing as I do. You betrayed it to me last night when you returned my kiss.'

'Yes, well, that's only because I haven't been kissed for a long…' Cassie stopped and bit her lip, suddenly realising she had just tripped over one of her very own lies…

CHAPTER FIVE

SEBASTIAN came across to where she was standing, and, taking her chin between his thumb and index finger, lifted her face to meet his gaze. 'So there is no current man in your life,' he mused. 'What other lies have you told me, hmm?'

Cassie felt her heart kicking erratically behind her chest wall. Her mouth dried up, her throat locked tight and her breathing came to a shuddering halt. 'Just that one…' she said, mentally calculating how many falsehoods she had told him within the space of less than twenty-four hours.

'I wonder what other little secrets you are keeping,' he said, still holding her gaze with the piercing scrutiny of his. 'Like where you live, for instance.'

Cassie swallowed. 'Where I live is no secret.'

'If so, then why was it when Stefanos dropped you at your house last night you failed to enter it but slipped out of sight up a lane before he could follow you?'

'Um…I…'

He smiled at her knowingly. 'Are you frightened Aristo's future king might call around for a spontaneous visit, hmm?'

You bet I am, Cassie thought in stomach-lurching dread. 'I'm sure you are far too busy to make house calls to commoners, much less ex-criminals,' she said, her tongue darting out to moisten her bone-dry lips. 'Besides, you wouldn't dream of drawing press attention to yourself in such a way.'

His thumb began stroking the underside of her chin, back and forth in a movement that was as potent as a mind-altering drug. 'I am tempted to risk it,' he said, looking at her mouth. 'For you, *agape mou,* I think I would be tempted to risk a great deal.'

Cassie felt another shock wave of reaction roll through her. 'You don't mean that…' she said. 'You hate me for…for betraying you. Why would you risk your reputation and your credibility for someone like me?'

He picked up a strand of her hair and tucked it behind her ear. 'Why indeed?'

'Sebastian…' she said raggedly as she put a hand on his chest to hold him back.

His much larger and broader hand covered hers, almost swallowing it whole. 'One night, Caz,' he said in a husky voice. 'Just give me one night.'

Cassie scrunched her eyes tightly shut to ward off the overwhelming temptation of being in his arms again. 'Sebastian…' *I want to, oh, how I want to!* She was so dangerously close to confessing. How could he not see it? The temptation he was dangling in front of her was overwhelming. To have one night with him, one night to keep her going for the rest of her life would be a glimpse of heaven.

'Look at me, Cassie,' he said softly but no less commandingly.

She slowly opened her eyes. His were impossibly dark and surprisingly soft; as if somewhere deep inside there was a part of him that had not yet exchanged his love for her for hate. Would one night reawaken everything he had felt for her in the past? Or would it do as he hoped and expunge her from his system once and for all?

'You're asking too much,' she said in a scratchy whisper. 'Way, way too much.'

'I want to feel it again, Cassie,' he said, running his hands down her bare arms to encircle her wrists. 'Remember what it was like between us?'

Cassie remembered too well, that was half the trouble. Hardly a day went by when she didn't think of the explosive magic she had felt in his arms. She had not known her body could respond so feverishly and so uninhibitedly until he had made her his. Her one brief foray into physical intimacy with another lover when she was seventeen had nowhere near prepared her for the cataclysmic response Sebastian's touch evoked. Even now with his long fingers curled around the slender bones of her wrists she felt the power and potency of him through the fine layers of her skin. She ached with the memories of his lovemaking, the way he had made her beg for release at times; she had almost screamed at him, tearing at him with her fingers until he had thrust her through the door to physical paradise. Oh, the pleasure she had felt in his arms! Shivers skated down her spine as she recalled just even one erotic moment of being possessed by him.

'You can't tell me it was like that for you with other men,' he continued when she didn't answer. 'I have had lovers before and after you, Cassie, and it was never the same. There is amazing chemistry between us. It makes everything else pale in comparison.'

'You're chasing a fantasy, Sebastian,' she said. 'We've both changed. We're not the same people now.'

'We might have changed but this is one thing that certainly hasn't,' he said, and, swooping down, covered her mouth with the crushing urgency of his.

Cassie knew she should pull out of his hold. There were a hundred reasons to push him away, but somehow she couldn't quite do it. The moment his lips met hers she felt the rush of need consume her. Her senses leapt with each stroke and glide of his masterful tongue, reducing her to a quivering wreck within moments. Was there no cure for this madness? she wondered dizzily. Everything about him felt so right and perfect. The pressure of his kiss, the movement of his hands from her wrists to her waist, then to just beneath her breasts, not quite touching but near enough to make them start to tingle and swell in anticipation.

She whimpered as his mouth continued to ruthlessly and passionately plunder hers, the lascivious dart of his tongue sending her crazy with the need to feel him in that secret heart of her that throbbed and ached for his possession. She leaned into his tight embrace, her arms going around his neck, her fingers threading through his thick dark hair as she returned his kiss with an ardour that more than matched his.

'You still want me,' Sebastian growled against her mouth, barely lifting his lips high enough to get the words out. 'I can taste it in every kiss we have shared.'

Cassie shivered as his warm breath fanned her swollen lips and she opened her eyes and looked up at him dazedly. 'I've always wanted you…'

One of his hands cupped her breast, cradling its gentle weight while the pad of his thumb began to roll over her engorged nipple. 'I swore I would never allow you to reduce me to this again,' he said, nibbling at the lobe of her ear with knee-wobbling deftness. 'But I can't help it. When I am with you I feel like I am going to burst like a trigger-happy teenager.'

Cassie felt the hardened probe of his erection pressing into her belly and felt a wave of desire wash over her, leaving her trembling with the force of it. She reached for him, her fingers skating over the waistband of his trousers before they went lower.

He groaned at the back of his throat as she outlined his rigid form through the fabric of his trousers, his reaction inciting her to roll down his zipper. He sucked in a breath, his hands on her ribcage grasping at her for purchase as she gently peeled his underwear away.

She could smell the erotic musk of his arousal, the skin stretched so tightly over his length her fingers trembled as she stroked him. He was so strong and powerful and yet her caressing touch brought him to life in a way she found totally exhilarating.

He groaned again, the deep, almost primitive sound fanning the flames of her desire for him. 'You have to stop, Cassie,' he said between ragged breaths. 'I can't take any more.'

Cassie ignored his plea and continued to caress him, but his hands came down on her shoulders and held her aloft. She looked up at him uncertainly. 'You don't want me to…?'

His dark eyes glittered with rampant desire. 'I want you to but not here and not now,' he said. 'You will come to me next Thursday. I will make sure we will not be disturbed. You can stay the night.'

She lowered her gaze. 'I can't stay the night…'

He brought up her chin with a determined finger. 'I will send a car for you.'

'You're not listening to me, Sebastian. I can't stay with you.'

'Why not?'

She bit her lip searching for a plausible excuse. 'I have to work the next day. I don't want to compromise my work situation. If I turn up late I could lose my job.'

'You will not lose your job,' he said. 'Besides, I have already requested your presence at the party I am holding for the children on the following Friday at the palace.'

Cassie's eyes rounded in alarm. 'The party is on Friday?' she asked. '*Next* Friday?'

'Yes,' he said. 'That was what Stefanos confirmed when he brought in our lunch. I wanted to do it sooner rather than later as with the coronation preparations my diary will not be so easy to juggle in the weeks to come. We are going ahead with it, otherwise it could be weeks or even months before I can see to it.'

Cassie was finding it hard to hold his gaze. She had to fight not to show how deeply disturbed she was by the news of the party. What if one of the staff mentioned to Sebastian she was Sam's mother? She could hardly tell Sophie and Kara and the others not to mention it, otherwise they might begin to suspect something. She would have to be so vigilant, keeping close to Sam the whole time. That was all she could do.

'I can't stay overnight,' Cassie repeated, chewing at her lip even more desperately. 'I will have to start work earlier on Friday to prepare the children for the party.'

'All right,' he said after a tense pause. 'I will agree to have you returned to your house after our date.'

Our date.

Cassie's mouth twisted at the euphemism. 'You've really changed, Sebastian. You never used to be so cold-bloodedly ruthless.'

'If you find me a little more ruthless than before you have only yourself to blame,' he countered. 'You did a good job on me, Cassandra Kyriakis. Whenever I become involved with a woman I take control at the start and I make sure I still have it at the finish.'

Cassie clenched her hands by her sides, her fingertips digging into her palms almost painfully. 'I'm not going to be your latest whore,' she said with a last stand of pride. 'I'd rather be locked up again for the next twenty years than suffer that fate.'

He had the gall to laugh. 'Oh, such feisty words, but do you have any idea of how foolish you are being?'

'It can't be any more foolish than agreeing to lie on my back for you to paw me whenever you like,' she shot back.

'Do you think I want it to be this way?' he asked as a flicker of anger lit his gaze from behind. 'I wish I could look at you and feel nothing, but that's not the way it is.'

'It's your pride,' she said. 'You want to rewrite the past because I…because…' she lowered her eyes from him '…I wasn't faithful to you.'

'It is not my pride,' he ground out harshly. 'I want you because I have never wanted anyone else like I want you.'

Cassie swallowed back her anguish at his grudging confession. She felt exactly the same way about him, but the secret of their son yawned like a deep, unbridgeable canyon between them. If he found out about Sam now Sebastian's whole life would change irreparably.

All she had to say was: *Five years ago I had your son.*

Cassie felt close to tears. She could feel them building at the back of her tight throat, their burning presence a stinging reminder of how much she had loved Sebastian, even though he had ignored her one point of contact with him via her letter, even though he had trashed her character all over again by offering her a short clandestine affair so similar to the one he had offered her six years ago.

'I really need to get going,' she said, fiddling with her watch.

He stepped closer and traced the pad of his index finger down the slope of her cheek. 'One week,' he said, locking gazes with her. 'Believe me, Cassie, I will not let this rest until I have one night with you.'

Cassie wished she had the strength and will power to say no. Any other person and it would have been so easy. But didn't she owe it to him? She'd had his son. She might not ever be in a position to inform him of it, but surely she owed him an hour or two of her time so she could one day tell Sam what sort of man his father was without revealing his true identity.

She had been lucky so far. Sam was surrounded by children

who had not just one parent, but *no* parents. It hadn't yet occurred to Sam to ask why he didn't have a father, but she knew in the years to come he would no doubt do so. She had no idea how she would handle the subject. Lying to her little boy seemed morally wrong, and yet wouldn't it be equally morally reprehensible to destroy Sebastian's lifelong goal of ruling his people by informing him he had a love-child?

'I guess if you want to see me on Thursday it could be arranged...' she said, feeling another piece of her heart curl up and die.

'I want to, *agape mou,*' Sebastian said, and brushed a soft kiss to her mouth. 'I want to very much.'

A knock sounded at the door and with a rueful expression he put her from him gently and strode over to answer it.

'Excuse me, Your Royal Highness,' Stefanos said. 'I wasn't sure if you were aware of the time. You have a meeting with the royal council in just less than fifteen minutes.'

'Thank you, Stefanos,' Sebastian said. 'You have timed it well. Dhespinis Kyriakis is just leaving. Could you ensure that she gets back to the orphanage safely?'

'Yes, indeed, Your Highness.'

Sebastian watched as Cassie picked up her purse and self-consciously straightened her clothes, her cheeks slightly pink and her eyes avoiding his as she brushed past.

'Until Thursday, Cassie,' he said so only she could hear it.

She stalled briefly, her fingers tightening on her purse, but then with a small, almost imperceptible nod she continued to move past him and followed the aide down the echoing corridor.

Sebastian puffed out his cheeks and let the breath escape in a long thin stream, his hand raking down his face in an effort to get his senses back into line. The last hour had been pure madness but it had proved one thing if nothing else.

What he had said to Cassie was right.

As stupid and misguided as it was, he was prepared to risk a very great deal to have her back in his arms, even if it was only for one night.

At the meeting a short time later Sebastian sat forwards in his chair, tapping his pen on the desk impatiently, his frown heavy. 'So there is still no sign of the Stefani diamond?' he asked his official council.

'I am afraid not, Your Highness,' the senior official answered soberly. 'The coronation plans are still in place but it makes things rather difficult.'

Sebastian had no time for someone stating the obvious. He knew what was at stake. The icon of the royal house of Karedes was the priceless Stefani diamond, the biggest of the rare pink diamonds found on the neighbouring island of Calista. The fact that the Anstan half had mysteriously disappeared was causing great mayhem in the royal household, for tradition had it no one could become King without the Stefani diamond in their coronation crown. King Zakari of Calista was already hunting for the Anstan half of the diamond, and if it was discovered he could unite both Aristo and Calista into the Kingdom of Adamas once more. This made it all the more imperative for Sebastian to solve the mystery and find the missing diamond.

'I want the investigation to continue until every person who ever handled the coronation crown is interviewed,' he instructed his officials. 'And of course there is no need to remind you of how this must remain within the palace walls. I do not want a press leak about this.'

Once the council meeting was over Sebastian called Stefanos aside. 'Two things, Stefanos, that I wish for you to see to immediately,' he said. 'Firstly, I would appreciate it if you would assist Demetrius in drawing up a guest list with each of the children's names on it and their carers. I would also like a small gift prepared for each child, appropriate for their age and gender. I will leave it in your very capable hands.'

'Yes, Your Highness.'

'Secondly, I would like you to make some enquiries for me,' Sebastian said, 'discreetly, of course.'

'But of course, Your Highness.'

'I want you to find out where Cassandra Kyriakis is living and if or when she was last involved with a lover,' Sebastian said with a determined set to his jaw.

'I will see to it immediately, Your Highness,' Stefanos said. 'Will that be all for now?'

Sebastian nodded as he clenched and unclenched his fingers inside his trouser pockets. 'For now,' he said, silently grinding his teeth.

After a quick word with Angelica, Cassie went into Sam's bedroom and sat on the edge of his bed, looking down at his innocent little face, so blissfully peaceful in sleep.

As she gently stroked the hair back off his forehead she thought of those first harrowing weeks in prison, how she had tried to adjust to being constantly under surveillance, not to mention the sleepless nights and terror-filled days. And that fateful day three months into her sentence when the prison doctor had called her down to the prison surgery for the results of the blood tests that had been ordered the week before. The news of her pregnancy had been an unbelievable shock. For several stunned days Cassie had been certain there must have been a mistake—a mix-up at the pathology laboratory or something. She couldn't possibly have been pregnant. She had been on the contraceptive pill since she was seventeen. She had not missed a period and apart from some breast tenderness and grumbling nausea and tiredness she had no other symptoms that could not have easily been put down to other causes. Stress, not eating, the death of her father…that last horrendous scene when he had tried to… Cassie had skittered away from memories, trying to keep a steady head in a world that had seemed intent on spinning out of her control, determined to find some other plausible reason why her body was so out of whack.

But in the end there had been no escaping it. The news of her pregnancy and the subsequent birth of Sam had thankfully—and in Cassie's opinion miraculously—never been leaked to the press. The prison authorities had made special dispensation for her to keep the baby with her until he was of nursery-school age, when he had been fostered out until her release.

At least Cassie had been able to get Sam back, which was not always the case with other women. She thought of the frayed photograph Angelica kept by her bedside of the dark-haired little boy, Nickolas, she had lost custody of during the height of her drug addiction. The boy's father had disappeared, taking Angelica's only reason for living with him. It had been four and a half years and Angelica still didn't know if her son was dead or alive.

Cassie bent forwards and softly kissed Sam's smooth brow. 'I am not going to let anyone take you away from me again,' she promised in a whisper. But the words seemed to echo faintly, as if fate had been listening on the sidelines and was already thinking of a way to step in once more.

CHAPTER SIX

'YOUR Royal Highness, I have that information you requested,' Stefanos said as he brought in Sebastian's coffee a couple of days later.

Sebastian lowered the newspaper he had been reading and gave his aide his full attention. 'What did you find out?'

'Cassandra Kyriakis is living at a small flat in Paros Lane with a former drug addict, a woman by the name of Angelica Mantoudakis. Apparently they met in prison but the Mantoudakis woman was released two years ago. She works at one of the local hotels as a housemaid.'

Sebastian's brows came together. 'What about a man?' he asked.

Stefanos shook his head. 'There is no man. However, there is a small child, a boy of about five or so.'

Sebastian straightened in his chair, a cold hand of unease disturbing the hairs on the back of his neck. 'A boy?' he asked, frowning harder. 'Who does he belong to?'

'I made some further enquiries and found out that Angelica Mantoudakis gave birth five years ago to a boy called Nickolas,' he said. 'I wasn't able to find out much else. The neighbours pretty much keep to themselves in that area, but one of them did say she sees Cassandra Kyriakis taking the little boy with her to the orphanage each day to the nursery school there, one assumes because the Mantoudakis woman's hours at the hotel prevent her doing so herself.'

Sebastian hadn't even realised he had been holding his breath until he let it out in a jagged stream of relief and something else he couldn't quite identify. 'Thank you, Stefanos,' he said. 'You did well.'

'The council have still not come up with any clues to the whereabouts of the Stefani diamond,' Stefanos went on. 'There is a private investigating team working on it, as well as Prince Alex, but so far nothing has come to light.'

Sebastian felt his jaw tighten all over again. He had lain awake half the night, wondering if the diamond would ever be found in time. No matter how discreet the private investigators would be he was under no illusions as to how long it would be before someone suspected something was amiss and rumours began to circulate. They had perhaps already begun to do so. Sebastian wanted the start of his rulership of Aristo to be as smooth as possible. He wanted to build the confidence of his people, to show them he was nothing like his autocratic father, but would listen to the various concerns brought to him from the community and act on them promptly and appropriately. He had a vision for Aristo, a vision he had nurtured from when he had first started to realise his destiny. He had been born to rule this island and he would do so with strong but considerate leadership, but unless the Stefani diamond was found, his coronation could not go ahead.

'Keep them on to it,' he instructed his aide. 'And make sure they keep their heads down while they are at it.'

'Certainly, Your Highness,' Stefanos said, and after a pause added, 'I have just been talking to Demetrius about the orphanage party. The director of the orphanage was delighted with the invitation as you are the first patron to have made such a magnanimous gesture.'

Sebastian waved away the compliment. 'They are children, Stefanos,' he said. 'Little defenceless children with no one to look out for them. It is the very least I can do.'

'Yes, indeed, Your Highness,' Stefanos agreed. 'So is the dinner with Cassandra Kyriakis going ahead for Thursday night? I will have to let the chef know.'

'It is going ahead,' Sebastian said, leaning back in his chair. 'I want to take her to Kionia for a picnic.'

Stefanos lifted his brows for a nanosecond. 'I will see to it immediately,' he said, and left.

Cassie was hovering near the window when the long, black, sleek car pulled up in front of the flat on Thursday evening. She scooped up her purse and light wrap and made her way outside even before the driver could get to the front door to ring the doorbell.

The uniformed driver opened the passenger door for her with a blank expression, and she slipped inside, coming face to face with Sebastian, who was sitting on the plush leather seat opposite hers.

'I can see you are in a hurry for our date, *agape mou*,' he observed with a benign smile. 'How flattering.'

Cassie rolled her eyes in disdain and shifted her knees so they weren't brushing against his. 'That's not the case at all,' she said with chilly hauteur. 'I didn't want to draw attention to myself or to you. Can you imagine what the neighbours would make of me going off in a limousine?'

'I take your point,' he said, still smiling. 'Would you like a drink? I would offer you champagne but you would not drink it, *ne?* But there is fresh orange juice or mineral water.'

'Orange juice would be lovely… Thank you.'

Once he had poured her a chilled glass of juice and handed it to her, Cassie settled back in her seat and tried to relax her shoulders. She took a covert look at him over the rim of her frosted glass as she took a small sip of her drink. He was wearing taupe-coloured trousers and a white open-neck shirt, the sleeves rolled up to almost his elbows giving him a handsome-without-really-trying look that was nothing short of heart-stopping. She felt her breath come to a skidding halt in her chest just looking at him. He was cleanly shaven, his curly black hair springy and damp from his recent shower. The citrus-based fragrance of his aftershave drifted towards her and she couldn't stop the flare of her nostrils to take more of the alluring scent in. How could a man so casually dressed be so overwhelmingly masculine? she wondered. The breadth of his shoulders, the taut flatness of his abdomen and the long muscular length of his thighs were an over-whelming reminder of his potency as a full-blooded man in the prime of his life.

'How was your day?' he asked.

Cassie lowered her glass with an unsteady hand. 'M-my day?'

His mouth tilted in a disarming manner that reminded her so much of Sam she felt her stomach muscles involuntarily tighten.

'Yes, Cassie, your day,' he said. 'Did you work at the or-phanage?'

'Yes…'

'How was Nickolas?'

Cassie looked at him blankly. 'Nickolas?'

He set his glass down on the flip-top rest at his elbow. 'Your

flatmate's son,' he said. 'The one you take with you to the orphanage nursery-school each day.'

Cassie licked her suddenly arid-dry lips.

'Um…he's…he's…how…how did you find out…about
him?'

'I had my aide Stefanos make some discreet enquiries
about who you were living with.'

Cassie felt her heart pumping so erratically she was sure
he would hear it, but she forced herself to hold his penetrating coal-black gaze in any case, even though every instinct
inside was screaming for her to avoid it. 'So,' she said with
an attempt at nonchalance she was sure had fallen well short
of the mark, 'what else did you find out about me?'

He picked up his glass once more and twirled it in his hand
in an indolent manner. 'Your flatmate is an ex-prisoner. A drug
addict, apparently. Hardly the company you should be keeping
if you are serious about turning your life around, now, is it?'

Her chin came up at that. 'I hope you're not going to hold
her past against her,' she said. 'Angelica is one of the most
genuine and loving people I have ever met. She deserves a
second chance.'

'Is she clean?'

She set her mouth. 'Yes, she is.'

'She would want to be, given she's the mother of a small
child,' he commented imperiously.

Cassie listened to her deafening heartbeats reverberating
through her eardrums: *kaboom, kaboom, kaboom…*

So he assumed Sam was her flatmate's child, she thought
with somewhat cautious relief. That was a good thing…for
now. As long as she could maintain the charade with
Angelica's cooperation for the next few weeks until she left
the island for good things would be fine…or so Cassie hoped.

'Did you meet her in prison?' he asked.

'Yes.'

'So the child was with her in prison?'

'Um…' Cassie mentally crossed her fingers at yet another one of her little white lies. 'Yes…'

He gave her a studied look for a lengthy moment. 'The little boy whose drawing you gave me the other day,' he said. 'Did he come from a criminal or violent background?'

Cassie's hand trembled slightly as she reached for her glass of juice. 'Not directly…'

One of Sebastian's brows hooked upwards. 'Meaning what exactly?'

'His mother would never dream of being violent towards him.'

A frown appeared on his brow. 'But I thought you said he was an orphan?'

Cassie stared at him for a heart-stopping moment. 'Um… I…I…' she gave a tight little swallow '…did I?'

He gave a single nod. 'You did.'

'Oh…well, I must have got him confused with another child…or something…'

'What is his name?' he asked.

Cassie's heart gave another pounding thump. 'N-name?'

'The little boy who gave me the drawing,' he said. 'What is his name?'

She ran her tongue across her lips. 'It's…er…Sam.'

'I am looking forward to meeting him tomorrow at the party,' Sebastian said. 'I have organised a magician to entertain them as well as a gift for every child and the mandatory balloons, sweets, cakes and ices.'

'That's very generous of you,' Cassie said, her heart still pounding sickeningly. She could even feel a fine trail of perspiration making its way between her shoulder blades. 'I'm sure they will have a wonderful time and remember it for the rest of their lives.'

'I would like to make it an annual event,' he said. 'And I would like to visit the orphanage as soon as it can be arranged.'

'I am sure the director will be delighted to have you do so,' Cassie said, even as her heart gave another gut-wrenching lurch of dread. The party at the palace was risky enough, but if Sebastian wandered around the orphanage on an official visit someone was surely going to inadvertently let the cat out of the bag over who Sam's mother was. Cassie had already told so many fibs. It was getting harder and harder to keep each brick of untruth in place. Any minute she felt as if the wall of lies she had built would tumble down and crush her. Even the way Sebastian looked at her in that unwavering way of his made her wonder if he suspected something was amiss. At times she felt as if it were written in block letters on her forehead: *I am the mother of your little son.* All Sebastian had to do was keep looking at her in that piercing way of his and he would surely see it.

Just the way he was looking at her now...

'Have you guessed where I am taking you?' he asked after a few moments of silence.

Cassie leaned forward to look out of the window. They had moved well beyond the town and were heading to the Bay of Kounimai where she knew the Karedes family had a private holiday retreat at a place called Kionia. Sebastian had never taken her there before but in the past he had told her of the secluded beauty of the villa with its fabulous views over the rough water of the passage separating Aristo from the neighbouring island of Calista. 'Are we going to Kionia?' she asked as she sat back in her seat.

'Yes,' he said. 'I thought we could both do with some privacy.

I had Stefanos organise a picnic for us. It is a pleasant evening with not too much sea breeze so we can enjoy the sunset.'

'It sounds lovely,' Cassie said. 'I can't remember the last time I went on a picnic. Sam's always asking me to—' She suddenly stopped, her heart thudding like an out-of-sync timepiece.

Sebastian cocked his head at her. 'Sam? You mean the little boy who drew me the picture?'

Cassie blinked at him, her brain whirling and spinning out of control. 'Um…he's…Angelica's little boy,' she finally managed to croak out.

He gave her a quizzical look. 'I thought his name was Nickolas,' he said. 'Or at least that's what Stefanos said it was, but then he could have got it wrong.'

'N-no, that is right…' Cassie hastily mortared another lie into her wall of deceit. 'Angelica's son is called Nickolas but…but he prefers his second name…'

'Like my sister prefers Lissa or Liss instead of Elissa,' he said.

Cassie felt her tension gradually start to dissipate, but even so her stomach felt as if a hive of bees had taken up residence inside. She felt as if each wing were buzzing against the lining of her stomach, the threat of a thousand stings making the trail of perspiration along her backbone feel more like a river. 'Yes…exactly like that…'

'I told her I ran into you,' Sebastian said. 'She's been in Paris studying. She came home for our father's funeral and Kitty's wedding, but now she's in Australia working for a friend of Alex's, a businessman by the name of James Black.'

'How is she?' Cassie asked, thinking with more than a pang or two of shame of the wild-child antics Lissa and she had got up to. It was hard to remember now who had encouraged whom, but Cassie suspected she was the one who had been held most responsible.

'You know Lissa,' he said with a rueful twist to his mouth.

'If there's a party she not only wants to be there but she wants to be the centre of it. She wasn't too keen about being packed off to Sydney but we all thought it best if she had some time in the real world. I just hope it irons out some of her wilfulness. She has always been a little too independent for her own good.'

Cassie looked down at her hands for a moment. 'I am sure the experience of travelling and working abroad will be wonderful for her. When you are next speaking to her…I mean, if you think it's appropriate to mention you have seen me, please tell her I send my regards.'

The car growled its way into the wrought iron fortress of the Karedeses' private hideaway, making the silence inside all the more intense. Cassie felt the press of Sebastian's watchful gaze and forced herself to bring her eyes back to his.

'No doubt she will contact you in due course,' he said, still with his dark, penetrating gaze trained on her face. 'When my father found out about the postcards she sent he strictly forbade any further contact while he was alive, which I think Lissa feels guilty about now. That is probably why she hasn't as yet contacted you.'

'I understand,' she said. 'We were probably not a good mix when I think about it. We brought out the worst in each other at times.'

'She was always very fond of you.'

Cassie felt her heart contract. 'I was…I *am* still very fond of her,' she said, and then unguardedly added, 'We had more in common than she probably realised.'

He gave her one of his narrow-eyed looks. 'What do you mean?'

Her gaze skittered away from his. 'The children of high-profile parents often have a lot in common. We are constantly followed by the press and anything we do or say is used against us. I think Lissa and I were alike in that we got fed up with it all and tried to get out there and live like other normal teenagers. But of course we could never be normal, Lissa more so than me. She, like you, has royal blood running through her veins.'

'You are right, of course,' he said. 'I too had to pull in my horns, so to speak. The weight of responsibility does that to you after a while. Even if my father had not died so unexpectedly I was already feeling the urge to settle down.'

Cassie felt a pain like a rusty switchblade go through her. Sebastian had already mentioned a suitable wife had been selected for him. She could see him married to a beautiful woman who was everything she was not nor ever could be: gracious, well-bred, with an immaculate reputation, well educated and comfortable in every social situation. No doubt his wonderfully suitable wife would bear him an heir and a spare, maybe even another couple of gorgeous children who looked just like Sam…

Even if she was thousands of kilometres away as she had planned, how on earth would Cassie bear it?

Sebastian instructed the driver to set up the picnic in a secluded spot near some tamarisk trees that provided a shelter of sorts a short distance from the stately royal holiday residence.

Within minutes a table with crisp white linen was set up, sparkling crystal glasses and crested silverware set out in preparation for a meal fit for…well, royalty of course, Cassie thought wryly as she watched a solid silver vase complete with red rose being placed in the very centre of the table. It was certainly nothing like the picnics Cassie had been on in the past, with floppy paper plates, plastic forks and knives that wouldn't cut through melted butter let alone anything else.

The food provided by the royal kitchen was nothing short of delightful, every morsel was a work of art in itself, and artfully arranged to entice even the most jaded of appetites.

Sebastian led Cassie to the silky fabric-covered chair opposite his, and, once he was sure she was comfortable, took his own seat, instructing the driver-cum-waiter to serve their meal.

Cassie had not felt in the least bit hungry, but as soon as the tiny dishes appeared in front of her she found herself partaking of a feast that was beyond belief. Char-grilled octopus, garlic mussels, plump prawns skewered on tiny sticks with a lime and coriander marinade, ripe olives and semi sun-dried tomatoes, followed by pesto-encrusted succulent grilled chicken with a variety of lightly steamed vegetables, and to top it off a vanilla bean crème caramel custard with plump summer berries.

Cassie had declined all alcohol, but the absence of fine wine had not for a moment taken away from the delectable feast she had partaken of. With her stomach replete and her taste buds still zinging with the fresh and fantastic flavours she had consumed, she felt as if she had been transported into another realm. After years of stolid prison food served haphazardly by other inmates, with the nagging suspicion of someone tampering with the meal as a payback for supposed misdemeanours, Cassie had not realised how much she had missed out on until now.

Did Sebastian have any idea of what he took for granted every single day? Meals were put in front of him morning, noon and night, nutritious, gourmet and delectable meals prepared by world-renowned chefs. He had never had to bargain or bribe to get a mouthful of food for himself, nor had he ever had to beg, borrow or steal to provide a tiny treat for his little son.

Sebastian poured himself a small measure of red wine, watching the fleeting emotions passing over Cassie's face. She had been very quiet during the meal. He had watched as she had taken tiny bites of each morsel with her small white teeth, her eyes lighting up as she savoured each mouthful, chewing slowly, as if wanting the flavours to last as long as possible. She used her cutlery with the grace and elegance of someone brought up with a refined sense of dining. He had met and dated women who had spent a year in a finishing school who had less class and poise than Cassie, which was a credit to her father, he supposed, given Cassie's mother had not been around.

'Was it lonely for you growing up without a mother?' Sebastian asked, hardly realising the question had fallen from his lips until the sea-washed silence was broken by it.

Her eyes moved upwards to meet his, a shadow of something dark and mysterious lurking in their startling emerald depths. 'I'm not sure it is possible to miss something you have never had,' she said in an offhand tone that didn't quite do the job of convincing Sebastian she meant it. 'I had a series of nannies who looked after me when my father was at work. I had toys and entertainment, more than most kids have, or at least certainly more than the kids I deal with now.'

Sebastian surveyed her features as he cradled his wineglass in his hand. 'You didn't answer my question, Cassie,' he said.

Cassie shifted her eyes from his and inwardly frowned. Why was he doing this? In the past he had hardly ever asked her about her life as a child. They hadn't had that sort of relationship. Their love affair—strike that—*sex* affair—had had nothing to do with getting to know each other as people. It had been lust that had driven them into each other's arms, a forbidden lust that had made it all the more exciting. Cassie's body quivered as she thought of the things they had done and where they had done them. The thrill of being discovered had been part of the adrenalin rush.

Cassie shifted in her chair, her face averted from the all-seeing gaze of Sebastian's. 'I guess it would have been nice to have had a mother…especially during adolescence,' she said, absently fiddling with the edge of the tablecloth. 'I try not to think about it too much. Lots of people don't have mothers and survive. I am hardly unique.'

'No, that is true, but you have never really talked about what it was like for you as a child,' he said. 'I guess I should have been more mature back when we were involved and asked you. But then like a lot of young men with hormones on their mind I didn't get around to it.'

Cassie wasn't brave enough to meet his eyes. She knew in any case what she would see there: desire, hot and strong, perhaps even stronger than what he had felt for her before. What she couldn't understand was why. She was the last person he should be considering associating with. She had a black mark on her name that would never go away, no matter how far away from Aristo she travelled. Her life was never going to be the same again. Not that it had been all that crash-hot to start with.

Cassie had spent years of her early childhood desperately trying to please her father to no avail. She couldn't quite recall how old she had been when she had changed her tactics and begun to rebel against him instead. All she could remember were the fights, the vicious slanging matches that had nearly always ended with her being—

'Cassie…' Sebastian's deep voice jerked her out of her torturous memories.

Cassie blinked at him, trying to recall what they had been talking about, her mind still back in her bedroom with her father's puce features glaring at her, his mouth a tight white line of livid rage, spittle pooling at the corners, his teeth audibly grinding together as his closed thick fist had raised, ready to strike…

She swallowed a painfully tight swallow that tore at the tender lining of her throat, her eyes skittering away from Sebastian's. Nausea roiled in her stomach, her blood pressure dropped so low she could feel the sensation of fine grains of sand shifting in her extremities. She was going to faint... No...hang on a minute...she was holding on...but only just... Breathe...deep and even, that was the way to do it. It had been years since she'd had a panic attack. She knew the drill; it just took a little discipline and focus to pull it off.

Breathe...in...out...in...out...in—

'Caz?' Sebastian leaned forward across the table and took her ice-cold hand in his, his brow furrowed in concern. 'What's going on? You've gone as white as a sheet. What is wrong?'

Cassie forced her lips into a smile but it made her face feel strangely disconnected from her mind. 'Nothing,' she said in what she hoped sounded like an offhand manner. 'I forgot what we were talking about. I was thinking about something else.'

He was still frowning at her. 'Whatever you were thinking about must have been distressing for you,' he said. 'Was it something to do with your time in prison?'

Cassie sat back in her chair and crossed her legs. She was as close to crumbling as she had ever been, but some tiny rod of pride kept her spine upright. 'You seem to be rather fascinated with my prison life,' she speculated. 'Is that because you harbour some sort of fantasy about an ex-criminal? Sex with someone from the slammer. It has a sort of ring to it, don't you think?'

Sebastian felt his desire for her rise in his body with the force of an earthquake. It rumbled through him, it shook him, and above everything else—it challenged him.

He would have her.

It didn't matter how far apart their worlds were now. He would have her again to assuage this achingly tight need in his body that refused to go away. After all, wasn't that the way she had played it with him in the past? She had teased him, led him on and on until he had been out of his mind with lust.

It had all been a game to her, but he was going to play it by his own rules this time around, not hers.

Sebastian knew how her mind worked. She was as good as penniless now. Sure, she seemingly enjoyed working at the orphanage, but the Cassie Kyriakis he had known six years ago would have turned her nose up at such menial, poorly paid work. He just couldn't imagine her soothing sobbing infants or wiping dripping noses, much less changing dirty nappies. He even remembered her telling him at one point how she never wanted to have children, that she intended to spend her life constantly partying, making the most of the wealth her father had accumulated.

Sebastian hadn't let it bother him too much at the time; he had dated plenty of rich young women with exactly the same mindset. And he had been well aware of his royal duty when the time came to find an impeccable wife who would willingly bear his royal heirs. Not for a moment had he thought Cassie Kyriakis a likely candidate…and yet…

Sebastian gave himself a stern mental shake. So what if his physical relationship with Cassie had for all these years since been unsurpassed? That did not necessarily mean there was no other woman out there who could not meet his needs in the same way or better. Anyway, it was only the deluded romantic fools of the world who claimed there was only one perfect soul mate for each person.

What utter nonsense!

Sebastian would show how misguided such a philosophy could be. He was even prepared to bet he would be disappointed in a repeat performance with Cassie. Memories did that to you. They glorified the past until the real thing was often a let-down, making you wonder why you had craved it so assiduously in the first place.

God knew how many men she had opened her legs for

since him. It coiled his gut with writhing, vicious vipers of jealousy to think of the men she had been with during the time they had been secretly conducting their affair. How could he know how many men she had given herself to?

Yes, it was perhaps sexist of him to judge her by different standards from his own, but she had *lied* to him, damn it! She had told him making love with him was the most amazing, out-of-this-world experience, and fool that he was he had believed her. How many other men had she gazed up at with those shining emerald eyes of hers, her lips swollen with passion, and said the very same thing?

'Would you like some more water?' Sebastian asked with no hint of what he had been thinking evident in his polite, solicitous tone.

'No...thank you...' Cassie said, placing her napkin down on the table. 'The meal was delicious. Thank you for going to so much trouble. It has certainly raised the bar on any future picnics I might have in the future.'

'It was nothing,' he said with a wry smile. 'I didn't lift a finger. I wouldn't know how to make a canapé if you paid me.'

There was a stretched-out silence with only the raging sea below to break it. *Boom...crash...boom...crash...*

'What about coffee?' Sebastian asked over the suddenly deafening sound of the waves against the shore. 'Stefanos has arranged coffee and chocolates inside. I wanted to make the most of the sunset but the breeze has stiffened now the sun has gone down. You have goose bumps—would you like my jacket?'

Cassie didn't like to tell him the pinpricks on her skin were from apprehension rather than cold, even though, as he had said, the breeze from the rough water below had only recently picked up its pace. She could see the galloping white horses of the waves, each one racing to crash against the shore in a foamy, almost angry wash against the rocks and sand. But before she could refuse the offer of his jacket he was on his feet and behind her chair, covering her shoulders in the warm citrus-scented folds of his coat.

Cassie felt as if she had just stepped into his skin, so intimate was the gesture, the light but firm touch of his hands on her shoulders as he set the jacket in place rendering her speechless with longing for more of his touch. She breathed in the spicy fragrance, all of her senses suddenly hyper-vigilant, and her heart in very great danger of making the same mistake it had made six years before.

Sebastian escorted her on the short trip to the private royal residence, a massive villa with views from every vantage point. Stefanos was nowhere in sight, but Cassie assumed he had been given instructions to make himself scarce. She couldn't help wondering with a jab of pain how many other times he had been issued with the same orders while Sebastian entertained other women.

As if Sebastian had read her thoughts, he said as he led the way into the opulent foyer, 'I think you should know at this point you are the very first person I have brought here. This is the private holiday residence for my family, off limits to everyone except only close family and closely trusted friends.'

Cassie raised her brows at him as he closed the heavy door behind him. 'So, Sebastian,' she said. 'Which category do I fall into? Surely you do not consider me a close friend or a future member of the royal family?'

Tension travelled all the way from his darker-than-dark eyes to his chiselled jaw and then to his thinned-out mouth. 'Given our history, Cassie, you are not eligible for either of those positions,' he bit out tightly.

Cassie wished with all her heart she could reveal Sam's identity and throw the truth of their situation in his face to make him realise how much she was a part of his wretched royal family whether he liked it or not, but some remnant of self-respect and self-preservation prevented her from doing so. Instead she smiled up at him, a cool, calculating smile that gave him no clue to the turmoil going on inside her. 'I consider myself deeply honoured, Your Royal Highness,' she drawled with a bow of her head that deliberately fell short of the mark, delivering the insult she had intended. 'It is indeed a privilege to be considered worthy of gracing the highly esteemed private residence of the Karedes family, considering the lower than low background I come from.'

'Your background was nothing to be ashamed of until you took it upon yourself to degrade your father at every opportunity,' he said. 'His public role was made a hundred times worse by the way you behaved.'

Twenty-four years of Cassie's suffering threatened to come to the surface, like a volcano silently brewing until the temperature of the lava became too hot to contain. A catastrophic explosion was imminent, but somehow she was able to contain the emotion she felt to remind herself no one knew her father as she had known him. No one had heard the soul-destroying words he had flung at her in one of his many out-of-control tempers; no one had seen the bruises his hands, not to mention any other objects within his reach, had left on her body.

Sebastian had not seen the jagged scar low on her back her father had scored into her flesh that fateful day. It was like a tattoo of torment, the brand her father had left to remind her of how he had demanded total control of her, a control she had not given willingly and had fought every inch of the way as each strike of his belt had bitten cruelly and cuttingly into her flesh.

Cassie had been so proud that she hadn't cried. She had gritted her teeth until she was sure they would crack under the pressure. She had taken every vicious cut of the strap like a convict bracing for the cat-o'-nine-tails.

That had been her victory.

Her father could blame her for her mother's untimely death, he could blame her for having been a small, needy and insecure child, and he could even blame her for being an out-of-control, wilful teenager, but he could not blame her for re-claiming her life and that of her child. That had been her only solace. Her father had not known of Sam's existence. Her tiny precious son had been even to Cassie, unknown in her womb at the time of that dreadful scene. Whether her father would have acted differently if he had known she was carrying a royal baby was something she would never know.

But Cassie knew she had choices now and one was to keep a cool head. Sebastian's presence admittedly made that task difficult, but she had to keep a lid on her emotions, at all times and in all places.

She *had* to.

Cassie lifted her gaze to his, her spine not quite so rigid, her shoulders going down beneath the sheltering warmth of his jacket. 'My father was not a good father,' she said. 'He might have been a brilliant mayor and an astute businessman, but he didn't love and protect me the way he should have done. You didn't know him personally, Sebastian. You knew of him from what your father and other palace officials told you.' Her eyes misted over suddenly as she added in a choked up voice, 'But you didn't *know* him.'

Sebastian let out a rusty sigh and, taking one single step, gathered her to him. He rested his chin on the top of her head and wondered why the hell he still felt this way about her. She could go from a shrieking shrew to a lost little girl within a heart-beat. Then, to make things even more confusing, she could turn on the heat and turn into a sensual goddess, that pouting mouth of hers making him want to press his down on those blood-red lips and never stop kissing her, devouring her taste, the essence of her body, to feel the convulsions of her feminine muscles around him, making him pour himself into her. He could feel the movement of his blood in his veins; he was already hard against her and wondered why she hadn't moved back.

He felt her take in a breath, the brush of her breasts against his chest making him shudder with the need to fill her as he had done in the past.

He lifted her chin and looked into the sea-glass-green of her eyes, fighting not to drown in them. 'You are right,' he said. 'I didn't know him personally. He seemed very affable but I know from personal experience that what goes on in public is not always representative of what happens in private.'

She looked back at him, her gaze as unfathomable as the ocean pounding below. 'I'm cold,' she said and he felt her shiver under the touch of his hands.

Sebastian took one of her hands from where it was clutching at his jacket to keep it in place, and brought it up to his mouth. He kissed each of her knuckles in turn, a soft-as-a-baby's sigh caress that made her pupils grow darker than the sea raging below. 'Then let's go inside and warm you up,' he said, and, taking her by the hand, he led her inside the villa.

CHAPTER SEVEN

CASSIE stepped into the private study Sebastian opened a short time later, her senses heightened by his light touch as he took his jacket from her shoulders and laid it over a chair.

He came back to stand in front of her, his dark gaze meshing with hers as he took both of her hands in his. 'Not so cold now?' he asked.

She shook her head, her tongue darting out to moisten her lips. 'No…not cold at all…'

He settled his hands on her waist and brought her up against his body. 'I should pour you a cup of coffee,' he said, looking down at her mouth.

Cassie felt her lips start to tingle the longer his gaze rested there. 'Should you?' she asked.

He smiled lopsidedly. 'You do not fancy a coffee right now, *agape mou?*'

Cassie drew in a shaky breath, her stomach feeling hollow with a combination of nerves and anticipation. 'That's not really why I am here, is it, Sebastian?'

He placed his palm at the nape of her neck, his fingers warm and tempting on her sensitive skin. 'You still want to deny what is between us, Cassie?' he asked.

How could she possibly deny it? Cassie wondered. What

would be the point? Saying no to Sebastian Karedes had never been easy for her, now even more so. They both knew she was here because she wanted to be here. By stepping over the threshold of the villa she had stepped into his arms and would stay there for as long as he wanted her to. 'No,' she said, placing her hands on his chest as she met his gaze. 'I am not going to deny it.'

He brought his mouth down to hers in a slow-moving assault on her senses, waiting until she opened her mouth on a whimpering sigh before he began to stroke her tongue with his own. The erotic caress loosened her spine, her legs swaying beneath her as he deepened the kiss, each slow thrust and stroke of his tongue fuelling her desire until all she could think about was how it would feel to have him possess her again.

His kiss changed its tempo as soon as her hands pulled his shirt out of his trousers, his mouth grinding against hers. Tongues of flame licked along her veins as she responded by rubbing up against him, her hands going to his waistband, unbuckling him and uncovering him with her searching fingers.

Cassie swallowed his gasp of reaction as her fingers danced along his length, the satin strength of him so potently male, so aroused he was seeping with moisture. She played with him, squeezing, rubbing and stroking him while her mouth was being plundered by his, her heart rate soaring, her body slick and wet with need.

He muttered something unintelligible as he tore his mouth off hers, his dark eyes glittering with pent-up desire, his hands already lifting her skirt, his clever, artful fingers searching for the secret heart of her desire, behind the thin lace of her knickers.

She quivered against his touch, the smooth stroking of his fingers, curling her toes and arching her back until she was gasping out loud, the shock waves of release reverberating through her.

The ripples of reaction were still rolling through her as he backed her to the nearest wall, only stopping long enough to retrieve a condom from his jacket pocket on the way past.

Cassie shivered in delight as she helped him sheath himself, the urgency in his movements building her desire all over again.

She shuddered as he surged into her moist warmth, his thickness stretching her, sending wave after wave of rapture through her with each deep, pounding thrust.

He set a furiously fast rhythm, as if he were riding against an approaching storm, each rocking movement of his body in hers bringing him closer and closer to the point of no return. She felt it building in his body, the increasing tautness of his muscles, the sucking in of his breath, the contortion of his features as he hovered for that infinitesimal moment, before exploding his need inside her, each last thrust accompanied by a primal grunt of deep male satisfaction.

Cassie listened to his breathing as he held her against him in the quiet glow of the aftermath, wondering how she had lived without the magic of his touch for so long. Her body felt tender and swollen from his almost rough possession, but she would not have admitted it for the world. Let him think she was used to a quick tumble wherever she could get it. It would make their inevitable parting neater and cleaner, for him at least. It would never be anything other than heartbreakingly painful for her.

A chirruping sound broke through her reverie but it was a moment or two before she realised what it was. Her small purse containing her mobile was sitting on the chair where Sebastian's jacket was draped.

'Is that your phone?' he asked, easing away from her.

Cassie straightened her clothes. 'Um, yes…but it was just someone leaving a message.'

He frowned as he glanced at his watch. 'Who would be texting you at this time of night?' he asked.

Cassie hoped her expression was not revealing anything of the rapid pulse of panic she could feel in her chest. 'It's probably my flatmate, Angelica. She is no doubt wondering where I am.'

He was still frowning slightly. 'Did you tell her who you were with?'

'Of course not,' she said, dropping her gaze.

Sebastian lifted her chin between his thumb and index finger. 'Word must not get out about our assignation, Cassie,' he said. 'I hope I can still trust you on that.'

She met his gaze with a flash of resentment in hers. 'Do you really think I would announce to all and sundry I have been chosen to service the future King of Aristo wherever and whenever he pleases?' she asked.

Sebastian set his mouth in a tight line. 'You were with me all the way, Cassie.'

She tugged his hand away from her face. 'I want to go home.'

'Not yet,' he said. 'I haven't finished with you.'

She glared at him but he could see the up-and-down movement of her throat as her eyes darted to her purse again.

'Aren't you going to read the message?' he asked, pinning her with his gaze.

The point of her tongue swept over her lips. 'I'm sure it's nothing important…'

Sebastian moved over to the chair and, scooping up her purse, came back and handed it to her. 'Why don't you check it to make sure?'

She hesitated just long enough for his suspicion of her to be heightened. She was hiding something; he was sure of it now. Perhaps she had a lover in spite of what Stefanos's covert enquiries had uncovered. He felt his insides twisting with jealousy; he would *not* share her.

He watched as she opened the face of her phone, her fingers fumbling as she pressed the text-message-viewing button. Her eyes widened for a moment, before she gathered herself, her face becoming an expressionless mask as she closed the phone and slipped it back into her purse.

'Nothing urgent?' he asked, watching her closely.

'My flatmate is feeling unwell,' she said. 'I think I should go back now to make sure she is all right.'

Sebastian knew she was lying. He could feel it. Damn it, he could see it in her eyes, the way they couldn't quite hold his. But he had plenty of time to uncover her deceit. He had offered her an affair and as far as he was concerned it had started tonight and would continue for as long as he wanted. What they had shared had been a foretaste of the pleasure he would take from her until he was satisfied she would rue the day she had walked away from him and into the arms of another man.

'I will summon Stefanos to bring the car around,' he said and, striding over to the desk, pressed a button on an intercom system.

Cassie sat in the limousine beside Sebastian a few minutes later, her features schooled into indifference. Angelica had sent her the message that Sam had woken with a bad dream and had refused to go back to bed until his mother came home.

As the car got closer she felt her panic building. What if Sam heard the car pulling up and opened the front door? Or what if he had worked himself up into hysteria by now and could be heard from the street?

The car purred to a halt outside the flat, which, after the opulent luxury of the royal hideaway, looked even shabbier and more run-down.

'Are you going to ask me in for coffee?' Sebastian asked as he helped Cassie from the car.

Cassie swallowed and pulled her hand out of his, clutching her purse against her. 'It's late,' she said. 'I don't want to disturb Angelica.'

He stood watching her for a beat or two. 'Tell your flatmate I hope she makes a speedy recovery,' he said with an unreadable half-smile playing about his lips.

'I—I will,' she said and, turning, walked the short distance to the front door, the twin drills of his dark gaze boring holes into her back.

Cassie slipped inside the flat, closing the door behind her just as Angelica appeared in the narrow hallway. 'Is he all right?' she asked.

Angelica nodded. 'He went back to sleep almost as soon as I pressed Send on my phone. I hope I didn't interrupt anything important?'

Cassie shifted her gaze. She would tell Angelica everything at some point, but not now. 'No,' she said heading towards Sam's room. 'Nothing important…'

The children from the orphanage were excited for most of the following day about the party that afternoon. Cassie and her co-workers Sophie and Kara had a difficult time settling the smaller ones for their afternoon naps and even some of the older children had been unusually disruptive. Sam, on the other hand, was quiet and obedient.

Too quiet, Cassie thought with a pang of guilt. Had his nightmare last night been a result of her increasing unease over the past week? He was such a sensitive and intuitive child. He had wet the bed during the early hours of the morning, the first time in weeks, and he had been so ashamed he had tried to hide the evidence by spreading a towel over the sheets when she had come in. She had taken him in her arms and told him it was perfectly normal for accidents to happen and he wasn't to blame himself, but somehow she didn't think her reassurances had worked.

Cassie watched him as he stood in line to get on the bus the palace had sent for them. He had a frown of concentration between his small brows, making him look more like Sebastian than ever. Her insides twisted at the thought of them meeting face to face. Would Sebastian see something no one else had so far seen? she wondered. She scanned the two lines of children; so many of them had dark hair and dark eyes just like Sam. Her little son wouldn't stand out…she hoped.

The children quietened with awe as they were led inside the palace a few minutes later, the shuffle of their feet and the rustle of their clothes the only sound as they filed into one of the reception rooms which had been superbly decorated. Balloons hung in colourful clusters from the ceiling, the long ribbons attached making it easy for each child to reach to claim one once the party was over. The tables were loaded with party delights, fairy cakes, ice cream, chocolate and other treats that had every child bug-eyed with anticipation.

The Prince Regent was announced by one of the officials and Cassie held her breath as Sebastian came into the room. His gaze briefly met hers before he turned his attention to the children, who had been instructed to stand on his entry. She watched as he made a concentrated effort to put his young guests at ease. He soon dispensed with formality and moved from table to table, crouching down and chatting easily with each child as he gave them each a gift from the large bag his aide was carrying.

Cassie swallowed as Sebastian drew closer and closer to Sam. It seemed so obvious now they were in the same room together. The likeness was remarkable, startling…terrifying.

She hovered in the background, catching Sam's eye at one point and giving him an encouraging smile even as her insides churned.

'Hello, what is your name?' Sebastian said as he came to the child next to Sam.

'I'm Alexis,' the eight-year-old girl said with her usual precocity. 'And this is Sam. I'll open his present for him. He probably won't talk to you though, 'cause he's shy. He still wets his pants sometimes.'

Cassie felt her heart contract at Alexis's unthinking cruelty. Sam's cheeks were stained with colour and his dark brown gaze dropped in shame.

'Hello, Sam,' Sebastian said. 'I have been looking forward to meeting you.'

Sam's little head came up. 'Y-you have?' he asked in a whisper.

Sebastian's smile was easy and warm. 'Yes, it seems we have something in common,' he said. 'We both love to draw. I loved the painting you sent me. I have it in my study on my desk.'

A shy smile tugged at Sam's little mouth.

'You are much better than I was at your age' Sebastian said, still smiling, 'and you are not as shy as I was back then. I used to dread meeting people but after a while I got used to it. I am sure you will too.'

Cassie felt like hugging Sebastian; he couldn't have said anything better to put her son at ease. Sam was beaming up at him, his earlier shame all but forgotten.

She waited for Sebastian to move on, but he spent far longer with Sam than any other child. She held her breath for so long she saw a school of silverfish appear before her eyes. She blinked them away and forced herself to take a couple of calming breaths, but it wasn't until Sebastian moved on that she felt her shoulders come down in tempo-rary relief.

Sebastian worked his way through the tables until every child had exchanged a few words with him, the sound of happy laughter and presents being unwrapped filling the room with joy.

Cassie had done her best to avoid him, but she could see, now that the magician had begun his act, Sebastian had been stealthily making his way to where she stood at the back of the room. She pressed herself back against the wall, wishing she could become as invisible as the rabbit the magician had made vanish just moments before.

'He is very good, is he not?' Sebastian said, indicating the magician, who was now pulling a long scarf out of one of the children's ears.

Her eyes moved away from his. 'Yes…he is…'

'The children are delightful,' he said after a moment. 'I'm so glad this afternoon has been a success.'

'Yes…you've made it very special for them and at such short notice. You must have very efficient staff.'

'I hope it wasn't too short for them,' he said, turning to look back at Sam's table with a small frown settling between his brows. 'When I was a little child it was often the anticipation of a special event that was the best part.'

The silence stretched for several heart-chugging seconds.

'I want to see you again tonight, Cassie,' Sebastian said, turning to face her.

Her eyes darted away from his. 'Um…I can't see you tonight…something's come up. I'm sure you understand how—'

'I understand one thing, Cassie, and that is I want to continue our association,' he said with an intransigent look. 'For the time being at least.'

She moistened her lips with the point of her tongue, her gaze flicking to where the children were seated, staring up at the magician as if he had cast a spell on them.

Sebastian took her arm and led her out of sight of the

tables. 'Listen to me, Cassie,' he demanded softly but no less implacably. 'This time I am the one who will say when our affair is over.'

She clawed at his hand around her wrist, her eyes shooting sparks of defiance at him. 'It's too dangerous,' she said. 'Can't you see that? Last night was a mistake. We should not have been together. It's over, Sebastian. It was over a long time ago.'

'Mummy?' A small child's voice sounded from behind Sebastian.

A gnarled hand clutched at his insides.

Mummy?

Sebastian turned and looked down at the little dark-haired boy called Sam who was chewing on his lip as he looked up at Cassie.

'Mummy, I need to go to the toilet but I don't know where it is. Can you take me?'

Sebastian felt a cold sensation go down his spine, like slow-moving ice. He swung his gaze back to Cassie. '*You* are Sam's mother?' he asked in a voice that sounded nothing like his.

Her face was shell-white, her eyes darting about in nervousness. 'I—I was going to tell you…' she began.

He frowned at her darkly, his thoughts shooting all over the place. God, she'd had a child. Somehow that hurt more than it should have. How had she kept such a thing a secret? He had heard no mention of a child. Why had she told him the boy was her flatmate's child? Why had she kept such a thing a…

He looked at the small boy again, his chest suddenly feeling as if something large and heavy had just backed over it and squeezed every scrap of air out of his lungs. He couldn't breathe. He couldn't speak. He stood frozen, every drop of blood in his body coming to a screaming, screeching halt.

Cassie had had a child while she was in prison, a child who

looked just like Sebastian. Thick, curly, black hair, dark brown eyes, olive skin and lean to the point of thin.

He had a son.

He had a child who had been kept a secret from him until now. Five years had passed and he had been robbed of every minute of his son's life. How many milestones had he missed? It tore at his insides to even think about them. When had he taken his first step? When had he said his first word? For God's sake, he didn't even know what day he had been born! Five birthdays had passed and he had not been there to celebrate any of them.

'Sorry, M-mummy,' Sam said with a wobble in his voice as he looked between them with eyes wide with worry. 'I tried to hold on but I had two glasses of lemonade. Will I get in trouble?'

'No…no, of course not, darling,' Cassie said, enveloping the boy in a hug. 'You're not in trouble at all. You're allowed to have all the lemonade you want.'

Sebastian watched as she slowly straightened, her eyes finally meeting his. He had thought he had hated her for what she had done to him before, but this was far worse. She had kept his son a secret, he could only assume deliberately. His mind began to reel at the thought of why she had left it this late. Had she planned to bring down the house of Karedes with a carefully timed press release?

He looked back down at Sam, the likeness hitting him over the head like a sledgehammer.

His son.

His son.

The words were running continuously in his head, like a recording stuck on one track.

He dragged his gaze back to Cassie's. 'We need to talk,' he somehow managed to get out past the thick, tight feeling in his throat.

Her eyes fell away. 'Not here...' She held the child close against her protectively. 'Not now.'

He clenched and unclenched his fists as he tried to keep control as she led Sam away. His insides were twisting as if a giant set of claws were attacking him. He felt a pain so intense he had to do everything in his power to keep a poker face in case anyone in the room picked up on his tension.

Sebastian had to think and to think fast. The party was almost over. He had to get Cassie somewhere safe so they could thrash this out. Anger rushed through him at the way she had lied to him, time and time again. She had given herself to him last night while holding this secret. That made him more furious than anything else. She had agreed to an affair with him to ramp up the stakes for him, so that when she dropped her bombshell the person who would pay the biggest price would be him. Damn it, he had already paid the biggest price. She had made sure of it by keeping him in ignorance of his own flesh and blood.

He pushed his anger to one side as he thought about that engaging little boy. *His son.* The words still felt unfamiliar on his tongue, he hadn't expected to say them for many years to come. But there was no mistaking that boy was his. Could no one else see it? *Had* anyone else seen it? His guts turned to gravy just thinking about the fallout from this. He had thought the leak about the Stefani diamond would be devastating, but it didn't even rate next to this.

Sam was a living, breathing image of himself. No wonder he had felt drawn to him. He had felt a connection that was almost visceral.

His stomach twisted again as he saw Cassie and Sam come back to where he was. The child was obviously picking up on the atmosphere; his little chin was trembling and tears began to shine in his eyes. How many times had Sebastian been exactly like that, clinging to his mother, tearful, fearful and unbearably shy?

'Is my mummy in t-trouble?' Sam asked, blinking up at Sebastian. 'She's not going to be taken away again, is she?'

Sebastian felt his heart tighten unbearably. He crouched down and put his hand on the little boy's shoulder, his hand seeming so big in comparison to the small thin bones beneath his palm. 'No one is going to take your mummy away, Sam,' he said, 'but I do need to talk to her. How would you like to come with her to my special hideaway for a few days? Have you ever been on a holiday before?'

Sam shook his head solemnly. 'No…'

Sebastian smiled and gently ruffled the black silk of his hair. 'Then it is about time you did. I will see to it immediately.'

Cassie cleared her throat. 'Excuse me, but I don't want—'

He straightened and cut his eyes to hers, gritting out in an undertone so Sam wouldn't hear, 'Do not speak to me until we are alone. You have a lot of explaining to do and I hope to God you've polished your explanation by the time I hear it or I swear there will be consequences that will not sit well with you.'

Cassie shrank back from the blistering anger in his tone. Her stomach caved in, her knees knocking together as she tried to control her erratic breathing. In spite of his assurances to Sam he could so easily take him off her. It would be the sort of revenge that would appeal to him. He had been denied all knowledge of his son for the first five years of his life. What better way to hurt her than to take Sam away from her indefinitely? She would end up just like Angelica, dragging herself through each day, her heart empty for the son she had lost and most likely would never see again.

Cassie watched in gut-wrenching despair as Sebastian strode over to Stefanos, his aide, exchanging a few words with him before coming back to where she and Sam were standing.

'I have arranged for you and Sam to be transported imme-diately to Kionia,' he said in a tone that warned her not to inter-rupt, much less contradict. 'I will contact the orphanage and offer them some excuse as to why you and the boy will not be returning.'

Cassie's eyes flared, but she kept her lips tightly clamped. She could feel the tremble of her son's thin shoul-ders under her hands and didn't want to cause him any more distress.

'M-Mummy?'

'It's all right, Sam,' she said, stroking his hair with an un-steady hand. 'I'm not going to leave you.'

Sebastian's glittering gaze challenged hers before he squatted down to speak to Sam. 'I have arranged for my old nanny to be at my villa,' he said. 'She will look after you any time Mummy cannot. She is lovely, just like a grandmother.'

'I don't have a grandmother,' Sam said, biting his lip.

Yes, you do, Sebastian thought with a mental wince. His mother was going to take this news hard. She would love Sam, it was not in her nature to do anything else, but accepting Cassie Kyriakis was another thing entirely.

He straightened to his full height to address Cassie once more. 'Stefanos will accompany you to your flat to pick up some essentials, but it is imperative that you speak to no one.'

'But what about Angelica?' she asked. 'I can hardly walk out without some sort of explanation.'

His eyes bored into hers. 'Does she know about this?'

She pressed her lips together, releasing them to whisper, 'No. I've never told her.'

Sebastian felt his spine turn to ice again. 'Does anyone know?' he asked, trying to keep his voice low. 'Anyone at the orphanage?'

She moistened her lips with the point of her tongue.

'Everyone knows he is my son but they don't know who the father is. I swear no one does.'

Sebastian wondered whether he could believe her. She had already told so many lies he was surprised she had been able to keep track of them all. It only demonstrated how adept she was at pulling the wool over everyone's eyes.

'I will see you this evening once you have settled Sam into bed,' he said. 'I have some other engagements now, but Stefanos is doing his utmost to clear my diary for the next few days.'

She gave him a mutinous look but he had already warned Stefanos she might try and escape with the child. He had instructed his aide to put her under lock and key until he returned. He wasn't going to risk anything at this stage. With a few choice words to the press Cassie could have made herself a fortune and brought down his rulership in one fell swoop.

The only question that niggled at him was why hadn't she done so already?

CHAPTER EIGHT

CASSIE paced the floor of the study where Stefanos had instructed her to wait for Sebastian. Sam was in bed, exhausted, barely putting up a struggle when the elderly but totally competent nanny Eleni had told him she would be babysitting him while his mother was downstairs.

Cassie's nerves felt as if they had been stretched beyond the limit. She was jumpy and agitated, the imposing walls of the luxury villa feeling like prison all over again. Her earlier distress had now turned to anger. As each minute dragged past she felt her rage escalating. Was he doing it deliberately? Making her wait for him like this, reminding her with chilling clarity he had all the power, all the control and all the cold-blooded ruthlessness to do what he wanted?

The door suddenly opened and she swung around. 'What the hell do you think you're doing locking me up in this place?' she railed as Sebastian came in.

Cassie had thought she had the highest score on anger until she saw the white-tipped fury on his face. He was in control but barely. She had never seen him so blisteringly, blazingly angry. His whole body was rigid with it, his hands clenched into tight fists, a pulse beating like a jackhammer in his neck.

'You cold-hearted, deceitful little bitch,' he spat at her malevolently.

Cassie took a step backwards, her voice locking in her throat.

He came up close, so close she had to fight every instinct not to shrink away. 'You lying little whore,' he went on brutally. 'I didn't think even you could go as low as you have gone, using a small, innocent child to cover up each and every one of your despicable lies.'

She swallowed tightly as guilt washed over her in scorching waves.

'It was all a game to you, wasn't it?' he said when she didn't speak.

She closed her eyes to escape the fire of his fury.

'Look at me, damn you!'

She flinched and opened her eyes again, her whole body beginning to shake. 'It wasn't like that…'

'What was it like, then?' he said with a curl of his lip. '"Here is a painting by a little orphan,"' he mimicked her voice. 'God, I could shake you until your teeth rattled for that alone.'

Cassie bit the inside of her mouth until she tasted blood.

'You lied to my face time and time again. How could you use a small innocent child to cover your back like that?'

'I know…' she choked. 'I'm sorry…'

His eyes narrowed to black slits. 'You are *sorry?* Oh, so that makes it all OK, then, does it, Cassie? You are sorry you forgot to mention you had my son five years ago but everything's rosy now it's all sorted out.' He raked a hand through his hair. 'God, give me strength.'

'I tried to tell you…I tried to but you didn't respond to my letter.'

His glare turned to a frown. 'Letter?' he asked. 'What letter?'

She swallowed tightly. 'I wrote you a letter as soon as I found out I was pregnant. When you didn't respond I assumed you weren't interested in hearing what I had to tell you. I didn't try again. It was too dangerous in any case. I could hardly write and tell you I was carrying your child—all my letters were screened.'

He gave her a cutting look. 'You were not going to tell me anything until you could do so for maximum effect, isn't that right, Cassie? I am just a matter of weeks away from being crowned as King. You could not have chosen a more devastatingly effective time.'

'No, that's not right,' she said. 'I wasn't going to tell you at all… Sam and I are leaving as soon as my parole is up. I've…I've already got the tickets.'

A menacing silence tightened the air to snapping point.

'So…let me get this right,' he said, skewering her gaze with his. 'You were going to take *my* child off the island never once telling me of his existence, is that correct?'

It sounded awful when he put it like that, Cassie thought. 'I thought it would be for the best,' she said. 'You're about to be King. I thought the last thing you would want to know about is a love-child.'

'Is that what you call him—*a love-child?*' he asked in scorn. 'But there was no love, was there, Cassie?'

She brought up her chin. 'I did love you.' *I do love you.*

His bark of a laugh was a bitter, horrible sound that echoed ominously in the room. 'Oh, yes, I remember now. You claimed to love me but you were opening your legs for anyone else who came along.'

'It wasn't like that…' she said in a barely audible voice. 'There was no one else.'

He came up even closer, so close she could see every dark fleck in his eyes and every spark of glittering hatred. 'Is there no end to your falsehoods?' he bit out. 'Do you think I would fall for any more of your despicable lies?'

Cassie felt the cold hand of despair clutch at her insides. 'I only told you that so I could end our relationship,' she said. 'I was afraid…'

'Of what?'

'Of…of how things were between us,' she said, not able to hold his gaze.

'I don't believe you. I don't believe a word that comes out of that perfidious mouth of yours,' he said. 'You are a liar just as your father always said you were. I was a fool to think otherwise. For years I have thought he was painting a worse picture of you to serve his own ends, but after this I realise everything he said about you was true. You have no conscience, no moral sense of what is right. Lying is second nature to you.'

'Yes, well, he would have known,' she shot back. 'It takes one to know one, doesn't it?'

He gave her a contemptuous look. 'You can malign him all you like because he can't defend himself. I know whose version I prefer to believe.'

Cassie felt her world start to crumble all over again. She had been so close to telling him what her father had been like, had told him more than she had told anyone, and yet now there was no way he would believe her if she told him the rest. The pain she felt was much worse than she could ever have imagined. It was as if her life, all of her suffering and despair had been a fantasy she had made up to protect herself.

Wasn't that always the way it had been? Everyone had always believed her father and they continued to do so even though he was dead. She'd had no one to defend her in the past and there would be no one in the future. Not even the one person she had wanted to understand her situation more than any other.

'Did you know you were pregnant when you ended our relationship?' he asked, still glaring at her furiously.

'No…I only found out after I was in prison. I had a health check done and a pregnancy test was standard procedure. The results came back positive. I was shocked. I didn't even know you could fall pregnant while on the pill.'

Sebastian heard the anguish behind the words and felt his anger loosen around the edges. She had been eighteen years old. Sure, she had acted like a streetwise slut, but finding herself pregnant and in prison must have thrown her for six.

'That's when I wrote to you,' she said, her eyes glistening with moisture. 'I asked to see you. I didn't think it would be appropriate to tell you other than face to face.'

'I received no such letter,' he said, still wondering if he should believe her. She was so good at this, damn her. She could even tear up on cue. He could feel the effect on him and could only assume it was deliberate. What she hoped to achieve he wasn't entirely sure. Perhaps a massive pay out to stop her from going to the press, but if he paid it how could he be sure she wouldn't double-cross him? And besides, he wanted to freely acknowledge Sam as his own son. The child deserved so much better than he'd had so far in his short life.

Sebastian felt his anger simmering all over again at how his son had been born in a prison instead of the palace where he belonged. God only knew what things he had seen or heard in those first formative years of his life, the people he had been housed with, the toughened criminals, the down-and-outs and dregs of society knew his son better than he did.

'You don't believe me, do you?' she said, the line of her mouth bitter.

He hesitated for perhaps a fraction too long to be convincing. 'I can only say if a letter was sent I did not see it. Someone must have intercepted it and destroyed it.'

'Your father?'

Sebastian considered it for a moment. 'I would not like to

think him responsible for such an act, but I have no way of proving it either way.'

'So you'd rather believe me capable of lying than sully your father's name with suspicion.'

He swore under his breath. 'Cassie, you have done nothing but lie to me from the moment we met,' he said. 'If I am having trouble believing you now, then you have only yourself to blame.'

Tears shone in her eyes. 'Please don't take Sam away from me,' she begged. 'He wouldn't cope with it, I know he wouldn't. Please…please don't take him away…'

Sebastian tried to harden his heart but it was impossible. She clearly loved the child and had gone through hell and high water to keep him. 'I am not going to take him away from you,' he said in a gruff tone. 'I can see he loves you as much as you love him. I just want some answers and I want you for once in your life to be honest with me. You surely owe me that?'

'I'm not sure I can trust you,' she said. 'You've brought me here against my will and locked all the doors behind me. I can't bear it.'

'There is no other way,' he said. 'I can't have this leaked out to the press.'

'Is that all that matters to you?' she asked. 'What people will think?'

'Damn it, Cassie, I don't care what people think. I am trying to protect Sam. He is totally innocent in all of this. I have missed out on five years of his life. How can I ever make it up to him? Where the hell do I start?'

Cassie felt so ashamed she hadn't factored in how Sebastian would be feeling right now. He had only just learned of Sam's existence. He had been robbed of so much and it could never be made up to him. She had been robbed herself when Sam had been taken away for the last year of her sentence and look how devastated that had left her. How much worse must he be feeling having not even known he had fathered a child until now?

'I haven't told him you are his father,' she said into the painful silence.

'Were you planning to tell him at some stage?'

'How could I?' she said in a broken whisper.

Sebastian scored another pathway through his hair. His emotions were all over the place. Every bone in his body was aching with the knowledge Cassie had borne his child alone. What if someone *had* intercepted her sole attempt to contact him? How could he blame her for not trying again since her first attempt had yielded nothing? Even her best friend, his sister Lissa, had deserted her at their father's command.

And there was Sam, shy little Sam who looked as if any moment he expected someone to destroy his carefully constructed world. His mother was everything to him, his anchor, just as Sebastian's mother had been to him. How could he swoop in and take control without considering the effect on that endearing little boy?

'He needs to be told,' he said heavily. 'I would like to be the one to do so.'

Cassie looked at him with worry, a dark shadow in her green eyes. 'You mean to acknowledge him as your own?'

He placed his closed fist against his heart. 'He is *my son,* Cassie,' he said. 'Do you really think I would turn my back on him?'

'No…it's just I thought with the coronation and all…'

'That is not important right now,' he said. 'I want to spend the next couple of weeks getting to know him. I have to come to some sort of decision over his future as well as my own.'

'I'm not asking you to give up the throne,' she said. 'I would never ask that of you.'

He studied her for a lengthy pause. 'Why did you agree to

another affair with me?' he asked. 'You knew I was his father—why dance with danger by getting involved with me again?'

She bit her lip and lowered her gaze. 'I knew it was dangerous but…'

'But?'

She brought her eyes back to his. 'I couldn't help myself…'

Sebastian hoped it wasn't another one of her lies. She looked exhausted, pale and fragile and nothing like the in-your-face Cassie of the past. She had been steadily shrinking from him from the moment he had stepped into the room, cowering almost, which made him wonder…

'Do you mind if I go to bed?' she asked, pinching at the bridge of her nose. 'I have the most appalling headache. It's been coming on all afternoon.'

'I didn't realise,' he said, frowning in concern. 'You should have said. I will get Stefanos to show you to your room. It is next door to Sam's and close to mine if you need anything during the night.'

'Thank you…'

'Cassie?'

She turned and looked at him, her face bleak and her eyes nothing less than soulless. 'Yes?'

'Thank you for not getting rid of him,' he said. 'You would have had many reasons to do so, but you did not.'

'I *could* not,' she said almost fiercely. 'Termination or adoption was never going to be an option for me. I had grown up without knowing my mother. It's been like a gaping hole in my life. I couldn't bear for my child to suffer the same.'

Sebastian could sense the pain behind the quietly spoken words. How had he not seen this about her before? But then he reminded himself their clandestine meetings had always been about satisfying an urgent physical need, they had not been about discovering intimate details of each other's lives.

He suddenly realised he had told her even less about his own life. He hadn't shared his frustration over his father's heavy handedness. He had told her nothing of the sense of duty that was at times burdensome. He had simply enjoyed a red-hot affair with her, not for a moment thinking she was anything but a good-time girl.

Sebastian could see how fragile she was now. She looked like a wraith with her too-slim body and long, blonde hair awry from dragging her fingers through it agitatedly. It awoke every protective instinct in his body to draw her close and offer what comfort he could.

'Cassie.' He reached out and touched her ever so gently on the arm, but she flinched away as if he had slapped her.

She looked at him, her tear-washed eyes glittering with a last stand show of defiance. 'I don't want to talk any more. I'm tired and my head feels as if it's going to explode. If you had a decent bone in your body you'd realise that and let me go to bed.'

He held her challenging glare for a moment before he let out a weary sigh. 'Of course,' he said, holding the door open for her. '*Kalinichta,* Cassie.'

She didn't respond, which he more or less expected, but it disappointed him all the same. He saw the shadows in her emerald eyes and knew he had played a huge part in putting them there. Now he wanted to know how on earth he was going to remove them.

CHAPTER NINE

CASSIE wasn't sure what had woken her only an hour or so later. The silence most probably, she thought wryly as she threw back the covers to go and check on Sam, who was sleeping next door. After years in a noisy prison she still found the quietness of night faintly disturbing.

She gently pushed open the door of Sam's room but came to a startled halt when she saw who was sitting beside the bed, with one of Sam's tiny hands cupped in his. 'Is…is everything all right?' she said in a low whisper.

Sebastian tucked Sam's hand back under the covers. 'Yes…I was just…checking him before I went to bed.'

Cassie waited until they were out in the corridor before she spoke. 'Haven't you been to bed yet? It's way past midnight.'

He rubbed one of his hands down his face, the scrape of his palm over his stubble sounding loud in the silence. 'No, I had some things to see to,' he said. 'How is your headache?'

Somehow the genuine concern in his voice made Cassie's skin tingle with awareness. So too did the fact she was standing before him in an almost sheer slip of a nightgown with only a light bathrobe covering it. 'It's gone… sort of…'

He lifted a hand and gently brushed back the hair off her

face, his touch so light she felt every nerve spring to life. She stood stock-still, not breathing, not thinking—just feeling.

'Do you fancy a drink or something?' he asked in a brusque tone, shoving his hand in his pocket as if he regretted touching her. 'I was just about to go downstairs and make one.'

She lifted her brows. 'You fix your own drinks?'

'Occasionally,' he said, his expression locking her out. 'Just because I have a late night doesn't mean my staff have to as well.'

'Did Sam call out?' she asked as he led the way downstairs. 'I checked him before I went to bed and he was fine.'

'No, he didn't call out,' he said. 'I just wanted to sit with him.'

'Oh…'

His eyes met hers. 'I do have the right to sit with him, do I not?'

'Of course…I didn't mean to suggest—'

He held open the door of one of the reception rooms, his eyes still boring into hers. 'There is no question over my paternity, is there, Cassie?'

Cassie felt the question like a slap across the face. 'No…there's no question at all.'

He studied her for a stretched-out moment. 'Under the circumstances royal protocol might call for proof.'

She held his piercing dark gaze, her heart contracting at the lack of trust she could see in his eyes. 'Go right ahead,' she said, stalking over to the middle of the room. 'I have nothing to hide.'

'Ah, but that is not quite true, is it, Cassie?' he said, coming over to where she was standing. 'You are rather adept at hiding things from me.'

Cassie took an unsteady step backwards. 'I told you I tried to tell you about Sam…'

'I am not just talking about Sam.'

She swept her tongue across her lips, her eyes automatically darting to the door. 'W-what are you talking about, then?'

'There,' he said. 'You did it just then. You get this cornered look in your eyes as if you think I am going to take a swipe at you. I used to think it was because of what went on in prison, but while I was thinking through some things this evening I realised I had seen that look on your face before.'

She straightened her shoulders with an effort. 'You have a rather threatening demeanour at times, Sebastian.'

'I would *never* raise my hand in anger,' he said, frowning darkly. 'You surely know that, Cassie. Have I ever given you a reason to think otherwise?'

'No…no, of course not,' Cassie said, thinking of how gentle he had been with Sam so far.

He seemed satisfied with her answer and after a moment he moved across to a drinks servery and poured some juice for her and a cognac for himself. 'Have you had time to have a look around while you have been here today?' he asked as he handed her the glass. 'It occurred to me that I didn't show you around last time you were here.'

'Not really,' she said, taking the drink from him. 'I wanted to spend the time settling Sam in—he was a bit nervous about coming here. Besides, I didn't want to get us both lost looking around by ourselves, and I wasn't sure what to say to the staff or what they knew about us so we kept to our rooms.'

'Eleni and, of course, Stefanos know Sam is my son, and the housekeeper who has worked here for most of my life, but that is all,' Sebastian said. 'I will take Sam on a tour tomorrow so he feels more secure. Finish your drink and I will show you around this floor. I think you will enjoy the views.'

Cassie followed him into the next room where the views from the large windows overlooking the ocean were stunningly beautiful, especially in the silvery darkness of a moonlit night. Lights from one of the passenger ferries to Greece or Turkey could be seen twinkling in the distance.

'Let me show you the view from one of the east-facing rooms,' Sebastian said. 'You can see the Port of Aquila on Calista.'

Cassie followed him into another room, which she took to be the morning room as there was an informal dining setting, as well as a large, comfortable-looking sofa where she could imagine members of the royal family would peruse the newspapers. He was right about the view, she thought as she looked at the angry sea below.

'As you see, it is very private,' Sebastian said from her left shoulder. 'The cliffs and rocks below make it impossible for anyone to access the grounds from the three seaboard sides.'

Cassie could feel the warmth of him standing so close and the deep timbre of his voice was like the melodious rumble of organ pipes. 'It is very beautiful here,' she said, more to fill the silence than anything else. 'And, as you say, very private.'

'Privacy is more valuable than you can ever imagine for people like me,' he said, still looking at the view. 'In fact I cannot put a price on it.'

Cassie picked up the wistfulness in his tone and turned to look at him, a small frown tugging at her brow. 'You sound as if you are not looking forward to being crowned as King and all it entails.'

He shifted his gaze from the window to mesh with hers, the edginess she had always associated with him evident in the way he held himself. 'No, that is not true,' he said. 'I am well prepared for the role and have looked forward to it for most of my life, but there are times…' He lifted one of his broad shoulders in a shrug that communicated everything and nothing.

'But there are times?' Cassie prodded.

His eyes moved away from hers. 'Come,' he said. 'I think you would like the library and the music room. Do you still play the piano?'

'I haven't touched one in years,' Cassie said as he led her to another room towards the western end of the house. 'I wasn't all that great at it in any case. I only did it because my father for…I mean…thought it was an essential part of a young lady's upbringing to have some proficiency in the arts.'

Sebastian held the music-room door open for her, noting how she had stumbled over her choice of words. He breathed in her scent as she walked past, a mixture of her heady jasmine and his sharp citrus that unleashed a host of memories from the lockers of his mind. He had showered every time they had made love in the past, but he could have sworn there were still times he could smell her in the very pores of his skin. He could still smell her on him from last night. 'Play something for me,' he said, letting the door close on a soft click behind him. 'Something to suit your current mood.'

Her eyes flicked to his, a camera-shutterlike look passing through them before they fell away and rested on the white grand piano. 'I'm not sure I can remember anything by ear…' she said, her teeth worrying at her bottom lip, her arms wrapped around her body like a shield.

Sebastian watched as she circled the instrument, like a wary opponent facing a much-feared foe. 'It's not going to bite you if you touch it, Cassie,' he said softly.

He strode over and pulled out the stool for her and once she was seated, or rather perched on the edge of it, he lifted the lid so the sound could reverberate throughout the spacious room.

Cassie opened and closed her fingers, her pulse like a drum beneath her skin. For someone who had lived the life of a party girl she knew she was doing a very poor job of playing the role now. She hated playing in front of an audience. She had only once played in front of Sebastian in the past and that had been entirely by accident. The apartment he had borrowed from a friend for their secret trysts had an old, slightly out of tune upright piano, and, arriving earlier than him one day, Cassie had sat down and run her normally rigid-with-fear fingers over the keys. Even she had been surprised by the poignancy of the cadences she had played, and it had been some minutes before she had realised Sebastian had been leaning against the door jamb, his dark, penetrating gaze focussed on her as he listened...

Cassie pulled away from the past and placed her fingers on the keys and started to play, stumblingly at first, hesitantly, like a small child at her first pianoforte exam. She had to remind herself her father was dead. He couldn't break a ruler over her knuckles now if she tripped over a note. He couldn't shout from another room with biting criticisms of her technique. He couldn't storm into the room and slam the lid down on the piano so hard she almost lost control of her insides in the most humiliating way of all.

No, he was rotting in hell where he belonged. Tears suddenly blurred her vision, but she played on, the notes rising and falling with each aching breath she took, her heart taking up far too much room in her chest as she thought of all she'd had in her hands and thrown away like stale bread crusts to the seagulls nesting on the cliffs below the windows.

Sebastian found himself transfixed. It was not just the music that was unusually poignant, but it was the fleeting shadows on Cassie's beautiful, model-perfect face. He was close enough to see the tears rolling down her cheeks, as if the music had touched her in a way she had not intended or indeed expected it to.

She had never cried in front of him in the past, not openly at least. He was well used to female tears having grown up with sisters; he understood more than most about the shifting of hormones and the moods that came and went like the tides. But that was a side he had never seen in Cassie. She had always been so in control emotionally, or had she? The devil-may-care attitude she had brandished about in the past was no longer a part of who she was now. She was quieter, watchful and deeper, like a shallow, bubbling brook that had suddenly turned a corner and become a deeply flowing river instead.

Careful, he lectured himself as another trill of notes sent the hairs on his arms upright. She was not for ever; she was just for now. He had to remember that, even if some secret part of him would have liked things to be different. He wouldn't have been the first royal to marry a commoner, but Cassie's past made any such alliance impossible. Was that why he was feeling this burning ache in his throat?

She looked so beautiful sitting there like that, her long slim fingers dancing over the keys as her confidence increased. He recognised a few bars of a Beethoven sonata but she suddenly stumbled over a note and froze like one of the marble statues in the gallery three rooms away.

'Cassie?' He stepped towards her.

She got to her feet, the piano stool almost toppling backwards in her haste. 'I'm sorry…' she said, not quite meeting his eyes. 'I was never very good at that piece. Too many sharps and flats…or something…'

Sebastian was beginning to think 'or something' just about summed Cassie Kyriakis up. He drew out a clean handkerchief, and came over to where she was standing with her arms folded across her chest, and gently dabbed at the tears on her cheeks. 'I think you played rather beautifully, Cassie,' he said. 'I didn't realise you were so talented. That is yet another secret you have kept from me.'

Her eyes watered up again, but before he could attend to the damage she took his handkerchief from him with a slight brush of her fingers against his, a rueful twist contorting the fullness of her mouth. 'Do you mind if I find somewhere to freshen up?' she asked.

Sebastian felt that tight knot in his throat again. She was holding him off; he wasn't sure why. Had he slipped under her guard, seeing more than she wanted him to see? So many clues were starting to make sense, like a crossword that had long been unsolved due to an unknown word. He could force it out of her, or he could wait for her to tell him. Something told him force was not the way to go. If what she had hinted at was true, and he was starting to suspect it was, she would need time and gentle handling to feel safe enough to reveal the full extent of her past.

'Sure,' he said, and led the way back out of the music room to the sweeping staircase. 'There is a guest bathroom on the next floor, second on the right. Take your time.'

She stretched her lips into a smile that looked almost painful. 'Thank you.'

He felt a heavy sigh bring his shoulders down once she had gracefully ascended the stairs, the invisible atoms of her perfume teasing his nostrils long after she had disappeared from sight...

Cassie leant back on the bathroom door and slowly slid to the floor, her head going forward on her bent knees, her shoulders shaking as she wrestled her emotions back into the steel chains she had long ago locked them in.

Who was she fooling? How could she possibly expect to be in Sebastian's presence after last night and not feel vulnerable? It wasn't just about him now knowing about Sam. She had been far too vulnerable when it came to Sebastian Karedes right from the start. But it was far worse now than it had ever been. He was starting to see things she had desperately kept hidden before. She had felt it in his steady, watchful gaze downstairs; the quizzical flicker in his eyes every now and again, as if he was trying to put a rather complicated puzzle together.

Cassie almost laughed out loud as she dragged herself to her feet. A puzzle, that was what she was. No one could figure her out because she liked it that way. What alternative did she have anyway? Who was going to believe her now?

There was a knock at the door and she almost leapt out of her skin. 'Cassie?' Sebastian's voice sounded out with deep strains of concern in it. 'Are you all right in there?'

She quickly blew her nose and tossed the tissue in the bin. 'I'm fine,' she said and came out, closing the door softly behind her.

The silence was like a mantle settling about them. Cassie could feel the soft cloak of muted light surrounding them. Shadows danced off the walls, tempting, taunting shadows that made her aware of how isolated they were. Sam was asleep upstairs with Eleni close by. There was no one around, no bodyguards, no lurking members of the press, just the silence and her lingering memory of last night in his arms. Could he feel it? she wondered. Was that why he was looking at her that way? His dark eyes scanning her features, as if looking for a chink in her hastily assembled armour?

'I have something to show you,' he said. 'It's in my room along the hall.'

Cassie put her hands up. 'Oh, no, you don't,' she said, backing away. 'Don't try that line with me. It's so hackneyed. I'm not going to see your etchings or your anything just so you can fast track me back into your bed.'

He lifted one brow at her. 'You think that's what I was doing?'

She gave him a narrow-eyed look. 'I *know* that's what you were doing. Go on, admit it. You were going to lure me into your parlour and one kiss would lead to another and then we both know what would happen. I told you last night was a mistake. We should never have given into the temptation.'

'Last night was not a mistake,' he said. 'I wanted you and you wanted me. Nothing has changed, Cassie.'

Cassie plugged her ears with her fingers. 'Stop it. Stop it right now, do you hear me?'

He pulled her hands down from her face. 'No,' he said, suddenly deadly serious again. 'You stop it and listen to me. *I want you.*' He spaced out the words for maximum effect and Cassie had to fight not to weaken as he continued. 'I know it's crazy and probably downright dangerous but I want you so badly it's like a pain in my gut that won't go away.'

Emotion clogged her throat. 'Please, Sebastian…' Her voice dropped to a desperate whisper. 'You don't know what you're doing…it's hormones…or something.'

He gave her a little shake and saw the flare of her eyes, felt the stiffening of her body and the quiver of her bottom lip before she got it under control. 'It's the "or something" I am worried about,' he said heavily, resting his forehead against hers. 'What am I going to do with you, Caz, my beautiful, complicated chameleon? What on earth am I going to do with you, hmm?'

Cassie felt like candle wax melting under a powerful heat source. Her bones loosened, her ligaments softened, her heart swelled and her resolve…well, it had been a little off centre in any case. 'You have to let me go,' she said, but it didn't sound anywhere near as convincing as she had wanted it to, it was too whispery, too don't-take-me-seriously-when-I-say-this. 'Now…right now…before we go in any deeper.'

It seemed a long time before he lifted his forehead from hers. He drew in a breath, an uneven one, which surprised her for she had thought it was just she who was struggling to keep the past back where it belonged.

He stepped back, just one step but it seemed as if a chasm had opened up between them. 'I was going to show you a photograph,' he said. 'In my bedroom, I have a photograph of you

I took one day when you weren't watching. I have never shown it to you. I didn't get the chance.'

Cassie's eyes went wide and her heart began to stutter, not unlike her voice. 'You…y-you have a photograph of me? You mean you didn't have a ritual burning when I dumped you?'

He winced at her choice of words. 'You know something? I hate that word. Dumped.' He spat it out like a mouthful of something vile.

She gave him an irritated look. 'Ended our relationship, then. Called it quits. Broke it off. Told you it was over.'

'But it's not over, is it, Cassie?' he asked in a low deep tone that sent a shower of remembered sensations down the entire length of her spine.

Cassie gritted her teeth. 'I *want* it to be over. Do you think I want to feel like this? You look at me like that and I—' She stopped, suddenly realising how she was betraying herself to him.

He stepped closer, just that one step but it bridged the chasm again. His body heat was searing a way through her clothes; his eyes were burning with promise, the promise of passion and paradise.

'And you what, Cassie?' he asked in that same sun-warmed satin-sliding-over-bare-skin tone.

Cassie sucked in a ragged breath and threw caution to the winds still raging outside. 'And I want you…' she said, not a whisper, not loud, but somewhere right in between.

The air was heavy, the silence so thick she could almost reach out and touch it. Instead she reached out and touched him, on the face, the soft skin of her palm making a raspy sound on the stubble that had grown there since he had shaved that morning.

She wasn't sure who made the next move after that. She had a sneaking suspicion it might have been her, but her conscience later on wouldn't allow her to admit it. Suddenly their mouths were fused, their bodies locked tightly together, their hands moving in wild, frantic desperation to get as close as humanly possible.

Cassie opened her mouth to the driving thrust of his tongue, met it with hers, tangling, teasing, tasting the promise of what was to come. She felt the surge of sexual energy streak through her body like a fire racing through thick, dry scrub, flames of need licking at every pleasure point in anticipation of his touch.

He had backed her against the nearest wall, his pelvis rock hard against her, grinding, pushing and probing until she wanted to scream with frustration at not having him where she wanted him most.

He lifted his mouth off hers long enough to say, 'I told myself it wasn't going to be like this.'

'Like what?' she asked, running her tongue over her lips and savouring the sex and salt male taste of him.

His eyes were so dark and intense as they held hers. 'In the past it was always so rushed between us,' he said, nipping at her bottom lip, tug, pull, tug, pull. 'Last night was the same. I told myself the next time together would be slow and sensual and something that neither of us will ever forget.'

Cassie didn't want to be reminded this was not going to be for ever. It was a just-in-the-moment thing. She knew that, but it was hard to think clearly when his teeth were doing that thing with her bottom lip and his hands searching for her breasts through the light but still annoying barrier of her clothes.

She reached down to stroke him through his trousers, the hard outline of his erection pulsing against her touch, reminding her of how big he was, and how her body, as slim as it was, had always managed to accommodate him.

Sebastian dragged his mouth off hers again. 'Not here,' he

said. 'Not here in the hall. I want you in my bed this time. Not against the wall, not against the kitchen bench, not in some cramped corner of someone else's house, but in my bed.'

Cassie brought his mouth back down to hers. 'A bed would be nice,' she murmured throatily.

'That's usually where this happens first,' he said, nuzzling against her neck. 'I don't think we've been together in a bed before.'

'Then it's about time we did something about that,' she said, sliding her hands down his chest as she popped each button on his shirt.

He shrugged himself out of it, and, kicking it aside with his foot, scooped her up in his arms and carried her to a room several doors down. He shouldered the door open in a classical-hero sort of way that did serious damage to Cassie's heart rate.

The mattress was soft, but he was rock-hard when he came down on top of her. 'You've got too many clothes on,' she said, tugging at his belt.

'So have you,' he said, and removed the problem with a deftness that was exhilarating.

Skin on skin.

Cassie could feel the pores of her skin opening to take more of him in. She could smell the musk of his body, the heat of it was driving her wild, but he was slowing down. She could sense it; each kiss was no less drugging but it was softer, lingering. Each caress of his hands was drawing out her response in a torturous way she had never experienced with him before. He cupped her breasts, rubbing his thumbs over the aching, tight points so leisurely she began to whimper in impatience. She wanted to feel his hot, moist mouth sucking hard on her nipples, to feel the almost savage scrape of his teeth, to feel the answering tug of her feminine muscles crying out to be stretched to the limit. She opened her thighs but he didn't do what she wanted or expected. He kept kissing her, on her mouth, her neck, her ear lobes, her collarbones and her breasts until she was panting and squirming and as close to begging as her pride would allow.

'I know what you want but I am not giving it to you,' he said, looking at her smoulderingly in between kisses. 'Or at least not yet.'

She arched her spine in an effort to search for his probing heat but, for the first time in her experience with him, failing. 'If you don't get inside me this minute I am going to…to…'

His laugh was a low rumble that made her longing for him all the more intense. 'To what, Cassie? Tonight I am going to take as long as I damn well like.'

Cassie smothered a groan of restlessness and gave herself up to the go-slow rhythm he was setting.

There was something to be said about taking your time, she decided a few breathless minutes later. She was becoming aware of her body in a way she had not done so before, even with him. She felt the flow of her blood to her feminine core, the way it swelled and ached and pulsed to be caressed. She shifted beneath him, trying to get him to give into the temptation of driving into her but he wouldn't do it. He kept moving away, not far, but just enough to make sure she felt the throb of his body, but not his full possession.

'You are doing this on purpose,' she said, mock-glaring at him even as she clutched at him. 'You want me to beg, don't you?'

He smiled and bent his head back to her breast, suckling, teasing and finally biting until every nerve in her body jumped to attention. 'If it's any comfort to you I'm having a hard time keeping control,' he said. 'I want to take you to the heights like I did last night, but I am not going to do it. Not this time.'

This last time… The words almost echoed in the silence.

Cassie shoved the reality aside. 'Do it now or don't do it at all,' she said with a steely glint in her eyes.

'You don't mean that,' he said, trailing a blistering pathway of kisses down past her belly button to the humid heart of her.

'Sure I d-do,' she said, sucking in a breath when his lips skated over her swollen folds. 'It's a woman's prerogative to change her mind at any time during the procedure.'

'I know the law, Caz,' he said, softly parting her. 'God, you are like an orchid, so beautiful.'

Cassie had always struggled with body issues. She'd had no idea how delicately she was made; the tidy secrets of her body were so different from his. There was no way he could hide his reaction to her, but she could hide hers from him, but only just.

Somehow she thought that was a good thing in the design of things. Women were far more vulnerable when it came to sex. She *felt* something when she shared her body with Sebastian. It was visceral, instinctive and totally consuming. Her heart was in it just as much as her body. She wouldn't be doing this now if she didn't care about him. It was a going-nowhere love, but this night would have to last for ever.

She knew that—he knew that.

She would *make* it last for ever.

She had gone through six years of hell and managed to survive. Another sixty or so wouldn't be easy, but at least she had loved and lost—it was supposed to be better than not loving at all, but somehow she seriously doubted it.

Cassie was jerked back to the moment when his tongue entered her, a lick first, then a gentle probe, and then a sensual onslaught that had her spine arching off the bed as an orgasm ripped through her unlike anything she had felt before. She gasped her way through it, her body disconnected from her mind as the sensations rocketed through her, leaving her boneless and shuddering with aftershocks.

'Good?' he asked with a smile that should have looked supercilious, but somehow didn't.

'Better than good,' she gasped out. 'One of the best…'

He moved up her body until he was within striking distance of hers. 'I think we should put that to the test, don't you?' he asked.

Cassie was almost beyond words. Her body was limp, but somehow still needy in spite of the earth-shattering response he had summoned from her. She watched as he applied a condom, the engorged length of him exciting her all over again.

He moved over her, his weight balanced on his elbows, his eyes glittering with need as he gently nudged her thighs apart. She arched her spine to receive that first wonderful thrust of his powerfully made body, a gasp escaping from her mouth as he began a torturously slow rhythm. Cassie dug her fingers into his buttocks, every sensitised nerve in her body begging for more speed to increase the delicious friction. He gradually increased his pace, his breathing becoming more hectic, and she knew with certainty he was coming closer and closer to losing control. She could feel the tension building in him, the muscles beneath her fingers tightly clenched before he took that final plunge. She was with him all the way, her hips rising to meet the downward thrust of his. She hit the summit first but he was right behind her, the shudders of his body as he emptied himself making her shiver all over.

Cassie listened to the sound of their breathing, wondering if he would say something, *anything* to fill the lengthening silence. But after a while she gave up thinking about it. She lay with him still enclosed within her, his face pressed against her neck, his warm breath tickling her skin as her eyelids gradually drifted down in total blissful relaxation…

Sebastian gently eased himself off her, disposing of the condom before he came back to stroke the tussled hair back off her face. Her soft mouth was swollen from his kisses, the faint flush of sexual pleasure still evident in her cheeks. This was the Cassie he had grown to love in the past. Only when her guard was down like this did he get a tiny glimpse of who she really was. She was complex, not shallow, she was troubled, not a trouble-maker, she was his Caz, the woman he could never have.

She stirred beneath him, her eyes opening to meet his. 'Seb?'

His smile was crooked. 'It's been a long time since you called me that.'

She touched his face with her fingertips, a feather-light caress that made his skin lift. 'That's because we can't go back,' she said with a hint of sadness in her voice. 'We're not Caz and Seb now. We're Cassie the ex-criminal and Sebastian the Prince Regent of Aristo, and never the twain shall meet, as they say.'

'It's not enough, Cassie,' he said, running his tongue across his lips as he looked deep into her eyes. 'I want more.'

Cassie swallowed tightly, hope like a raising agent in her chest. 'What do you mean?'

His expression was rueful as he tucked a strand of her hair back behind her ear. 'I thought once we did this a couple of times it would be enough, but it's not. I want you again.'

She stared at him, suspended between hope and despair. 'I'm not sure what to say...' she took another small swallow and added '...or what you are saying...'

He pressed a soft kiss to her mouth, a brush-like touch that made her lips tingle. 'I would like to have more time, Caz,' he said, 'a few more nights alone with you. That is all I am asking.'

'Why?' Cassie asked.

He raked a hand through his hair and let out a deep, uneven sigh. 'Because for the first time since I met you six years ago I am starting to see a glimpse of who you really are. I want to see more.'

Cassie lowered her gaze from his, her heart aching and heavy in her chest. 'There's no future in this, you know that. There can never be anything but an affair between us.' *And a very short and secret one at that,* she thought with another pang of despair.

He kissed her softly, lingeringly, before pushing up her chin to meet her eyes once more. 'Let's have what we can have for as long as we can have it,' he said.

Cassie left it far too late to say no. For a few pulsing seconds she had her chance, but she said nothing. But as his mouth came back down to claim hers she knew exactly why she hadn't.

She still loved him.

CHAPTER TEN

CASSIE was helping Sam with his breakfast the next morning when Sebastian came in. She looked up, knowing her cheeks were glowing from all the intimacy they had shared during the night before she had slipped back to her own room in the early hours of the morning while he had been sleeping.

He met her gaze for a pulsing moment before turning to Sam. 'Good morning, Sam,' he said, taking the chair beside him. 'Did you sleep well?'

Sam put his spoon down politely. 'Yes. I could hear the sea. Mummy said I might be able to go to the beach and build a sandcastle.'

'I think that would be a very good idea,' Sebastian said. 'But first I would like to talk to you about something very important.'

Sam's big brown eyes instantly clouded with worry. He looked at his mother, his chin starting to tremble. 'Have I d-done something wrong?' he asked in a thin voice.

Sebastian felt his chest tighten and took both of Sam's small hands in his, again marvelling at how tiny they were compared to his own. He looked into those deeply brown eyes so like his own and wondered if that haunted, terrified look was the outcome of his early years living in prison. How could he make his little boy feel secure? It would take months if not years and yet he had so little time at his disposal. 'You have done nothing wrong, Sam,' he said gently. Oh, God, where did he begin? How could he tell this small innocent child how he had let him and his mother down?

Five years.

He had missed it all. He hadn't even seen a photograph of Sam as a baby. He hadn't even thought to ask Cassie to show him one. Not that he had given her much of a chance to retrieve any. He had packed her and Sam away with barely enough time for Cassie to pack a few belongings together and tell her flatmate where she and Sam were going.

'Sam…' He cleared his throat and began again, 'I have recently found out I am your father.'

Sam glanced at his mother. 'But I don't have a father, do I, Mummy?'

Sebastian saw Cassie's throat move up and down. 'Darling…I have never actually said you didn't have a father…'

'No, but Spiro said I didn't have one,' Sam said. 'I heard him tell Kara.'

Cassie frowned. 'What did he say?'

Sam bit his lip. 'He said it was anyone's guess who I belonged to…'

Sebastian met Cassie's bleak gaze before turning back to Sam. 'You belong to me, Sam,' he said, giving the boy's hands a gentle squeeze. 'You will always belong to me, no matter what happens in the future.'

Cassie felt her stomach clench with dread. What was he implying? That any future of Sam's would be with his father and not with her? What else could he mean? There was no way Sebastian could have it all. They both knew that. That was why last night had been so poignant to her. This next couple of weeks would be all they would ever have together, as a little family. It would all too soon be over.

'So you and Mummy and me are going to always be together?' Sam asked with hope shining in his eyes.

'For the time being at least,' Sebastian said after a slight pause.

Sam's eyes began to water. 'Is Mummy going to leave me here?'

'No,' Cassie said stridently, glaring at Sebastian.

Sebastian put his hands on Sam's shoulders. 'Sam, I know this is hard for you to understand, but your mother and I are not married. But that does not mean we both don't love you. We do, very much.'

Sam gulped back a little sob. 'But I don't want to be anywhere without my mummy,' he said. 'Can't we stay with you? We won't get in the way, will we, Mummy?'

Cassie bit the inside of her mouth to stop herself from crying. 'Sweetie, it's not that simple…'

Sam's eyes were streaming now and his bottom lip trembling as he slipped off the chair and came over to her. 'But why can't you marry Daddy and then we can all live together?' he asked. 'I like it here. I can see boats from my bedroom window and there's a big garden. Eleni said there's even a pool.'

Cassie kept her eyes away from Sebastian's as she bent down and hugged Sam. 'Darling, your father is a very important man. It's just not possible for him to live with us all the time. He has to travel all over the world sometimes. But I am sure we'll sort something out, something that makes all of us happy.'

'I don't want to go back to the orphanage,' Sam said, starting to cry. 'I want to stay here with Daddy and you.'

Sebastian rubbed at his face, his throat tightening as he thought of how different things could have been if he had known six years ago what he knew now. He would have done anything to have avoided the pain he could see etched on his little boy's face. What sort of father did Sam think he was that he hadn't done a single thing so far to give him what he was entitled to?

Cassie was looking daggers at him, piercing him with silent blame for upsetting their child, and Sebastian could hardly blame her. He had handled things appallingly. Sam was far too young to understand the dynamics of the situation. He would need careful nurturing and protection until something could be sorted out.

For so long the search for the Stefani diamond and Sebastian's future coronation as King had been his entire focus. He had thought of nothing else but how he could lead his people, and yet now he was faced with an agonising decision.

How could he take Sam away from his mother, even for an access visit? Sam was insecure and painfully shy. Besides, what little boy didn't need their mother at that age?

And then there was Cassie. The young woman Sebastian had never been able to erase from his mind. The last two nights had brought it all back, the way she made him feel, the passion that flared so hotly between them. He had been surprised at how disappointed he had felt when he had woken to find she had gone back to her room some time during the early hours of the morning. He had lain there in amongst the crumpled bedclothes, breathing in her scent, his body aching to possess her all over again.

The people of Aristo would never accept her as his bride. They were going to have enough trouble accepting her as the mother of his son. Cassie's past was always going to be a stumbling block. But last night at the piano he had seen a side to her that was as far from the party-girl socialite as anyone could be. It made him wonder if he had been too hasty in his judgement of her, in fact if everyone had been too hasty. There was a haunting sadness about her, he had been noticing it more and more, especially when she thought he wasn't watching.

Eleni came in at that moment and with a few cheery words with Sam led him away to play with some toys she had found in the nursery upstairs.

Cassie turned and glared at him. 'Couldn't you have waited until Sam was feeling a little more settled before dumping all that on him?' she asked.

Sebastian raked his hand through his hair. 'What was I supposed to do?' he asked. 'There is no point lying to him. I am his father and I want him to know and accept that.'

'You wanted to stake your claim on him, that's what you wanted,' she said, flashing her emerald gaze at him. 'I won't let you take him away from me, Sebastian.'

'I am not going to do anything that will not be of benefit to my son,' he said.

Her eyes flared. 'Oh, and what is that supposed to mean? That it will be of much greater benefit to him to be away from his jailbird mother?'

'I didn't say that, Cassie.'

'You didn't have to,' she said. 'I can see it every time you look at me. You are thinking how the hell am I going to tell the world who the mother of my son is—isn't that right, Sebastian?'

He set his jaw. 'Look, Cassie, this is a difficult situation for both of us. I have so little time in which to get to know Sam before I have to announce his existence. I have missed out on so much and I need to do what I can to make up for it. Do you realise I haven't even seen a photograph of him as a baby?'

Her stiff stance relaxed a little. 'I brought some photographs with me,' she said. 'I grabbed them when Stefanos took us via the flat.'

Sebastian was surprised she had thought to do so, especially given the haste in which he had insisted his orders be carried out. 'I would like to see them,' he said, trying to disguise the lump that had risen in his throat.

'I'll get them,' she said. 'They're in my room.'

Sebastian's mobile started to ring and he unhooked it from his belt and glanced at the screen. 'I'll have to get this, I'm afraid,' he said. 'Can you find your way to my study? I'll meet you there in ten minutes.'

She gave a nod and slipped out of the room while Sebastian took the call, keeping his voice low as he spoke to Stefanos. There was still no news about the Stefani diamond but neither had there been anything leaked to the press about Sam. There were some photographs in the paper of the party and a short piece about Sebastian's role as royal patron, but thankfully nothing else, so far.

Cassie took the scrapbooks she had made and after a few wrong turns made her way to Sebastian's study. She stood outside for a moment, holding the books against her chest, trying to prepare herself for yet another emotional journey through time. Every time she looked at the photos documenting Sam's life she felt such an aching sadness that she hadn't been able to give him a normal start to life. Everything had been against her from the very start. Sam had opened his eyes inside the walls of a bleak prison, not in the richly furnished palace where by blood he belonged. There had been no one with her when she had given birth after twenty agonising hours of labour, no one but a gruff midwife and a particularly unsympathetic prison guard who had stood and watched every intimate detail with a sneering expression on her face.

Cassie had longed for Sebastian to suddenly burst through the door and come to her. She'd had to bite down on her lip until it was bleeding to stop from crying out for him as every contraction had rippled through her abdomen.

She had never missed her mother more than at that point when Sam had finally been handed to her. She had never even held a baby before, never knew how tiny they were, how vulnerable and precious and totally innocent. Had her mother lived long enough to hold her? she wondered. No one had ever told her. Had her mother looked down at her as she had looked down at Sam at that moment, and sworn to love and protect her baby no matter what?

The door of the study suddenly opened in front of her. 'How long have you been standing there?' Sebastian asked with narrowed eyes.

Cassie clutched the scrapbooks against her chest, her mouth going dry at the hardened look in his eyes. 'Not long... I got lost a couple of times on the way down...'

He held her gaze for an infinitesimal moment, before indicating for her to go inside. He raked a hand through his hair in that edgy way of his. 'I have a lot on my mind right now.'

'I can come back later if you would prefer,' she said, glancing back at the door.

'No.' He dropped his hand from where it had been to rub the back of his neck, the smile he gave her a little forced. 'Take a seat on the sofa. Would you like coffee or tea? I suddenly realised I interrupted your breakfast.'

'No, I'm fine...thank you...' Cassie sat on the sofa and held her breath as he took the seat beside her, his thigh brushing against hers.

'Show me,' he said, his voice sounding rough.

Cassie opened the first scrapbook, realising then how tawdry it looked compared to the gold-encrusted ones he most probably had of his childhood. She had never been able to afford anything more than these cheap books, although she had promised herself once she was off the island and had some money to spare she was going to buy some proper albums.

'This is just after he was born,' she said, the rustle of the page turning over the only sound in the room.

Sebastian looked at the photo of his baby son lying on Cassie's chest, his tiny body still streaked with blood and the waxy protective covering of vernix from the womb. He hadn't cried since he was a small child but tears came to his eyes now and he had trouble seeing through them. The photograph blurred and he swallowed deeply.

'And this is when he was about two weeks old.' Cassie had turned another page, thankfully without looking up at him.

He looked at the prison-issue blanket covering his son and felt another blade of guilt slice him. Photo after photo had the same devastating effect on him. Pictures of Sam playing within the barbed-wire-enclosed prison, inmates all around, some of them looking less desirable than others.

Cassie reached for another scrapbook and showed him some clippings of Sam's hair and even the minuscule crescents of his fingernails. Sebastian reached out and touched the hair with his fingers; the dark curls could have been his when he was the same age. Emotion clogged his throat and he had to swallow again to clear it.

'I don't have many photos of when he was four,' Cassie said, still looking at the open book resting on Sebastian's thighs.

'Why not?' he asked.

She looked at him then. 'Because that was the year he was taken away from me,' she said with an embittered set to her mouth. 'The foster parents didn't think to take photographs for me. Why would they? I was just a prisoner.'

Sebastian began to understand then some of what she had gone through. He had missed out on five years of Sam's life but she, too, had missed out. She had lost six years of her young life, and a whole year of her son's with not even a photograph to comfort her. No wonder Sam was as shy as he was and so frightened of being separated from his mother. In each of the photos up until he turned three Sam was a happy, smiling little baby and toddler. It was only when Cassie showed him the remaining photos, including the ones up to date, that Sebastian could see what that year without his mother had done to Sam.

'Can I keep these for a few days?' he asked after a moment. 'I want to get some copies made.'

Cassie wasn't sure, but she thought she could see a hint of moisture in the darkness of his gaze. 'Of course,' she said. 'But please be careful with them. I've already lost a photo or two where the glue has come unstuck.'

'I will make sure they are handled with the utmost care,' he promised. 'Thank you for showing them to me. I cannot tell you what it has meant to me.'

Cassie compressed her lips, struggling to contain her own emotions. She got to her feet and, wrapping her arms around her body, faced him. 'I wanted to give him so much more,' she said. 'He deserved so much more. I'm so worried he will never get over it...you know, being taken away from me. That year he went to the foster home...' She released one of her hands to brush at her eyes and continued raggedly, 'I couldn't protect him. What if someone had hurt him? What if someone treated him roughly like my father did to me? I wasn't there for him, Sebastian. I wasn't there to protect him like no one was there to protect me...'

'Your father...' he swallowed over the word as he got to his feet '...abused you?'

Cassie couldn't speak. Tears were suddenly blocking her throat, burning, aching tears that were spilling from her eyes and rolling down her face.

Sebastian reached for her, enfolding her in his arms, stroking the back of her head, murmuring soothing, meaningless words to her as the storm of her emotions passed through her. He felt every quake of her body; every broken sob tore at him until his own eyes felt moist and his chest too tight to breathe.

'I'm sorry…'

She tried to push away from him but, although he allowed her some room, he didn't release her. He held her hands in his, his thumbs stroking over her fingers. 'Tell me everything, Cassie,' he said softly. 'You are safe now. No one is going to hurt you. I won't allow them to.'

She looked up at him, her chin trembling so like Sam's he felt another deep wave of emotion swamp him. He had missed out on so much but he was starting to realise most of the blame for that was his. He'd fallen into the same trap as everyone else, judging her without really knowing her. All the clues were there now that he had the benefit of hindsight. Each letter to the unsolvable crossword now in place, and his gut churned at what those letters spelt.

'He broke my arm.' The words tumbled out and once they had started Cassie couldn't seem to stop. 'He broke my arm when I was four years old. On the way to the hospital he told me if I said a word to anyone about how it had happened he would do much worse. He told me to tell everyone I had fallen off my bed. I was so frightened. It wasn't the first time he had hit me, far from it. He was always hitting me, but after that he toned it down a bit. It wouldn't do to have anyone pointing their finger at him, now, would it? He was a high-profile man who made a great show of how much he loved his difficult daughter.'

Sebastian kept on stroking her cold, lifeless hands. 'Oh, Cassie,' was all he could manage to say. 'Oh, my poor, Caz.'

She continued speaking in the same flat, emotionless tone. 'By the time I was a teenager I deliberately set out to shame him. I couldn't tell anyone about the physical abuse but I could still get at him that way, or so I thought. I guess I didn't stop to think about the consequences for my own life…'

'You were a child, for God's sake,' Sebastian said. 'A terrified child with no one you could turn to.'

'The night we broke up…' She paused, her face a picture of pain at the memory. 'I felt I had no choice. My father had so many times renewed his warning…I thought about going to the police, but he was best friends with the commissioner. He had powerful friends everywhere. I had nothing to fall back on but an already damaged reputation.'

Sebastian's frown deepened. 'So you made up a parcel of lies about sleeping around to put me off the scent?'

She nodded. 'I'm sorry… It must have hurt you but I couldn't think of what else to do. I couldn't see any future in our relationship. I was going to leave as soon as I turned eighteen in any case. My father saw my packed bags and…and that was it.'

'He attacked you?' His words were more of a statement than a question.

'Yes…I thought he was going to…to…' She screwed up her face as if she couldn't bear to say the word out loud.

Sebastian felt another sickening wave of nausea roll through him as he suddenly realised what word she was avoiding. He put his arms back around her, holding her close, trying to comfort a pain that could not be comforted. 'I'm so sorry.' The words seemed so inadequate and yet he kept saying them. 'I'm so very sorry. I wish I had been able to protect you. I wish I had known. I wish you had trusted me enough to tell me.'

He put her from him again, looking down at her reddened eyes. 'Did you ever consider telling someone during the trial about what you had suffered?' he asked. 'You could have shown them the X-rays from when you were a child. Surely someone would have listened.'

She gave him the bleakest of looks. 'I considered it a few times but I could see the disgust in everyone's eyes. I was a tramp, a rebellious little slut who had brought shame and disgrace on her poor, hard-working father. It was all so daunting.' She sighed and carried on sadly, 'When I found out I was pregnant I realised why I hadn't put up much of a fight. I was so tired and sick and so overwhelmed with it all I just sat there like an automaton without offering a word in my own defence.'

Sebastian gripped her hands. 'I will speak to my legal counsel,' he said. 'I'll have your name cleared. I will do everything within my power to see proper justice is served.'

'No,' she said, pulling out of his hold. 'I don't want to go through it all again. I just want to leave Aristo.'

Three beats of silence passed.

'You will not be leaving.'

Her eyes flared and a pulse began to beat at her throat. 'What do you mean I won't be leaving?' she asked.

'I will not allow you to take my son away,' he said. 'I have only just met him. I need time to get to know him before I announce to the press my intentions where he is concerned.'

Cassie tried to keep her panic contained but it bubbled up inside her. She could see his point of view, but she couldn't allow herself to be imprisoned again, even in such a gilded cage as the Karedes private villa. 'I will not allow you to keep me under house arrest,' she said, glaring at him. 'I want to be able to come and go as I see fit.'

'I am afraid that is impossible,' he said with an intransigent set to his features. 'I have to take every precaution that this situation is dealt with in the utmost secrecy.'

'It's all about you and your precious throne, isn't it?' she threw at him.

'It has nothing to do with the throne,' he ground out in frustration. 'I want to spend time with Sam without the paparazzi shoving cameras in his face. He's shy and—'

'So that's my fault, is it?' she asked. 'It's all because of the terrible mother he has—that's what you're thinking, isn't it?'

He shook his head at her, his eyes going upwards as if for patience from some higher source. 'I wasn't implying anything of the sort,' he said, lowering his voice. 'When the time is right I will have no hesitation in announcing to the people of Aristo you are the mother of my child.'

She gave him a churlish look. 'Yeah, well, I bet you won't do it until you have the paternity test results in your hands.'

He let out his breath in a whistling stream, a signal Cassie knew from past experience, he was nearing the end of his tether. 'What would you do if the tables were turned? Answer me, Cassie. What would you do?'

Cassie felt herself backing down. 'I—I would do the same...' she said, so low it was barely audible.

'Say it louder.'

She lifted her chin. 'You heard.'

'Say it louder,' he commanded again.

Cassie tightened her hands into fists, her anger rising up like lava, her voice rising along with it. 'I said I would do the same. I said I would do the same. I SAID I WOULD DO THE SAME.'

Sebastian captured her flailing hands before they could connect with his face as he supposed she intended. 'Stop it, Cassie. It's over...shhh, *agape mou,* it's over. I'm not fighting with you. I pushed you too far. I'm sorry, OK?'

She choked back a little sob. 'Don't you dare be nice to me... I can cope with you when you're not nice...'

He gave a rueful smile. 'That is the problem, isn't it? You are not used to people treating you with respect and consideration so you put up a prickly don't-mess-with-me front.'

She tried to avoid his gaze but he countered it by placing a gentle hand beneath her chin. 'Don't shut me out now, Caz,' he said. 'Not now. You can trust me. You do know that, don't you?'

Her throat went up and down. 'I'm not used to trusting anyone…'

'I know but that has to change. It is important you learn to trust me so that Sam bonds with me. He takes his cue from you, don't forget.'

Cassie searched his face. 'Can I trust you not to take him away from me?' she asked.

'I could ask you the very same question.'

'I won't take him away without you knowing about it.' Her gaze slipped to his mouth. 'I wasn't sure if you would see the likeness. I can see it, but then I am his mother.'

'I see it.'

Her eyes flicked back to his. 'Does that mean you don't question you are his father?'

'Cassie, the paternity test is not for me,' he said, taking her by the shoulders, his thumbs rubbing softly against her bare flesh. 'I know he is my son. I felt a connection when you gave me the painting he had done for me. I couldn't understand it at the time. I had this sudden urge to meet this child. It became my entire focus.'

'Were you really as shy as he is when you were small?' she asked.

He stroked a finger down the curve of her cheek. 'I was for a long time. I grew out of it eventually and I am sure he will too. You are a wonderful mother to him, Cassie. You remind me so much of my mother. I can see how much he adores you. You are his world.'

'I love him more than you will ever know,' she said softly. 'He's really my only reason for living. Before I found out I was carrying him I wanted to…to…'

He placed a fingertip against her lips. 'No, Cassie, don't

say it. I can't bear to hear you say it. I hate to think of what you went through. No wonder you were so angry at me for not responding to your letter.'

She gave him another searching look. 'So you believe now I sent one?'

'That is another thing I mulled over after you left my bed this morning,' he said. 'It is obvious my father must have ordered my mail to be screened. After all, he blocked Lissa from contacting you. There can be no other explanation.'

Cassie felt her shoulders start to relax. 'I'm glad you believe me… It's been so hard having no one on my side…'

His hands moved down the length of her arms to encircle her wrists. 'I am on your side now, Cassie, don't ever forget that. I will do whatever I can to make up for the past.'

She wanted to believe him, but she knew he couldn't have everything his way. What would be his final choice? It was too painful to even think about. All she knew was he couldn't have it all, and neither could she. They would both have to make a choice, but somehow she knew his was not going to include her, no matter how much she prayed it would.

CHAPTER ELEVEN

CASSIE spent the next few days watching as Sebastian spent time with Sam. It was so moving to see them together, their dark heads bent close together over a puzzle or a book or a painting they had done, their smiles so similar. Sam was starting to blossom, his confidence growing as each day passed. He clearly adored his father and Sebastian made no effort to hide his very deep love for his son.

Cassie tried not to let it concern her but Sebastian had not asked her to sleep with him again. Was he trying to distance himself from her? It was so hard to tell. When Sam was around he smiled and chatted with her as any set of normal parents would do, but as soon as Sam was in bed Sebastian excused himself from her company, citing business to see to, letters to write, phone calls to make, anything, it seemed, rather than spend time with her.

It made her feel so terribly insecure, especially when she had revealed her past to him. Had he found it too hard to cope with? Was that why he was avoiding her? He preferred to think of her as a sleep-around-slut he could lure back into an affair, but not as a young woman who had been mistreated and shown injustice all of her life.

'Now, young man,' Sebastian said as he picked up Sam

from the floor and set him on his shoulders. 'I am going to take you upstairs to bed where you should have been well over an hour ago.'

Sam giggled as he dug his hands into his father's hair to keep his balance. 'Will you take me down to the beach again tomorrow?' he asked.

'Yes, and I will even show you a cave where my brothers and sisters and I used to hide things, like buried treasure,' he said.

'Will it still be there?' Sam asked, bending round so he could look into his father's eyes.

Sebastian smiled. 'If it isn't we will bury some of our own,' he said. 'Now kiss Mummy goodnight.'

'I want you both to tuck me in,' Sam said.

Cassie met Sebastian's gaze for a brief moment before she looked up at Sam so high above her. 'Let Daddy tuck you in on his own, darling,' she said. 'I have done it so many times and he has got a lot of catching up to do.'

Sam's forehead began to wrinkle in a worried frown. 'But I want you there too, Mummy.'

Sebastian hauled Sam down off his shoulders and onto his hip instead. 'Of course Mummy can help me tuck you in,' he said. 'Now what story do you want me to read to you tonight?'

Sam looked up at him with big brown eyes. 'Mummy told me a story about a prince who found a shoe after a party and he searched to find the beautiful girl who had lost it. Do you know that story?'

Sebastian felt his chest tighten. 'Yes, I know that one. It's called *Cinderella*.'

'That's right!' Sam said excitedly. 'Isn't Daddy clever, Mummy? He knows the same stories you know.'

'Yes, he's very clever, darling,' she said, her cheeks flushing slightly.

A few minutes later Sebastian rose from where he had

been sitting on his son's bed. Sam was fast asleep, his breathing deep and even, his angelic face a picture of contentment.

He watched as Cassie leaned over and pressed a soft kiss to Sam's forehead, her fingers brushing the hair back off his face, the look of love on her face making him feel another deep pang of regret for all she had gone through.

'Have you got a minute to have a chat?' he asked once they had both left Sam's room.

She gave him an ironic look. 'I'm the one with all the time on my hands, Sebastian,' she said with a touch of resentment. 'You're the one who is always too busy.'

'You are feeling neglected,' Sebastian said, blowing out a sigh. 'I am sorry, but being away from the palace like this means I have things to see to each night. When I've come to your room you have always been asleep. I didn't want to disturb you.'

Her forehead creased. 'You came to my room?'

He gave her a wry smile. 'You should not sound so surprised, Cassie. I thought I had made it clear how much I want you.'

She lowered her gaze a fraction. 'Yes, but I thought you had changed your mind…or something…'

He placed his hands at her waist. 'That is the whole trouble, Cassie,' he said. 'I want what I cannot have.'

She looked up at him, her eyes uncertain. 'I'm not asking for for ever, Sebastian.'

His chest rose and fell on another sigh. 'I know, and that is what concerns me the most,' he said. 'You and Sam deserve for ever. You both deserve the happiness that has been stolen from you.'

Cassie could see the struggle he was having played out on his face. He had deep shadows under his eyes as if he had not slept at all over the last few nights. She wanted to tell him how much she loved him but knew it would only make his decision all the harder to make. He was already carrying a load of guilt and was doing everything in his power to make it up to Sam. 'You are a fantastic father,' she said softly. 'Sam loves you so much.'

'I love him too,' he said, looking into her eyes. 'I cannot tell you how much.'

'I know how much,' she said. 'I feel that way too.'

His hands moved from her waist. 'I have something to show you,' he said. 'They arrived this afternoon.'

Cassie followed him downstairs to his study where he showed her how he had had all the photographs of Sam copied and reset into four leather-bound albums, each one with the gold crest of the Karedes family on the cover. She couldn't speak for a moment; she sat silently tracing her fingertip over the royal crest, wondering if this was part of the removal process. He was making the disparity of their lives and background all the more apparent. He was showing her where Sam belonged, where she could never follow.

'What do you think?' he asked.

She brought her gaze up to his. 'I think you are systematically trying to nudge me out of his life, that's what I think.'

His brows came together. 'What are you talking about? I had those done for you. I have another set made for myself.'

She got to her feet and crossed her arms over her chest. 'What have you done with the originals?'

'I threw them out,' he said. 'They were falling apart in any case.'

Cassie glared at him in fury. 'You threw them out? Is that what you're telling me? You threw my scrapbooks out?'

'Cassie, what is all the fuss about?' he asked. 'You would surely have replaced them yourself when you found the time.'

'You had no right to throw away what was mine,' she said, fighting back tears. 'I had to work hard to pay for those books. I had to barter with food and privileges to pay for them and now you've tossed them out as if they're worth nothing. Do you have any idea how that makes me feel?'

He came over to where she was standing. 'I think I am starting to get a sense of what you are feeling,' he said gently. 'You had so little to give Sam but you gave him everything you could. Those scrapbooks represented some of the sacrifices you had been forced to make. I am sorry, Cassie. I will call Stefanos and have him return them to you. It was wrong of me to assume they were not valuable to you.'

Cassie could feel her defences crumbling. Tears she had sworn she was not going to allow to fall were already falling, one by one, but before she could brush them away with her hands Sebastian got there first. With a touch so gentle he blotted each tear with the pad of his thumbs.

'I'm sorry,' she said. 'I shouldn't have been so touchy about it.'

His eyes darkened as they held hers. 'I do not know how to make it up to you, for all you have lost, for all that I could have prevented if I had taken the time to get to know you. I have been doing some research on your father. He had friends in so many high places it was no wonder you felt you had no one to go to. I had my aide request the medical records of when you were admitted to the hospital when you were four, and there was no record of you ever being admitted.'

Cassie felt her shoulders go down. 'I didn't stand a chance, did I?'

'I will get justice for you, Cassie,' he said, pulling her closer. 'I will leave no stone unturned until I do.'

Cassie was standing too close to him to be able to ignore the pulse of his body, and the thin layer of her clothes that shielded her form couldn't possibly disguise her own response to his nearness. She ran her tongue over the dryness of her lips;

her breathing going out of time, her heart tripping as his head slowly came down...

The press of his lips against hers was gentle at first, but as soon as he stroked his tongue across the seam of her lips everything changed. Passion flared like a combustible fuel exposed to a lighted taper. It streaked along Cassie's veins, thundering in her ears and pooling in her belly like liquid fire. She felt the hard probe of his body against the flimsy barrier of her gown, the intimate closeness making it all that harder to move away. His mouth was burning hot, his tongue insistent and determined as it conquered hers.

He backed her towards the sofa, his muscled thighs rubbing along hers with every heart-stopping step. She felt the cushions at the back of her knees and went down with barely a whimper, her mouth locked on his.

His hands peeled away the spaghetti-thin shoulder straps on her sundress, his mouth moving from hers to blaze down past her shoulders to her breasts. She bit back a gasp as the heated moistness of his mouth closed over her nipple, the sexy scrape of his teeth sending arrows of delight to her already-curling toes. She felt her body secretly preparing for him, the on-off pulse of her inner muscles making her wild to feel him deep and hard within her.

His mouth moved farther down her body, giving her small niplike kisses that sent her senses spinning even further out of control. She was writhing beneath his solid weight, desperate to get closer, her hands tearing at his clothes so she could feel him skin on skin.

He captured her hands and held them above her head, his dark eyes glinting with rampant desire. 'Don't be so impatient, *agape mou*,' he teased playfully. 'I am getting to that.'

'I want you *now*,' she said, arching up against him. 'You're taking too long.'

'It is all the better for waiting, Cassie,' he said. 'Can you feel it building and building?'

Cassie could and it was driving her crazy. 'I want to touch you,' she said. 'Let me go so I can touch you properly.'

His eyes burned into hers for a heady moment before he released her hands. 'Touch me all you like, Cassie,' he said, and shrugged himself out of his shirt.

Cassie needed no other inducement. She had his belt off and his waistband undone within seconds, her fingers enclosing him with just the right amount of tension to make him cut back a groan of pleasure. She moved her hand up and down, watching as he fought to keep control.

When he tried to stop her she pushed his hand away, and, giving him a sultry look, bent her mouth to him. She felt him shudder as she took the first strong suck, a whole-body shudder that sent shivers of vicarious pleasure up and down her spine. The tension in his body was electrifying; she could feel it building to explosion point. She could taste him, that salt and musk combination that was as erotic as it was irresistible.

'Enough, oh, dear God in heaven, enough,' he groaned and pulled out.

Cassie ran the point of her tongue over her lips, knowing it would drive him wild. 'Am I going too fast for you?' she asked with an arch look.

'Not fast enough,' he growled, and pressed her back down with his weight coming over her.

Cassie shivered as he pulled her dress off her body with a total disregard for the delicate fabric. She heard it tear but was too far gone to fully register it. He nudged her thighs apart, the first stablike thrust of his body ricocheting through her as he drove home to the hilt. He set a fast pace, but she delighted in every exhilarating second of it, her body on fire as her senses climbed to the summit of human pleasure. Every nerve was screaming for release, her legs were quivering, her back arching and her breathing choppy and uneven as he drove her to the edge time and time again, only to pull back at the last teetering moment.

'Don't make me beg,' she panted against his moist mouth.

'I want you to beg,' he said against her lips. 'I want you to scream at me to give you what you want.'

She bit at him, a playful puppy bite. 'Someone might hear us,' she said.

'I don't give a damn who hears us,' he said. 'Tell me what you want, Cassie.'

'I want you to make me come,' she said, pulling his head back down to hers.

He crushed her mouth beneath his, his body hard and urgent in hers as one of his hands went between their bodies to caress the swollen centre of her desire. Cassie bit back a cry as she began to soar, each smashing wave of release making her body convulse around him. She sobbed her way through it, the power of it unlike anything she had ever felt before.

He came close behind, his body tensing for the final plunge, every muscle under her fingertips bunching before he emptied himself.

Cassie let her hands skate over his back and shoulders in the aftermath, her heart still hammering, her breathing just as erratic as his. It was times like this she could almost imagine a different life for herself, a life where she would wake up each morning next to Sebastian, his legs entwined with hers, the essence of him still hot and wet between her thighs…

Her heart suddenly gave a sideways lurch. 'Oh, no…'

Sebastian eased himself off her. 'What's wrong, Cassie? Did I hurt you? Was I too rough?'

She gave him a wide-eyed look of alarm. 'You didn't use a condom.'

'I know,' he said with a rueful grimace. 'But I'm all clear, so don't worry.'

Cassie searched for her dress and underwear, trying not to let her panic take too many fast strides. 'I can't believe you didn't use a condom,' she said, tossing aside the sofa cushions.

'Cassie, I told you I won't give you anything.'

'No,' she said, turning her back on him as she reached for her dress lying on the floor. 'Or at least nothing you haven't already given me in the past.'

Sebastian didn't take in what she had said. He stared at the jagged white scar near her tailbone for what seemed like endless seconds. 'How long have you had that scar?' he asked.

He saw her stiffen before she turned to face him. 'What scar?'

He got to his feet and came over to where she was standing. 'I think you know what I am talking about. I've never seen it before.'

'Yes, well, I've never been totally naked with you before,' she said, flashing her green eyes at him in irritation.

He placed his hands on her shoulders to stop her from spinning away. 'You don't have to cover up for him now, Cassie,' he said in as gentle a tone as he could. 'If your father did that to you then you have no reason not to tell me.'

He felt the tremble of her body under his hands and his heart contracted when he saw fresh tears well in her eyes. 'Look, it was a long time ago and I'd rather just forget about it,' she said.

'How long?'

She bit her lip. 'The night I got home from breaking off things with you…'

Sebastian closed his eyes for a moment before drawing her close, his hands touching her as if she were a fragile work of art, his gut wrenching all over again as his fingers traced over the ribbed flesh of her back. 'I know it is of no comfort, but if you had told me it would have been me in that jail, not you,' he said. 'I would have killed him for what he has done to you. I swear to God I would have torn him from limb to limb.'

'I wouldn't have wanted you to do that,' she said, looking up at him.

Sebastian brought one of her hands to his mouth and brushed his lips over the back of her knuckles. 'Come with me upstairs,' he said. 'I want to spend tonight holding you in my arms.'

She looked as if she was going to say no, but then she gave him a smile tinged with sadness. 'I guess we should make the most of the time we have left…'

Sebastian didn't want to think about how each day was slipping through his fingers like fine grains of sand. All he could hope for was a few more days to keep Sam and Cassie close while he sorted through his options. Everything had happened so quickly and he was still coming to terms with it all. Not just Sam's existence but how his feelings for Cassie were rising up to the surface after years of being shoved down.

He led her upstairs to his bedroom, closing the door softly behind them. 'I was thinking about having a shower,' he said. 'Would you like to join me?'

'It's all right,' she said, perching on the edge of his bed, not quite meeting his eyes. 'I'll wait until you're finished and then have one.'

It struck him then, how shy she was. No doubt ashamed of how disfigured her body was by that horrible scar. His gut clenched all over again at what she had suffered at that madman's hands. 'No,' he said, keeping his voice steady but only just. 'You go first. I have a couple of calls to make in any case.'

When he came back she was lying in amongst his pillows, looking small and fragile and uncertain. He came over to her and, picking up one of her hands, brought it up to his mouth, kissing her palm and then each of her fingers in turn. 'I just checked on Sam,' he said. 'He was fast asleep.'

Sebastian leaned forward and pressed a soft kiss to her forehead. 'I am going to have a quick shower. Don't go to sleep on me now, will you, *agape mou?*'

She gave him a small smile but there was still that haunting air of sadness in her green eyes. 'I won't.'

Cassie waited for him, her heart feeling like an engine in her chest when he came back out of the bathroom, dressed in nothing but a towel tied loosely at his hips. He was so magnificently built, so commandingly male. He dropped the towel and turned back the sheets to slip in beside her, taking her in his arms and holding her close for a long time without speaking.

She listened to his breathing, heard his heartbeat pounding against her cheek, storing away the clean male scent of him to comfort her in the lonely years to come.

She had thought he had fallen asleep but slowly his hands began to move over her, slow, gentle caressing movements, a touch that was almost reverent.

'Your skin feels like silk,' he breathed against her ear.

She shivered as his mouth sealed hers in a kiss of passionate possession, his tongue meeting hers in a slow tango that stirred her deeply.

He lifted his mouth off hers to kiss each of her breasts, taking his time, his tongue rolling and licking and tasting her until her back was arching off the bed.

He moved down her body, dipping into the cave of her belly button before going to the secret heart of her, tasting her, teasing her until she was gasping her way through a shattering release.

Cassie wanted to pleasure him but he seemed in no hurry to have her do anything but lie there and have him worship her body. He kept pushing her hands away, kissing her into silence, stroking all of her tension away with the glide of his hands.

At one point he turned her over. She resisted at first but he kissed away her doubts and gently turned her onto her stomach. She felt each and every kiss as he travelled down the length of her spine, his lips lingering over her scar, as if he wanted to take away the pain of the memories it had scored on her brain, much less her skin.

When he turned her back over he could see the tears in her eyes and dabbed them away with the edge of the sheet. 'I wish I could make the past go away for you, Cassie,' he said. 'I want to bring this out in the open, to tell the people of this island how unjustly you were treated.'

She moved out of his embrace. 'It's over and I need to move on for Sam's sake. I don't want him to know about any of this, that's why I want to get right away where no one knows me. He's already heard too much.'

'Cassie, I can't allow you to leave Aristo until I think it is appropriate,' he said with a frown. 'Surely you understand that?'

'I do understand the situation you are in and I am making no demands on you other than to give me my freedom.'

His eyes warred with hers for several tense seconds. 'I am not going to let you walk away, Cassie. If I have to lock every door you are behind, I will do it.'

Cassie swung away in fury, ripping the sheet off the bed to cover herself. 'I suppose not using a condom downstairs was part of your insurance policy, was it?' she bit out bitterly.

'What?'

She turned back to look at him. 'I'm not on the pill, Sebastian, so you had better start crossing your fingers and hope and pray that lightning doesn't strike in the same place twice.'

Sebastian stared at her for a stunned moment or two. 'Do you think it's possible?' he finally managed to croak out. 'Where are you in your cycle?'

'There is never a safe time,' she said. 'If I fell pregnant on the pill, God only knows how quickly I will do so without it.'

He raked a hand through his hair. 'I need some time to think about this…'

'Why don't you get back to me in, say, six years?' she said with an embittered look.

He set his mouth. 'I know I probably more than deserve that, Cassie, but I did not intend for you to be put in such a compromising situation. Not the first time and certainly not now.'

'Do you think I wanted this to happen all over again?' she asked. 'You were the one to suggest we rake over the coals of the past by sleeping together again.'

He knew she was right. He had pressured her into an affair that could only have one outcome.

'I can say no to anyone else but you,' she said. 'I hate you for it.'

He moved over to her, taking her by the upper arms, his hold firm but gentle. 'I know you hate me, Caz. I hate myself, to tell you the truth. But hate is going to get us nowhere. It is important for Sam that he sees us getting along as any other mature and sensible couple would do.'

'But we're not a couple,' she said, wriggling out of his hold. 'We never have been and we never will be.'

Sebastian couldn't read her expression, which frustrated him more than he wanted to admit. What was she implying? That she wanted something more permanent, had *always* wanted something more lasting? His mind whirled as he thought about all the obstacles they would face if he presented her to the public as his chosen partner. And there was Sam to consider. How would he cope with suddenly being in the spotlight? Sebastian knew the people of Aristo would never accept Cassie Kyriakis as their queen. Even if he hired every top lawyer to clear her name he wasn't sure if it would achieve much. People formed their own opinions and were loath to change them, even if a solid case was put before them.

As to his own feelings, well, Sebastian was still trying to sort it all out in his head. He had been so determined to right the wrongs of the past with a short-term affair with her, but it had blown up in his face upon finding out about Sam, not to mention the harrowing details of Cassie's home life. The love he had felt for her six years ago had been locked away—he had thought for ever. He had duties to face, responsibilities and expectations he had been schooled and prepared for all his life. Walking away from all that was rightly his and expected of him by the people of Aristo was not something to be taken lightly.

And there was his brother Alex to consider. He and his wife Maria were expecting the birth of their first child in a day or two. Alex had always expressed his reluctance to take up the throne. How would he feel if Sebastian gave him no other choice?

'Cassie, it is not my intention to imprison you, anything but. You will be safe here without the press hounding you. Believe me that is my only motivation, to keep you and Sam safe.'

'All right,' she said on an expelled breath. 'You've got two weeks but that's all.'

CHAPTER TWELVE

'DADDY says I can have a real paint set and brushes and a...a...*weasel* all to myself!' Sam announced proudly as he came running towards Cassie one morning four days later.

'Easel,' she said as she bent down to kiss his forehead. 'It's called an easel. A weasel is a small furry animal.'

'Oh...' Sam went on excitedly. 'I've got a new tip truck and a kite Daddy and me are going to use on the beach and Daddy promised me I can have a camera all of my own when I am six.'

Cassie forced a smile in spite of her inner turmoil. How could she tell Sam this week of indulgence was soon to end? She had no doubt Sebastian would continue contact with his son; he had made that very clear every night they had spent together. In such a short time he had established a loving relationship with Sam that had many times brought tears to her eyes. It made what she had missed out on during her childhood all the more painfully apparent. But in spite of the tenderness and passion they had shared night after night Sebastian had mentioned nothing about her place in his life. Cassie knew Sam would always be known as the king's love-child, a mistake from his past, the one blemish he couldn't erase. And as the child's mother she would be shunted sideways; there would be no place for her once he stepped up to the throne.

'Daddy's going to have breakfast with me,' Sam said. 'I'm going to have pancakes. He said I could have anything I wanted.'

'Darling…' Cassie took his hands in hers. 'I don't think it's—'

'It's all right,' Sebastian said from just behind her. 'I'll deal with this.'

Something about his demeanour alerted her to an undercurrent of tension. He had brought it into the room with him, like a blast of cold air when someone opened a door leading into a warm room.

He crouched in front of Sam. 'Sam, Mummy and I have some things to discuss. Eleni will see to your breakfast this morning but I promise I will have lunch with you instead.'

'What sort of things do you have to talk about?' Sam asked with a worried look between his parents. 'I'm not going back to the orphanage, am I? I don't want to go back. I like being with you, Daddy, and Mummy does too, don't you, Mummy?'

Cassie forced her mouth to smile in response. 'I love being anywhere you are, darling.'

'I know you like being here, Sam,' Sebastian said after glancing for a moment at Cassie. 'I love having you here with me.'

'Can I stay for ever?' Sam asked with hope shining brightly in his chocolate-brown eyes. 'I love you. I'll be very good. I promise. I won't wet my pants any more. I'll try really hard. Really, *really* hard.'

Sebastian felt his heart lodge itself halfway up his throat so he could barely speak. 'Sam, you don't have to do anything but be yourself,' he said. 'I love you just the way you are.'

'So I'm not going to be sent away?' Sam asked.

Sebastian could feel the tension coming off Cassie standing at his left shoulder. 'Here is Eleni now. I will come back for you later.'

Cassie watched as Sam scampered off towards Eleni before she turned to face Sebastian. 'Nice one, Karedes,' she sniped at him. 'How to bribe a little kid away from its mother in just over a week. God, you make me sick.'

A flicker of anger passed through his dark eyes as they clashed with hers. 'I am doing no such thing. Come into the study out of the hearing of the staff.'

'I know what you're doing,' she said as she trotted to keep up with his long strides. 'You're making Sam so dependent on you he won't even notice when I'm gone. That's what your plan is, isn't it? To get me out of the picture as soon as you can. You're showering him with toys and giving him choices and opportunities I could never give him. It will make him think I don't love him the way you supposedly do.'

He frowned down at her. 'You consider what I feel for Sam is not genuine?'

She captured her lip between her teeth. 'No...no, I'm not saying that... I know you love him and he loves you.'

'How could I not love him?' he asked, holding open the study door for her to pass through. 'He is so engaging and so innocent I want to protect him as much as possible. He has been through so much for one so young. I am doing what I can to make it up to him.'

'I don't want him to be hurt,' she said. 'He doesn't really understand the circumstances of your life. He thinks things will continue as they are, but they can't and you need to prepare him for it.'

He closed the study door and, moving across the room, picked up a newspaper. 'If you did not want to see Sam hurt, then why on earth did you do this?' he asked, handing her the paper.

Cassie stared down at the headlines. There was a photograph of Sam on the front page with: FUTURE KING'S LOVE-CHILD REVEALED BY EX-PRISONER CASSIE KYRIAKIS emblazoned beneath. She looked up at Sebastian's glittering gaze. 'You think *I'm* responsible for this?' she choked.

He folded his arms, one ankle crossing over the other as he leaned back against his desk in an accusatory manner. 'Don't play games with me, Cassie. I know, in spite of what we have shared over the last couple of weeks, deep down you have always wanted to get back at me for how I let you down. But using Sam as a pawn is taking things a little too far. The press have gone wild with this. There are camera crews and television vans at the gate as we speak.'

Cassie took an uneven swallow. 'I didn't speak to anyone… How can you think I would do something like this?'

'Have you spoken to your flatmate in the last couple of days?'

Cassie suddenly remembered the call she had received from Angelica a couple of days ago. Angelica had heard rumours circulating and had wanted to know what was going on. Cassie had confessed all and had sworn her to silence, trusting her implicitly to keep Sam's paternity a secret.

'Cassie?' Sebastian's voice was brittle. 'Have you spoken to Angelica about this?'

'Yes, but she would never—'

He let out a stiff curse. 'And you trusted that junkie?' he asked incredulously.

She set her mouth. 'Yes, I do, as a matter of fact. I trust her more than I've ever trusted anyone.'

His eyes remained hard. 'Do you recognise the photo?'

She looked at it again. 'Yes…yes, I do,' she said. 'It's one of the ones I lost somewhere.'

He hooked one dark brow upwards. 'Lost or sold to the press via your drugged-up flatmate?'

She put the newspaper down with an unsteady hand. 'Angelica is not a drugged-up junkie. She is my best friend—she stood by me when no one else could give a toss.'

'That's what this is about, isn't it?' He waved the paper in her face. 'I didn't stand up for you when you needed me to so this is payback time.'

'How could you possibly think I would betray you or Sam in such a way?' Cassie asked, tears starting to spring to her eyes as she looked deeply into his. 'I love you both too much to ever do that.'

He went very still, his eyes losing some of their hardness. 'You love me?' he asked huskily.

Cassie pressed her lips together. 'I'm sorry... I shouldn't have let that slip out. I don't want to make things any more complicated than they already are.'

He pushed himself away from the table. 'Is this a new thing or an old thing?'

'Me loving you?' she asked, sweeping her tongue over her dry lips uncertainly.

He nodded without speaking, but she saw his throat rising and falling over a swallow, as if her confession had stunned him, but he was trying to conceal how much.

She twisted her hands together. 'It's an old thing...six years to be exact...I have always loved you, Seb.'

The silence hung like an axe over Cassie's head. She held her breath, wondering what he was going to say in response or if he was going to try and ignore her declaration of love because of the circumstances that made it impossible for them to ever be together.

'Remember I said the first night we spent together I had a photograph of you that you hadn't seen?' he said in a tone that had softened considerably.

'Yes...I forgot to ask you to show it to me,' she said, and felt her cheeks grow warm as she remembered why she hadn't thought to ask. She had been too distracted making love with him to think of anything but the pleasure he had made her feel.

He walked over to a table where a frame was sitting next to a vase of flowers. He came back over and handed her the frame and she looked down at it for a long time without speaking. It was a side-on shot of her, standing looking out to sea close to sunset, some strands of her long hair blowing across her face. Cassie could remember the exact day. It was two days before her father's death. She had gone down to the shore after a particularly nasty argument with him. He had raged at her over something insignificant and petty, slapping her across the face, not hard enough to leave a mark but enough to make her skin burn for hours afterwards. Once he had gone upstairs to drink himself into oblivion, as had become his habit, she had slipped out to walk along the beach, knowing if she stayed out long enough he would be asleep by the time she got back.

She had walked along the shore, stopping now and again to look out to sea, agonising over what to do about her relationship with Sebastian. How ironic he had captured the very moment she had decided to end their affair. She had stood there, mentally rehearsing what she was going to say to him, word by word, over and over until she had felt confident enough to convince him every lie was true.

Cassie had known one of Sebastian's hobbies was photography. She had seen several shots Sebastian had taken in the past, but there was something about this photograph that showed how talented he really was. He had not only captured a moment in time, he had captured a mood and made it almost tangible.

Cassie felt tears stinging at the backs of her eyes for how much her life had changed in the space of those next two days. She had been so young, so lost and alone in spite of all the people she had surrounded herself with.

To conceal her emotions she handed him back the frame with a stiff smile. 'You should have told me you were taking it,' she said. 'I would have fixed my hair at the very least.'

He looked at the photograph for a moment before putting it aside. 'I was about to call out to you but then I stopped. I decided to capture your image without you knowing you were being photographed.'

'Why did you keep it?' Cassie asked after a tiny pause.

His dark eyes meshed with hers. 'Have you ever had an item of clothing in your wardrobe you don't wear any more but still don't feel quite ready to discard it?'

She gave him an ironic look. 'I am quite sure you are not the one in your household to sort through your socks and underwear drawer. You have numerous servants who do that for you.'

His smile was a little crooked. 'Yes, perhaps you are right. There are not many things I do for myself these days.'

'Including choosing a wife?' Cassie wished she hadn't let it slip out, for she was sure she sounded as jealous as she felt.

He held her gaze for an interminable moment. 'As future King I am expected to marry and marry well. But I will have no one else make the final choice for me.'

A silence began to thicken the air.

'I have a meeting with my brother Alex later this morning back at the palace,' Sebastian said. 'In time I will be making my own statement to the press about Sam.'

Her eyes flared in alarm. 'What?'

His mouth was set in a determined line. 'I want to present Sam as my son. I don't want him hidden away as if I am ashamed of him. I am not. He is my flesh and blood.'

'But what about what I want?' she said. 'Do you have any idea of what the press will do to me? They'll crucify me all over again. I know they will. Look at what they have already said. How can I stop Sam hearing that stuff about me?'

'I realise the implications for you, Cassie, and I will do my best to defend you.'

'You weren't too keen on defending me a few minutes

ago,' she threw back. 'You were accusing me of selling this scandal to the press. It just shows how little you know me.'

'I apologise for jumping to conclusions,' Sebastian said. 'I didn't think it through logically. You are the last person to have spoken to the press. My absence from the palace has no doubt added to the speculation along with the issue of the missing diamond.'

'What missing diamond?'

Sebastian waited a beat before telling her. She had a right to know what he had been facing over the last few months. He could trust her to keep it quiet, of that he was now sure. Her love for him was something he had not been expecting, although it warmed him to the very core of his being. He just wanted a few more days to give Alex time to think over the proposition he had put before him.

'So can't you be King without the diamond?' she asked once he had finished.

'The coronation is still being planned, but there is no guarantee the diamond will be located in time,' he said. 'This must go no further than these four walls, Cassie.'

'You can trust me, Sebastian.'

He bent down and brushed his mouth against hers. 'I know I can, *agape mou*,' he said, and, touching her briefly on the curve of her cheek, added gently, 'I just wish I had trusted you from the beginning.'

The news about Sebastian's love-child went on for several days, which rather ironically made Cassie glad he had insisted she stay at Kionia with Sam. She had hardly seen Sebastian over the last four days; he had come back late at night, spending long hours in his study or pacing the floor of his room. She had wanted to go to him so many times but felt if he wanted to be with her he would have said so by now. In spite of her confession of love, he had not spoken of his own feelings. She was left in limbo, wishing and hoping for something that deep down she knew could never be.

The day of her parole came and she came to a decision. She called Angelica, who agreed to meet her and Sam at the front gates of the hideaway just as the guards were changing shifts. It was a risky move, but Cassie felt if she didn't leave now it would make it all the more difficult for Sam in the long run. She packed the things she had brought plus as much of what Sebastian had given Sam as he could fit into two bags.

While Eleni was occupied elsewhere, Cassie carried the bags downstairs, but just as she was about to store them in a cupboard the front door opened and Sebastian came in.

His eyes went to the bags in her hands. 'What are you doing?' he asked with a heavy frown.

She put the bags down and faced him determinedly. 'I am leaving with Sam,' she said. 'Nothing you say will stop me. I have made up my mind. My parole is up. I am a free woman.'

'You were going to just walk out without saying goodbye?' he asked in a flintlike tone. 'You weren't even going to let me speak to Sam?'

Cassie could feel the anger coming off him but stood her ground. 'You've barely seen him for the last few days,' she said. 'I thought it best to get out before he becomes even more attached to you.'

'You thought it best to take my son away from me?' he barked at her. 'How could you think that was the best thing for Sam, or even me for that matter?'

'We don't belong in your life,' Cassie said, holding back tears. 'The press have gone on and on about my background. I can't bear it any more. I can't even look at the paper now without feeling sick to my stomach.'

'So you haven't seen today's paper?'

She shook her head. 'No…no, I haven't…'

'There's an exclusive interview with someone from the orphanage called Spiro who claims he slept with you several times.'

Cassie felt her despair hit an all-time low. 'And you believed him?'

He let out a gust of breath after a tense moment. 'Of course I don't believe him. I have reason to believe he is the one behind the press leak.'

'Thank you for believing me,' Cassie said, blinking back tears. 'I can't tell you how much that means to me. No matter what happens I won't let Sam forget how wonderful you have been to me.'

He gave her an unreadable look as he unfolded the newspaper again. 'Since you haven't read the rest of the news I think you should know my younger brother Alex and his wife Maria had a baby girl late last night,' he said. 'They have called her Alexandria.'

'Oh, that's lovely news,' she said. 'I hope everything went well with the delivery.'

He drew in a breath as he tossed the paper to one side. 'Yes, it all went very well. Alex was over the moon, raving about the birth, how he cut the cord and held his daughter before anyone else touched her. It was obviously a very moving experience for him, and of course for Maria.'

Cassie bit down on her lip as she saw the raw emotion on his face. Even though she had shown him all the photos she had of Sam she knew it would never make up for him not being there as his brother had been for his wife for the birth of their tiny daughter. She even wondered if he truly had forgiven her for not trying harder to contact him about the pregnancy. Although he had shown amazing compassion over what she had suffered at the hands of her father, there was a part of her that suspected Sebastian had yet to process his feelings about having a love-child to a woman his people saw as not fit to stand by his side as his future queen.

'I have to leave, Sebastian,' she said into the creaking silence. 'Surely you see that? This will all blow over once Sam and I are off the island. It's the best way—the *only* way. If you truly love Sam then you will let me take him away where he can't be hurt by all the speculation and innuendo.'

Sebastian knew she was right about Sam. He was far too young and vulnerable to cope with the press, but how could he let his little son go? He had only just started to get to know him. There was so much he didn't know and would never know if he was not in close contact with his little boy. He felt as if he were being torn in two. Whatever decision he made was going to affect someone adversely.

And then there was Cassie. How could he let her leave now that he knew what he felt for her, what he had always felt for her? The last couple of weeks had shown him how much he had misjudged her. His guilt was like a yoke about his shoulders; he couldn't shake it off no matter what she said to exonerate him. There had been so little time to right the wrongs of the past, if indeed they ever could be righted.

He had already spoken to his legal advisors about clearing Cassie's name, but they had not been overwhelmingly positive. They had argued that it would look as if the Prince Regent of Aristo was manipulating the system in order to whitewash his mistress. Sebastian recognised it was politically sensitive, but he was more concerned about doing the right thing by Cassie and Sam. But perhaps the right thing *was* to let them leave Aristo, at least until the scandal died down a bit.

'All right,' he said, releasing a jagged sigh. 'I will let you and Sam go, but I must insist you keep me informed at all times of where you are. I will see that you are both provided for, and I would like to see Sam when it can be arranged. I would also like to spend some time with him before you leave in the morning.'

'Of course,' Cassie said, swallowing against a groundswell of emotion. He was letting them go. He had made his choice and it did not include her and Sam. But then why was she so heart-wrenchingly disappointed? Hadn't she always known she and Sebastian were never going to be together? She had known it from the very first time they had met six years ago. Sam's existence didn't change anything—why should it?

Sebastian had responsibilities that went back for centuries. Royal courts had dealt with this sort of situation many times before. The mistress and child were taken care of well out of the eye of the public, and in time completely forgotten.

Sebastian came up to her and, bending down, pressed his mouth to hers in a soft kiss that tasted to Cassie of goodbye. Her lips clung to his for a brief moment, as if trying to delay the final moment of separation.

She stood back from him and gave him a wry look. 'I guess it would be rather tacky to say at this point, thanks for the memories.'

The movement of his lips was nowhere near a smile, more of a grimace of regret. 'Thank you for my son,' he said in a deep, rough tone as he touched her on the cheek in a finger-tip caress.

Cassie knew if she didn't move away now she would crack. She pulled her shoulders back and pasted a smile on her face. 'Thank you for my freedom,' she said, and turned and walked up the stairs.

CHAPTER THIRTEEN

CASSIE was besieged by the press on her way to the ferry with Sam the next morning. Sam was already in tears, not quite understanding what was going on. Sebastian had spent some time with him earlier, but he had left before Cassie could see him one last time. Eleni had said he had been called away to something urgent at the palace, but Cassie had wondered if the old woman had been told to say that so Sebastian could avoid saying goodbye.

'But I don't want to leave Daddy,' Sam wailed as she tugged him along the gangplank to board the passenger ferry.

'Sweetie, it's just not possible to stay here,' she said, fighting back tears of her own at some of the vicious insults still being thrown at her from the wharf.

Cassie kept her head down as she showed their boarding passes to the ticket officer, her hands shaking so much the passes rattled like leaves in a stiff breeze.

Finally they were on their way, and Sam out of sheer exhaustion fell asleep on her lap, his face still blotchy from crying. Cassie sat stroking his hair, tears rolling down her cheeks as the island began to shrink as the ferry cut through the choppy water.

'Dhespinis Kyriakis?' A woman of about thirty seemed to

come out of nowhere. 'Do you mind if I sit down next to you and your little boy?'

Cassie could hardly say no as the seat next to her was vacant; in fact it was the only vacant one on that side of the ferry. 'If you like,' she said, and cuddled Sam closer.

'I heard what people were saying back there on the wharf,' the woman said after a moment.

Cassie tightened her mouth as she looked at the woman. 'If you have something to add to what has already been said, then forget it. I have heard it all before.'

'I am not here to insult you,' the woman said. 'I am here because I want to set the record straight. You see…I knew your father.'

Something about the woman's grim tone made Cassie's eyes widen in interest. 'You…you did?'

'I used to work for him ten years ago,' she said. 'He continually harassed me, threatened me and even on one occasion physically assaulted me, but every time I tried to report it, he circumvented it by smearing my reputation by spreading rumours around the council chambers. I was too young and inexperienced to know how to handle it, so in the end I left. It took me years before I found my feet again. I've only been working as a journalist in London for the last couple of years.'

Cassie felt her back stiffen. 'A journalist?'

'Please don't be worried,' the woman said. 'I was visiting relatives on Calista and heard about the Prince Regent's love-child. Your name leapt off the page. I knew when I read you had been imprisoned for the manslaughter of your father that there had to be more to it than that. I wanted to meet you, to interview you so you can tell your side of the story so you can receive the justice you have so far been denied. I will back you up and by doing so receive the justice I, too, was denied all those years ago.'

Cassie chewed at her lip. Should she do it, for Sam's sake if not her own? After all, he would be the one who had to live with the stigma of having an ex-prisoner as his mother. If she could clear her name it would be one step in the long road to recovering her life. And not just her life, but this young woman's who had also suffered at her father's hands. 'I'm not sure where to begin…' she said.

The young woman offered her hand. 'My name is Alexia and I always think the best place to start is at the beginning.'

Sebastian got down to the wharf just as the ferry was disappearing into the distance. His eyes blurred but not from staring at the shrinking vessel, nor was it because of the onshore breeze.

Behind him his bodyguards were pushing back against the assembled crowd, some of whom were holding placards with disgusting words and phrases written on them about Cassie.

Sebastian strode over and, ignoring the protests of his security team, faced the loud-mouthed crowd. He was aware of cameras flashing and every word he said being recorded, but he no longer cared. He tore strips off the gathering of people, telling them of the injustice Cassandra Kyriakis had suffered, not just at her father's hands all her young life, but at the hands of the courts who had wrongly imprisoned her just because she had tried to protect herself from her father's violence.

The crowd gradually began to disperse, like a pack of dogs that had been heavily chastened; their tails were between their legs as they slunk away.

Stefanos opened the car door for Sebastian. 'You do realise that will be all over the press tomorrow, Your Highness?'

Sebastian gave him an I-couldn't-care-less shrug. 'If it is I will not be here to read it,' he said with a set mouth.

'May I ask where you will be, Your Highness?'

Sebastian glanced at the palace and then back at the faint

outline of the ferry. 'I will give you one guess,' he said with a slowly spreading smile.

'Does that mean you will require the royal helicopter, Your Highness?'

Sebastian turned to look at his aide. 'You bet I will,' he said, still smiling. 'Take me to the heliport immediately.'

Once Cassie had settled Sam for a nap in the tiny villa she had chosen on the Greek Island of Ithaki, she came out to the terrace to breathe in the clean, salty air. The less populated island had appealed to her, for, although it didn't have a great choice of tourist-friendly beaches, the lack of tourists meant she and Sam could melt into the background until she decided where to finally go to rebuild her life.

The sound of footsteps behind her made her turn, her eyes going to the size of saucers when she saw Sebastian standing there.

'Are you out here to weave your shroud?' he asked.

Cassie frowned in bewilderment. 'Pardon?'

Amusement danced in his eyes. 'You don't know the legend of Penelope and Odysseus?'

'Yes…sort of…'

'The ancient island of Ithaca, now known as Ithaki, was Odysseus's long-lost home,' he explained. 'Legend has it Penelope sat waiting for him to return to her, weaving a shroud to keep her suitors at bay, for they believed he was dead, and she had told them once the shroud was finished she would choose one of them. But each night she cleverly unravelled her work while she waited for Odysseus to return.'

Cassie felt something move inside her chest. 'I wouldn't know the first thing about weaving….'

'Perhaps that is a good thing,' he said, 'for I would not want this particular suitor to be put off.'

She kept staring at him, trying to make sense of his words, hope like a tiny flickering flame inside her, struggling to warm the chill of the heartache she had suffered in leaving that morning.

'Aren't you going to say something?' he asked.

She pressed her lips together for a moment before she returned her eyes to his. 'If you've come to see Sam I'm afraid he's just settled down for a nap,' she said. 'He was a bit seasick on the way.'

'I would love to see Sam, but first I would like to talk to you.'

Cassie shifted her weight from foot to foot, her teeth having another go at her bottom lip. 'Look, if it's about the journalist I spoke to on the ferry across—'

'It's not about a journalist, and if you spoke to one then it can't have been any worse than what I said to the paparazzi and your send-off crowd down at the wharf,' he said with a wry twinkling smile. 'I am almost looking forward to seeing tomorrow's papers.'

She frowned at him. 'You spoke to the press?'

He gave her a tender look. 'Did you think I would not defend you, *agape mou?*'

Cassie didn't know what to think. She was struggling to contain her emotions, her heart was beating so hard and so fast her head felt as if it were spinning.

Sebastian came up to her and took her hands in his. 'Caz, I should have said this the day you told me about Sam—in fact I should have told you when you told me about your father and his treatment of you.'

She looked into his eyes. 'T-told me what?'

'You can't guess?'

She shook her head.

He brought her hands up to his mouth, pressing a soft kiss to each of her knuckles as he held her gaze. 'I love you,' he said. 'I have loved you for so long it felt like a limb was being torn off when you and Sam left. I was called back to the palace over some minor issue that was trumped up as being urgent because I suspect everyone knew I was going to stop you from leaving if I spent another minute with you.'

'We have no future, Seb,' she said. 'You know that. The throne is—'

'Empty until Alex makes up his mind whether he will take it or not,' he said. 'I do not want to rule unless you are by my side. You complete me, Caz, in a way no one else has or could ever do. This is not just about Sam—I need you to know that. If the people will not accept you as my wife then I will gladly relinquish the throne and all it entails.'

Cassie couldn't believe what she was hearing. She wanted to slap at her head, to make sure she hadn't imagined it. 'Your...*wife?*' she finally managed to croak. 'You want me to marry you?'

He smiled at her with love shining in his eyes. 'As soon as it can be arranged,' he said. 'We have been robbed of so much time. I want to make you my wife and start working on a brother or sister for Sam. We can be a family at last. It doesn't matter to me if it is on Aristo or somewhere else. But I suspect, after what I said to the press this morning, you will become the princess of the people in no time at all.'

Cassie couldn't hold back the tears; they dripped from her eyes as she hugged him close. 'I just want to be *your* princess,' she said.

He wrapped his arms around her, holding her tightly against him. 'You have always been my princess, Caz, the princess of my heart.'

There was the patter of little footsteps on the terrace, and a little voice squealed, 'Daddy! You've come to visit!'

Sebastian smiled as he scooped his little son up into his arms. 'Not just to visit, Sam,' he said, hugging him tightly. 'I am here to stay.'

* * * * *

We chatted to Melanie Milburne about the world of THE ROYAL HOUSE OF KAREDES. *Here are her insights!*

Would you prefer to live on Aristo or Calista?

I would definitely like to live on Aristo! All those beaches and majestic buildings such as the Karedes Palace and secluded hideaways.

What did you enjoy about writing about the Royal House of Karedes?

I really enjoyed getting to know the characters and seeing them develop as they realized their destiny, in particular Sebastian, who had so much pressure on his shoulders. Cassie was one of my favorite heroines as she was so courageous and her love for Sebastian had withstood almost impossible odds.

How did you find writing as part of a continuity?

It is always an amazing privilege to be part of a continuity knowing you are amongst brilliant authors and that you have been specially chosen to join them. It's quite daunting in fact!

When you are writing, what is your typical day?

I am quite a disciplined person (some would say obsessive!) so I like to get all my other tasks out of the way before I write. I swim first thing and then catch up on e-mails and do any shopping that needs to be done, plus take my dogs for a walk. I usually write all afternoon with lots of breaks for cups of tea and cookies.

Where do you get the inspiration for your characters?

I am a voracious reader and a people-watcher so I guess I would have to say a combination of life and reading, both fiction and nonfiction. Often it is just a phrase I have read that triggers a "what if" question in my head and then away I go.

What did you like most about your hero and heroine in this continuity?

I loved Cassie's spirit, which in spite of all she had suffered had not been broken. I loved Sebastian's self-sacrifice in that he was prepared to give up his right to the throne for the woman he loved.

What would be the best—and worst—things about being part of a royal dynasty?

I have a friend whose sister is a princess so I know how hard it is to have any real privacy. It would be so difficult to have hundreds of cameras thrust in your face all the time and not have any normalcy in your life. No ducking out for a coffee and shopping, for instance. But then a handsome prince more than makes up for it, right?

Are diamonds really a girl's best friend?

No, I think a loving partner who stands by you no matter what is a girl's best friend. Diamonds are definitely a bonus though!

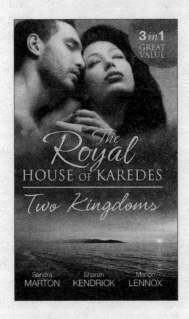

Tall, Dark and... Yours!

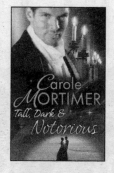
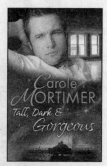
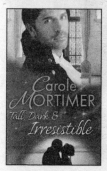

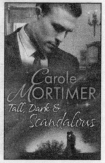

MEET THE
AUSTRALIAN ALPHAS!

Pick up the first title of this sizzling new
Australia collection by the wonderful

Emma Darcy

**Available at
millsandboon.co.uk**

Discover more romance at

www.millsandboon.co.uk